BY
BLOOD

ALSO BY ELLEN ULLMAN

Close to the Machine

The Bug

BY
BLOOD

ELLEN ULLMAN

FARRAR, STRAUS AND GIROUX   NEW YORK

Fic
Ullman

Farrar, Straus and Giroux
18 West 18th Street, New York 10011

Distributed in Canada by D&M Publishers, Inc.
Printed in the United States of America
First edition, 2012

Library of Congress Cataloging-in-Publication Data
Ullman, Ellen.
    By blood : a novel / Ellen Ullman.
        p.   cm.
    ISBN 978-0-374-11755-9 (hardback)
    1. Adoptees—Fiction.   2. College teachers—Fiction.   3. Identity (Psychology)—
Fiction.   4. Triangles (Interpersonal relations)—Fiction.   5. San Francisco (Calif.)—
Fiction.   6. California—History—1950—Fiction.   7. Psychological fiction.   I. Title.

PS3621.L45 B9 2012
813'.6—dc23

                                                                        2011041626

Designed by Abby Kagan

www.fsgbooks.com

10   9   8   7   6   5   4   3   2   1

ONE

1.

I did not cause her any harm. This was a great victory for me. At the end of it, I was a changed man. I am indebted to her; it was she who changed me, although I never learned her name.

My involvement with the young woman in question began several years ago, in the late summer of 1974, while I was on leave from the university. I sought to secure for myself a small office in the downtown business district of San Francisco, where I intended to prepare a series of lectures about *The Eumenides*—The Kindly Ones—the third play in Aeschylus's great trilogy. A limited budget brought me to the edge of a rough, depressed neighborhood. And my first sighting of the prospective office building—eight begrimed gargoyles crouched beneath the parapet, their eyes eaten away by time—nearly caused me to retrace my steps.

Yet there was no question of my turning back. Immediately upon my arrival in San Francisco, a month earlier, a great gloom had descended upon me. I had arranged my leave in great haste; I knew no one in the area. And it must have been this isolation that had engendered in me a particularly obdurate spell of the nervous condition to which I had been subject since boyhood. Although I was then a grown man of fifty years, the illness, as ever, cast me back into the dark emotions of my preadolescence, as if I remained unchanged the desperate boy of twelve I had been. Indeed, the very purpose of the office was to act as a counterweight to this most recent spell, to get me dressed and out of the house, to force me to walk on public streets among people, to immerse myself, however anonymously, in the general hum of society; and in this way, perhaps, sustain the gestures of normal life.

It was therefore imperative that I do battle with my trepidations. I suppressed my fears of the neighborhood and my distress at the building's dreary mien. We were in the midst of the Great Stagflation, I reminded myself. The whole city (indeed the entire country) had a blasted, exhausted air. Why should the building before me not be similarly afflicted? I therefore turned my gaze from the eyeless gargoyles, told myself there was no reason to be unnerved by the shuttered bar on the ground floor (whose sign creaked in San Francisco's seemingly perpetual wind).

Somewhat emboldened by these mental devices, I took the final steps to the entryway.

I opened the door to a flash of white: a lobby clad entirely in brilliant marble. So clean and smooth was this marble that one had the sudden impression of having entered a foreign landscape, a snowy whiteout, where depth perception was faulty. Through the glare I seemed to see three cherubs floating above the elevators, their eyes of black onyx, which, as I watched in fright, appeared to be moving. It took some moments to understand what hung before me: elevator floor indicators, in the form of bronze cherubs, their eyes circling to watch the floor numbers as the cars rose and fell.

To the right of the elevators was a stairway, above it a sign directing visitors to the manager's office on the mezzanine. I climbed this short flight—its marble steps concave from years of wear—then I followed the manager into the elevator and rode with him up to the eighth floor (the cherubim ogling us, I imagined). He led me along hallways lined with great slabs of marble wainscoting, each four feet wide and as tall as an average man of the nineteenth century. Finally we stood before a door of tenderly varnished fruitwood, its fittings—knob, back plate, hinges, lock, mail slot—all oxidized to a burnt golden patina.

The room he showed me was very small. The desk, settee, and bookcase it contained were battered. The transom above the door had been painted shut. But I had already decided, on the strength of the building's interior materials—clearly chosen to withstand the insult of time—that this would be my office. So with the manager's agreement to restore the transom to working order, I signed a one-year lease, to commence in three days, the first of August. And then throughout the first weeks of my tenancy, while I struggled to regain my footing and begin my project, I was calmed by the currents of dark, cool air that flowed through the transom (the sort of mysterious air that seems to remain undisturbed for decades in the deep interiors of old buildings), and by the sight of the aged Hotel Palace across the way, where I could, in certain lights, see the doings of guests not prudent enough to close their shades.

Each weekday, I rode downtown on the streetcar, anticipating the pleasures of sitting at my desk, the rumble of the traffic eight stories below me. Before reaching the city center, however, one had to pass a grim procession of empty storefronts, vacant lots, and derelict buildings—a particularly blighted district. Nevertheless, despite the proliferation of

such neighborhoods, the good San Franciscans seemed to rouse themselves each morning to perform at least the motions of civic life, producing an air (however false) of gainful industry. This impression of restorative
public energy helped me to put myself aside, so to speak, and by month's
end I had made progress on my lectures, producing my first coherent set
of notes.

Then, shortly after Labor Day, as I sat down to draft the first talk in
the series, I found that the acoustical qualities of the office, previously so
regenerative, had abruptly changed. Cutting through the pleasant social
drone from the streets below, superseding it in both pitch and constancy,
was an odd whirring sound, like wind rushing through a keyhole. And
just audible above the whir, coming in uneven and therefore intrusive
intervals, was a speaking voice, but only its sibilants and dentalizations—
only the tongue and teeth, as it were. I am certain it was only the general
darkness of my mood, but I felt there was something mocking and threatening in this sibilance, for the sound drew me to it the way a cat is lured—
psst, psst—for drowning.

I jumped up from my desk determined to know the source of these
intrusions. Immediately I suspected the doors to the adjoining offices.
My room, small as it was, had two interior doors to what were once
communicating offices, both doors now kept locked. Aside from noticing the fine wood of which they were made, I had paid these vestigial
entryways no attention, as I had never heard anything issuing from
them. Indeed, I had had no awareness of the other offices at all, my goal
in securing my own room having been, as I have said, to find a place outside of my own life, so to speak, to immerse myself in a general, anony-
mous social sea.

Now forced to consider the reality of the tenants around me, I went out
into the hall. The stenciled letters on the office door to my left identified
its occupants as "Consulting Engineers." I moved my ear closer and
heard nothing, but through the frosted glass in the door's upper portion
(unlike my office, many doors retained their original etched-glass panels, with finely wrought patterns), I could make out two heads moving,
as if over a desk or drafting table. The only odd thing I noticed about
this office was that its number was out of sequence, being 803, whereas
mine was 807, and my other neighbor's 804. I then recalled the building
manager saying, when I signed the lease, that tenants, as they changed
offices over the years, were permitted to take their numbers with them

as long as they remained on the same floor, their suite numbers obviously constituting some kind of property or identity. And indeed, as I looked around the hallway, I saw that the office numbers were a complete jumble, 832 next to 812 next to 887, and so on, indicating that the lessees had proved themselves loyal to the building and to the eighth floor but were otherwise restless and inconstant. I wondered for a moment if I should want to retain 807 in the event that I should move away from my neighbor, and I decided that I would, for there was something orderly in the descent from eight to seven passing around zero, and, in the number 7, perhaps an aura of luck.

Rousing myself from these distractions and resuming the surveillance of my neighbors, I came to the office on my right, number 804. As I drew closer, the whir became unmistakable, as did the voice. There was no glass panel in this door; its gold letters simply read, "Dora Schussler, Ph.D."

I stood immobile in the hall for some seconds. My first association with the designation "Ph.D." was that this Dr. Schussler should be an academic like myself, and that she and I should coexist quite well, her time being spent in the quiet pursuits of reading and writing. Why, then, was there this whirring, and this persistent hissing? And why hadn't I heard it from the first, on the day I inspected what was then my still prospective office, thereby preventing me from being bound to such an incompatible neighbor?

These questions (posed to myself with an aggrieved, affronted, indignant air) distracted me from seeing the truth of my situation, which became clear only as I stared at the swirls of the ancient, wear-darkened broadloom that lined the hall. I recalled the first time I had ever heard a sound like the one issuing from Dr. Schussler's office, which had been many years ago, in the office of one of the many therapists I had had reason to visit during the course of my life. In the waiting area, there had been a small beige plastic machine, placed on the floor, which had given off just such a whir, its role being to blur the clarity of the spoken word that might be audible from the therapeutic offices, thereby preventing anyone, as he waited, from understanding what was being said within (though I myself, still a young man, often tried to overhear, telling myself such curiosity was natural). With great force, the whole period of time surrounding my meetings with the psychotherapist came back to me, and I could see quite clearly the little yellow lamp she kept on a low table beside her, and the vine that covered the single north-facing window, its leaves perpetually trembling.

I did not wish to recall this portion of my life, especially not at the office where I had sought to escape the great black drapery of my nervous condition. Indeed, finding myself tied to such an enterprise seemed to me an evil joke, as I had wagered both my emotional health and my professional reputation against the efficacy of the therapeutic relationship. Over the course of thirty-five years—meeting weekly, twice a week, sometimes daily—I had looked across small rooms into the bewildered, pitiable faces of counselors, therapists, social workers, analysts, and psychiatrists, each inordinately concerned about his or her own professional nomenclature, credentials, theories, accreditations; all of them, in the end, indistinguishable to me. Now, still battling the hooded view of life that had haunted my family for generations, I had come to the conclusion that their well-meaning talking cures, except as applied to the most ordinary of unhappinesses, were useless.

What now could I do to separate myself from this Dora Schussler? How could I escape her analysands with all their fruitless self-examinations, beside whom I was now obligated to spend the remaining eleven months of my lease? I had no legal recourse, I realized. I could not go to the manager and say I had been duped, my neighbor had been hushed, paid off to silence the babblings of her profession on the day I had first surveyed the premises. The situation of my room had not been maliciously misrepresented. I had engaged the office in August, iconic month of the therapeutic hiatus. It was now September. Dr. Dora Schussler, Ph.D. and psychotherapist, was back at work.

2.

Still standing in the hallway, I leapt to an uncharacteristically hopeful thought. I dared believe that the piercing, sibilant voice coming through Dr. Schussler's door belonged to the current analysand, not to the analyst (as I chose to call them, indiscriminately, since I was not inclined, as I have said, to be impressed by the naming conventions of the psychological professions). I reasoned that if it were the patient whom I had been hearing, all I had to do was be away from the office for one therapeutic hour per week, a mere fifty minutes, and the situation would be tolerable. Somewhat reassured, I went back to my room to wait for the conclusion of the current session and the beginning of the next.

Yet, as the remaining thirty minutes of the session crept by, all manner of alarming thoughts intruded. I shuddered at the consideration that, though the horrid voice might indeed be that of the patient, she (for the voice seemed to me eminently female) might be undergoing a true, orthodox, Freudian analysis, which meant she would be coming to whisper and cluck her problems at me every day of the workweek. It then came to me that the therapist's name was Dora, the name of Freud's famous hysteric. Surely, I reasoned (using the absurd, self-defeating logic that always ruled during nervous episodes), Dr. Schussler was a Freudian, the dreadful voice would haunt me daily, my work at the office was ruined, my dwindling financial resources were committed without recourse, and I would have to return to my empty house in a dreary neighborhood, where it was mortally dangerous for me.

In this foolish but inevitable manner, I escalated my own fears, growing ever more agitated, until I was startled by the slam of Dr. Schussler's door. I then heard the patient tread past my office, the ding of the elevator bell, and finally, rising into my awareness as if it had suddenly been turned up in volume, the whirring torrent of the noise machine.

I forced myself not to become fixated upon the sound. This was difficult, because the whir, which had seemed so constant upon first hearing, now appeared to have patterns within it, coming in rhythmic waves. And there was something teasing about these subtle rhythms, a kind of phantom music that seemed to play just below the level of audibility, all the more seductive for being not quite music, a melody just beyond reach, vanishing when I gave it direct, analytical attention. Only through the greatest mental discipline could I consign it to the background, willing it to become part of the general sound atmosphere, along with the rumbling trucks below, the shrill of a traffic policeman's whistle, the honking horns. This cognitive effort was exhausting, even for the brief ten minutes of the interclient interval. When I relaxed in any measure, looking up from my notes or glancing across the way to the windows of the Hotel Palace (where a maid was assiduously wiping a table), the quasi-musical patterns returned, luring my attentions.

So it was that the subsequent ding of the elevator came as a relief—or, I should say, at least an exchange of anxieties. For now I waited expectantly to see if the next client would be the solution to the problem of the sibilant voice. This new analysand walked past my own door; Dr. Schussler opened hers; and the patient entered the office. Due to the strong air currents that always blew through the hallways, the door closed with a wall-rattling slam (an annoyance, since I myself was always mindful of the draft, closing my own door in respectful silence). For one moment, there was only the whir of the sound machine and the noise from the street. Then, fulfilling my worst expectations (as life would always do, said my depressed illogic), the awful sibilance returned. And there was no escaping the conclusion: The horrid sound was produced by the tongue and teeth of Dr. Schussler!

I would move, I thought. I would carry my 807 down the hall, or I would accept another office on another floor, pursuing any avenue to get away from this therapist, counselor, psychoanalyst—whatever she wished to call herself. I was about to look for the building manager, demand he place me in a different room, when suddenly everything went quiet.

It was the sound machine: abruptly stopped. And in its absence was a stillness so crisp that I could hear the suggestive, teasing, slip-sound of a single tissue being withdrawn from a Kleenex box.

Then a voice, which said, Thanks. You know I hate that thing.

And a reply: So sorry. I do forget.

3.

I was so startled by the clarity of the sounds coming from the next office—I could hear a sigh, an intake of breath, the lifting of a haunch, indeed to the extent that I knew with utter certainty that both client and analyst sat upon leather—that I could not move for several seconds. What was I to do about this sudden, forced intimacy? Perhaps I should have coughed or jostled a drawer, so that they, hearing me, would know the extent to which I was hearing them. Yet I sat still. And in a brief instant, through some quirk of reasoning (no doubt related to the generally twisted logic of my mood), I convinced myself that my making noise would be an imposition upon them, that my presence would inhibit them, and the only way for analyst and analysand to continue their work undisturbed was for me to keep my existence a secret.

Supporting my decision was the fact that I understood almost nothing of what they were saying. Charlotte, Roger, Susan—who were these people? The hotel, our arrangement, the old project, the meeting, the assignment—references to empty space. How could I see myself as a trespasser when I had so little comprehension of what I was overhearing? Ten minutes passed with a discussion of scuba diving (the patient had or had not done this before?). Then she circled back to "the assignment" and "the old project." Dr. Schussler of course would know the meaning of these references, or would have to pretend she did, since that was a therapist's most basic function: to keep the thread of her patients' stories, to remember all the names, relationships, and events, to absorb (somehow) the infinitely expanding expository action of an ongoing life. But it all meant nothing to me. I was like a person who had happened upon a novel fallen open at random.

So it was that I simply sat and listened to the sound of their voices— Dr. Schussler's, in particular, her spat-out *T*s and whistled *S*s. Of course! She was German. This explained the mysterious dentalizations and sibilance that had intruded over the whir of the noise machine. But now I could also hear what the machine had masked: a calm—even soothing— resonance, something throaty in it, a tone pleasantly raked by time. Her accent confused me. I had spent a sabbatical year in Germany, living in the home of a professor of linguistics, and I had come to understand that a hard *S*, like the doctor's, was characteristic of a resident of Hamburg. Yet her unhurried syllables and soft tone were more indicative of Bavaria or, perhaps, Switzerland. I wondered if she had been born in the Baltic region and had moved to the south, or perhaps vice versa, for my knowledge of German was insufficient to discern which part of her accent was dominant, so to speak.

Her patient, however, was altogether American, with the flat accent of the Midwest—from somewhere along the rim of the Great Lakes from Buffalo to Detroit. Her cadence and inflection were like those of my female former graduate students, and I therefore took her to be in her mid- or late twenties. At some point in her young life, she seemed to have unlearned the worst aspects of her native region's speech, for she had softened the jaw-breaking growl that passed for an *R* in that part of the world, and had widened the mashed, dipthonged *A* (a horrid sound, as if you pinched your nose while saying *ee-yeah*) into an airy, open, monosyllabic *ah*. The effect, altogether, was of a provincial who had acquired culture, at an out-of-town university perhaps. Now and then, her acculturated layer slipped—an *A* going nasal, an *R* growing teeth—which was not at all an unpleasing phenomenon, as it let one hear past her creamy alto into a core of watchfulness and vulnerability.

I merely let the sound of these voices play over me, as I have said, allowing the mentioned names and places to come and go without attempts on my part to understand their referents. The patient meandered; Dr. Schussler replied occasionally with friendly nonchalance; and in this way more than half the session passed. Then came a moment I distinctly understood. The doctor's voice abruptly changed; her accent turned harsh; her tone pointed, as she said:

So, have you thought further about our discussion before the break?

A long pause followed. And as I waited to hear the reply, I realized I had distinguished this moment because of all the therapists and analysts who had insisted upon asking me this same demonic question. And I recalled how much I had detested it: this constant looping backward in time to the last therapized hour, as if everything that had happened in the intervening days or week was not real, or not quite as real as the life lived inside yellow-lamp-lit rooms where ivy trembled at the windows. My goodwill toward Dr. Schussler retreated. I found myself allied with the young analysand, with her resistance: What force there was in the annoyed sigh she gave off! And what a long moment she took to lean over and slowly withdraw a tissue from the inevitably close-by box.

I know we agreed we'd go back to it after the break, the patient finally said. But I've changed my mind. I think I've avoided it all my life for good reason. I don't see how it will help for me to get into it now.

Dr. Schussler made a small, throaty sound but said nothing. There was now another pause, as analyst and analysand sparred to see who could longer endure the silence. Of course it was the client who gave way:

I really don't see the relevance of that to who I am now, she said. I don't want to go there. I told you. I don't see the point. I've made my peace with it. It's a fact, like where I grew up or the color of my eyes. Please, I don't see why you keep coming back to it. I told you. Some things should just remain a mystery.

I was naturally enticed by the idea of a mystery, as anyone would be, and I hoped she might reveal at least the nature of this secret. But for some seconds, the analysand did not speak. She only stirred in her chair (was she lying on a couch? I thought not; something about the quality of her voice made me think she sat upright), and then she immediately changed the subject.

The topic to which she leapt was an argument with one Charlotte, a name that had already come up several times during the session. It seemed that she and Charlotte had argued over the arrangement of food in the refrigerator. Then the patient complained that Charlotte always left the kitchen-cabinet doors open. Finally, she decried Charlotte's continual invasions of her privacy, saying, She talks to me all the time. When I'm in the bathroom. When I'm in the shower. While I'm washing dishes and can't hear over the water. That booming voice: it follows me everywhere.

I thought this Charlotte must be her roommate. With whom else does one have such dull domestic spats? Dr. Schussler had obviously heard much of this before, for she inquired whether the two women were following the ground rules they had established. As her client went on to reply, it was clear that the doctor was as bored as I with the course this session was taking. She signaled her disengagement by continually shifting her weight in her leather chair, sending out squeaks and creaks that somehow connoted a jeering disapproval.

Finally, she intervened. Remember, said Dr. Schussler. We did talk about whether you were going to take seriously these incompatibilities.

It is not simply a matter of housekeeping standards. Charlotte is a bicycle messenger, and you are a financial analyst. She has barely completed a junior college course in accounting, and you have a master's degree in business administration and econometrics. She accuses you of being a "collaborator" for not being open at work about your lesbianism.

(Lesbians!)

She jeers at you for wearing "straight" business clothes. She says you think like a man. These are serious problems, as you yourself have said, and they are not going to disappear simply because Charlotte thought you were "stunning," as she put it.

Yes, said the patient. Totally true. You're right. But just the same— she paused—all that bicycle riding has given her a truly amazing pair of legs.

The doctor coughed.

The thighs, most especially.

Silence from the therapist.

And let's just say that I immensely enjoy all the many ways she considers me stunning.

Her analyst *tssked*. You know what I mean, she said.

Oh, all right. I do. Of course I do. We're completely different. We have nothing in common. It's ridiculous in so many ways. But when we take our clothes off . . . when the sex is so very good . . .

Lesbian sex! I experienced a moment of extreme titillation, for there is no one who is not curious about homosexuality, and especially about lesbianism, if one is a man. I felt my groin tighten and my penis begin to stir, bodily acts about which I could do nothing. One might as well try to stop one's heart from beating as attempt to prevent this involuntary rush of blood to one's manly parts, especially when one has been presented with an image of two women, naked, their beautiful legs, their breasts, the hidden places into which they—and so forth. Although I considered my reaction altogether normal—as I have said, any man in my position would have responded similarly—when the tumescence proceeded briskly, I became quite alarmed. Further engorgement would require me to stand and adjust my trousers—and then all would be lost. My chair would creak; they would hear me; I would never again learn about lesbian sex, or indeed any other aspect of the patient's life. I would be plunged back into loneliness in my dreadful house by the sea. I therefore forced myself to think of the two women in their roles as squabbling roommates—the disputed refrigerator shelves, cabinet doors, shouts over running water—arguments so banal as to dispel the deepest desire and compulsion.

Oh, Charlotte's all right, the patient was going on (to my relief, as I began to wilt). Really. You're making too much of the surface differences. I know we've talked about it, but maybe the problems aren't insurmountable. It's just that she's so steeped in the politics of lesbianism, the radical idea of it, she can't exactly think for herself, react for herself. It's as if her body belongs to some community, not to herself. She's forever coming home from a meeting of one collective or another, and she has this struggle model in her head. Everything must be fought for; an action must always be planned. The personal is political, she never stops saying. I keep trying to tell her the reverse is not true! But then she says to me, Everything worthwhile requires a fight. Honey, don't you *want* to struggle?

Now the patient burst out laughing, as did the therapist, and it was all I could do not to laugh myself. The women's liberation movement was in a period of great militancy; the streets of the university were often filled with short-haired women marching with their fists in the air. And it was absurd to imagine these stalwarts going home to struggle over the correct way to arrange a refrigerator. (I preferred to imagine them otherwise, as I have said.) But the therapist did not permit this diversion for long, as she was clearly intent upon drawing her patient into deeper waters.

Yes, said Dr. Schussler pointedly. All that is true. But remember what you said not long ago: Charlotte chose you. You are not sure that you would have chosen her in return. The doctor's voice then softened: And this does bring us back to the subject we were discussing before the break. Remember how we talked about the ways this mirrors your relationship with your mother, this profound sense of otherness?

The client snorted her impatience. She loudly drummed on the arm of her seat with her fingers and turned herself this way and that amidst much creaking of leather. I told you, she said finally. I don't want to go into this again. I *like* not knowing where I've come from. I *like* it. Every child thinks it must have been switched at birth, these can't possibly be my real parents, it's all a big mistake. Well, I just happened to have more evidence than they do. Mine really aren't my parents. I told you this a hundred times: I am not adopted! I have *mysterious origins*!

Dr. Schussler took in a breath and then released it. For several seconds, neither client nor therapist moved. They had arrived at last at the heart of the matter. But alas the hour was too far advanced. What came next were the softly murmured words with which every therapy session inevitably ends: Our time is up, the doctor said.

4.

So this was the mystery the patient wished to keep hidden: She was adopted! Improbable as this may seem, it was her adopted status, not her lesbianism, that produced in me the keener excitement. For my best friend while growing up, Paul Beleiter, had been adopted, a fact he had worn as a badge of identity. I was overjoyed to think of him! When we were fifteen, Paul escaped from our meager town. His parents had threatened to withdraw financial support if he did not prepare for a course of engineering; he shrugged them off as one would shed so many ill-fitting clothes. He moved into the rooming house of an old widower, then on to an existence all his own: Manhattan, a scholarship to a special high school of art, Greenwich Village, friends who smoked Gitanes, Jewish girlfriends with haloes of frizzy hair.

How I had longed to follow him! It was the time in my life when my ancestors had already put their damp hands on me. Any hope that I would not emulate my father was dashed (or nearly so) when I followed not his example (alcohol and pills) but the more elegant method of Virginia Woolf: into the river with stones in my pockets. I was appointed with my first mental health practitioner (she of the ivy trembling at the window). And there was Paul, already a man on his own terms, graceful and full of laughter, freed from the strict, brittle people who had raised him.

I was certain it was the adoption that had given him the courage. Paul was not adopted as one would say "I am Protestant" or "I am from Michigan," but as a quiddity, an indwelling trait that set him apart from we poor, owned, claimed children of our mothers' wombs. His alien genes had blessed him; they had given him the knowledge of his difference, his singularity. Now it thrilled me to think that I, sitting quietly behind a thin door, could follow the psychological turns whereby my dear friend had extricated himself from the engulfment of family; whereby he, like the patient, had come to the realization: These are not my parents.

If Paul—and now the patient—could extricate themselves, why not I? Why could I not learn the art of being parentless from these adoptees: these very models of self-creation?

At that moment, it seemed to me that my relocation to San Francisco had not been a stumbling error after all. The sudden leave, the dismal house by the beach I had rented, the ad in the newspaper that had led me to this strange office building in a rough neighborhood—each of these steps now seemed a requisite stage in a propitious process designed to bring me to Room 807, to the adopted patient, and, through her, to a possible release from the clammy hand of ancestry. Such a release had been the quest of my many psychological explorations; and to think that now I sat so close—physically and psychically—to the nub of this matter filled my heart with the first true joy I had experienced in decades.

Yet my happiness alarmed me. I was drawn to the patient, excited by the thought of an intimacy such as the one I had had with Paul, but a deeper intimacy for my being hidden and therefore more liable to know her secrets. But I was simultaneously ashamed of that excitement. My crouch behind the wall was too familiar, a stance too close to the postures of my darker nature; to impulses I had pledged to resist.

I ached as I considered it—to lose this grand opportunity of escaping my progenitors!—yet my pledge was made. Not to honor it could lead me farther into the shadows. How clever were the crows of my nervous condition: to thus show me a path to freedom but one that led directly through their realm, so to speak.

I therefore resolved, steadfastly, to avoid the patient's sessions. But here I faced another difficulty: I had no idea when the patient's next therapy hour might be. Did she come once a week, twice, daily? For that matter, what other patients, coming at any time of any day, might similarly want Dr. Schussler to turn off the sound machine and whose privacy I might therefore also breach, behind whose lives I would crouch in silence?

I could not decide on a plan of action; the office was to be a refuge for me, as I have said, a place where I might pierce the isolation that had so exacerbated my current nervous spell. Nonetheless, before Dr. Schussler's next client could arrive, I left the building and made my way to Market Street, there to begin the long, rumbling ride on the N Judah streetcar out to its terminus at Ocean Beach.

The car rocked westward, and by degrees the fog closed in on us. At first, there were only small puffs of low-lying clouds blowing across the sky, which caused the sun to blink on and off disagreeably, glare one moment, sun-blindness the next. The intervals of darkness grew gradually longer, until the drifts finally coalesced into a bank of cloud; so that by the time I alighted at my stop by the Great Highway, with the ocean just beyond, the insatiable fog had completely swallowed up the sun. There was a stiff wind. My teeth were gritted with sand as I walked the three short blocks to the small house with peeling paint I had rented, sight unseen, during my hasty departure from the university. The idea of living by the sea had seemed recuperative. Never having visited San Francisco, I had had no idea that the Sunset District, through which I now walked, was a treeless neighborhood of cheerless houses, where the fog swirled relentlessly and the wind blew without cease. I arrived home and tried to calm myself by reprising my expansive moment at the office— the joyful certainty that I had come to San Francisco and Ocean Beach for a purpose—but all night long the wind rattled the windows, and I found no peace.

The next evening, a Thursday night, I tried to return to the office at a time when Dr. Schussler's hours would certainly be over, eleven o'clock. But the moment I approached the building, I was on my guard. Bordering the office building was a great expanse of vacant lots, twelve square blocks of weeds and trash, the remains of a blighted neighborhood that had been demolished years earlier in a wave of so-called urban renewal. During the day, I had often come upon a bedroll or a tent or the remains of a cook fire. But now, by night, the site looked like the campground of a defeated army, as indeed it was. Desperate veterans of the Vietnam War had joined the ranks of the usual beggars and alcoholics— many veterans still wearing bits of their uniforms, a shirt, a jacket, insignia attached, all filthy now. Here they squatted in threes and fours by small fires, cooking their dinners among the ruined foundations of vanished buildings. Many eyed me, there being no one else about, and I hurried past. But at the entrance to the office, I found two drunken men sprawled in the doorway. As I reached across them to let myself into the building with my key, one of them abruptly turned over and grabbed the hem of my coat. I tried to pull away, but the man held his grip, growling at me, Hey, mister! Gimme your money! Gimme your money! Then he flopped on his side and passed out again, too drunk even to rob me. I stepped back, shaken. In an empty streetcar, I took the long ride home, resolving I would never again go to the office by night.

I next tried the weekend. The hubbub from the nearby shopping streets was reassuring, providing the general social context I had sought at the office. But the empty building was disquieting. The lobby stank of stale cigarette smoke, as it never had during the week, the sort of ghost-smoke that lingers in bars and badly aired hotel rooms, although the small bar-and-grill on the ground floor had been shuttered for a decade. The creaky elevators were often out of order, and I was afraid of becoming trapped between floors with no one there to hear me. As I worked, I kept hearing the ding of the elevators but never the tread of anyone getting on or off. Now and then, doors would slam up and down the corridors, yet I never saw anyone in the halls. I looked out to find only the empty, block-long hallways that, at their distant ends, disappeared into an odd, hazy, indoor twilight.

The next morning, Sunday, I rode up in the elevator with great apprehension. Rising floor by floor, I became more comically distressed. For I suddenly saw myself as a big, circus-decorated balloon that was designed to expand as it rose and then spectacularly explode. I knew this image was ridiculous, yet I simultaneously could not shake its efficacy. It was the same problem I had faced throughout all the long years of my therapies, when I had learned to be aware of my own thoughts and feelings, even to the extent of understanding why I was having those thoughts and feelings—their root causes, the curious emotional subterfuges through which certain emotional propensities install themselves in the psyche—yet, withal, finding myself powerless to change them. The dark emotions seemed to be part of my body, instinctual, issuing from the cells as surely as saliva or blood or urine, and with as little conscious opportunity to intervene in their production. By the time I reached the eighth floor, all I could do was step out into the corridor, look up and down the empty twilit halls, press the elevator button once again, and ride my way back down.

I spent Monday in the house, avoiding Dr. Schussler and her patients, and by Tuesday, while the wind and sand still knocked at the windows, the reasons that had prompted me to lease the office reannounced themselves with renewed urgency—indeed, I felt there was a grave risk in my staying home for another day. I had been in my nightclothes since Sunday afternoon; I hadn't washed; I hadn't shaved. On Tuesday night, in a nameless rage, I had smashed all the cheap glassware the owner of the house had left for me. I knew that Wednesday morning, whatever else I might do, I had to go back to the office.

As the N Judah carried me away from the beach, I awaited that moment when the fog would drift, thin, lift, and clear. Finally in sunlight, I thought of the cool white lobby that awaited me, the benign cherubs gazing down from elevator lintels, the man-high wainscoting standing marble-hard outside my office door. And above any other anticipation was my desire to hear the analysand's voice once again; for she was, after all, the only person in all of San Francisco I could say with any truth that I knew.

So it was that at eleven o'clock on Wednesday morning, which last week had been the patient's appointed hour, I sat very still in my office, sipping air in the smallest quantities respiration would allow, awaiting the next installment of her therapy. The sound machine gave off its torrent; the patient walked past my office; the door to Dr. Schussler's office slammed shut. And then, after the sound machine ceased its roar, came the sudden, exciting silence.

5.

I'm tired today, the patient began. I don't know why I'm here. I shouldn't have come. I didn't sleep well. My stomach hurts. I have a headache.

Are you ill? asked Dr. Schussler.

No. A hangover.

Silence.

I went to the bar last night. A Little More. I hate that place. I don't know why I go there. I think I just want to look at the old-style girls, with their makeup and their breasts out to here. Next to the so-called politico lesbians, they're so sexy. Not a flannel shirt in the crowd last night. God, I'm so tired of women who don't look like women.

After a long pause, Dr. Schussler asked, Doesn't Charlotte look like a woman?

The patient sighed. Have I been talking to a wall? She's a politico. Short hair. Flannel shirts. Jeans. Sturdy shoes. *Struggling.*

But you said . . . Her legs . . .

Muscular. Dyke's legs. In Doc Marten's stomping boots. I told you, she loves it when I call her a dyke, but she squirms if I call her a woman. For godsakes, the whole idea for me was to be with a woman. Like Colette said, If I wanted to be with a man, I'd be with someone who could do a pee-pee against a wall.

The therapist said nothing.

What's the point, the patient went on. What's the point of talking about this anymore. We've talked about it ad nauseam. The entire lesbian community talks about it ad nauseam. Butch, femme. Sexy or sex object. I'm so tired of this. I don't belong in this so-called community. I want a regular life. I don't want to change the world, I just want to go to bed with a woman! But I've told you this, I've told you this.

Yes, said the doctor. You have told me. But sometimes we must go over and over things before their meaning is clear.

I told you. I told you. Over and over. Two years of coming here just to say the same things again and again. I don't even know why I come to therapy. What a waste of time. A waste of money. I'm not getting anywhere. I should get out of here, not waste my time today. I should go.

After a pause, Dr. Schussler said: Naturally, I would like you to stay, if only to work through this mood, this anger and impatience that takes you over. But of course you can leave anytime you like. As we have discussed, this is all for your sake, not mine.

The patient blew out a breath. Sorry. I'm sorry. Like I said, I'm in a bad mood. I shouldn't have come. I'm just going to bitch at you, so I should probably get out of here before I get abusive.

But why would you get abusive toward me?

Oh, don't play that therapist game with me. You know very well what I mean. We've discussed it a million times, like everything else. I'm about to tell you to fuck off, so I'd better go before I do.

The therapist gasped softly (this profanity evidently had crossed some prior limit). But immediately the doctor righted herself. She took a long breath, then said in an even tone: All right. Perhaps. If you think that is best. You can go. But before you do, let me ask you one thing. Do you think this anger, this feeling of getting nowhere, of not belonging, has anything to do with the last session, with my bringing up the subject of adoption?

The patient breathed in and out several times.

Fuck no! Why do therapists think everything is about therapy? I went to a bar and wanted to make love to a woman in high heels, all very wrong in the world I live in for some stupid reason. That's what it's about. But hey, you're so hyped up on this adoption thing, I'm not sure you're even hearing me.

Perhaps you are right, said Dr. Schussler.

Then I'm leaving, said the patient.

If you must, said Dr. Schussler.

I guess I have to pay for the session anyway.

(Ah, money, I thought. The patient's revenge: reminding the therapist we've paid for her, like a whore.)

Yes, you must, the doctor said.

6.

What an exciting session! I could barely contain myself while the patient slammed the door behind her and the sound machine came on again. Beautiful legs in stomping boots! Women in high heels! Old- and new-style lesbians! As if sex had a fashion that waxed and waned with the design of shoes.

Throughout the long week that followed, I waited with almost unendurable anticipation for the patient's return. For I wondered what new drama would ensue. I was certain I had come in on her therapy at just the right moment, one of those mysterious fulcrum points: a pure, Aristotelian shift in the plot wherein the therapeutic story of the patient's life was about to turn. All my years of therapy told me this was true. Something had pressed up against her denials and evasions for two long years, and now—with all the inevitability of Oedipus killing his father—she must give way.

On the following Wednesday, therefore, I arose early and took special care to dress in comfortable, loose-fitting clothes (the better to sit absolutely still during any inadvertent titillation). I brought with me a small seat cushion (also for comfort during my immobility). It was barely nine in the morning when I boarded the N Judah; quarter of ten when I came within sight of our building's eyeless gargoyles.

It was a dangerous time, hard upon the interclient interval. Dr. Schussler often left her office between patients, for a restroom visit, I assumed, or a coffee at a nearby cafe, and it was imperative that she not encounter me entering my office. My presence in the hallway, my body before the door so close to hers, would force upon her the very fact of my existence, my face and physique giving visual form to any sound she might hear. Yet she must not imagine a body in Room 807; she must believe the room holds nothing but air.

Accordingly I slowed my steps. Upon entering the lobby, I scanned the persons about, wondering if one woman or another was Dr. Schussler. Over the weeks, a certain picture of the doctor had grown in my mind— nearing sixty, a slight limp (which I heard as she walked by my door), gray hair, perhaps a bun—an image simultaneously particular in certain details but vague overall, the way a character in a novel, barely described, can yet occupy a distinct place in one's mind. In short, I thought I should recognize her. Yet it was necessary that she not notice me in any particular way, even as a regular presence in the building. I had to be part of a crowd, an ordinary man in gray clothing: nothing. I was practiced at this; my nervous condition had given me a wealth of experience in the art of nonbeing.

I waited before the three elevators, watching the eyes of the cherubs circulate, an effect that had not entirely ceased to unnerve me. Eight other people waited. None among them was a woman who agreed with my image of the doctor; neither did she appear as one elevator and then another disgorged its passengers.

I therefore took the next car to the eighth floor and softly walked to my office. As I had practiced for the last weeks, I took extraordinary care with the keys and the lock and click of the door—always a tense moment. The mechanisms were old and not entirely reliable; I had learned to use a plastic card to control the release of the latch. Now having entered, I appointed my chair with the cushion, and then sat down to wait, listening all the while to the whir of the sound machine and the doctor's shushuations.

The ten o'clock patient left. At the stroke of eleven—a nearby church bell bonged out the hour—the doctor's sound machine promptly ceased. I stilled myself. Nothing but silence issued from Dr. Schussler's office. A minute went by, then two, three, four: excruciating minutes for anyone expectant and immobile, as I was. The time moved on to five past, six past, seven past, eight. And now from the other side of the door came an odd, teasing, slippery sound. It vanished, then returned—a rubbing, *slip-slip*—then vanished again.

I was suddenly frightened. What if I had gotten everything wrong? What if the great, dramatic turning point in the patient's therapy was not to be a grand story but an abrupt ending? With dawning dread, I remembered: the patient's sense that years had gone by, that nothing had changed, that nothing would ever change—how often had such feelings led me to abandon whatever therapist, psychiatrist, counselor, analyst, social worker, doctor who had dared to presume I might be happy? The patient could leave Dr. Schussler. She could abandon me.

And now again came that rubbing, cicada-like *slip-slip*.

Then another sound, a scrape.

My nostrils were suddenly filled with the scent of phosphorus; now of smoke. A cigarette: Dr. Schussler was smoking!

I no longer smoked—my stale-tobacco smell had become too memorable—but my nose was yet lined with countless receptors for the bitter, brilliant, desperate, dangerous scent that now came sliding under our adjoining door. I knew at once, with utter certainty, that Dr. Dora Schussler was smoking not a Kent, nor a Marlboro, nor a simpering Kool or Newport, but that she inhaled nothing other than a Pall Mall or a Viceroy—Viceroy, I decided—so tuned was I still to the tender shadings of my former addiction. I could all but see the pack, the gold medallion pendant from a V-shaped pin. And along with this sudden visualization of her cigarettes, I could picture the doctor herself: leaning back in her chair, lifting her head, exhaling, tipping the ash into the ashtray, crossing and recrossing her legs. Of course. That was the slip-sound I had been hearing: the slide of nylon upon nylon.

I was immediately becalmed. It was as if a long, long snake had curled under the door and wound one end around the therapist and the other around me—so joined did I feel to the experience of Dr. Schussler's cigarette: every breath she took, in and out, lung to lung. I inhaled her assurance. There was no need to worry. If not today, then next time: The patient would return.

And, soon enough, there came the ding of the elevator, the footsteps running down the hall, the therapist rising to open her door, the slam as the draft banged it shut.

Oh, hell, said the patient. I'm so sorry. A ridiculous argument at work. You know how I hate being late.

7.

Sit down, said the therapist.

It was the third derivative, said the patient.

But of course. Sit down.

The patient took her seat with a great puff of a cushion.

Carl kept questioning our historical curve analysis, the patient went on. Get rid of that function on the third derivative, he says. But Marsha refuses. It's done; it works; leave it, she says. But then Peter insists, Let's consider Carl's input. But Paul agrees with Marsha, and says, No, we tested it; it's working; our model is predictive. And so everyone is arguing in my carrel, and no one hears me when I'm saying, Stop, I've got to go. Then even more people pile in.

The patient rambled on in this vein: Peter, Marsha, Carl, Sasha, William, Paul, John, Larry. If Dr. Schussler knew these people, she simply let their names go by, as did I, since they meant nothing at all to me. The patient spoke, besides, of secular trends and intermediate trades, of waves and quadrants and regression curves, not to mention various incomprehensible three- and four-letter acronyms, which, I presumed, pertained to her company's insider terms relating to stock-market technical analysis and econometrics (subjects about which, again, I knew nothing).

But no matter. The sound of her voice soothed me. The curling remains of Dr. Schussler's cigarette still threaded the air, floating by like the patient's incomprehensible words. I simply sat still and enjoyed the tone of her voice, which played above the words like the sustain of a majestic chord. And there was something else, a little tremolo, the deep, inner unease I had noticed on that first day. For even as she raved on, it seemed that the little watchful person who stood guard over her speech had remained at his post, at attention, carefully ushering her confused As and Rs into the proper halls of culture.

She continued on for some time about her problems at work: a project that was late, a manager who disliked her, a woman in another group— was she perhaps a lesbian? Charlotte then made an appearance: another argument, this time initiated by someone's failure to fold the sheets (whether it was the patient or her girlfriend who had so shirked her duties I could not tell).

As I sat listening, I considered how odd it was to know such intimate details about a person's life yet have no context in which to place them. The voice that emanated from Room 804, the characters described, the situations and events—it was as if I were tuned to a radio play, a disembodied story floating in the quickening of my imagination. And what an odd narrator this story had, how risky, from a critical point of view; how much more conventional if she were only a financial analyst, or only a lesbian, or only an adoptee, if she did not have this odd mélange of characteristics living uneasily inside her. As the minutes went by, I kept pondering this, and saw the great difficulty in the work of the therapist: making a whole from the evidence of the broken pieces we bring them, these disparate stories that hold dark meaning for us, these unhappiness samples.

The patient was quiet for some seconds. Then:

Pretty dull stuff? she said to her therapist.

Not at all (lied the doctor).

But I suppose you'd like me to talk about what happened last week.

Silence from the therapist.

About my running out, the patient went on.

Dr. Schussler still said nothing.

You know, said the patient, I wasn't late because of last time.

The therapist gave a little laugh. No, she finally said. Of course not.

It wasn't . . . Oh, all right. Maybe. Maybe it did. I wasn't exactly in a hurry to get here.

A long pause ensued.

It's that adoption business, the patient finally said. You're driving me crazy over it. It's not like I haven't looked at it before. There were times when I tried to find out about my past. I mean indirectly, in my own way, as I had to.

When Dr. Schussler gave no response, the patient went on:

I looked into the process of adoption, when I was young, thirteen, still in boarding school. It's a good story. I'm assuming you'd like me to tell it.

But of course, said Dr. Schussler.

I thought you would, said the patient.

Dr. Schussler did not reply.

I thought you'd be overjoyed, said the patient. I thought you'd be encouraging, pushing, probing.

The doctor laughed. What can I probe, since you have not yet said anything?

Yes, yes, all right. I'm sorry. I'm playing games, aren't I?

Well, no, said the doctor after a pause. I do not think it is a game at all. I think you are doing exactly what you need to do. I think you sense, correctly, that this subject will be unsettling to explore. And that you will explore it how and when you are able.

The patient gave a little hum. And I could feel the waves of gratitude pouring forth from her. (If only my own therapists had been so giving! I thought.) Thank you, the patient said at last. Because I've been feeling you've been short with me, that you've been disapproving of me. As if you're getting bored with me. As if I couldn't be an interesting client if I didn't explore my "mysterious origins."

Dr. Schussler inhaled sharply, and for some time she said nothing. I heard her shift in her chair; there was a crinkling sound; and I knew it could only be the Viceroy pack she was seeking: a cigarette, to help stave off the next thing that must happen. For everything now depended upon her reply. If Dr. Schussler did not admit to her own failings and humanity—if she hid behind the therapist's ridiculous game of asking, So why do you think you thought that I had disapproving thoughts about you?—this therapeutic relationship, like so many of my own, would die.

The pause went on: eight seconds, ten, twelve. A fire truck wailed below then dopplered off.

Yes, Dr. Schussler said at last. I may have been . . . perhaps I . . .

She fell back into the cushions of her chair.

You know, she said, in our profession . . . it is often hard to know when to press on and when to let go.

(*Mirabile dictu!*)

Now the patient drew a breath. Do you think . . . she began.

Yes? asked the analyst.

Do you think it's time . . .

What?

That I dealt with—

Your adoption? I do, but—

Find my mother? Do that whole nasty thing where I blow up my family and hers, and make everyone unhappy?

No, no, no. Not that—

Then what?

I mean—

What else can you mean? Once you open this door, you know there's no way in hell to close it.

I glanced at my wristwatch, and to my dismay saw that the patient's hour was now gone. Then I remembered how often I had done the same: allowed myself to approach the brink only when I knew I could soon back away. There is some instinctive internal clock, some narrative curve, we analysands surely follow, so that we may have the fortitude to tell the story of ourselves another day.

We will have to explore this next time, the doctor gently said.

8.

I was filled with happiness—why deny it? The plot was turning, just as I had predicted. And it was now about to address the subject of my most ardent hopes: how the adoptee creates himself (or herself, in this case). I would learn how one separates from parents of all sorts, "real" or adoptive. And surely that path had to lead through the canyons of genetics. Even my dear friend Paul Beleiter had spent a year wondering over his blood relatives. How could one not? Such is the desire—irresistible, physical, cellular—to find one's likeness; to know whence came this eye, this brow, this dimple in the chin, or, for that matter, this talent, this compulsion, this madness: whatever one feels is indelibly engraved within.

Yet it was also imperative that the patient, like Paul, investigate the birth parents as an *idea*—an exploration confined to thoughts, dreams, images in the mind. The slabs of flesh of her actual parents would debase her quest, I thought. If she found those whose genes she carried, she would be surrounded by yet more people owning the perquisites of parenthood—a whole coterie with the power to grant her joy, or snatch it away. Paul had never found his parents. Later he told me of his relief: What if they were only ordinary? he said. And I replied: What if they were monsters? He laughed and said: That would be better.

All now depended upon the skill of the analyst. The success of the patient's endeavor, and my own, required that Dr. Schussler lead her patient through the ravines of inheritance without letting her stop there, so to speak. She must not stimulate in her client a thirst for her "true" mother, for that would transform those gloriously "mysterious origins" into a banal reality of blood. But I had no faith in the powers of the psychological professions, as I have said. Who was this Dora Schussler that she would presume to take on the role of psychic guide?

I feared for the patient. I rode the streetcar up and down Market Street; I went from my house to the office and back again; the weekend went by and then came Monday, Tuesday. And all through, the patient's words hung in the darkening of my thoughts: *Once you open this door, you know there's no way in hell to close it.*

Wednesday morning came; I trembled in my office; at last the patient arrived. The doctor wasted no time in returning to the subject of their prior meeting.

What we want to do, she said as they began, is probe your *feelings* about being adopted. We want to understand adoption's effect upon who you are now, upon your relationships with your parents, your friends, your lovers, and, most of all, upon your inner concept of yourself.

The patient laughed.

I already know adoption's effect on my feelings.

But really, said Dr. Schussler, we are just—

It hasn't had any effect. There is some deep-down way that my parents—my adoptive parents—don't affect me at all.

(Yes! I thought.)

That can't be so, said the analyst.

Oh, really? What do you know about it?

The doctor exhaled, annoyed. Then she said: Of course it is my job to know just a little about these things.

But aren't you supposed to listen?

Of course.

Then listen. There is some way that I am distant—unconnected—to my family. I will never be like them. Some core part of me is alien to them. I am . . . alone.

(Exactly! I thought. The apartness Paul had always spoken of, that sense of being a singularity in the world!)

Precisely, said the doctor. It is just this sense of being unconnected that we need to explore.

Please just listen! It's the story I wanted to tell you last week before we ran out of time.

The analyst stirred in her chair. Yes, dear, she said in an odd voice.

What's that about? said the patient.

What? said the therapist.

That "yes, dear" business—and don't say, What do *I* think it's about.

The doctor laughed. You have said many times that when your mother is resisting you, she says, Yes, dear.

Hell. I don't want to talk about Mother. What I'm talking about is older. Original. Built in. Before Mother, before Father, before school. Before I even learned to think in words. As if it came out of my bones, my nerves, my skin. Original—she gave a laugh—like sin.

The analyst sat back amidst a great commotion of creaking leather. Please, she said. Go on.

9.

It was Christmastime, the patient began. I was thirteen, home from boarding school on winter break. I don't think Mother even kissed me before she said, Don't unpack. We're going to New York. A holiday! she sang. But I had an assignment for school, due after the break, and there I was in New York, in a hotel, sharing a room with Lizabeth,

(Lizabeth?)

who chattered at me all the time when she was little.

(Ah, a sister, it seemed.)

It had to be a report of a visit to a hospital for some reason—yes, we were studying the medical professions—and now I had to find someplace in New York. There was a Yellow Pages in the closet of our hotel room, where I found a long list of hospitals, column after column. How would I choose? Presbyterian Such-and-Such, Jewish Center for This-and-That, Mary Mother of So-and-So—then suddenly one name jumped out at me.

She paused.

The Manhattan Hospital for Foundlings.

Foundlings! she went on. What an old-fashioned word. It made me think of newborns left on doorsteps. Of Baby Moses in the reeds. And wasn't there this medieval practice where infants were put in some sort of lazy-Susan-type thing and spun anonymously into a convent?

Here the patient stopped, and I thought, Surely Dr. Schussler will participate now, despite the patient's request that she merely listen. For what a grisly image the patient had conjured up: helpless infants in a trap of clanking iron, surrendered to the cold care of nuns.

The patient gave off a little laugh. Or at least that's what I remembered from some medieval history class, she said. I mean the lazy Susans.

Again she waited.

(She's asking for help, I thought. Help her, Dr. Schussler!)

So I called them, the patient went on. The Hospital for Foundlings. I was transferred around, and finally I had an appointment with someone— was her name Mrs. Waters? Yes, let's say it was Mrs. Waters.

I didn't tell my family where I was going—oh, well, yes; they knew I had an assignment and that I was going to a hospital. But I lied about the name. I told them it was something like "General Hospital." They never paid much attention to me, so lying was easy.

I had to lie, you see. Adoption could not be mentioned in our family. Never—along with many other forbidden topics that came under the rubric of what Father called "interpersonal matters." Of course everyone knew I was adopted. But it was not to be discussed, not to be mentioned. But Father could not control everyone, much as he would have liked to. There was always the occasional stupid person meeting us for the first time who would say, Now which one of you is the real one?

Oh, yeah, said the patient with a laugh. I always used to think, Lizabeth's the real one and I'm the phantom. How do you do, ma'am. Shake hands with me and I'll give you a good squeeze to show you how real I am.

(Lizabeth. The sister. A "natural" one. How horrid for the patient to be followed by a "wet" child!)

The patient laughed again.

Besides, she quickly went on, it was very easy to keep the fiction going. From the outside, we seemed such a well-matched family. Father with his sandy hair and blue eyes. Mother also blue-eyed and blond—and getting chemically blonder by the year. Lizabeth still towheaded, her hair so light her eyebrows disappeared. And there I am: blond, too. Well, "dirty blond," Mother was sure to point out; perhaps we should fix that, she'd say. And then there were my hazel eyes. Don't squint so, she'd always say. It makes your eyes go dark.

The patient stopped.

I . . . Never mind, she said.

So Mother gave me money for a taxi, the patient went on, to get to the hospital—the subway was out of the question, said Father; perverts were everywhere in New York. The hotel doorman helped me into a cab, and then I rode up a broad, bustling avenue. I have no idea which it was, only that life was exploding all around me. People, cars, trucks, buses, taxis, horns, shouts, lights; policemen blowing their whistles and waving their arms to hold back the crowds: a magnificent craziness. It was cold, snowing; the taxi window fogged. I couldn't bear having it between me and the world. So I rolled it down and rode with my head stuck out in the air like a dog. The snow swirled around in the windy street, and all the people and cars seemed to swirl with it, me along with

everyone and everything, and I had a moment—oh!—that I thought
signaled the opening of my life at last; the sort of moment I thought
would come again and again and again.

Ha, said the patient. She paused.

What? asked the doctor.

(What? The doctor had to ask "what"? Of course it was the adult
understanding that such moments did not come again and again!)

Nothing.

(The doctor let it pass. Fool!)

Anyhow, said the patient, then went on:

Finally—too soon—we came to the foundling hospital. It was at the
back of a gated courtyard; I had to circle and circle the building, tramp-
ing in the snow, before I found the door. I went to a reception desk,
asked for Mrs. Waters, and was given a seat in a large waiting area. It was
crowded with women and babies; noisy with the babies' cries; steamy
with the heated, melted snow from everyone's boots and coats and hats.
The minutes went by, and soon the pile of winter clothes in my lap began
to thaw. I began to panic. I imagined my skirt with a large wet stain right
in the front; my white blouse gone see-through, everyone able to see my
bra, which I had just started wearing that year. My sweater sleeves would
hang damp, my skirt would look like I'd just peed in it, my new stretchy
bra would be on view for everyone to see—the little red rose in the
middle like a bull's-eye. I wished suddenly that I had never come here,
had never lied to my parents, had never done anything relating to foundlings or babies or children or adoption. I prayed earnestly to be transported back in time, to the hotel room with Lizabeth, where we would
be planning our outfits for an outing to a museum.

Suddenly, a tall woman loomed over me. I was staring into the crotch
of a very fitted skirt in a nubby sort of fabric, the skirt clinging in an
hourglass sort of way, so that I could see very clearly the woman's hips
and panty line, even the bumps of her garters. Now a hand came toward
me. I'm Mrs. Waters, said the woman. Let's see if we can't help you with
that project of yours.

She was wearing a skirt suit and the highest heels I had ever
seen. Her hair was nearly black, cut to chin length. She wore deep red
lipstick—she was beautiful in a frightening sort of way. I somehow found
my own hand from under my pile of clothes, offered it to her in return,
and stood up awkwardly, trying to hold on to my coat and scarf and hat,

and at the same time keep everything in front of me, to hide the water stains.

I followed Mrs. Waters across a wide lobby. Along the way I checked myself and saw, to my enormous relief, that my skirt and blouse were only wrinkled and damp, not wet through. And now I could concentrate on the sight of Mrs. Waters's high, high heels as they clicked their way across the white marble floor.

She led me into an elevator. It was very dark in there—black glass panels, black floor, pinpoint lights above—so that all I could see of Mrs. Waters's face were her cheekbones, everything else disappearing into black sockets. It seemed that we rode up for a long time, silently, just a whistle of a ventilator coming from somewhere, finally arriving at a floor Mrs. Waters called "the wards."

The elevator door opened to blinding light: bright, greenish fluorescent lights leading off in long trails across what seemed a mile-long ceiling. And noise. Hundreds of cries and wails and screams. Under the trail of the lights, I saw what looked like an endless line of cribs. It took me a moment to understand what I was looking at: ward after ward of babies, room after room, row after row. I had never seen so many babies in my life. And were all of them "foundlings"? I asked Mrs. Waters, Are all of these babies without parents? And she said yes. And then I asked, Where did they come from? From the courts, she said. From unwed mothers. From lawyers and social workers. From the police, who sometimes found infants in trash bins.

(Trash bins! Dr. Schussler: Where are you?)

Trash bins! said the patient. My God! Then before I could get over this, Mrs. Waters led me back into that night-dark elevator, where she turned a key in a lock on the elevator panel and then pressed a button for a floor. This lock, the darkness, brought back the anxiety I had been feeling while I had waited to meet her. And in the confinement of the elevator, during the long, quiet ride, with only that whistling ventilator— I suddenly felt that I was in extreme danger. I clutched my damp clothes and held my breath, the way I did as a kid passing a cemetery, as if just inhaling would let in whatever horrible thing was out there. All at once it came to me that I was making a terrible mistake. I was trespassing. I was doing something totally, completely, utterly forbidden: finding out where abandoned babies came from.

The elevator door abruptly opened, and now I had no choice but to follow Mrs. Waters, who clip-clopped ahead of me down a long, stark hallway, finally opening a door and waiting for me to enter. It was very dim in there, almost as dark as the elevator, and I could make out several people sitting before a panel full of knobs and buttons, some sort of controls, I thought

This is where we test the children, said Mrs. Waters, gesturing as she said this toward what at first had seemed to be some sort of screen but that I now saw was a glass, a one-way mirror, and on the other side, being looked at by the people in the booth or control room, were several babies— I don't mean babies, exactly; they were sitting up by themselves, so maybe they were six months old or so. I found all this very strange. Those babies, the people observing them, the darkness, the locks, the knobs and buttons—what were they for? And what exactly did they control? Although there was nothing at all sinister about what the babies were doing. They were sitting there playing, in a patty-cake sort of way, with blocks and stuffed animals and puzzles and colored shapes, all very normal. And it seemed they were mostly enjoying themselves, just a few tears now and then, but only in that quick way children have of crying when they're thwarted for a minute.

Then Mrs. Waters explained the purpose of the booth: They were investigating the psychological health of the children. We need to understand them before we can offer them for adoption, she said. We place the children in both comfortable and less comfortable conditions. We want to see how they react, whether they're sturdy or fearful children, or maybe truly disturbed, all of which has a bearing on what we would tell the prospective adoptive parents, or if we would consider them adoptable at all. For instance, we can make the room instantly dark, or we can introduce a very loud noise, and see what is called their "startle" response. Strange people can suddenly walk in; or already-reliable people can play with them, then suddenly leave. We're stressing them psychologically, it's true, but only briefly and under the most controlled conditions—and all in the interest of placing them in suitable, happy homes.

Mrs. Waters stood over me, so tall, so imposing. The investigators kept their backs to me and said nothing, only adjusted the controls before them. And I looked over at the babies, playing, trusting, all unsuspecting, about to be put through some terrible gauntlet before they could leave this strange hospital and find a home. Which one, I wondered, was the unlucky one: the one who might not be "adoptable at all"?

At that moment, several people entered the room on the other side of the glass, picked up the babies, and carried them away—I don't know where they went. Then Mrs. Waters said, Why don't you sit here quietly, and you can watch us put the next batch through their paces.

And so the next "batch" came in, three babies of about the same age as the previous group—girls, each one held by a woman. The women put the babies on a table and sat down beside them, and then they played with the babies, each woman with the baby she had carried in. This went on for some time. They played coochie-coo and patty-cake and hide-and-seek behind their hands. The women held up squeaky toys and rattles, balls and stuffed animals. They kissed and hugged the babies, who were laughing and squealing.

Then at some point—there must have been a signal I wasn't aware of—each woman picked up her own version of the same appealing toy, a sort of head with feathers and shiny bits, which rattled and squeaked as the women played with it in front of the babies. All the babies reached out eagerly to touch the toy. But the women just kept holding it, shaking it, rattling it. Then the women reached down and picked up something from the floor, which turned out to be tall metal cylinders. After giving the babies one more chance to see and reach for the toy, each woman placed her toy in her respective cylinder. Then they stood up and left the room.

For a moment, all three babies just looked at the cylinders, which really were quite tall in comparison with their little bodies, almost the whole length of their arms. Then one, the little girl in the middle, reached right in and retrieved the toy. The baby on the left patted the outside of the cylinder, gave off some quick cries and tears, then began tentatively exploring it, gradually going deeper until, with a great cry of glee, she came up with the toy in her hand.

But the last baby . . . the last one could not bring herself to reach inside. She began wailing and screaming and hitting the top of the cylinder, so hard I thought she would make her hand bleed. The happiness of the other two babies just seemed to make her more miserable, because she watched them, saw their happiness, their delight, then screamed and hit her cylinder again and again. I thought I had never seen such misery in my life, such raw, terrible unhappiness, her whole body turning nearly inside out with cries.

I looked at the researchers. How could they put this child through such a trial? None of them spoke. They just watched and took notes, while this baby was tortured with desire for the toy they themselves had made her want.

Finally I turned to Mrs. Waters and asked, What does this show? What does this tell you? She nodded at one of the researchers at the control panel, who said, That this child is very fearful. That she's afraid to explore, is easily overcome by stress, even when given a great deal of love and attention. It's too bad. She'll have a hard time in this world.

Here the patient stopped and sat there breathing haltingly, as if she would cry—but no. At once she regained control of herself, and said:

So I knew I was looking at the unlucky one.

She paused.

Born unhappy. Built in. Original, like sin. In her bones and blood and skin. And nothing would ever change that verdict: She was going to have a hard time in this world. I looked at that little baby—she was still screaming; why didn't somebody soothe her now, for God's sake?—and I wondered: What would I have done? How deep and dark and terrible that cylinder must have seemed. Would I have been able to do it: reach in and find the shiny little happiness at the bottom?

10.

The elevator bell *ding*ed out in the hallway.

It's time, isn't it? the patient said.

The doctor hummed softly. I am afraid so, she said.

What bad timing, said the patient.

You can call me, said Dr. Schussler. You know you can always call.

The doctor stood, then her client.

I have that—

I remember, said the therapist.

Bad timing!

Yes, the doctor said. Certainly not the best.

You can call, said the analyst. Please. Do not hesitate to call.

The moment the door closed behind the patient, Dr. Schussler lit a cigarette and dragged on it deeply, three times. Before the curl of her smoke could reach under our communicating door, she picked up her phone and dialed. The rotary phone ticked off the numbers: two? eight? five? The rest of the pulses went by too quickly to count, and I soon heard the therapist say:

Dr. Gurevitch? Dr. Schussler. Yes. Thank you. I am so happy to have caught you in. You received my— Of course. Yes. In particular I am hoping we can . . . three. The patient coded as three. You see— Aha! Yes. Eight o'clock? Until then. Yes!

She hung up the phone, then threw open the window—airing out the office, I thought. Moments later she closed the window, opened her door, and said "come in" to her twelve o'clock. Their voices disappeared behind the rush of the sound machine.

11.

I sat stunned. *Born unhappy. Built in. Original, like sin.* These words kept reciting themselves in my mind until I thought I must have said them myself. The sound machine was on; I might move about, but I did not, could not. The patient and I were kin, I suddenly knew, spawn of the same cursed line: the tribe of the inherently unhappy. How early one knows this! Too early, too young; she at thirteen, I at twelve. All unexpectedly the realization comes; that damned day; that indelible sight; that unreachable, shiny little happiness.

The nearby church bell tolled the slow strokes of noon. At the twelfth, my heart began to race. Sweat sprang out upon my neck and back. The weather had turned unaccountably hot; one day the late summer's fog chilled the city as usual; the next came a dry, hot wind from the east, sending temperatures above ninety degrees under merciless skies. Even the cold breath of the old building's soul had been vanquished by the heat. Yet the sweat that clung to me was chillingly cold. There was nothing I could do. I could only watch as my black mood descended upon me the crows, so delighted, flapping down for their meal of carrion. They pecked at my wishes, as they did always; sucked the world empty of hope. I thought of the weight of inheritance that had fallen upon the patient—so heavy, so like my own—and my dreams for her self-creation seemed doomed, a small, flapping bird chained to a stake at the foot.

The clock sounded one, then two. And only then, after Dr. Schussler left for her luncheon break, did I stand and try to calm myself. I took a turn about the office, visited the men's room, then walked the length of the corridors: two long, perpendicular hallways—the building was shaped like a carpenter's rule—where at the far end of each hall there gathered a dim, perpetual twilight. I could not return to my cottage by the ocean—the hot weather had beckoned hordes to the beach; their loud radios plagued me; motorcycles raced up and down the Great Highway without cease. I could only stay at the office, which I did, lying down as best I could upon the small settee, settling in before the therapist returned for her three o'clock patient.

The afternoon wore away. The sound machine kept up its empty breathing; Dr. Schussler spat out her *Ts*, hard-hushed her *Ss*. A faint current of hot air stirred the venetian blind, setting it to knock softly against the casement. Spears of light hit the walls, then vanished, then speared again in the uneven rhythm of the bare breeze. It seemed to me that I had seen and heard all this before: the stabs of light, the knock of the blind, the rush of *Ss*. A voice sounded in my head. When you're adopted, said the voice, you don't look like anyone. The sound machine took up the rhythm of the breeze, playing a deceptive melody. And all at once I knew how this moment had come to be, where it had happened, long ago.

I did not want to go there in my mind. I looked out the window—a statue on the roofline of the Palace, a naked man, loins draped—then looked away.

12.

The weather turned on us again. The heat subsided; there was one clear and temperate day; and then it began to rain. I had no idea that rain could fall with such steady determination, hour by hour, day after day. What kind of devilish place had I come to, I wondered, where humid fog could turn to sere heat and then to monsoon rains all within the space of a few weeks? A wet gloom now seemed to have settled over the city, and while San Franciscans went about their business as usual (the N Judah rumbled by; passengers ascended and descended; cars dashed by on the Great Highway), the fifth deluged day found me still in bed, in dirty pajamas, watching rainwater seep under my door. Out on the beach, no one appeared but a single haunted soul in a black hooded jacket: a suicide, I thought, surveying the sea for riptides.

Only the thought of the patient's return enabled me to rise from my bed, dress, make my way under the drenched gargoyles, through the white lobby, past the black, circling eyes of the cherubs, to my office, there to await the rich cream of the patient's voice.

In my absence, the radiators evidently had come aboil, for now they chuffed and clanged as steam surged through the building's aged pipes. The dry heat was almost unbearable. I envied the man in the Hotel Palace across the way, who, as I watched, threw open his window and, heedless of the rain, stood naked to the street.

I doubted that the man could see me—I kept my light off, lest Dr. Schussler look up and see the glow at her neighbor's window—yet I could see him clearly. His body protruded past the plane of the window directly opposite mine, and the gray light of the sky cast an even, silvery tone upon his skin, so that he appeared to be made of marble, one of the statues that lined the hotel's venerable roof. He was tall and well made, muscular yet not overly so: the sort of body that would neither repulse nor intimidate if encountered in the locker room. A look of pleasure passed over the man's face, which he lifted up to the sky and rain. Then, his face still uplifted, he took his genitals in both hands.

Not since boyhood—since Paul, my best friend—had I seen another male touch himself. I gaped as the man fondled his testicles and stroked his penis softly, almost absently. After some moments, he encircled the base of his penis with the thumb and forefinger of one hand and began to pull upon it with the other. He gave himself long, full, strong pulls, and his member responded by steadily growing in length and girth. He continued in that full, slow rhythm until his penis achieved an impressive size, protruding some inches into the narrow width of New Montgomery Street, so that he seemed very near to me, almost at a touching distance, the eye of his penis looking directly at me, as it were. All the while, he kept his face uplifted to the sky, blinking with delight as drops played upon his eyelids, his mouth opening and closing as if to taste the rain. My own member begin to stir—it was normal, I told myself; I was responding to the memory of my boyhood games; also sex begets sex; the sight of the man's penis, of his pleasure, his delight, merely made me think of my own.

But then, suddenly, without ever quickening his rhythm as I would have done near the end, the man closed his eyes, arched his back, gave one great thrust, and ejaculated forcefully into the air.

His seed dripped from the ledge.

I shut my eyes in disgust.

13.

When you're adopted, you don't look like anyone.

It was Paul, Paul Beleiter. We were in his bedroom. The light that pressed against his venetian blinds was the hot sun of an August day. From down the hall came the static of a drifting radio station, a melody now surfacing, now fading, then a stern voice: talk of war in Europe. Paul and I did not listen. We were boys, twelve years old, indolent in the last days of summer.

When you're adopted, Paul was saying, you don't look like anyone.

We were sprawled across his wide bed. I looked at Paul: sculpted lips, curls of near-black hair, smooth skin—swarthy, a shade too dark for the liking of his adoptive parents. His nose was pointed, his eyes too close together, fortunate imperfections that gave him a ferocious gaze. No, he didn't look like anyone, not even the other boys. He towered over us; his beard was beginning to show; his voice was already lowering—he was years beyond us, it seemed. His father was pale and slight; his mother pallid, tight. Why would he want to look like them?

He was angry. Something about some art classes in New York; a scholarship he'd won; his parents forbidding him to go. We were stranded in Ovid, our town named for the poet. But the artists who had settled and named the place were long gone. Now only fields and dairy cows stretched out in the heat beyond the window; farmers and the people who sold them things. Paul's father sold tractors, mine insurance. At least we didn't have cow shit on our shoes, we said.

They don't know anything about art, I said to Paul.

I'm never going to be like my parents, said Paul. Never.

He leaned down, reached under the bed, and came up holding a box, the sort that once might have held a pair of boots.

Look at this, he said.

He held a stack of clippings. Then one by one he laid them on the bedspread. They were photographs, no story attached, no caption. Here and there, the newspaper name was printed on a clipping's border: the *Ithaca Journal*, the *Cortland Standard*, the *Elmira Star-Gazette*, the *Finger*

Lakes Times, the *Olean Times-Herald.* Some clippings were white, some faded, some yellowed—Paul had clearly been collecting these for years. We were very best friends; why hadn't he shown these to me before?

Horrible, isn't it? Paul said.

I don't—

What happens to people when they grow up.

Now I saw it: an adult and child in each picture, the child remarkably like the adult who was clearly the parent. Uncanny resemblances. Faces captured at two distant moments in time.

Amazing, I said.

Keep looking, said Paul.

For what?

Here. Look what happens to a dimple.

It was a picture of a cute little boy of about five. His happy, dimpled face relaxed on his father's shoulder. The father, too, had dimples, but the formerly endearing little dots had deepened, were now surrounded by desiccated skin, hanging sacs of flesh.

And look what happens to that adorable pudgy cheek, said Paul.

A sagging jowl, I saw.

And look at that little girl's pretty fair hair.

Her mother's was thinned, dyed, dry.

And this one, he said.

A holiday picnic. A mother holding a little girl on her lap. Beside her, the grandmother, holding a little boy. Three generations, one face. The curve of a tender cheek, softened, then sunken. Wrinkles slowly etching themselves into the skin above the mouth. The girl's round little eye, hopeful; the mother's eye, drooping at the edges; the grandmother's, disappearing into a sea of folds.

And on it went: A little roly-poly boy sat upon his father's fat gut of a lap. A girl with twinkling eyes looked into the crow-marked eyes of her mother. A beanpole of a boy in the embrace of a father whose wrinkled skin hung from bony arms. A tiny puff in a cheek become a sorry fold. Small lips now a mean line. Cute buck teeth grown into embarrassments. Tiny flaws, invisible in the freshness of youth, now magnified, exaggerated, dominant in the parent: the terrible work of time that awaited the child.

Paul picked up this first set of clippings and replaced it with another— another catalogue of the decay, desiccation, bloating, wrinkling, graying, fading, and shrinking that awaited the poor innocent spawn of his parents' blood.

How can anyone stand it? said Paul. I mean, how can you look into the face of your parent and know you're going to turn into *that*?

I leapt away from the bed and went to the window, where I drew back the blind and stood squinting into the brilliance of the yard. I watched birds peck at the grass, leaves ruffle in the breeze, a cat dive into a patch of underbush, as I tried not to think about my mother, who just two months before had tried to "do some harm to herself," as my aunt had put it. While at the hospital, sitting among my relatives and listening to their talk, I had learned things about my grandmother—that she had locked herself in a running car in a closed garage. And about my great-uncle on my father's side, who had jumped off a roof; about my mother's grandfather, who had given away all his money one day in a manic fit; about another great-aunt, who had thrown herself in front of a car. While waiting to hear about my mother's condition, my aunts and uncles and adult cousins had gone on describing manias, depressions, obsessions, compulsions—it seemed our family had long bloodlines of mad people stretching back in time, suicides running in our veins the way blue eyes were passed down in saner clans. Throughout, my father sat there without speaking, closed, withdrawn, as he had been for the past year. I looked around this circle of my relatives. I saw my eyes here, my chin there, my cowlick rising from the crown of Uncle John's head. My aunt Selma once said I had the temperament of Uncle Harry: Did this include whatever bad thing he had done with his gun?

I said to Paul: Everyone says I look exactly like my mother.

He started, sat back on the bed, put down his clippings. He knew—he had to have known—how I longed to be like him, how dearly I wished not to know that what had happened to my family—to my mother, to my unspeaking father—could also happen to me. I longed for him to walk over to me, embrace me, at least pat me on the shoulder, and say, Don't worry, you're your own man, you never know.

But of course we were just boys, twelve years old, and so what, really, could he do or say? Paul quietly retrieved the clippings, put them in the box, and slid it back under the bed.

Let's play our game, said Paul.

I don't feel like it.

He reached for me. Sure you do, he said.

14.

I came back to myself. I heard truck engines idling in the street below, horns honking, a squeal of brakes, the airy breath of Dr. Schussler's sound machine. I looked down at my watch: ten past eleven. I had not heard the church carillon chime the hour; the sound machine still whirred; the patient was not there. I looked across the street at the hotel: The man was gone. The window opposite was shut, the curtains drawn, no glow showing from within. From the roofline, the statue looked back at me: the naked man, the cloth about his loins.

I waited all through the day; the patient did not come. Then through the night. I returned the next day and waited, and then the next. And still the patient did not come.

All the while, I thought of her, and of the analyst who had enticed her into exploring the actual situation of her birth. And suddenly I thought the patient should flee, quit this therapy, return to the calming shadow of her mysterious origins. There she could imagine her parents to be anyone—brilliant mathematicians; fierce-minded analysts; dark-souled bisexuals, perhaps, who had passed on to her a woman's love for women—ancestors who would understand implicitly the person she felt herself to be.

She should be more like Paul, I thought, reveling in the unknown possibilities of her future. Everyone has his own genetic fate written inside him—his own complement of mental predispositions, weaker organs waiting to fail, more or less likely routes upon which he will encounter death. But what good does it do to know it? Knowledge is not a relief. The burden is not lessened by the sense of its not being one's own fault, not a failure of will, of intent, of virtue. One is just as subject to this fate, the fate of this body, its Furies.

15.

The week was gone. The rain went on, intermittently now; the black-hooded man daily haunted the beach; the sound machine never ceased its empty breathing. I sat in the office in the dark of the raining days and nights, and did not look out the window, afraid that I might see again the apparition of the naked man, since apparition I believed him to have been, a conjuring out of the absurd black stew of my mind.

Another week, and I began to believe that I had conjured up Dr. Schussler as well, that the hiss that came from the adjoining office was merely a sound produced by my own ears; that I had even conjured up the patient, that there had never been an adopted lesbian woman struggling to understand herself on the other side of our common wall—how else could my mere wish that she flee make her disappear?

Only some compulsion brought me back, day by day, to sit at that desk in the office. For this, at least, I thanked my blood, all the ancestors who could not see a carpet without arranging the fringe, a sofa without aligning the cushions, a shoulder without picking lint. I watched the rain, avoided looking toward the windows of the Palace, pretended to work on my lectures, whose words now seemed worthless to my eyes. How much time had passed? I didn't care. I merely sat. What day was it? I had no idea.

When suddenly, one mid-morning, the sound machine stopped.

I did not trust the silence. Had I dreamed it?

But there was Dr. Schussler's German-accented voice clearly saying, Welcome back! How was the trip?

And then came the young, deep, watchful voice—so rich! so lovely!—for which my whole being had been yearning.

16.

I don't know how to begin, the patient said.

Perhaps, said Dr. Schussler, you might tell me about the trip—

The convention. Great. Granger spoke, the god of econometrics. A speech about time series data, stationary and nonstationary series—oh, it's too complicated to explain. But it made me wish I'd studied with him at U.C. San Diego instead of going to Wharton.

The patient paused.

And from there we went to our prospective client. The Brighton Fund. Which went well. Very well, actually. They were impressed with our models and immediately subscribed.

Wonderful! You must be so pleased, after all the arguments about . . .

The function on the third derivative.

The doctor laughed. Yes, that was it.

The patient shifted about her chair, then fell silent.

And there is something else? asked the therapist.

The patient took a breath, released it. A lot more happened on this trip.

Yes?

Well . . . since our business was finished so quickly, I decided not to come back right away. I . . . went to see my family.

The doctor hummed but said nothing.

You know how rarely I see them, said the patient. I talk to them on the phone maybe three times a year. Like I've told you. When they call, I figure someone must have died. So I don't know what got into me. All I know is, I was free, not far away, and I went.

And? asked the doctor when the patient did not immediately go on.

And I asked my mother about my adoption.

Oh, my!

(Dr. Schussler must have jumped in her seat; her chair produced a squall of creaking leather; I myself could barely hold still.)

The patient said nothing more for several seconds.

And? the doctor prompted once more.

I can't tell you what a bitch my mother was, said the patient.

17.

It was Sunday evening, said the voice I loved, a windy day, she went on.
The patient was sitting with her mother in a room they called the den,
a small addition whose walls were pierced on three sides by windows
("pierced by windows": my patient's lovely phrase). The trees had begun
to turn. Fingers of drying leaves kept scratching at the window glass
("fingers of leaves": also the patient's beautiful words). Her mother sat on
a recliner that faced the television; the patient across from her on a small
sofa. Between them was a glass coffee table covered with delicate glass
figurines and ceramics: a ballerina, an old woman selling balloons, a
clown, a breaching whale, an owl, a rose, a ballet slipper.

Her mother had just come into the room and was still fussing with
her skirt, trying not to wrinkle it as she settled into her recliner. When
she was satisfied with her efforts, she said to her daughter:

You know, you'll get me a glass of ice water.

It was her future imperative tense, the patient explained to Dr.
Schussler. My mother foresees something that will occur in the future,
and you have no choice but to enact it.

Her mother had come home from the beauty salon, where they had
created for her a hard, round, fiercely yellow helmet that was supposed
to be beautiful hair.

What do you think of it? asked her mother, gently patting her helmet
with one hand as she received her daughter's proffered ice water with
the other.

Not too big? she asked.

Well, maybe a little, answered the patient.

Oh, I don't think so. You know, we women don't wear our hair loose
and tousled like you girls.

We're women, Mother.

Well, I think of you as girls. I can't change the way I think. You're
my girl.

Your hair is fine, Mother.

Not too sprayed?

Your hair is fine, Mother.

Her mother said while lighting a cigarette: Today the dry cleaner told me I always look so nice. Not like the other women in their housedresses and curlers. I don't understand how women can let themselves be seen like that.

Her mother was wearing a pearl-gray wool suit, lapis lazuli beads, a peacock brooch pinned to her shoulder: gold, inset with gemstones. The skirt was tight, to show off her trim figure.

You always look lovely, Mother.

There's a certain illusion a woman has to maintain, dear. A little powder and paint goes a long way. Don't forget that, darling. Remember that when you get married.

I'm never going to get married, Mother. You know that I—

Dammit! her mother said. We are not going to discuss that in this house! How many times do I have to tell you?

I wanted to kill her, the patient told her therapist. Really I did. At that moment I thought I would jump up and strangle her. The weight of all those lies, all those silences—I thought there was no way out but to kill her. I suppose I wanted a kind of revenge. How many years had I spent telling her she was beautiful, trying to fill that black-hole need in her— unquenchable, endless—meanwhile sparing her any little upset about me, about who I really was. Bringing up the adoption would hurt her back—that's what I'm thinking now. But at the time I only knew how blind angry I was. Her refusal to see me, know me. I just felt, I'm not going to let you get away with it anymore. And I said:

So. Tell me what you know about my adoption.

I said it just like that, the patient told Dr. Schussler. Right out. Nothing to prepare her.

But then we both froze, as if we'd been caught in a spotlight doing something wrong. Her cigarette stopped in midair. Dead stop. I confess I enjoyed seeing her freeze up like that. Then, oh so slowly, Mother reached down and put her ice water on the glass coffee table, placing it carefully among the delicate figurines.

What makes you bring that up, dear?

Didn't you think I'd be curious? I asked her. That I would ask some-time?

The cigarette went back into motion. She inhaled, coughed once, then blew out a line of smoke. Funny, she said at last. I don't suppose I've thought much about it in years. I mean, it all happened so long ago. I don't even think of you as . . .

Adopted.

Yes. Adopted.

I watched her deepening lip lines, the patient told her doctor. You know, the wrinkles on the top lip, hard lines straight up and down from nose to mouth.

Mother, you told me never to make that expression. Lip—

Lip lines! Ugly! She laughed. Thank you, dear.

But you've got to tell me, the patient persisted. Tell me what you know.

Her mother's mouth contracted again. I'll have to discuss this with Father.

Why with Father?

I just do.

Why? He doesn't own this story.

Her mother looked up at her with an expression the patient had never before seen on that carefully made-up face. Was it fear?

Or does he? the patient went on.

Her mother crushed her half-smoked cigarette, stood up, straightened her dress, patted her hair.

It isn't too big, is it?

No, Mother. It's not too big.

And the color?

Perfect.

Her mother stepped one way, then another, then picked up her glass of water. You know, she said, you'll take this and put this in the dishwasher. She gave the glass to her daughter and started out of the room. But she abruptly paused at the threshold.

We went through an adoption agency, her mother said from the doorway.

She was looking down as she spoke, at her skirt.

But what adoption agency? the patient asked her.

Oh . . . Let's not . . . She was still concentrating on the skirt, brushing it with her hand.

Oh, darling, it was so long ago, she went on. I really don't remember. Something connected with a Catholic charity.

Catholic! said the patient. But what do you mean—*Catholic*?

Oh, you know. After the war there were so many little babies need-ing homes—

Orphans?

Well. Yes. Or, you know. Men would come home on furloughs.

Bastards.

Darling! What a thing to say!

Well, what else?

Her mother kept brushing her skirt.

And why a Catholic agency? the patient asked her mother. Father hates Catholics. He's practically pathological on the subject.

Her mother looked up briefly. Sweetheart! Do you think something like the religion of the *agency* would keep us from adopting you? It doesn't necessarily mean that you were born Catholic. Do I have a stain here?

Where?

Here.

Her mother indicated a spot on her left thigh.

I don't see anything, the patient said. And you didn't ask?

What?

If I'd been born a Catholic.

Something passed over her face, said the patient. A little squint. A tightness in her mouth. So brief and subtle that, if I'd blinked, I would have missed it.

Heavens, no! she said. We so wanted a child. We were so happy to have you!

But Father hates Catholics. Rabidly!

Really, there's nothing to say. We didn't care, darling!

She sang it out, the patient said. *We didn't care, dahling!*—playing Nora Charles in *The Thin Man*.

And at that she left the room, calling out over her shoulder:

You ought to pack, dear. Early flight tomorrow.

18.

'I'he bitch—she wouldn't say another word about it, said the patient. Until the moment I got into the taxi, she wouldn't even look me square in the face. So isn't this great, just great. Look what I found out for all my troubles: Now I'm a goddamn Catholic!

Not necessarily Catholic, said the therapist in a calming voice, just as your mother said. In any case, what would it matter?

What would it matter? Matter! You know I was brought up hating Catholics! You know that. My father's hatred is irrational, relentless. It's not like a normal person's prejudice. It's a . . . racial hatred. My whole upbringing. All the times I told you about. When I couldn't stay at Mary's. And the summer with a "preponderance of them." And the fight we had over the "papist cultists."

The patient continued in this light—the man named O'Reilly, the Irish mafia, the summer camp across the lake, that "Danny Boy" song— butterflying from one reference to the next. She and the doctor had evidently dissected these incidents many times before, so no clarifying information was forthcoming, and I therefore tried to listen as I had done in the past: letting the unexplained names and events go by without heed, allowing myself to be soothed by the sound of the patient's voice.

But as the references went on—that girl in school, the professor, the people on the next block, the wedding, the sweet-sixteen party, that shop lady—I grew increasingly annoyed at the cryptic turn this session was taking. The patient had gone away without explanation—tortured me with her absence—only to return and make it clear she had a life I could not comprehend. She owed me an explanation! How dare she simply run on—the summer in Utah, the couple at the hotel, my friend's best friend—with all these trinkets, these little pebbles of life! I understood: Yes, her father hated Catholics. She has proven her point. Must she keep going on? Why wouldn't Dr. Schussler stop her? What pettiness the patient was displaying! She was supposed to be my champion, my athlete in the arena, strong in her battle against the mere situation of birth. But she would not get far if she did not move on from this pitiful evidence-gathering!

Then all at once I was frightened. How quickly I could come to hate her—she who was moments ago my icon of self-creation. I must be careful, I thought. I have traveled this path before. I must not go there. I therefore forced down my anger; sat still as my annoyance ebbed. It took all my self-control, but I succeeded, congratulating myself that I had changed, that I could be otherwise than I'd been. I tuned my ear to the lovely pitch of the patient's voice, her beautiful whiskey alto, and once again let it play above me as music, staccato now, legato then, *piano* and *forte*. My dear patient, I thought, forgive me! And how my heart contracted when she suddenly sobbed and cried out:

I don't understand! How could they get me from a place they hate? How could they? I know it sounds crazy, but I feel I'm tainted. That Father looks at me and sees this mark: Catholic.

But you are not changed, said the therapist. Your being, your self, is the same, whether you came from a reed basket, a Protestant church, or a Catholic agency.

This has nothing to do with who I am! shouted the patient. It's a mark on me *before* I was anyone. No matter what I am!

She was breathing forcefully, and I thought she would finally cry. But she contained herself and fell silent.

Seconds passed. Traffic noise rose as if to fill the gap.

She was lying, of course, said the patient at last.

Your mother, said the doctor.

Yes. Mother. I could tell she knew a lot more than she was saying. But I couldn't get anything more out of her. She just did her *dahling* thing and brushed me off—ha! Like the skirt.

The patient paused.

And why did she tell me just that one detail, she continued, the Catholic agency, and nothing more? To get back at me. Get back at me for bringing up the forbidden subject of adoption.

It's not allowed, you see. Adoption. Forbidden. I'm not to remind her of something—I don't know what it is, but the adoption brings up something she hates too. Something bad happened. Something bad she wants to forget. So she had to hurt me. For bringing it up. Hurt me.

The patient stopped, breathing very hard now, nearly crying, but again containing herself. Five seconds went by. Then she burst out:

Why did I ever get into this? I told you I didn't want to! I knew it would be bad—knew it. Why did you—you!—get me into this?

The therapist said nothing.

Is the hour over? asked the patient.

If you wish, said the doctor. We only have a minute or two.

Then it's over, said the patient, who strode out the door and slammed it shut.

Even before the elevator arrived, Dr. Schussler was on the phone, trying to reach that Dr. Gurevitch.

19.

Oh, my poor patient! What a force of anger thundered in her steps as she passed my door! I could hear her breathing—steaming with the tears she would not shed—coming toward me then receding as she circled before the elevator. It was all I could do to keep myself still. I wanted to throw my arms about her, comfort her, provide her with shelter. My avatar, doing battle for me. And who could help her? That damned therapist! That Dora Schussler, analyst or psychologist or therapist—whatever she wished to call herself—and again I wondered, Was she up to the noble task of guiding my dear patient?

Or would there be a task at all? The seven days seemed twenty. I could do nothing but worry about the patient's return—I feared once more that she might break off the therapy, abandoning me to my loneliness in that terrible cottage by the sea. As the days went by, I kept hearing the hot anger in the patient's breath, which somehow mingled in my mind with the shushing of steam from the office radiators, the hiss of tires on the wet pavement below, the whisper of rain at the windows, the rush of Dr. Schussler's machine—all around me the sounds of the patient's broken heart.

Wednesday came at last. The doctor smoked. The sound machine went silent. Again came the slish of stockings, the exhalations of smoke, the window raised and lowered as if a semaphore telling the patient: Come. Come now. Once more the church bell played the carillon. Then the strokes of the hours: each seeming to say, no, no, no.

The minutes passed: one, two, five, fifteen. Would she never come?

Then: ding, elevator door, thud of steps, rattle of the door handle, and—slam!—the sound I had so resented but six weeks ago (could it be only that recently?), now so thrilling.

She burbled on about work—but no matter. She was here. Stochastic models and secular trends, Bayesian logic and probabilities, time horizons and intermediate "tops"—fine, anything she wished to discuss, I don't need to understand (I sternly told myself), only let me hear the sound of her voice. As the talk of work went on, the doctor tried all her therapist's tricks to return to the land of "last time"—as we were saying; we really should discuss; do you want to talk about?—yapping all about her client like a sheepdog. Finally she herded her charge into the desired fold, there to find the patient's resistance as fierce as ever.

What's there to talk about? Father hates Catholics! So he will always hate me. I'm marked—marked indelibly as something he cannot love.

Let us try to look at this another way, said the doctor. Perhaps he'll love you all the more for "rescuing" you.

Huh! the patient replied. Absurd. How many times do I have to tell you the story about the "papist cultists," or my friend Mary?

But—

But nothing. I'm certain about this. I might as well have a tattoo of the pope on my forehead!

The conversation went on in this vein, but the therapist could not budge the patient from her syllogism: Father hates Catholics; I'm branded as Catholic; therefore Father hates me. She replayed it throughout the hour, "stuck in a single organization of events," as several of my own mental health professionals had put it when confronted with my own stubbornness. Seeing it from the other side (from behind the wall, as an observer), I understood the obsessive quality of such an attachment, something comforting in holding on to a smug, all-seeing knowledge, even a sad or hurtful one; something that let the patient control the precise amount of pain she administered to herself—playing her own executioner, as it were.

So the session wore itself away, as did the next, which began with the repeated trope, the therapist attempting to challenge it, the patient resisting, and so on, until the therapist gave in. She let the patient turn to other subjects, in this case her girlfriend, Charlotte, their arguments, the complicated social alignments among their friends. And another hour was gone.

The following week reprised the pattern: the broken-record recitation of her father's hatred for her, then a jump to more quotidian matters.

Finally nudged away from this recital at one session, the patient turned to economics. The great difficulties our country was facing. Rising prices at the same time as stagnating business activity. A combination so new it required the creation of a new word: stagflation. She wondered how she could adapt her models to this "anomalous macro situation" (if

I am transcribing all this correctly). She worried about the new Japanese imports—the word "econobox" had just entered the lexicon with the arrival of the first Datsuns; about high oil prices, lines at gas stations, the fear, the sense of the economic world as we know it coming to an end.

And what do you feel about all this? asked the therapist.

Come on. What do you think I feel?

Tell me.

Despair!

Do you think this has anything to do with what you learned from your mother?

A snort. Silence. Another run for the door.

Still she returned. Week after week she made her way to Room 804, the lodging of her psyche, where she successfully avoided any surgery to remove the knife she herself had thrust into her heart. At the next session she instead turned back to her problems with Charlotte, who kept calling the patient "a bourgeois" each time she tried to talk about her work, its difficulties, its challenging appeal.

(At least say "bourgeoise," I thought, the female form, hating this Charlotte all the more by the second, if only for her ignorance of foreign languages.)

Do you ask yourself, interjected the therapist, why you stay with someone who so clearly does not accept who you are?

Yes, yes, the patient said with sighs. All the time.

But yet you stay.

Yes. I stay.

So I must bring this up again. Do you see how this mirrors your relationship with your mother? Did you not say that you brought up the subject of adoption—wanted to hurt her—because she will not accept who you are?

Right, said the patient. I did. Mother.

Suddenly an ambulance came wailing, its cry echoing between the buildings on our narrow street. Patient and doctor waited while the siren quavered away toward a distant corner.

Wonder what's going on out there, said the patient.

Hmm, said the doctor. And in here?

You mean this room?

No. (A rustle of fabric.) Here.

Ah! The patient laughed. You mean inside.

She paused.

Inside me.

Once again she fell silent.

Horns blared in the street. The last seconds drifted away.

Until next week, the doctor softly said.

20.

But next week, the patient was late yet again. And as before, the minutes crept by, my anxiety rising all the while. Silence reigned in Dr. Schussler's office. She had turned off the sound machine, then sat, waiting for her patient.

At exactly twenty past eleven (according to my watch), Dr. Schussler lit a cigarette and turned on the sound machine. What was she doing—giving up on the patient? Was she just sitting there with her Viceroys, enjoying a smoke, glad to have a free hour on the day before Thanksgiving?

For we had arrived at that time of year, the last week in November, and I longed to hear my dear patient's voice one more time before the assault of the holiday. She had mentioned, buried amidst the evasions of the past weeks, that she was doing something she never did: going home for Thanksgiving. Surely, then, she would need fortification from her therapist before facing the question of her origins—for how could she not raise the issue, there, in the presence of her adoptive family, of her father, the man at the head of the table with the carving knives who will think "Catholic!" (she believes) each time he looks at her?

Why did she not come? And what time signature was Dr. Schussler following that twenty-after should signal the end of the patient's allotted period? Would she be turned away if she should come now, or in ten minutes? I dared not leave the office for fear that Dr. Schussler might do the same at any moment, and I had not given up entirely my hopes for the patient's arrival. So I was forced into a simmering uncertainty and sat immobile in my chair, afraid for myself and for the patient, for I felt we should not be cast alone into the madness of the holidays.

I am not certain what came upon me, but I was suddenly racked by what seemed to be hiccups, silent hiccups; tears welled up in my eyes; I began to shake all over, as if in the grip of a seizure. I panicked—was I ill? I looked at my wet hands and could barely comprehend why they should be so—such was my long divorce from the experience of crying. My nervous condition had always draped the world in too bleak a bunting to allow for tears, since true sorrow is impossible without the hope of happiness. And here I was—crying! I was so glad at the return of this simple human expression that my eyes immediately dried and my sobs vanished; and then I was desperate for the tears to come again!

In the midst of such comedy—I'm happy I'm crying! Now I'm miserable that I'm too happy to cry!—there came a knock on the therapist's door. Then another, and a series of impatient raps. I could not hear the doctor's response—the sound machine still played—but several seconds later I heard the door open. There was a discussion at the door—the machine blew fog through their voices—and all I could distinguish was something about drinks and a party. Were they talking about an office party? Was that the patient's excuse for coming late?

I was not to know, for that horrid Dora Schussler, forgetting her client's wishes, let the sound machine play on after she had closed the door behind the patient. All I yearned to hear was reduced to sibilance and dentalization, the tongue and teeth of the therapist piercing the whir, and the occasional bass hum, like the sound of a television heard late at night through a hotel wall. And beyond all that was my dear patient! Her needs, her fears, her emotional preparations for the family visit—all was smothered by the machine.

When suddenly came silence.

Then the therapist's Germanic voice:

We must end early, she said.

Yes, I remember, said the patient.

Then more silence; then a faint sound of breathing, growing stronger; then:

Oh, why did I waste this session! the patient cried out. I needed to figure out what I'm doing. What I'll say, if I'll say anything. Oh, God! I wasted it.

She said no more, only kept breathing deeply without coming to tears.

I am so sorry, dear, said the doctor. We have to stop now.

Yes.

You have the emergency number. If you are overwhelmed, please call. You know you can always call.

I know.

I will be here for you, said Dr. Schussler.

The therapist stood, then the patient.

Oh, God! exclaimed the patient. Why did I blow this session? What am I going to do?

There was a rustle of fabric.

Please don't try to hug me, said the patient. I don't want to be touched right now.

21.

Again the patient circled the vestibule, awaiting the elevator. As before, her breathing came toward me and faded away—toward me and away—her breaths still laden with unshed tears. Oh, how I longed to stroke those sorrowing shoulders that did not wish to be touched; how I wished she could find the way to her tears.

Suddenly the impulse to follow her took hold of me. It was as if my flock of crows—my large, fat, shiny crows, the sort that look like small vultures—as if they had flapped up from a dense tree to cut crazy angles around me and shout, *Her! Her! Her!* (So did the desire present itself to my imagination, which, as I have said, was morbid and afflicted at the time.) *Her! Her! Her!* All the many psychologists, counselors, therapists, and psychiatrists who had plied their trades upon me would have trembled to learn what had become of their charge, the ruinous uses to which their work had been put. *Her. Her. Her.*

The elevator was a conspirator; still it did not arrive; still the patient paced the hall; there was yet time for damage to be done.

I struggled against the impulse. I thought of the day I had first entered the building, the flash of white, the lobby as immaculate as my desire for normalcy; the cherubs who floated above, their circling eyes watching over all the inhabitants; the sheets of marble lining the corridor in procession; beyond all, the cool inner breath of the place, which sighed, *It will be all right here.*

And at last I was freed; finally came the twin whispers that signaled my release: the shush of the elevator doors closing, the suspirations of the sound machine come on once again.

22.

The horrors of the holiday lay before me. Turkeys, Pilgrims with muskets, smiling Indians, cornucopia, families at table—images taped to every shop window; disgustingly cheerful music spilling from every door. I found no relief at the office. The management had installed some sort of loudspeaker through which treacled an endless round of holiday songs—*chestnuts roasting, no place like home, to grandmother's house, laughing all the way.* The lobby was empty, yet the music played on, and the black eyes of the elevators' cherubim circled without cease, while empty cars rode up and down, up and down (the call buttons pressed by whom?), trolling for passengers who did not exist. Even a sane man, I thought, would consider suicide in such a situation, if only for the pleasure of never again hearing "Jingle Bells."

Thanksgiving Day itself dawned gray and cold. The downtown district was deserted but for the desperate men who haunted the streets wrapped in dirty blankets. The next day came up sunny, and shoppers inundated Union Square. I joined them and let myself be jostled as I mingled among them, finding myself pulled in the currents toward Macy's or Nieman Marcus, Bullock's or the Hound, Joseph Magnin or I. Magnin; offered foulard ties and perfumes in purple bottles, chiffon scarves and fine leather briefcases, tennis sweaters and felt hats with narrow brims, each with a small feather in the band; even fine satin lingerie for "my lady."

I left the stores and sat down upon a bench in the corner of the square. On the bench perpendicular sat a young woman and a lovely doe-eyed boy of about twelve—the girl's brother, it seemed. He had crow-black hair and smooth, coffee-colored skin—I imagined the family had come from somewhere in Asia, perhaps Indonesia. He was slim and angular, with impossibly long fingers for a boy his age. He fidgeted and glanced about as the girl took out her makeup case and began to apply a deep-purple tint to her lips. She had dyed her hair blond, which altogether ruined her prettiness, I thought, as the shade she had chosen—a brassy yellow—clashed with the warm brown of her skin. Nonetheless, I tipped my hat to her, and she responded with a dazzling smile. The boy ignored me.

When the girl was done with her makeup, they rose and started off across the square. I soon found myself rising as well and ambling off in their direction. I had no intention of doing so—I was completely unaware of my actions for the first ten minutes—but I soon realized I was following the girl and boy in and out of the department stores that surrounded the square.

I tried to stop myself. I had pledged not to do any such thing. But (said the voice I could not still) that pledge had been made in the darkness, and here we were in sparkling daylight, amidst a crowd, so what harm could be done? Besides (the voice continued), I had already followed many shoppers in and out of the stores, and the girl and boy were but two more. And the pair seemed to be retracing the very route I had taken—Macy's, Bullock's, Joseph Magnin, I. Magnin—such repetition making the act appear all the more familiar and normal. So it was that I trotted on behind them, as they examined a sequined sweater, a pink silk scarf, a pair of men's pigskin gloves in a deep cognac (very expensive), a black leather briefcase, a woman's purse in red suede, and ties of various description. Now and then, the young woman allowed herself to be sprayed with perfume, so that the scent that trailed behind her was like that of an overgrown garden wherein every flower had once bloomed and was now rotted.

It was at the I. Magnin glove counter—the boy was trying on a pair in brown suede—that the woman finally wheeled and turned to me:

What in the world are you doing? she demanded. Are you following us? I will call a guard!

(What could I say? Could I tell her mine was a harmless compulsion? Who would believe me by now?)

Forgive me, I replied. I was simply overcome by your beauty.

Her purple lips firmed with indecision, then relaxed, lay flat, and suddenly swept up into a smile. She touched her brassy curls; blushed; melted.

Why, thank you, she said.

The boy rolled his velvet eyes.

How foolish women are, I thought. This one was like all the rest. Now she would let me follow her anywhere.

23

Her! Her! Her! My crows mocked me throughout the weekend, even into Monday and Tuesday. *Her! Her!* they taunted, laughing, and put before me constantly the face of the Indonesian girl; the doe eyes of her brother, which haunted me with their cool, adult disdain. *Do not go to the patient,* whispered my unshakable companions as Wednesday morning dawned. *You are not worthy of her.*

Yet, as the hours of the morning progressed, my disquiet rose, to the extent that I preferred the mockery of my Furies to the doom-beat of my own heart. I hurriedly dressed; I raced to the streetcar; the next I knew, I was stepping down at the corner of Market and New Montgomery. My gargoyles came into view, crouched and dirty as they shouldered the roofline; then my cherubim, whose circling eyes I watched in alarm as I realized the time, which was so close to the top of the hour and the start of the patient's session. I had to reach my office immediately! At last one angel eyed the large *L* of the lobby; finally the elevator opened its doors, disgorged its passengers, and waited to be filled again.

I entered first; a few others followed me; the doors began to roll closed. Then one hand after another poked through, forcing the doors to roll back again. Hand by hand, passenger by passenger—the cab filled so slowly I thought I might scream. I was pushed to the back wall; bodies pressed in all around me. Finally it seemed we would leave when—there was but a three-inch slit to go—a slender hand knifed through.

I had but a moment to see her face—a delicate young woman, brown-haired, brow sweated, cheeks flushed—but a shock went through me. For reasons that made no sense, I was instantly certain she was my dear patient. Now, as the elevator swept up the shaft, I had to think quickly. Was that hair an ordinary brown or the "dirty blond" of my patient? Was she the right age? Did she seem to match the alto voice that flowed through the adjoining door? If only she would speak! Say "getting off" or "excuse me." And if she were indeed the patient, my problem was more acute, I realized. What would I do? Follow her out of the cab, then try to disappear down a hallway as she turned toward Room 804? If so, I would not be able to get into my office unheard—I would miss the session and never know what happened at her visit home for Thanksgiving!

The elevator stopped at the mezzanine. The young woman (my patient?) stepped out to let others leave, then deftly stepped back in, performing this little dance as we stopped floor by floor, each time giving me a momentary view of her profile, which was nearly hidden behind an unruly shock of hair. Did the patient ever speak of having curly hair? I could not remember. And I still did not have a plan of action as we rose and the woman remained with me, the back of her head now right before my eyes, so that a scent of something floral—camellias—rose from her. But I could not recall my patient ever giving off a strong scent! Surely I would have noticed a scent so sensual—nearly the scent of my Indonesian girl! Was this an olfactory mirage, the very air mocking me? We came to floor five, then six, and the young woman remained with me yet, my heart racing all the while, in panic or excitement—I could not tell which.

There were but four of us left in the cab. We came to floor seven. The elevator seemed to float, taking minutes to find its stopping place. At last the doors rolled open—and my young woman stepped out.

I leapt out of the elevator at floor eight and moved swiftly down the corridor. The sound machine still played! I had time, then, to perform the careful legerdemain of keys and plastic card that allowed me to enter Room 807 unheard.

My heart had barely stilled itself when, taking my customary chair, I realized the woman's exit on the seventh floor meant nothing. She might indeed be my patient. She might simply be visiting the ladies' room—available on seven but not on eight—before coming to her session. And so it was that, as the sound machine was silenced, and the patient did arrive at last, I could not concentrate on the opening words of the session.

For a sudden double-mindedness came over me. Two images of my dear patient began to war in my mind: first the rather ordinary face of the young woman in the elevator (a flushed cheek, a sweaty brow), then the vague yet delicate and lovely place in my imagination in which my dear patient had always lived. First one image then the other vied for ownership of the creamy sound penetrating our wall, the images alternating with great frequency, back and forth, the mundane to the heavenly, until it seemed the effort of holding in my mind one, then the other, would cause me to disintegrate.

I made a decision: The young woman on the elevator was not my patient! Such plainness could never be attached to the whiskey voice that filled my ears with pleasure. No scent of camellias—this was the evidence that fed my certainty. All at once, the plain face withered away; I was bathed in the cool, dark pool of my imagination wherein floated my dear patient; and I heard her therapist laugh and say:

Of course I can.

And the patient reply: I don't know how to begin.

24.

Start anywhere, said the therapist. Go in any direction.

No, no. That's what's making me crazy, replied the patient. It keeps coming back to me in pieces, flashes. I thought that here—with you—here, the only place . . . I need to unravel it. Go in order. In my mind. In line. Straighten it out.

All right.

Make it coherent. It's all incoherent.

All right.

The patient said nothing for some seconds.

It's so noisy here, she said at last. Funny how you don't notice it, and then you do.

A chorus of horns suddenly rose from the street.

Did I make that happen? asked the patient. You see, don't you, how weird I am.

I see you are distressed.

Yes.

A long pause.

Distressed, said the patient.

Just start at the beginning, said the doctor.

But what is the beginning? My mother told me what she knows, but it's not the beginning. It's a middle. Somewhere in the middle of a middle. A long way from the beginning. I don't know if I'll ever find the beginning.

25.

They were in the den as before. It was the Sunday after Thanksgiving, early evening. The trees had lost their leaves but for a few ugly stragglers, "wrinkled shapes against the twilight," said the patient, who then laughed at her attempted poetry.

We had the same seats, she went on. Mother on the recliner, me on the loveseat, the table full of glass figurines between us. The television was on—*Miracle on 34th Street,* that sentimental piece of crap. Can't they even wait until December to trot out the crappy Christmas movies?

I'd held off saying anything, she went on. Maybe it was self-protective. I didn't want a big blowup, and then still have to be there for three more days, or else have to change my flight, pack a bag, rush off in some noisy, dramatic scene. So if I was going to say something on this trip, it was now or never. Father and Lizabeth were at the mall. Mother and I were alone for the first time all weekend.

Earlier that day, we'd visited the Rushstons—you remember, my parents' old friends. Mother was still all put together: tomato-red bouclé skirt, white silk blouse, pearls. She even kept on her high heels, Bruno Maglis, red fabric to match the skirt. She sat with her feet tucked under her—heels and all—smoking, sipping a cup of tea, watching that terrible movie as if she'd never seen it before. Never took her eyes off the screen. Maybe she was nervous, too. Yes, now that I think of it, I suppose she was as afraid as I was.

Afraid? asked the therapist.

To break . . . I was going to say, To break the ice. But the break would be more . . . thorough.

In what way?

With the whole conception of who I am . . . Was.

The patient stopped for several seconds, as if her silence could ward off what was about to happen.

Well, she said, rousing herself. So we come to the part of the movie where all the mail addressed to Santa Claus is brought into court, where Kris Kringle is on trial, or whatever the bearded fat guy's name is. The post office has sent all the Santa mail to Kringle. Then the judge has to rule that, well, since the United States Post Office believes he's Santa Claus, he really must be Santa Claus. And Mother starts to tear up. Then comes the part where the little girl gets her dream house with her dream parents, and the fat guy's eyes are twinkling, and by then Mother is out-right weeping.

And I was suddenly really pissed off—it came out of nowhere, bang, one minute I'm simply annoyed and then—what? Pissed as hell. There we were with a real-life drama between us, and she's lost in this—what? This fantasy sorrow. That crap emotion. She never shows emotion, WASP that she is, except times like this: fake feelings, show feelings, canned tears.

So she's crying, and she says to me: Honey, you'll bring me the tissues.

The tissue box was on the bookcase, closer to her than to me, but she had to sit there and command me in her future imperative: You'll bring me the tissues.

I went and picked up the box, but I didn't hand it to her right away. I stood there with the box just out of her reach and said: You know, Mother. You're going to have to tell me more about my adoption than the Catholic-agency thing.

She looked up at me as if she were coming out of a deep sleep.

What was that, dear? she said, wiping a cheek.

The adoption. You can't just drop the "Catholic" business on me, then say nothing else.

Give me the tissues, dear.

You have to tell me more. I know you know more than you've said.

The tissues, dear! You will give me the tissues!

I handed her the box, and she started wiping her eyes and blowing her nose. I could tell she wanted to hand me the dirty tissues, as if I'm the mother, taking away baby's snot rags, but I'm sure she saw the look on my face and didn't dare.

You have to tell me more, I said.

Oh, my darling, she answered. Why do you want to go into all that business? It was so long ago, I don't even think about it.

You don't think about it. But you dropped something on me, now I have to think about it. So you can't just leave it there.

But why, dear? It means nothing, as I said.

Because it explains how Father feels about me—or doesn't feel, to be more exact.

What are you talking about?

He . . . He's uneasy with me. About me.

What are you saying? Father loves you!

I was still standing over her. The television was still playing, and all this is happening with the commercials blaring behind us. A really loud one came on, and I had to yell over it:

He hates Catholics! And every time he looks at me, he sees a Catholic baby. So he hates me! It explains everything!

Mother's face dropped. Her head fell back on the recliner. She stared at me, for a second or two almost uncomprehending. Then she began shaking her head slowly, back and forth, her mouth open, but no voice was coming out, just her lips mouthing, Oh, no, Oh, no. Until finally she said:

Oh, my God, baby. You don't really think that. Oh, no. God. Oh, God, no.

She picked up the Space Commander and clicked MUTE.

It was suddenly very quiet. I could hear the branches scratching at the windows, the wind rustling through the hedges. Mother began looking around her seat, and I realized she was looking for all her used tissues, which she balled up and put in the empty teacup.

You know, darling, she said, handing me the teacup with the balled-up tissues, you'll put this in the dishwasher, and then you'll make me a martini.

What—now?

You make the best ones, dear. Everyone says so. It's so good to have you home. I always sleep better when the children are home. Make me a good martini—and one for yourself—and then I'll tell you everything.

26.

The patient found the Smirnoff in the freezer, behind the Beefeater gin her father's pals liked to swill. The bottle, then the ice: everything felt burning cold. What had she said to change her mother's mind so quickly? She felt like a child who'd made the big mistake: step on a crack, break your mother's back. It was all she could do to put the ice and vodka in the shaker, add a drop of vermouth, swirl around the ice cubes then toss them out, spear the olive with a toothpick. It had to be made just so: just as Mother had taught her that summer when she was thirteen, when she had carried the martini glasses so expertly on a tray, never spilling anything, serving Mother's friends as they lounged on the patio, smoking cigarettes in long plastic holders.

Isn't the first sip always the best? said her mother, taking the martini in two hands and holding up the glass for scrutiny. That first one you have to take carefully or else spill it? She bent her lips to the rim and siphoned off the top quarter inch. Ah, darling! No one makes these quite like you do. What—you didn't make one for yourself?

By then the sky had become quite dark, and the branches were black against the windows. Her mother looked up to exclaim, My, how dreary it is to have the sun down at five o'clock!

The patient sat listening to the scratch of the leaves and watched her mother sip her drink. It seemed to her that many minutes passed in this way, in a suspense of scratching and sipping—little clawing sounds, she said to her doctor.

I felt that everything was very fragile, she said, that if I moved, everything would fall apart.

What everything? Dr. Schussler asked.

Everything, everything, the patient said. My life, my identity, all the things you think are solid—suddenly you realize you could have been someone else. Anyone else, depending on the family that took you in. Rich or poor. State junior college or Ivy League M.B.A. Catholic or Protestant. Or, God knows, maybe Baptist, Holy Roller, the child of tongue speakers or snake handlers. I felt like I was back at the foundling hospital, sitting there in the overheated lobby with my wet clothes in my lap, waiting for Mrs. Waters. Sitting there afraid, afraid of being exposed.

Exposed as what? the doctor asked.

A fraud. A construction. An arbitrary set of facts.

(How glorious! I thought, as I listened on my side of our common wall. She knows she is self-created!)

But is it not also true, said the therapist, that we discussed some core inside you, something that felt alien to your family, something that remained unchanged despite the pressures put upon you to be one thing or another?

(Yes! Self-driven, immune to the mere circumstance of birth!)

The patient breathed in and out. Yes, she said at last. But there was something else. I looked at Mother, in her lovely outfit, with her perfect yellow ball of hair, her nails polished a pale pink, her red high heels, all this on a Sunday evening at home. I watched her drink; I saw the way she put the glass down on the tabletop so carefully. And I knew then that she was afraid. I suddenly wanted to protect her—and realized I've always been protecting her.

Protecting her from what? the doctor asked.

Oh, from all the pain opening up this subject would cause her.

Cause *her* pain? Dr. Schussler asked.

I'm assuming it had to be hard, to get a child to adopt, to suddenly have this little alien put in your arms. You don't know where she came from—a human meteor dropped from the sky. Maybe she's a demon seed, the patient said with a laugh.

Well, perhaps, said the doctor gently. Perhaps it was hard for your mother at the beginning. But then she was rewarded for whatever difficulties she might have gone through. After all, said the therapist after a long pause, she had *you*.

The patient gasped. Me! she said.

She fell back into her chair.

Me, she repeated softly.

She was silent for some time. I'd never considered that, she finally said.

And your mother then goes on, said the doctor, to find that she is a fortunate woman, who has been given not a demon but a treasure.

The patient laughed. Oh, I wouldn't go that far.

Yet there was no doubt that the thought of her worth had fallen upon the patient with the force of revelation. The timbre of her voice brightened; the cadence of her speech strode forthrightly on. For now, fortified with her new understanding, she seemed to take courage as she resumed the story of her mysterious birth.

27.

As I said, we were in the den, the patient went on.

Dark had fallen. The wind was blowing. The patient knew her father and sister might come back at any moment. Beyond the kitchen, the rooms of the big house were in full night, still unlit. Mother and daughter sat across from each other, the glass coffee table between them, each in a separate pool of light from two small lamps.

Her mother put down her drink and seemed to stare at something far off behind the dark leaves. Then she lit a cigarette, dropped her used match into the ashtray, and said: Sweetheart, you'll empty this, please.

By the time the patient returned, the martini was half gone.

Her mother sighed. Oh, sweetheart, this was all so long ago. I don't even recognize the person I was then.

She kept staring out the window. And the patient knew, while her mother still looked at whatever was holding her gaze, there was still a chance. She could stop all this, say forget it, never mind. But it was already too late: Her mother was exhaling her smoke, clearing her throat, touching her beads, firming her mouth.

The first thing you need to know is that your father was born a Catholic.

I thought I'd heard wrong, the patient told Dr. Schussler. She'd said it so quickly, blurted it out. All I could say was, He was born *what?*

He was born a Catholic, she repeated. His father—

Grandfather Avery?

Grandfather Avery was a devout Catholic—

What? Why didn't Father say so?

Because he and his father became completely estranged.

Her mother stopped to sip her drink, then said: Over me.

I never knew Father's father, the patient said to the doctor. He died before I was born, my parents always told me. And no one ever talked about him. A few pictures once fell out of an old album, a thin, bearded man, that's all I thought of him, and otherwise he didn't exist for me. So I couldn't bring this nonperson back to life, I mean in my mind, and didn't stop to notice Mother's face, and didn't realize how long she'd paused.

But now I think something like thirty seconds must have gone by before she went on to say:

Your father converted when he married me. And because of this, his father cut him off. Completely. You see, your grandfather was not just a Catholic, but a traditionalist Catholic. Mass twice a day, confessions, rosary beads, murmuring Latin in the dark in a haze of incense. Bleeding Jesus crucifixes everywhere, even over the bed. Horrid to have the image of a man—even if he is the son of God, he's a man—horrid to have a man nailed at the hands and feet bleeding over your headboard. That was their house, and it was what your grandfather expected of Father. Not only that, but the whole family was part of a group preparing to move to some big piece of property in southern Illinois. Five families were going, and your father—with a proper wife, not someone like me—was expected to join them. Your grandfather was a single man then—your father's mother died long before all this happened—and he was going to be the patriarch, the wise layman leading the flock under the guidance of their guru priest. You see, it was a cult, a religious cult, although people didn't call it that in those days. They just said they were "forming a religious community."

I couldn't speak, said the patient to her therapist. I didn't know what to think. I couldn't imagine Father in a situation like that. He's so sophisticated, looking more like David Niven every day, with his pencil mustache and cashmere sweaters, his virgin wool slacks breaking just so over his soft Italian loafers. Mr. Architect with plans rolled up under his arm. Mr. Perfect WASP. All I could manage to say was:

I can't imagine it—*Father*?

Yes, said Mother. Father grew up like that. And he hated it. Hated them. They were evil to me, and to him, when he brought me home. All they could think of was the money they'd spent sending your father to architecture school in the expectation that he would build them their compound in the wilds of southern Illinois. People think "the Midwest" when they think Illinois, they think Chicago, but southern Illinois is the Bible Belt, right above Kentucky; it's the South. They were going to a place called Mount—something with a C; I can't remember; I suppose I've blotted it out—to their mount, there to be surrounded by Baptists and Lutherans, practically one church for every ten people, and teach them all the way back to the One Holy Apostolic Catholic Church.

Mother laughed, bitterly, said the patient. Then she took three long pulls on her martini and tipped the last drop into her mouth.

Mother! I said to her. You promised you'd go slow on that stuff.

She lit a cigarette. Do you want to know all this or not? she asked.

Yes, I said.

So let me do this my way.

Then she sat quietly for a while, smoking, just looking out the window. And I could see the bad memories coming back to her, crawling between her eyebrows and cracking her lips like ice. She went on to tell me about all the humiliations Grandfather's family put her through, how they took her into a chapel and made her kneel for two hours as they prayed over her and nearly suffocated her with incense, how they tried to make her promise she'd become a Catholic and when she refused, they locked her in a basement—

Locked her in a basement? Dr. Schussler interrupted.

Yes, in a basement, as the whole group, twenty adults or more, argued above her—she could hear them stamping and shouting, and at one point she actually feared for her life!

Mein Gott! said the doctor.

And finally Father decided he was the one who was going to convert, to become a Presbyterian and marry Mother. And both of them were banished. That's the word Mother used: "banished."

Mother said: They told your father, You are dead to us.

Then her mother paused, smoked, sighed.

Well, she went on, luckily my family was kinder and helped us get started. They helped your father set up his practice, helped us buy our first house, and, well, begin the life you know.

She looked out into the dark.

And that's the story, she said at last.

The TV had been on the whole time, the patient told her therapist. Muted, just the picture flashing over us, as if we couldn't stand to be alone with ourselves. I looked out to see whatever Mother was looking at, and all I could see was our reflection, a mother and a daughter projected out beyond the glass, flickering in the light of the TV. They looked happier than we were, nice and normal, mother and child on a Sunday night in front of the TV. And all at once it came to me that I'd been so startled to learn about Father that I'd forgotten I still hadn't learned anything more about my adoption.

But Mother, I said, what does all this have to do with me?

Again she looked at me as if out of a deep sleep.

You? she asked. Her brow wrinkled instantly. Her lips turned into staccato lines. Then—it was so clear; amazing; I could see the WASP de-emotion machine come to life—her brow smoothed out, her lips turned up in a big smile, and she said:

But darling! Don't you see? It shows you that Father's hatred of Catholics has nothing to do with you! Aren't you happy you know this?

Happy, I repeated.

But something was wrong. I'd seen that lie sweep across her face. Maybe a minute went by, and finally I said to her:

But Mother, if Father converted when you two got married, how is it I came to you through a Catholic agency? Because by then Father was no longer a Catholic.

I had hit it exactly, the patient said to Dr. Schussler. I could tell because her bright-lie face collapsed. She looked suddenly . . . I suppose "haunted" is the word.

Are you sure you want to know all this, honey? she said. I mean, some things are best left alone. Sometimes it's good not to discuss every-thing the way young people do these days.

Mother! There's more to tell. I can see it in your face.

Yes. There's more.

She sighed.

Yes. More. All right. But, you know, first you'll make me another one of those swell martinis. And you'll make one for yourself, sweetheart—dry and very cold, just like the last?

28.

I went into the kitchen and didn't know what to do, she said. I hated her drinking. I hated that she made me a party to it—made me her bartender. But I knew she wouldn't go on without another drink, and so I went through the whole martini routine again, the mixing and the shaking, and the carrying in on a tray.

Oh, thank you, darling, Mother said. I love when you serve me with a tray. It's so very dear of you to do these little things that please me. Come and let me give you a kiss.

I knelt down beside her, so I could give her the glass without spilling any, and offered up my cheek, which she air-kissed, saying *Mwa!* like Dinah Shore.

The agency, Mother, I said, sitting down again. The Catholic adoption agency.

Yes. The agency, Mother said, meanwhile holding up her glass for inspection, looking for the required thin floes of ice.

You always make them just right, she said.

Mother! The agency! I said again.

She took her first sip—she even said "Ah!" like a thirsty person—then she said:

Well, I told you that there were these Catholic babies in Europe that had come under the care of the Church during the war—

You didn't say Europe. I thought the babies were here. You didn't say Europe.

Didn't I? Well, they were in Europe. The war ended, and the children had come under the Church's care under various circumstances—

Orphans and bastards.

Won't you please stop with that! If you want to know the story, just let me tell it.

Yes, Mother.

Don't go jumping in and running ahead the way you always do.

Yes, Mother.

All right, then. So.

She took a sip of her drink, then another.

So. Somehow the whole group around your grandfather, Grand-father Avery, was in touch with someone from the Catholic Church, a high muckety-muck, someone "highly placed in the Church hierarchy," he was told. And this functionary was arranging for the children to be placed in Catholic homes, both in Europe and here. It was all very hush-hush because . . .

She paused, looked out the window, then took a pull on her martini.

Because, well, I don't know why, come to think of it.

It was a lie, said the patient to Dr. Schussler. It was clearly a lie. She knew why. But if I interrupted her again, I knew she'd walk off—she does that rather than get angry. So I let it go, and she mumbled on a bit, covering up. You know people are lying when they say too much about a simple thing. Finally she said:

In any case, the adoptions had to be done quickly, for the sake of the children, obviously, so that they would have parents instead of living in a church orphanage or a monastery. You may not have realized it, honey, but Europe was in ruins after the war, really devastated, people hungry, getting over losses of loved ones, businesses wrecked. So it wasn't a situation where people were lining up to take in babies. On the contrary. That's why so many were sent over here.

Shipped over like cargo, I said.

Will you stop that!

So I was one of them, I said to Mother, sent over here from the ruins of Europe.

Don't talk like that, darling. People cared about you, and all the little children without families.

But how did I get from Grandfather Avery's crazy group to you—to you and Father? You said you were estranged from Grandfather. And that Father wasn't even a Catholic anymore.

Her mother gave her a stern look.

Really. I think it's best not to go into all these details from the past. You know, sleeping dogs and all that. She patted her hair, fingered the silk of her collar.

You can't stop here, Mother.

Think about it, dear. We can talk some other time, perhaps, if you decide you want me to go on.

Don't be ridiculous. I'm orphaned somehow in the madness of the war. I'm in a monastery or an orphanage. The Catholic Church then ferries me to America, to this Catholic cult, as you called it, and then—what?

What, her mother echoed.

She smoked, then said:

Well. I'll just say it: There was some problem with the first adoption.

First adoption?

Her mother took a deep breath.

All right. You wanted to know.

She paused.

You were adopted first by your father's father.

What? Grandfather Avery?

I was reeling, the patient said to Dr. Schussler. That thin, bearded man I'd never given a thought to, a fading picture, a dead man no one mentioned: Suddenly he's my father.

Yes, dear. He adopted you. But only briefly. A few months. There was . . . a problem with the adoption.

What problem?

Mother picked up her martini and took three long pulls from it, until only the olive remained at the bottom.

I never actually knew at the time, she finally said. All that was between your father and his father. Father kept many things from me in those days. Back then I assumed it was because of Grandfather's age—he was forty-seven, and that was considered very old for a father in those days. And because he wasn't married. And maybe because they found out that the guru priest the group followed had been defrocked—I forgot to tell you that, about the defrocked priest. All I knew was there was a phone call out of the blue from a member of your grandfather's group asking Father to get in touch with them. After that, your father met with his father for the first time in a year, and when he came home he asked if we would take the child.

The child. Me.

Yes, dear. You.

And you said yes, the patient said.

Well . . . not immediately. Your father and I weren't ready for a child then. We were . . . having problems.

What sort of problems?

I shouldn't say any more, sweetheart. Your father wouldn't . . . There are some things that are private, dear, between a husband and wife. Remember that when you get married.

Come on. You know I'll never get married. Unless someday I can marry—

You will not say that in this house! I told you that. You will not mention it again!

What choice did I have? the patient said to the doctor. I had to exchange one silence for another.

All right, I said.

Now—Mother adjusted her collar, retying the bow—do you want to know the story or not?

Go on, I said.

She looked right at me, her eyes a little blurry—from tears or martinis, I couldn't tell.

You see, she said. I wasn't really ready to have a child.

You didn't want me?

Please don't interrupt! I didn't know it was you yet! It wasn't you, as you are. It was just the idea of having a baby—I wanted Father and me to enjoy some time together, since the beginning of our marriage had been so difficult. You can understand that, can't you?

I thought about it, and said I did.

But then, I went on, what changed your mind?

Well then, her mother said. Father came home and put you in my arms. I looked into your big eyes. You were so beautiful. Your skin was so soft. You wanted to get down and crawl—you were so ready for life, so hungry for it! And, what can I say? It only took a minute. I fell in love with you.

Her mother looked squarely at her. I really did, you know. Fall in love with you.

I knew I should go over and hug her, the patient told Dr. Schussler. This really should have been a breakthrough moment. The whole thing: Violins. Tears. Hugs. But I could not take it in: this sudden expression of love, out of nowhere.

How old was I? the patient asked her mother.

Let's see, you were crawling already. So maybe five, six months.

And was I big?

Not too big, not too small. Her mother smiled. Just right.

What color was my hair then?

The smile faded. Like now, she said, brownish—dirty blond.

Mother and daughter sat in silence as the house suddenly shuddered in a gust of wind.

Is there a picture? the patient asked.

Her mother looked up. A picture?

Of the day I came home.

I don't know why there should be a picture.

It's the day you "fell in love with me," remember? You have all these pictures of Lizabeth the day you brought her home from the hospital.

Her mother looked out beyond the leaves again.

No, there wasn't a picture, she said.

And why didn't you and Father ever talk about all this? Why was it such a big secret?

Mother kept gazing off into the darkness. It was a long time before she answered. Then she said:

I guess I wanted to believe that you started with me.

She had spoken in a soft voice, very tender, full of longing. But something was wrong, the patient thought. Her mother's eyes were strangely clouded. She kept looking out the window, into the dark, and her mouth slowly contracted.

Lip lines, Mother, the patient said.

Lip lines! Ugly! Thank you, dear, her mother said, spreading out the skin above her lip with her fingers. And then she fell silent.

So there's more, said the patient.

Yes, there's more.

Go on, the patient said.

Are you sure, darling? There are some things it's best not to know.

But you've started—

Yes, I've started. What was I thinking? Now that I have begun—

You have to finish.

I have to finish.

You can't stop now.

No, I don't suppose I can. Not even for another martini, she said with a smile, much as I would dearly love to. All right. Yes. I have to go on.

I was very happy for the next two months, her mother said. You were a joy, Father was busy with his work, just starting his practice, and I could stay home all day and care for you, play with you, watch you grow.

I don't remember the exact circumstances, but one day I was looking for something on your father's desk. One of the drawers was always kept locked. I don't know why I suddenly felt I had to open it. At our last house I knew your father always kept the desk key taped under the center drawer. And sure enough, I looked, and there was the key.

Among the papers in the drawer was a file with a cover embossed with a curious logo: letters that spelled out C-O-R-P-U-S—CORPUS— below that Jesus on the cross in the center of a globe, and below that the Virgin Mary and child. All of which I thought was odd, having both the crucifix and the Virgin, and also CORPUS. Body, body of Christ. I opened the file and saw a letter from a Bishop M.—no last name, just the initial—to someone named Bill Ryan, whose title was given as President, Catholic Overseas Rescue U.S. I don't remember the exact wording, but the gist of the letter was that Bill should understand the need for utter secrecy in the matter—what the "matter" was wasn't made clear in the letter. So naturally I had to turn the page.

Her mother reached for her glass. Oh, right. Empty, she said.

Go on, her daughter said.

So I turned the page. It was a photostat of a document in German. There was a date, sometime in 1946. And then another date. My hands started shaking. I could barely keep from tearing the paper, they shook so hard. Because the second date was one I knew as well as the beating of my own heart. December 26th—

My birth date!

Yes, your birth date. It was a birth record of some kind. My hands were trembling, as I said, shaking uncontrollably. Until that moment, you see, I had known nothing about you except a birth date, and that you were German—

German? You didn't say German. Only from Europe.

Didn't I? Well, yes. Germany. Father had told me you were brought over from Germany. So I knew that you were German, Catholic, and needed a home. And of course, after being your mother for two months, that you were darling, energetic, bright, and adorable. Here suddenly was the fact—maybe it wasn't a fact; I made myself hold certainty away for a minute—that you weren't just someone else's child before I knew you, but the child of one woman, a specific woman, a woman in particular.

You saw her name?

No, dear. Not her full name. Just a first name and initial. Maria G. That was it. That was all. And now: Did I want to turn the page? As I said, I wanted to believe you started with me. Ah, denial. The great glory of denial. But denial must be whole, entire, untouched. It was already touched.

My mother's name was Maria! said the patient.

See? said her mother. See how quickly denial evaporates? Already she's your mother, not me.

Oh, God. I didn't mean—

Oh, don't worry, dear. Of course. What else can you call her? Your womb? Your egg incubator? Your—

Birth mother, supplied the patient.

Yes, birth mother. Her mother clicked her tongue. That's what all those adoption groups call it. But what an awkward nomenclature, darling. Don't you think it's rather brutal—this concentration on the bloody act of birth? Why don't we simply call her Madame G.

The patient laughed. I've studied a little German, Mother. I believe that should be *Frau* G.

Said her mother: I told you not to smile like that. It's disgusting. Your gums are so low. You shouldn't show those disgusting gums when you smile.

29.

A knock on the doctor's door startled us all. Dr. Schussler and the patient jumped in their seats, and it was all I could do to keep still myself. I looked at my watch in amazement: In all my years of therapy, I had never known a single one of the therapeutic breed to proceed past the very tick of the fifty-minute hour. Yet here it was noon, full noon, two hands on the twelve.

Dr. Schussler went to the door, opened it. Two minutes, she said very softly out into the corridor. The door closed, and her next client's footsteps pounded down the hall.

Ah! We cannot stop here for an entire week! the doctor said.

(No, indeed! I thought. We cannot stop here!)

Oh, God, said the patient. Is the hour already up?

Ach. I am afraid so.

There came the sound of pages turning.

I had a cancellation for tonight, the doctor went on. Eight o'clock. Can you come back then?

The footsteps came pounding back, then stamped outside the door.

Yes, said the patient, rising to her feet. I'll come back then.

30.

Your mother had just insulted you once again, said Dr. Schussler as they resumed at eight.

Oh, yes indeed, said the patient. She thinks my gums are disgusting. Can you imagine how impossible it is to be a happy person if your mother thinks your smile is disgusting? Anyway. Never mind this for now. Getting back to where we were.

There was a pause. Then she resumed as if the many hours had not intervened:

Mother asked me to make her another martini. No, didn't ask. It was the usual command: You know, you'll make one for me, sweetheart, dry and very cold, just like the last.

So I made yet another martini, circling the vermouth around the glass then tossing it, shaking the vodka until it was ice cold—the whole routine of Mother's perfect martini. All the while, I was aware of wanting to prolong each step—perform the ritual exquisitely well, be the world's most perfect bartender. Because I knew we'd go back to the story about the ruins of Europe, defeated Germany—all its horror. I knew what was waiting for me. How could I not know what was waiting for me?

I put the drink on the tray and looked at it for a moment: It was clear and icy, something immaculate in it, unclouded. This may seem silly but I suddenly wanted a clear, clean life filled with martinis, like Mother's. I would wear high heels and skirts; I'd learn to wear makeup, learn how to chitchat at cocktail parties; I'd get married to some unassuming man—be normal, regular, like everyone else, which all at once seemed what I'd always wanted: to be normal and regular, not odd, not adopted, not an unhappy genetic alien set down among cheerful people. For a moment I even wondered if my being gay was just another admission of defeat.

Defeat at what? asked the therapist.

At being normal.

Do not do this to yourself, said the doctor. Now you are punishing yourself.

Yes, said the patient after a long pause.

As her client remained silent, Dr. Schussler said: So you made the martini and carried it to your mother.

Yes, said the patient. I did it as if in a dream. Some other person was carrying that tray, not spilling a drop of the drink, getting kissed for it. Someone else clicked off the TV. And that person said:

All right, Mother. What else was in that file?

Wait, sweetheart. That first sip. Ah! Perfect, as always. All right. Now. What else was in that file.

Mother put down her glass and looked out the window, where our neighbor's light was now shining through the leaves.

How many times have I asked Jim Bracket to put a shade on that horrid porch light! she said. It's brighter than a bloody streetlight. There must be some regulation about how bright a residential light can be!

Mother, please.

Her mother sighed. Yes, I know. I know I'm stalling. But you see how hard it is for me to go on with this. I promise I won't get drunk. I'll drink this slowly. But let me say to you now: Don't you think you know enough already? You came from Germany. Your mother's name was Maria. Somehow she lost you—it was wartime; perhaps she died. Isn't that quite enough to know?

Was it? Was it quite enough to know? For one last time, the patient told her therapist, she felt the pull of secrecy, the thrill she had felt during all those years of having *mysterious origins*: the vague, wonderful stories she had recited in the back of her mind. Mothers and fathers had paraded by—nobles, movie stars, singers, artists, intellectuals—as her tastes in parents had changed over the years. Sometimes they were named Wilhelmina and Reginald, sometimes Fighting Bear and Little Feather. At twelve, she had imagined herself the secret illegitimate child of Jo Stafford; at fifteen, the unknown daughter of Virginia Woolf. Then, at sixteen, the happy images had suddenly faded, and the idea of her parents had become a hazy story of a woman who had an affair with a married man, got pregnant, and had to give up the baby for adoption when the scoundrel wouldn't leave his wife and marry her.

Now all those old parents were suddenly banished.

Now there was Frau G.

Wasn't that quite enough to know?

If she stopped here, and learned no more, she thought, there would still be stories she could tell herself, plausible stories about Frau G. Perhaps she was a very rich woman, a cultured woman, who lived in a grand apartment in Berlin. Yes, of course. She was a liberal-minded woman, not a Nazi, and the intelligentsia of Berlin had flocked to her drawing room, where each Tuesday evening she held a salon. Her husband was on leave when she was conceived; and then, tragically, he died at the front. The war ended, and Frau G. now found herself without her fortune, all the banks of Berlin having been looted, all the records lost, the mark worth not a pfennig. Sitting in the ruined drawing room where she had held forth over so many happy gatherings, her belly grown large and heavy, the lovely Frau came to the reluctant and awful decision to give her baby away, to give her to someone who could give the child what she had had before the war: a happy, prosperous home.

But I was too old for all that now, said the patient to her doctor with a laugh. The ridiculousness of the story was too apparent. I knew I couldn't make up any more special parents.

So I said:

You can't stop now, Mother. What else was in the "secret" file?

Yes, sighed her mother. I know. I can't stop now. I knew this day would come sometime. And, oh, hell—she laughed—here it is.

She took a small sip of her drink. All right, now, dear. Collect yourself. So. I looked at the next page. I should tell you it was a very odd document. Very strange. It was mostly blank. There wasn't even room on it for information. Just a stark little piece of paper. Maybe five by seven inches. Gray and already crackling. Wartime paper. I picked it up very carefully—as I said, my hands were trembling—and scanned it all over for something more, anything more. But there were just some short sentences in German, maybe two, and what looked like an official stamp on the right-hand corner.

And then you turned the page.

Yes, after I stared, dumb, at the words in a language I don't understand. After I had stared so long that the letters turned into nonsense squiggles—yes, then I turned the page.

Her mother fell back in her chair, let her head lean against the headrest of the recliner. The next page, dear, she said, was a dossier. It was in English, no name, only a number—307—and I assumed of course that this was more information about the . . . about you.

She smiled at her daughter.

But then I read on and saw that couldn't be true. I saw a birth date. Her smile fell. May 17, 1921.

So it was about—

Yes—

My birth mother—

Frau G., dear.

My mother, the patient said to herself.

Please go on, she said aloud.

Her mother took a sip of her drink, then went to take another.

Mother. Slowly, you said.

Yes, she said, putting down the glass.

Yes. What else. There was more, a little more. Place of birth: Berlin. Last known residence: Celle. Then there were spaces for information about the child's father. Father's name: Unknown. Father's date of birth: Unknown. Father's last residence: Unknown. And so on about the father: unknown, unknown, unknown.

So Frau G. had been born in Berlin and had last lived someplace named Celle. Nothing was known about your father. And the next line on the dossier said this: Date of surrender: May 18, 1946.

May 18th. Isn't that just one day after her—after Frau G.'s birthday?

How quickly you memorize it! For all the times you forgot mine.

Oh, God.

Yes, her mother said, running her polished index finger around the rim of her glass. It appears to have been her birthday.

And what did it mean—surrender?

Surrender. That's the term they use for when a woman gives up a baby. She surrenders it. Horrible. Another one of those brutal adoption terms. As if people didn't have any feelings. Terrible! Let's agree never to mention the word again.

She—she gave me up the day after her birthday?

So it would seem, dear. And now, darling, it's time for another sip.

The patient watched helplessly as her mother downed the rest of her martini, then sat there considering the olive at the end of the toothpick.

Mother. Please.

Yes, yes. We have to go on, don't we? Ever forward. Onward! She ate the olive.

Mother!

Yes, well. The next part of the dossier described Frau G. physically. It listed her height: five foot five. Weight: about one-twenty—slim, I remember thinking. Eye color: blue. Hair color: blond. Complexion: fair. Like us, I thought. Like Father and me: blond, blue-eyed, and fair. Physical defects: none. Genetic diseases: none. Mental health: excellent. I remember thinking, How can her mental health be excellent when she is . . . when she is giving up her baby? And then I realized they meant she wasn't schizophrenic or hysterical, or some other gross mental problem they worried about at the time. People feeling sad, or even tormented . . . This wasn't considered a mental health problem in those days. Only feelings. People thought of them as only feelings.

She looked out into the glare of Jim Bracket's porch light while the shadows of the leaves scrabbled over her face. She crossed her arms over her chest. And when she spoke again, her voice was level, and a little cold.

I really should have started here, she said. No point in holding off. Very stupid of me. The last line on the dossier was "Religion." Mother's religion.

Not Catholic, said the patient.

Yes. Not Catholic. She looked at her daughter.

Jewish, it said. Jewish.

This is what I'd been holding off the whole time I was making the martini, the patient told Dr. Schussler. Now I couldn't keep it away, of course. She'd said the word, and that was that.

So me, I said. So I'm Jewish too.

No, no! You were baptized. And from that moment, you were Catholic.

And before that—Jewish.

Her mother stood, smoothed her dress, sat down, then exchanged the places of two little glass figurines, the ballerina with the balloon seller. I didn't know it until I saw the file, she said at last.

What do you mean, you didn't know it? asked the patient.

Her mother said nothing. I don't understand, the patient said.

Her mother sat forward, ran her fingertips over the ballerina's legs. Of course, I didn't either. I . . . Well, when I found out, you can imagine how I felt—

You?—

—standing there, coming across the fact that your mother was Jewish. What *you* felt?

I leafed through the rest of the file, her mother went on. Correspondence, some of it in German, to and from that Bill Ryan person, one letter with a Vatican letterhead. It was more than I could take in, more than I could conceive of. I closed the file. That logo. Catholic Overseas Rescue. Who was being rescued? And from what?

All this took place in the morning. I had to wait all day for your father to come home, eight hours before I could ask him what the hell this was all about. The day seemed to go on forever. You were very fussy, crying over everything. I must have changed your diaper ten times. I couldn't understand what was the matter with you.

I was a nuisance.

No.

A nuisance. You fell out of love with me just as quickly as you fell in love. Look what you were stuck with: a Jewish baby.

Don't be silly. You were ill or something. I couldn't soothe you. You wouldn't be soothed.

A bother.

No. I paced up and down with you, bounced you up and down, held you, and still you kept on crying and crying until I thought I would go crazy until your father came home.

At last you went down for a nap. At last I heard Father's key in the door. Before he had his hat off, his coat off, I was asking about you, your mother, Jews, Catholic Overseas Rescue. Rescued from what? I demanded to know.

He was furious. How dare you go into my locked drawer! He threw his briefcase at me; I had to jump back so it wouldn't hit me. It was very heavy, loaded with papers, and I stood there stupidly for a moment looking at it sprawled at my feet. Meanwhile Father is hollering, How dare you! You stupid idiot. You'll ruin everything. You stupid cow!

He spoke to you like that? the patient asked.

Yes. He did. In those days. When he was still fresh from the influence of his father and that horrible group.

And then?

Then I followed him into his office, still demanding to know what was going on. He tore off his hat, his coat. He kept shouting, You idiot! No one's supposed to know. Not even you. He pounded the desk. He bent his chair back. He picked up an ashtray—glass, heavy—and raised his arm to throw it. Not at me! I yelled. And he crashed it to the floor.

Upstairs, you started crying. Wailing.

You'd better go tend to her, Father said.

But I wasn't going to be dismissed so easily. I went upstairs, checked you, saw you were all right, then picked you up and carried you into the office.

Father eyed me as I came in, but now I had you in my arms, the baby he'd . . . the baby we went to so much trouble to bring into our lives. I sat down on the side chair, he at the desk, as if we were there for an appointment.

You fussed and whimpered, almost too big to hold in my arms.

I thought she'd have blue eyes, Father finally said.

Maybe too soon to tell, I answered.

They're going dark, aren't they? He leaned over and looked at the big bundle in my lap. He gave a laugh, then said to me: They told my father she'd be a blonde. What an ass. He believed it when they told him the child was "pure Aryan."

(Dr. Schussler gasped.)

Tell me, I said to your father. What are you hiding from me?

He sat back in his desk chair—it had a high back, and he rested his head for a while. Then he reached out his hand to you. He caressed your soft hair, your sweet soft skin, ran a finger over your brow, and looked into your sparkling eyes. You started laughing. He tickled you. You laughed some more. He kissed you. You see, darling, no matter what anyone thought they wanted or didn't want, there you were. And we fell helplessly in love.

Her mother's eyes moistened and slowly overflowed, and finally one pendulous tear fell to the edge of her blouse. She looked down at the perfectly round spot in the white of the silk.

You'll bring me a tissue, dear?

Thank you, darling, her mother said, after dabbing at her wet spot, then handing her daughter the crumpled tissue for disposal.

But you still haven't told me what he said.

Her mother sighed. You see, sweetheart, at that moment I wasn't sure I wanted him to go on. There we were, our little family, you being the delight that you were. And I wasn't sure . . . but yes, I did ask him to go on.

So here is the whole story, dear. As quickly as I can tell it. The Church took in all sorts of children during the war, not all of them Catholic. While they were under the Church's protection, most of them were baptized—they considered it a religious duty, evidently, though to me it seemed highly impertinent . . . Well. Never mind that.

In any case, she went on, all of the Jewish babies were baptized—immediately. And when the war ended, the Church was afraid their families would come looking for them. Some archbishop had made the decision: The Jewish children were not going back, even if their parents came for them.

So I was stolen! said the patient, already looking toward the end of the story.

Will you wait, dear! You wanted the whole story, and here it is. The Jewish children were not going back, even if their parents came for them. And especially if it was only aunts and uncles or distant relations looking for them. Or worse, there were community organizations and religious congregations—synagogues—looking for the Jewish children who had been given to the Church for protection. And they wanted them back, to send them to Palestine. You can understand how that wouldn't necessarily be in the best interests of the children, giving them to organizations that would send them into Palestine, a contested zone. You know, the British were trying to keep the Jews out, to please the Arabs; and there were bombings, and terrorist actions. Certainly no place for an infant. You can understand why the Church wouldn't want the babies to go there, can't you? The archbishop said if by chance a child had not been baptized for some reason, it could go back. But no baptized Jewish child was to be given back. Period.

So I *was* stolen! said the patient. My mother probably died in a concentration camp, and the damn Catholic Church stole me away before any of my relatives could find me!

No, no. Father told me you were . . . given up in a displaced-persons camp. A D.P. camp, they called it. So this had to be after the war, after the camps were freed. So whatever happened, your birth mother didn't die there, in a . . .

Concentration camp. Can't you even say it? Concentration camp! But is it supposed to be some kind of relief—that she didn't die in one?

Yes, dear. I would think so. Some relief. Your mother survived the war, she was in a displaced-persons camp, probably having great difficulties, and she gave you up to the Church so you would have a better life. You weren't stolen. Father promised me you weren't one of the stolen babies. At that time, no one was trying to get you back.

At that time? You mean someone came for me later?

No, darling. No one ever came for you.

And then her mother looked away.

I can't describe it, the patient said to the doctor. The emptiness I suddenly felt. The sense of being abandoned—it's always there. Part of being adopted is the knowledge that you were given away by someone. Abandonment is always in the background, a sort of platform that all the other feelings are stacked on. But now . . . It wasn't a feeling but an actual fact. My mother dropped me off at the church and never came back. No one . . . no one ever came for me.

So I was abandoned, I said to Mother.

Surrendered, dear, she said.

Then she sat quietly, only gazing off through the window. Jim Bracket had turned off his porch light, and now the world outside the room was completely black. The wind was down, and the leaves only trembled a little now and then. I felt as if a blanket had been thrown over my head and I'd already breathed in all the air that was under it. I thought I might faint—although I've never fainted in the whole of my life. But now I suddenly understood how women really might just wilt and fall down.

But then I realized there was still more to the story.

But how did I get from Grandfather to you? I asked Mother. You still haven't told me that.

Mother looked at me. She was so unhappy. It was all the unhappiness I was ever afraid of giving her by asking about my adoption.

Darling, she said. This part is the hardest, I think.

Go on, I said.

You see, Grandfather thought he was taking in a Catholic child. He had not been told about the baptized babies—

And when he found out I was Jewish he—

He asked if Father and I would take you.

He junked me!

Darling, no—

He wanted some Aryan and got a dirty Jew! God. What a joke!

Sweetheart. Why would you say something like that?

But why give me to you? Why in the world give me to you and not to some charity, some—

Father said his father put it this way: If you're so happy not being a Catholic, how about going all the way and being Jewish?

So it was all about their feud. Father took me to get back at his father! No, dear.

He wanted to prove a point, so he took me. He didn't want me. You didn't want me. It was all just payback, wasn't it?

Oh, dear darling. You must not see it that way. In any case, what does any of that matter? As I said, the moment you came into our lives, all that fell away.

But you can't stop knowing something, can you?

That's right, dear. That's right. But not talking about something helps you forget, a little, then a little more as time goes by. She looked off into the dark. That's why I never wished to tell any of all this.

She'd barely finished her sentence when we heard the keys in the front door.

Mother fixed her eyes on me. And for some few seconds, we seemed so close to each other, both of us together, afraid, because now what would we do? Tell Father? Lizabeth? Make this story a regular part of our lives? The keys went on jangling, the dead bolt clacked open, and we still looked at each other, alone in our little private world for a little while more. The door blew open. We're home! Father's voice boomed out across the house.

Mother stood, came toward me, bent down, and I thought she might kiss me. Then her mouth went to my ear, and she shout-whispered: *You will not tell Father!*

She went into the kitchen. Hello, darling, she sang out. Show me what you and Lizabeth bought today.

Make us martinis! Father called out.

Lizabeth came into the den, gave a quick hello, flipped on the TV. Mind? she asked.

Okay, I said.

A screaming commercial came on, music, blaring. From the kitchen came the sound of packages being opened, the *tink* of glasses being taken from the shelf, the fridge opening and closing, the happy sound of ice cubes crackling open from the tray. Everything around me was swirling into normal. Lizabeth, Mother, Father—their lives would just go on as they always had. Shopping trips, Sunday evenings by the TV, yet another round of martinis. But I sat there in the den, unable to move, as if I was already in my other life. Me, with my eyes gone dark and my dirty blond hair—dirty! All I could think was: I'm a Jew, I'm a Jew, I'm a Jew.

31.

The patient fell silent, and then doctor and client shifted in their seats, as if returning to the present. A thin shaft of light from under our adjoining door sent a ray across the carpet of my dark office; and every time Dr. Schussler crossed her legs, as she was doing now, she cast jagged shadows across the floor. The silence, the play of shadows, went on for some long seconds; when suddenly the patient said:

Are you . . . possibly . . . Jewish?

The doctor took in a breath.

I know . . . it's not usual . . . but . . . the patient tried again. Mother told me, and suddenly I need to know who I'm talking to. What do they think about Jews? Like my grandfather. Hating Jews. And Mother, who thinks it's so vile that she has to hide it from the neighbors and the ladies at the club. Or maybe someone I'm talking to is Jewish. So I don't have to worry about being hated.

I could all but see the standard therapeutic expression installing itself on Dr. Schussler's face, the slightly shy, apologetic, but altogether forbidding smile that says unequivocally: I am not going to tell you.

You're German, the patient said, or at least you speak German. It meant nothing to me before: where you came from, even who you were—are. But now. With all this. So you're German. And if you're not Jewish . . .

That smile: I could feel the steel of it through the wall.

It would help if you were Jewish, the patient said.

The jagged shadows played across the floor.

You see, I don't know any Jewish people, the patient pressed on. I've met Jews, of course, but I've never been close to one. I have no idea what it means to say, I'm a Jew.

From the Hotel Palace across the way came the forlorn wail of the doorman's taxi whistle.

It would help if I could talk to you about what it means to be Jewish.

Dr. Schussler fell back against the cushion of her chair.

Ach! she breathed. Who I am is not important. We are here to discuss who you are.

The doctor stood.

Oh, God, said the patient. It's time for me to go, isn't it?

(Well past time, I saw by the glow of my watch dial.)

The patient remained seated. I don't want to go out there.

The taxi whistle called again.

She laughed. Please don't make me go.

She withdrew a tissue from the box.

Call me if you need to, the therapist said.

The patient stood. Then she paused in the doorway. There was a rustle of fabric.

Please don't hug me, she said. What is this hugging thing you've gotten into? It's weird, this hugging.

Then she left, slamming the door behind her.

Dr. Schussler immediately lit a cigarette, picked up the phone, dialed. This is Dr. Schussler again, she said after a time. Have you given Dr. Gurevitch my last message? Yes. I see. But—I understand. Please say it is urgent. Yes, the same message. Patient three.

32.

Now came disaster. All through the patient's session, something had teased at the back of my throat. By evening, it was a hot scratch. Whatever it was then invaded my nasal passages—a mere cold, I hoped. But the next night I awoke shivering: a hundred and two, said the thermometer I always kept with me when traveling (one never knows when affliction will come upon one). An hour later, the bed was soaked, and again I lay shivering under my wet sheets. One hundred and three, said the thermometer.

Morning found me aching in every joint. The *San Francisco Chronicle* (which I stole from my neighbor's doorstep) said some dreaded Asian flu had descended upon the population. And it was clear that I had been claimed as one of its victims.

Five days remained before the patient's next session: I was determined to attend, no matter how ill I might be. But then came sneezing, then coughing; and along with these symptoms—noisy, irrepressible symptoms!—came panic. The sound machine was no match for such explosive sneezes, such exclamatory coughs. If I should go to the office—at any hour—I would be discovered.

Wednesday came, and I was desolate. The flu had not relented; my cough was thunderous. There was no recourse but to stay home, in my miserable cottage, watching the rain that dripped daily from a soaked, leaden sky. There I thought of nothing but the patient, the convoluted emotions she must be experiencing, the torments of being cast into one identity—*Catholic! Father hates Catholics!*—then another—*Jewish! Grandfather hates Jews!* (What relief I felt that I myself had not succumbed to my own family's suspicion of Jews!) The utter cruelty of the Catholic Church, stealing the Jewish babies it had taken under its protection. Then the double-dealing of her grandfather, his prejudices, his despicable desire for a "pure Aryan" child. The patient as an Oedipal object traded between father and son. At every turn, someone to reject her, hate her, abandon her. And only two sessions remaining before the Christmas break—two castrated, fifty-minute hours—and nothing but the therapist's skills to rescue the patient from the landslide that had fallen upon her.

Then, no sooner did I think of the therapist's skills than a frightening thought threaded its way through my consciousness. I could not stop hearing the end of the session—or rather, what had happened after the session's official closing. I recalled Dr. Schussler's haste in reaching for the telephone, her words rushing forth, a quaver in her voice, so uncharacteristic of her usual Teutonic control. Gurevitch: She was trying to reach that Dr. Gurevitch. It was "urgent," she said. And, in a terrifying instant, the other moments in which I had heard "Gurevitch" stood before me, each a signpost marking the next step to hell.

For I knew in that moment that Schussler was seeking "consultation." Each call had been made after a difficult session with the patient; each was more insistent than the last. The doctor was in trouble. She could not handle the patient who lay before her, heart open on the table. She could not guide my dear patient's journey, and she knew it. *Consultation.* But it doesn't matter what those therapists, analysts, counselors, doctors, psychiatrists call it; they need some other doctor to save them from the mess they have created for themselves. What they are seeking is help.

I knew about such things. One of my own dear practitioners revealed to me that she had been seeking consultation on my case, explaining she had overidentified with me, her personal "issues" clouding "our work." Her father also had committed suicide, she felt compelled to tell me. Thank you very much—*bitch* (I thought; I was twenty-five and still said such things). Why tell me? Why not just bear your own travails silently? I quit that therapist, but not before asking if she should not pay me for the insights I had given her.

Now I realized that Dr. Schussler could indeed be as incompetent as my former therapist—and what fear for my dear patient descended upon me! The patient's passage (and mine) was made more perilous than ever, since we could not rely upon the person who made the desperate calls to Gurevitch. Once more I asked myself: Who was this Dr. Dora Schussler, this clinician who had presumed to force the issue of adoption and then found herself so unprepared for its aftermath?

Everything I thought I knew about Dr. Schussler suddenly vanished. The particular place in my mind in which I had carried her image all these months—empty. Most likely she was not sixty, not mature, not experienced. That limp: A person may develop a limp at any age. She could be thirty. That bun I had always presumed: a fantasy. She might have straight long hair, parted down the middle, playing over her shoulders, like many women today.

I was unmoored, for I was forced to revise my entire narrative—backward, a backward revision—which put in doubt all I had imagined to have come before. Must I now see all the therapy sessions with a different Dora Schussler; call her (in my mind) not "doctor" but "Dora"; see a short skirt barely covering those legs she crosses as she smokes? Could Dora be—this thought terrified me—could she be the sort I would have followed across Union Square?

33.

Dreams: I could not tell if I was waking or sleeping. The fever spiked and sweated down, spiked and sweated down, and the rest of the week I recall only as episodes of shaking chills and the misery of drenched, cold sheets that no one comes to change. I spent the dark hours floating on the rim of sleep and wandered through daylight in a haze, during which time I could not tell what was real—that knocking at my door right now: Was it my neighbor come to complain about the stolen newspaper? Or a phantom remnant of a dream, flotsam that had drifted by on the verge of sleep? The knocks came again. And again. They must be real, I thought. I dragged myself to the door. No one. The empty beach, the leaden sky, the restless back of the ocean, rising and falling like a great beast, from here to the rim of Asia—source of the scourge that had laid me low.

I played the radio. Day and night. It was my only contact with the world. The landlord had left behind an old, wooden, fabric-fronted radio, some of the fabric torn. The tuner often drifted between stations, so that everything I heard emerged out of static and returned into it, almost in rhythm with my fever, the static seeming to bury me under storms of snow just as the shaking chills grabbed hold of me. Talk shows, panel discussions, news—I tried to hear anything that was broadcast live, anything that chattered on. Even the stations full of shouted commercials: no matter, as long as it was a living announcer who did the promotion, reciting now, in this moment, if only to hear the yelp of humanity. Then the radio tuner would drift, and I would be cast off again into the emptiness of electronic noise.

Through the shivering curtains of static came whispers of strange reports, horrors and chaos, murders, women forced to watch their boyfriends knifed to death, then killed themselves by multiple knife thrusts, killed slowly, painfully, so that they had time to feel each assault and know they were going to die. Murders as trophies: random shootings of white people by black men in some bizarre organization where they earned "wings" for killing whites. Political murders: underground groups plotting bombings, assaults, robberies. The heiress Patty Hearst: kidnapped. I had been lost in my own wanderings since my arrival in San Francisco, not even pausing to glance at newspaper headlines. Were these emissions from my radio true events or figments of my fevers?

The radio reports faded in and out, so I could not learn who was speaking, and exactly of what. But their reality gained favor as similar stories drifted in over the hours: couples on lovers' lane killed in their cars; the knife murder, the same woman, tied up and speared over and over again, as if the world could not get enough of her horror. Taunting letters sent to the local newspapers by the killer, daring the police to catch him, his name hidden in cryptograms still undeciphered, his signature a circle and cross: rifle crosshairs. The Zodiac, he was called. All this was transmitted to me in peripatetic fragments, blinking lights diffused in fog: the letters, the ciphers, the crosshairs, the count of the victims—thirty-seven, the killer claimed.

Also fluxing through the hiss, in single words and phrases, were speculations about the killer's identity: Loner. Voyeur. Fear of women. Obsessional. Meticulous. Compulsive. Abused. Family history. Abuser. Mental illness. Dysfunction. Sexual. These words floated at me and hovered in the cold air. Then, in one stunning moment of transmission clarity, the static vanished and the speaker said: We believe he may be connected with a university, since the first attack happened near a college campus.

The breath froze in me. I shivered with a chill that did not come from my fever. Was this a description of . . . myself? In terror, I wondered if I was indeed the brutal killer; if in blacked-out hours I had committed such horrid crimes and then cleansed them from my memory; if I had indeed become what I had always feared my obsessions would make of me.

No, I told myself. No! I had been accused of . . . not that, not yet, please God. But what would keep me from it? The university had forced me to take a leave while they investigated. How far had I gone? I swore: I had touched no one! But once the complaint was lodged, I understood the fear I had aroused—no, "aroused" is not the right word; the correct description is the fear I had "created." For the object of my attentions had no reason to be afraid of me, had every reason to rely upon me as a trusted guide and advisor. And therefore there was no question of any "arousal." There was only the terrible darkness within me, which he had seen and, rightly, feared.

Only the patient can save me, I thought. She is all that is still decent in me. She is my trial, my test. I will not harm her! As long as I can hear her voice; as long as she makes her way to Room 804 to tell her story; as long as I may be near to her; as long as I may know what happens to her—I will be all right, she will be all right. We have nothing to fear.

Wednesday came again, the patient's last session before the holiday break. If I did not go to the office I would not hear her voice again until the end of the holiday break. How I needed her! How I ached for her! Yet my fevers and coughs continued—I could not go. My damp bed was my prison.

I turned off the radio. But the night did not give me rest. Again I skimmed the rim of sleep, tortured by images that grew more violent by the hour.

When Thursday morning came, I knew I could stay home no longer. I could not remain alone with my crows circling me, with their taunting call, *Her! Her! Her!* I resolved to go to the office. The sound machine would play; its whir would hide my stifled coughs. The patient would be gone, but still there was my dear office—its polished marble, varnished fruitwoods, balustraded stairways—all I had to help me.

34.

I bundled myself in sweaters and rode the N Judah. I debarked at Market and New Montgomery Streets, and the gargoyles came into view. Soon the entry was before me, the whiteness of the lobby: a bleach against the stain of my dark thoughts.

But then there came a shock.

A guard was stationed in the lobby!

The marble reception desk had been empty all these months, and now suddenly there stood a tall, well-built black man, wearing a black suit and tie, no insignia on him, but his stance and demeanor leaving no doubt that he was a security officer.

He turned as I entered; he stared at me. His skin was dark brown and smooth, his face absurdly handsome: a doo-wop crooner's face, a teenage-idol sort of man. At the same time, there was something menacing in his look, all the more frightful because I could not precisely locate the threatening feature in his almost-pretty face. Perhaps it came from his bearing, which was erect and muscular, or his powerful-looking hands, which he held clasped before him.

You will sign in, sir, he said to me in a commanding bass, indicating the sign on the desk that said, "All Visitors Must Check In at Reception."

But I am not a visitor, I replied. I am the tenant in Room 807.

I pointed to my name on the building roster that hung behind him.

He turned to it, then back to me, his face absolutely impassive. And for several seconds we stood beneath the ogling cherubs, he towering above me, as he weighed my veracity.

May I have identification, sir? he said.

I was affronted, yet frightened. I retrieved my university identification card. He looked at it, at me, then finally handed back the card.

Go on, sir, he said, his face still showing no emotion, waving me toward the elevator that had just arrived, which I entered guiltily, as if I truly were an imposter invading the building for illicit purposes.

My hands shook as I performed the delicate act of opening my office. I could barely control my breathing as I took my customary seat at the desk. My haven, my welcoming lobby with its whiteness and goodness—assailed!

A hostile force had arrived without warning. I would have to pass by the man every day, twice in and twice out, including the luncheon I normally took in a nearby cafe. Perhaps I could arrive very early and leave very late, and not go out for lunch. But what were his hours? Did he come on duty at four in the morning, five, six, seven? Leave at four, five, six? And for what reason had he been hired in the first place? Perhaps there had been an incident, a robbery, a shooting—a murder!

In this manner did I prosecute my madness, pursuing it vigorously, for the fearful stories that had emanated from my radio seemed to have followed me to the office, where, in my absence, a sudden need for security had apparently appeared: murderers circling us, bombers plotting, kidnappers tracking their prey. With only the fiercest self-control could I calm myself. I told myself that all downtown buildings of any size had guards or receptionists; ours had been the odd one; and now we were simply like everyone else.

No sooner did I still myself when there arose yet another impediment to my peace. The sound machine was whirring; above its rustle came the clicks and hushes of Dr. Schussler's Germanic speech—but what image of her should I hold? Again I was horridly double-minded, as I had been with the patient. Was this Dora a young woman of little experience, or the woman of a certain age I had first envisioned? Was there a long skirt or a mini; flat shoes or heels; flowing hair or bun? The two visions, each the inverse of the other, flashed in my mind like those double neon signs lighting one set of words, then another. I would go insane, I thought, if I could not pick one image—or perhaps construct a third possibility—in any case be released from this migrainous flashing in my head.

The old one! I decided. Nylon stockings—young women no longer wear nylon stockings. The slish and slide were the evidence! As for the consultation she was seeking, that did not mean she was a beginner, a young woman starting her practice. A therapist can be incompetent at any age—I, of all people, should know that. And slowly the old Dora Schussler reestablished herself, from the shoes and stockings up: sensible heels, nylons, mid-length skirt, blouse, face of a decent-looking woman of sixty, gray hair, bun.

I passed the day in feverish reverie; the hours slipped away; darkness pressed against the windows. I looked at my watch: nearly eight o'clock. The guard was surely gone for the day. I heard Dr. Schussler's seven o'clock patient leave, and, once the eight o'clock was safely installed, I planned to make my exit. So it was that I sat bundled in my sweaters, coat, scarf, and hat, despite the steam that clanged through the radiators.

The next patient arrived. I stood. I went to the door and was about to take the door knob in my hand, when suddenly the sound machine fell silent. And a deep alto voice said:

Thank you for seeing me tonight.

35.

My dear patient!

    I am glad you could come on such short notice, said the doctor.

    (And there I stood before the door, bundled up for the cold!)

    Sorry about yesterday, the patient said.

    (What had happened yesterday while I lay in my sickbed?)

    The doctor made a reassuring sound.

    (The door was still open; they stood so near me, naked to the corridor.)

    Of course I'll pay, said the patient with a laugh.

    (Had she run off again in midsession?)

    I'm a little drunk, she said.

    Dr. Schussler did not immediately step back from the doorway.

    We went out for drinks after work, she went on. One too many, that's all.

    The doctor remained standing at the opened door.

    If not for the coming break, she said, I would ask you to leave right now.

    Oh, yeah, the patient said a little sloppily.

    Are you all right? asked Dr. Schussler.

    Oh, yeah, said the patient. I'm fine, great, terrifically all right.

    Two or three seconds passed.

    Come in, the doctor said.

36.

Dr. Schussler closed the door, and the patient fell into her chair with a great sigh of the leather cushion.

What is happening? asked the doctor.

The patient seemed to shuffle her feet on the carpet. A driver in the street below leaned on his horn.

Shit! said the patient. What the hell's wrong with that guy?

The horn went on.

Really. What the fuck is wrong with him?

The horn continued; then stopped.

I have something to tell you, said the patient.

Yes?

You won't believe it.

Yes?

Last Friday night . . . I went to this Jewish—what do they call it? Temple.

She stopped; again shuffled her feet against the carpet.

Oh, my, said the therapist. And how was that?

I was late. I took a seat on a back pew—pews! What a surprise. Didn't expect that. Not sure what I'd thought Jews would sit on—benches?— but there were pews, like church.

She paused.

And of course there was no bleeding Jesus. But otherwise . . . Big domed building. Ladies dressed up in mink coats. Organ. Playing hymns! Same old chorus of middle-aged women with their vibratos wobbling from here to the next county. Except for the tiny bits of Hebrew— transliterated, so you don't even have to know it—*ba-ruch* something something *bow-ray pa-ree*—that can't be right, *paree*, like Paris. Except for those Hebrew bits, Mother would have felt right at home. I could just see her taking the coffee and tea afterward—no milk, though. Some-thing about kosher. But what could be not kosher about milk I have no idea. Coffee-Mate. Terrible stuff!

You stayed afterward for coffee? asked Dr. Schussler.

Why not?

Did you meet—?

No one. No one talked to me. Except to say good *shabbose*—is that how you say it—*sha-BOSE*? Mother. Right at home. But my grandfather—she gave a laugh—I don't even know him, never met him, but couldn't stop thinking about what Mother told me. How much he would've hated the place. Too well lit. Too much light on the subject. Needed his *mysterium tremendum*. Mass in Latin murmured in the dark, misted by incense. Everyone kneeling before the crucifix, Jesus hanging over them, suffering, sacrificed, bleeding his dark red human blood, blood they drink in communion—how primitive is that! Body of Christ, body of Christ. *Corpus Christi.* CORPUS. The scum group that took me in then bounced me out. Banished me, like they banished Father.

Then she fell silent. For some thirty seconds, there were only the honking horns in the street, the cough of the radiators.

I don't want to be a fucking Jew, the patient said at last.

Jewish, said Dr. Schussler. Somehow it is better to call someone *Jewish* than a *Jew*.

All right. I don't want to be fucking *Jewish*. Happy now?

Dr. Schussler sighed. It is very difficult for us to do our work if you come here after drinking.

Oh, I know.

We can't—

I know, I know. We were having fun, is all. That last round. That's the one I shouldn't . . . I know.

The radiators clanged.

What am I going to do? the patient went on. I don't want to be Jewish, but I don't even know what that means. Like I said, I've never even known a Jew—fuck! A Jewish *person*. Is this going to be some PC thing, like we can't say gay anymore but only gay-lesbian-bisexual?

I am not familiar with that stricture, said Dr. Schussler, so I cannot reply to your question.

No. Really. Are you going to correct me every time I say *Jew*?

You can say *Jew* whenever you like.

All right. Good! There. One thing a little easier. So I'll say it again: Jew. I've never been close to a fucking Jew.

The therapist shifted in her chair, crossed and recrossed her legs.

Well, of course you went to a boarding school, she said finally, but perhaps there were Jewish children in your neighborhood?

Oh, no, said the patient. Our neighborhood had covenants.

Covenants—as in the ark of the?

The patient laughed. Obviously you haven't lived anywhere with a homeowners' association. Conditions, covenants, and restrictions—C, C, and Rs. Rules of the association.

I do not—

No Jews.

Ah.

No Jews, no blacks, no Hindus, no Mexicans. Not even Catholics were allowed.

I see.

Even by the time the covenants became illegal—

There was history, supplied the therapist.

Yes. Right. History. People lived where they lived.

A fait accompli, said Dr. Schussler. And what about college? she went on. You went to a big university.

A sorority.

And I might suppose no—

No Jews. Right. Fuck! No *Jewish women*. It wasn't a rule—

Just history.

Yes. Right. History.

Then graduate school, said Dr. Schussler. Your Wharton M.B.A.

Many, many, many, many Jews, said the patient. Goldbergs and Cohens and Levines and Steins from here to kingdom come. A sea of men with black hair, big noses, and eyeglasses. I had no idea, when I decided to go into business, that I would be joining a Jewish club.

The doctor gasped.

Something wrong?

Dr. Schussler coughed. No. Something in my throat.

You're sure?

The doctor coughed again. A little bronchitis, she said.

It's the "Jewish club" business you're reacting to, isn't it? It's like I said there's a Jewish cabal, right?

What is your opinion?

Shit! Here we go again!

Dr. Schussler said nothing.

Dammit, won't you tell me what you think! Well, who gives a shit what you think. Goddamn PC business in the lesbian world about who's working-class and who's not. Can't even say what you think. It was a god-damn club. All that talk of being a *mensch*, all those holidays they took off, everyone knew all about them but me. High holy days. Passover. The one where they eat outside in a—what? *Soo-kah?* Those little bean-ies they wore. *Kippah. Yarmulke*—do you have any idea what the differ-ence is between a kippah and a yarmulke? I moved out west to get away from it. I may not be in the center of the markets anymore. I may have to get up at five a.m. to watch the tickers. But at least I'm away from all that.

The therapist took a breath, then released it. But did you not tell me, she said, in this very room, that you came out to San Francisco to meet women?

I—

To be part of—

Well—

The sexual revolution, the gay revolution.

Yes, said the patient.

Yes.

So? asked the patient.

So perhaps you are doing a bit of backward revisionism. You are startled by the news your mother gave you. You are having trouble as-similating it. And so you are trying to reject it, in whole cloth, by revising your history, trying to see it as a rejection of Judaism itself.

Humph, the patient said.

Rich Jews, brainy Jews, large noses, eyeglasses, Jews running the business world, said the doctor. These are stereotypes, as I am certain you know. Dangerous stereotypes.

I told you I didn't really know any Jews. Stereotypes—that's all I have.

Do you really want to rest with these ideas? asked the doctor. Do you not wish me to challenge them?

And I didn't like Jewish women any better than I liked the Jewish men of Wall Street. Charlotte used to drag me to all those meetings. Noisy, pushy Jewish girls, shouting slogans.

Noisy, pushy: These are more stereotypes, said Dr. Schussler.

Stereotypes usually exist for a reason, you know.

The doctor sat back and heaved a great, defeated sigh.

But why are you doing this to yourself, dear?

The patient snorted. So what am I supposed to be doing to myself?

Making yourself out to be so hateful.

This gave the patient pause. When she replied, it was with a softened voice:

But I am hateful, don't you see? I am full of hate. I was brought up to hate Catholics and Jews, and then I find out I may be Catholic, then no, it's even worse than that—I'm a Jew! For godsakes, what am I supposed to feel?

The doctor waited for the patient to go on. After her client said nothing for several seconds, she said:

I am afraid you can only feel this bewilderment for now. I am afraid there is no recourse but for you to feel it.

Feel it, echoed the patient.

It seemed, for the moment at least, that the therapist was not doing such a bad job after all, for the patient now sighed heavily, balancing on the rim of her emotions, about to "feel it."

When she suddenly exclaimed:

But what was *that*?

37.

I had coughed! A sudden, explosive cough had escaped my chest!

All that while I had been poised there, sweating in my outerwear, afraid to move a muscle, standing equally on each foot, so as not to creak a floorboard . . .

All that while, I had controlled my breathing, because I stood so close to our common door, and my labored breath might give me away . . .

All during that half hour I had allowed the sweat to roll uninhibited down my body, for fear even the rustle of my overcoat would be heard . . .

Only to be betrayed by my own chest! A tremendous cough! Which erupted out of me and barked once into the night like a tethered dog.

It was loud! said the patient. What was it?

My God, I don't know, answered the therapist.

It sounded like it was right in this room, said the patient.

Why, yes it did, said Dr. Schussler.

They shifted in their seats.

Well, I don't see anything, said the therapist.

(I shivered, my sweat ice-cold.)

And I don't hear anything now, said the patient.

But it was odd, said the doctor. It did seem to be coming from right there.

(I could feel them looking at our thin door. I all but saw the doctor's hand stretched out in my direction, her finger pointed at me.)

Seconds passed. Horns played in the street below.

(I must be quiet! I must stay hidden!)

The doctor sighed. In any case, she went on, shifting back around in her chair, I hope you understand the reasons for the hatred—the self-hatred—you have expressed.

Yes, said the patient. And then again no, I don't.

(But still she stared at the door. I could feel her eyes on me. Oh, how

I wanted her gaze! All the same, I begged her inside myself, Turn around, my dear patient. Forget I exist!)

But I still haven't told you the worst thing, she went on, shifting back in her seat (at last).

She laughed.

Charlotte's breaking up with me.

38

Mein Gott! said the therapist. Why did you not say?

I think I want to pretend it isn't happening.

The patient sighed, and sat back.

Charlotte got me a surprise Christmas gift, she said.

Yes? said the therapist.

Yes, right. Not like her at all. Charlotte and her fear of being "bourgeois," which seems to include anything with a bow. So, yes, very unexpected. She'd written "Merry Christmas!" and "Happy Birthday!" on an envelope—scrawled, in smudged pencil, but still, a gift. I opened it.

She laughed.

It was a confirmation for a one-week stay at this Russian River resort, she went on. Some cabins under the pines. A famous place for *wim-min* and *wim-mine*, spelled W-O-M-Y-N. Granola lesbians, whose greatest goal in life is to have a piece of land, a goat, and goat cheese. It's all *wim-min*, wim-*mine*, and baby dykes—and just the sort of place Charlotte knows I hate.

(I stood holding my scarf over my mouth, to stifle any sound, and listened, fascinated, despite the patient's distress. How interesting that a category as seemingly solid as "lesbian" could contain all these various admixtures! The "old-style girls" the patient had admired at the bar called A Little More: high heels, red lipstick, "breasts out to here," she'd said. The "politicos": politically active, short hair, flannel shirts, "stomping boots." And now these new types, these "granola lesbians" with their goats; and what did she mean by "baby" dykes?)

Asked the doctor: And where would you like to go on holiday?

Somewhere warm, the patient replied. Charlotte knows this. I think it was the first thing I told her about myself. That I love swimming in the sea, tennis, golf, cocktails under the stars, my girlfriend and I naked under our silky dresses. The patient gave off a cynical laugh. Why in the world did she take up with me? Charlotte ridiculed me. You want to go to a third-world country, she said, where poor people in waiter's jackets serve you piña coladas. You're nothing but a Dinah Shore lesbian! she shouted at me.

(Yet another type! This one, she went on to explain, described a well-to-do lesbian who looks "straight," has her nails done, and drives to the Dinah Shore Open women's golf tournament in a Cadillac.)

Finally the doctor said: But let us return to the point. The question is not why she took up with you. The question is, Why did you take up with *her*?

The patient did not answer for some seconds. The sounds of the street filled the pause: the blare of car horns, the roar of a truck's engine, the machine-gun rhythm of a jackhammer from some far sidewalk.

What is wrong? asked the therapist.

Charlotte gave me an ultimatum.

And? asked the therapist.

She said, either come with her or consider our relationship over.

There was a moment of silence, then:

How terrible of her! said Dr. Schussler.

You think she's being terrible, too, don't you?

Of course I do. I think it is very selfish of Charlotte not to consider your needs, after what you have been through emotionally.

That's what I thought. How could she do this to me? Now, when she knows what happened with my family . . . now . . . no sympathy for me . . . called me anti-Semitic! When she knows how much I need . . . oh, God, a holiday . . . enjoy Christmas . . . as a Jew? And with all my work . . . she makes fun of that, too . . . all the hours . . . I'm so tired . . . Oh, God, how I need a rest.

And she succumbed to tears.

They were drunken cries at first, bleary and whiny, but still: At last she had found her way to her tears.

Dr. Schussler let her patient cry without interruption. In any case, there was no reversing the flow of those tears. All that the patient had kept bound up inside her: now pouring forth in uncontrollable wails and sobs. It was an awful sound to hear, like the roar of a deadly swollen river. So much loss and helplessness. Loneliness so much like my own. I imagined her cries resounding in the corridor, through the halls, down the elevator shaft, to the cherubs with their black, startled eyes.

I glanced at my watch; only ten minutes of the session remained. Dr. Schussler must not lose control of the clock again, I thought. She was performing rather well; her consultation with Dr. Gurevitch seemed to have had some good effect (against all my expectations). Yet she again seemed unable to manage the hour; her patient was sobbing uncontrollably—and she must not let the patient walk out into the cold of Christmas alone, raw. I could barely stand still. Perhaps I should move, I thought, make noise—cough—somehow shift the therapist's attention, even at the risk of losing my position as a silent audience, even at the risk of losing the patient, my life's blood. I loved her so much that I would do anything.

The therapist sat without moving; the patient wept quietly now. And then came our savior: With only minutes remaining, the church carillon played the three-quarter hour.

Dr. Schussler stood; walked over to the patient.

Here you are, she said. Here are more tissues.

The patient laughed. Thank you, she said, beginning to blow her nose, cough, inhale deeply—all the things people do to try to bring their endless sobbing to a temporary end.

What do you think I should do? the patient asked between gasps and hiccups. I mean about the vacation. Why do you think she's doing this? I don't understand.

The doctor sat quietly for a moment. I could hear the words she was not saying: Charlotte wanted to break up but was making the patient do it for her. The patient was not ready to hear this; how good of the doctor to keep this to herself.

Finally the doctor laughed. Well, she said, I can tell you without any hesitation that I do not believe you should go to that granola resort.

Ah, sighed the patient. Thank you.

You did not need my permission.

No, said the patient between ebbing sobs. But I need your help.

The therapist inhaled, exhaled. Do you want to stay home? she asked finally.

Home? the patient echoed.

A sob stabbed her.

Home? You mean that place where I'll be eating breakfast alone under Charlotte's Holly Near posters? Where you can't open the cupboards without getting buried in an avalanche of saved yogurt containers? And all the avocado pits. No avocado eaten in our house ever escaped the fate of getting speared all around with toothpicks and hung in jars like prisoners. In every windowsill: empty Hain's sesame-butter jars breeding ugly, scraggly roots.

The therapist laughed. All right, what are Andie and Clarissa doing?

Going to Puerto Vallarta, the patient said between lingering gasps and sniffles.

Can you join them?

Andie's college friend was supposed to go with them, but now she has the flu. Andie says I can have her room.

Perfect! said the therapist.

You think I should go with them?

It is a nice resort, yes?

Yes. Fancy. Balconies overlooking the ocean, pools with swim-up bars. She laughed. Poor people in white jackets serving piña coladas.

Then she began to weep gently again. But Charlotte . . .

Charlotte, said the therapist.

This means I'm leaving Charlotte, said the patient.

Perhaps yes, perhaps no. She may or may not mean what she said. You can find out after the holidays. The doctor was quiet for a moment. Then she said: But you must do what is best for you. I believe you need rest and the support of good friends like Andie and Clarissa.

Yes . . . but . . . I feel so alone.

And she softly wept.

The therapist spoke gently while her patient gently cried, counseling her patient to be careful, monitor her drinking, take no drugs, be mindful of whom she befriended.

I will be here for you, the doctor said in a firm voice. Any time, day or night, you may leave a telephone message for me. If it is an emergency, you must do so. Now you will promise—swear!—that you will call me if you come undone in any way.

The patient coughed, blew her nose, laughed. I swear, she said.

They stood. I heard the analyst walk over to the patient, then there was a rustle of fabric. Thank you again, the patient said, her voice slightly muffled, as if it came through whatever stuff covered the nook of Dr. Schussler's shoulder.

39

I waited. Dr. Schussler did not turn on the sound machine. It seemed an eternity before she gathered her things, turned off the lights, and went home. I stood all that while in my overcoat, sweating under my many layers, finally tumbling into the street. I coughed my way toward Market Street.

Puerto Vallarta. A small travel agency down the block from our building had a sign in the window: a five-night package, airfare and hotel included, the "luxury hotel" shown on the poster boasting "all balconies facing the ocean." It was just as the patient desired: balconies, breezes, her silk dress fluttering across the sun-browned skin of her body. I had never noticed the agency's existence; there was no reason I should have. But now: Puerto Vallarta.

Although it was nearly nine o'clock, a light showed from within. I stepped into the shop.

Its atmosphere could not have been more unlike the posters of bikini-clad models that covered the walls. At a piled-high desk sat a woman of about my age smoking a long cigarette that dangled from her lips. She and her desk comprised the whole agency, a tiny space into each surface of which had seeped the grime of the street and the reek of age-old cigarette smoke.

Help you? asked the woman, the cigarette remaining in her lips as she spoke.

I stood by her desk—the side chair was piled as high as her desk—and inquired about the package in the window.

Which one? she asked without looking up. I got lotsa packages.

I indicated the trip to Puerto Vallarta, in particular the hotel shown in the poster in the window.

Too late, she said, her cigarette dropping ashes as it dangled. Sold out.

Before that moment, I was certain I did not actually want to go to Puerto Vallarta. I had merely been inquiring, I thought; only wished to feel closer to the patient, know more about the details of her trip, perhaps even what she would spend, what she could afford, therefore the style and conduct of her life. But upon learning that this agent could not help me, the sweat began to boil on my skin; coughs suddenly wracked my chest. *Her! Her! Her!* sounded in my head, growing ever louder, so that my coughs seemed to come from far away, from deep underwater. I could barely hear my own voice when I said:

That is very wrong! Why is your sign still in the window? You should not advertise what you cannot deliver!

She looked up.

Mister, she said, Christmas is around the corner. Everyone knows you have to book in advance. I can get you to Mazatlán, if you want.

How dare she! I thought. What was this Mazatlán? Who is this hag to thwart me?

I do not want to go to Mazatlán—wherever that is, I said with a shout. I want to go to Puerto Vallarta, you liar!

The woman put down her cigarette, stood, one hand on her desk drawer.

You got a problem, mister?

I imagined there was a gun in that drawer. Could she hear the crows calling in my head?

Forgive me, madam, I said, as politely as possible—the cawing still sounding—but I resisted now. Resisted.

It is only my deep disappointment, I said, meanwhile concentrating on making my voice higher, friendlier. Of course it is not your fault, madam.

And I fled the shop.

The N Judah was nearly empty. I sat under the bright fixtures and saw but a few passing lights and my own reflection in the window, the look of which horrified me: hollow-eyed, slack-cheeked—the face of someone who could harm an aging travel agent?

By ones and twos, the other passengers disembarked, until I was alone with my face in the window. Never had the patient seemed so far away. Was her good halo banished so quickly, within a mere slip of time, between nine o'clock and nine fifteen? I stepped down at the Ocean Beach terminus; the doors closed behind me; the streetcar rattled off.

40.

With the patient gone for the holidays, there was no recourse but to resume those of my activities one might designate as "normal." I would go to the office, traveling to and fro at regular hours. I would keep myself among crowds. I would wear my gray suit and overcoat, put on the narrow-brimmed hat with the feather in the band that I had bought after Thanksgiving. So attired, perhaps my Furies would not recognize me; would see an average man walking on a public street.

Yet immediately I faced an obstacle. To arrive at the office at regular hours meant encountering the security guard, that blot upon the refuge that was my lobby. I was not ready to withstand his scrutiny; not yet able to face the menace I felt emanating from his pretty countenance. I therefore delayed my departure for the office, hoping to time my arrival with the comings and goings of the lunchtime throng, and thereby evade the gaze of Mr. Handsome (as I had taken to calling him in my mind). His face haunted me all during my ride on the streetcar, as I again tried to ascertain what it was particularly that gave him such an air of threat. Perhaps it was the perfect, too-square jaw, like that of a plastic action figure—it made him seem not quite real, a G.I. Joe, a fantasy of male power. Or the eyes, which were fixed and penetrating. Or the mouth, perhaps, almost a girl's carved lips, absurdly full and curved for a man of his stature.

I waited outside the lobby doors, in an area where the guard could not see me unless he turned and craned his neck, and I peered through the glass to see if a crowd had assembled. I was fortunate. Many were waiting for the elevators, and then two cars arrived at once, creating a perfect traffic jam of people trying to get off jostling those trying to get on. I entered, pushed past the security guard in the midst of this confusion, and was the third person inside a waiting elevator car. The car began to fill around me.

Then the guard reached his hand inside.

Step out, please, sir, he said.

It was an order. Yet I answered:

But you know me!

I do not, sir, he said. Please step out.

He held the elevator door open. The eyes of all the other passengers fell upon me.

I stepped out.

Again the guard indicated the sign-in book.

But you know me! I repeated, once more showing him my name on the roster.

He scrutinized me as before, his lovely lips set in a firm line, only his eyes going back and forth, dark orbs like those of the cherubs. As time ticked on, I began to fear for my safety, for it came to me: He can see through me! He can hear the noise in my head! He knows the dark acts of which I may be capable!

I saw his brow narrow, just a hair's width. Meanwhile his gaze remained set upon me. It was impossible to know what he was about to do. I saw that was the source of his power: His beauty mesmerized; one could not read his face; would a smile or a knife be the next thing one saw?

Go on, sir, he said at last, but noncommittally, as if to say, I will get you next time.

I do not know how I passed the day. Dr. Schussler's office was quiet, no patients, no sound machine, and the emptiness of the adjoining room made my loneliness feel particularly acute. Finally night fell. The guard would be gone. I went down to Union Square to lose myself amongst the crowd.

A tall Christmas tree stood in the center of the square, as did a Jewish candelabrum, its eight lights already lit. I could only wonder what the patient felt as she gazed upon that Jewish symbol. Last year, it was probably no more to her than a civic show of ecumenical spirit. But now, while crossing the square, as she would have to do to negotiate the shopping district, did she find the candelabrum oppressive? Wish she could return it to its former irrelevance? Mexico offered the patient many opportunities for relaxation, I thought, not the least its relative shortage of Jews.

But I could not long retain these thoughts of the patient. All around me a sort of frenzy seemed to be in progress. Great convoys of shoppers went by in furious motion, sailing in noisy groups, as if something desperately needed to be purchased and the shops might close at any moment. The crowds were full of shouting young men. Heavy shopping bags kept clipping me behind the knee. I was pushed into the street by a raucous, half-drunken group; no sooner did I regain the sidewalk when I was pushed aside by another. A passing car spattered my pants leg with mud.

I fled the square and wandered in the now-dark business district, where I soon found myself before a grill with a long wooden counter, at which sat a row of gentlemen who were taking their dinner. As this seemed to be the sort of establishment where a man dining alone might feel comfortable, I went in, joined the gentlemen, and contentedly passed two hours listening to the banter between diners and waiters, who, it seemed, had acquaintanceships of long standing.

It was when I left the grill that something seemed to change in my very metabolism. It might have been the effect of the deserted business district, where the stoplights blinked their reds and yellows into empty streets. Or perhaps it was the faded frivolity of Union Square, where discarded wrappings were trapped in the shrubbery, and a large blown bow, like some horrid spider, skittered across the sidewalk. I only know that, before I knew what I was doing, I hailed a cab, settled in my seat, and asked the driver, Would you perhaps know a bar called A Little More?

The driver put his arm on the seatback and did a slow turn around to look at me.

Sir, are you sure you want to go there?

I was not sure of anything. My body seemed not to belong to me.

Yes, I said. Please take me there.

The driver said nothing as he drove us across Market Street, proceeded what seemed to me east and south for several blocks, then traveled under an elevated roadway. We came to a district I had never seen before, a wide boulevard lined with warehouses, now dark. Then we turned up a short street that dead-ended into a parking lot.

Are we there? I asked. Where are we?

The driver gestured toward the far side of the parking lot. Back that end, he said.

I paid the fare.

Want me to wait? the driver asked.

Why would I want you to wait?

Okay, sir. You know best.

And he drove away.

41.

Once the sound of the cab faded off, I could hear music spilling out of a doorway. The night had turned cold and blustery, and as I crossed the crowded parking lot, the music came and went, blown about by the wind.

In the entranceway was a woman sitting on a barstool, who stood at my approach.

You lost, buddy? she asked.

She was an average-looking woman with a pleasant face, wearing a white shirt and chinos, with a parka around her shoulders—nothing to identify her as a lesbian, to my eye. Her manner was not exactly hostile, but she was wary and a little amused, I thought.

A friend asked me to meet her here, I said.

Another woman came to join her. She looked precisely like my idea of a lesbian: big, heavyset, mannish. The words "bull dyke" came to mind involuntarily. What's he doing here? she said to the first woman.

Says he's meeting a friend.

They both laughed, looked me up and down, and finally the first woman sighed and turned to me. Too bad we can't keep you out legally, she said. Cover's five bucks, Mr. Friend of Somebody.

I gave her the money, and she stamped my hand with something out of a children's printing set: the image of a giraffe. Then I was free to enter, but as I went by, the big woman pulled me aside and said, Be good, little buddy. I'm keeping my eye on you.

I found myself in a large, darkened room, standing before a crowded dance floor. A revolving mirrored ball hung from the ceiling, casting circling pinpoints of light on the dancers, as they too swirled about, so that for a moment I felt dizzy, as if it were the floor that was moving, not the ball or the dancers. The room was hot and smoky, throbbing with the beat of music I knew was called disco. And as my eyes became accustomed to the dim light, I could see that the dance floor was ringed with small tables, each one filled with a small group of women who crowded around the tiny circle of the table, holding cocktail glasses and bottles of beer. So many women! I thought, for there were perhaps two hundred or more in the room, filling not only the dance floor and the tables but also the bar area behind me, where ladies stood four deep as they pressed forward to place an order with the busy women bartenders.

And all of them are lesbians! came my next thought. For there were charming ladies of every variety, far outnumbering the "bull dykes" whom I had always imagined were the typical sort. There were women in neat pantsuits—businesswomen, they seemed. And many "old-style girls," who looked just as delectable as the patient had said, in their tight sweaters and red lips, curvy, like lounge vamps of the fifties. There were tiny Asian women, who seemed to be in pairs in which one partner took the role of the man and one the woman. And women who simply looked fresh and athletic, as if they had just come from the clubhouse after a swim—could these be "Dinah Shore lesbians"?

By far the largest group were the "politicos": women with short hair and flannel shirts who, to my mind, looked not like women but like tender preadolescents. Many had stripped off their shirts and danced in their undershirts, cotton muscle shirts, braless nipples bobbing sweetly beneath the surface of the cloth. The word "youths" came to mind as I gazed upon them—not "boys" or "girls" but "youths"—for they seemed to have stopped themselves at that delicate moment just before the terrible descent into the divide between male and female: girls who could still run around unashamed in their underwear, boys whose cheeks were still soft with down. And as I watched the couples sway on the dance floor—to a popular slow song, "Midnight Train to Georgia"—I could not understand why the patient was so resistant to their charms. For I found them adorably sexy, with their short haircuts with cut-in sideburns and cute little cowlicks, their tight blue jeans, bodies pressed tightly together as they moved to the rhythm of that aching, plaintive song. And, thrust between each other's legs, a knee seeking a tender spot.

Was Charlotte here? I suddenly wondered. She might be relaxing amongst her goat-lady lesbians. Then again, about to find herself newly single, she might be one of those women in blue jeans, her knee already exploring the inner thigh of someone new. And which of these women had the patient flirted with, on those nights when she had had one too many: that woman wearing a dark, tailored pantsuit? Or, better yet, that one there: a blowzy vamp showing cleavage? It thrilled me to think that this is where the patient had stood, right on the edge of this dance floor, gazing into the many faces of female allure.

The room suddenly seemed very crowded, for all at once there was a cloud of women around me. Their bodies were so close that I could smell their perfumes and hair gels and sweat, and I did not try to move away, for I confess it was a very pleasant sensation: to be so surrounded by so much female flesh, the occasional brush of a breast against my arm, the rub of a backside, a hip to my thigh. Without actually dancing (which would have been strange, since I was alone), I tried to sway with the crowd, just slightly, if only to go unopposed with the movement all around me. I felt myself being drawn from the margin of the dance floor slowly toward the center, and again I let myself be taken by the overall drift, for it seemed odder to force my way out than to let the situation be as it was: twirling lights, undulating women's bodies, a high, sweet voice singing *I love to love you, baby.*

Then the music changed to something faster, and a cry of happiness rose from the throats of the women all around me. They danced with a wilder energy, throwing their arms about, singing along with the chorus. *Voulez-vous couchez avec moi, ce soir?* In the tighter press of bodies, I began to be elbowed now and again, but I thought nothing of it, as there was now a kind of abandon in the dancing, a joyousness, and I—a man amidst this happy throng of women—was surely an obstacle to their pleasures.

I tried to edge my way off the dance floor. But the crowd was now quite thick, and I had not gone two steps when I was sharply jostled. Sorry, said a woman, giving me a tight smile. She was a politico type, and after I mumbled a "sorry" of my own, it seemed to me that her girl-friend, another woman in an undershirt, threw her partner directly against me. They both laughed, then danced away; and before I could consider what had just happened, I felt an elbow to my ribs. Instinctively stepping aside, I received a jab in my back. I twisted around, and an arm flew into my neck. Oops! came a voice behind me. I tried to see where this had come from, but suddenly a foot came down upon mine: the high-heeled shoe of a blonde in a tight skirt. Sorry! she sing-songed as her partner swept her away.

The women seemed to be pressing in around me. The dance floor cannot really be as crowded as all this, I thought, as I was bumped from one side, then from the other. I tried to move away, to an area that might be more open, but I was soon stepped on again, by a businesswoman in sensible pumps, then by the combat boots of a bull dyke. A tiny Asian woman, giggling, reached out a graceful foot and pressed it upon my toes, then howled with delight, like a child at a balloon dance.

And still the women seemed to press in, to the point where I could not move, even to defend myself from the next spike heel to the instep, the flung arm that hit me in the face, the fist that landed on my throat. The heat became overwhelming. The smell of their bodies and lotions was now sickening. The feel of their bodies upon mine—the tight jam of flesh on flesh—was now causing me a kind of panic, as I was terrified that I might unintentionally touch a breast or a thigh and so bring upon myself some sort of physical retribution. I wanted desperately to leave, but no matter how I turned and turned, the women's bodies trapped me in place, and I seemed to drift ever farther from the edge of the dance floor, from the entrance, from the red glow of the exit sign, which I watched recede into the distance as I was swept into the depths of the room. Still the music throbbed and the lights swirled and the blows fell upon me, and I could not find my way out of this mass of women, who, I saw, were laughing at me.

I was about to cry out, when a loud voice shouted from the far side of the room:

Take it easy, girls. Don't gangbang 'im!

All the women stepped back, just an inch, and I was able to turn around and see where this voice was coming from. It was the bull dyke from the door, parting the crowd with her arms. She was laughing. Don't gangbang 'im, girls, she kept repeating, and soon the crowd took up her laughter in a rippling wave that washed over the dance floor. Is that what they had been doing: gangbanging me? Finally the big woman reached me and put a meaty hand on my arm.

You better get outta here, mister, she said, still laughing, before these girls stomp you to death.

I moved in her wake toward the door. But still the women were gathered around me like clinging fog. Creep! someone said in my right ear. I turned in the direction of the voice, and immediately to my left someone said, Letch! I turned my head again, and directly into my face a woman spat, Pervert!

Go on, mister, said my rescuer. Just keep moving.

At the doorway, she raised an eyebrow at me, which was pierced by a tiny ring. And remember, little buddy, she said in a kindly voice, it'll be worse next time.

I hurried across the parking lot, shivering as my sweat met the cold night air.

I marched down the short street to the dark boulevard, then stopped, searching for evidence of the elevated roadway, for any sign of the route that cab had taken. I walked in one direction then another, striding, the taunts of the women sounding in my head. *Creep. Letch. Pervert.* That's what the students at the university had called me. But it was all wrong, very wrong. I always went alone to student haunts. I never approached— never even thought of touching anyone. The boy intrigued me, that was all. It was only my way of trying to understand him!

Somehow I came to the elevated roadway. Somehow I found the route the cab had taken, Folsom Street, I thought. Not a block from the roadway was the neon sign of what seemed to be a diner. Hamburger Mary's, it said. I opened the door to a rush of warm air.

Table? asked a waitress.

I slid gratefully into a booth, took a menu, asked for coffee. As I sat and felt the blood coming back into my hands, I noticed there were many men in leather jackets in the diner, some with chains on their wrists and around their necks. After the waitress brought my coffee and took my order, I asked her, Is this some sort of biker hangout?

She laughed, a hoarse laugh. You don't know where the hell you are, do you, honey?

I ate a hamburger, fried potatoes, a salad, finding myself starved despite my dinner earlier in the evening. Feeling warmed and fortified, I asked for the check, paid it, and prepared to go back out into the night to find my way home. It was only when the waitress brought my change that I noticed it: her height, the size of her hands, the Adam's apple that bobbed at her throat.

She must have seen the look in my eyes, for she said, Honey, you don't look so good. Let me call you a cab.

Then she shrieked: You're a cab! You're a cab!

Her laugh was so shrill that I instinctively slid to the far side of the booth. I looked over my shoulder and saw that the other patrons, the men in leather and chains, were glancing over, amused, but otherwise showed no interest. Was this a common occurrence? Could anyone wander in from the street for a hamburger and find himself pressed against the wall while a looming man-woman shrieked at him in utter ridicule?

Please, I said. I'll just—

Oh, don't be so sensitive! She had abruptly stopped laughing. I'll let you know when your cab's here. Don't worry. Nothing's going to happen to you.

42.

I could not bring myself to go home. Not knowing where else to go, I asked the taxi driver to take me to the Palace. The hotel must have a bar, I thought, where I could prepare myself for the long ride out to Ocean Beach. But in the lounge I found only two drunken men accompanied by three prostitutes. Stretching out behind them, all across the back bar, was a large, garish mural painted by Maxfield Parrish: the Pied Piper leading children up a rocky promontory. There was something grotesque in this larger-than-life-size Piper with his hooked nose, the children's phony, chub-cheeked innocence, the impossibly purple sunset behind them; the live prostitutes painted almost as shamelessly as the mural. I fled the bar, crossed the street, stepped over the desperate men sprawled in the doorway, and rode the elevator up to my office.

There I lay in the dark, trying to make myself comfortable on the small settee. The Palace's rooftop pink-neon sign, three stories high, loomed over the window. The first letter A was defective, and I watched the restless oscillation of Palace, P lace, Palace, P lace, as I tried to empty my mind of the evening's events.

I must have dozed off, for the next thing I knew, I was being startled awake by a thundering slam. It took me a moment to realize it was a door closing. Then, hearing footfalls on the other side of the wall, I knew the slam must have come from the door to the next room—Dr. Schussler's office!

What would Dr. Schussler be doing at her office late at night on the Friday before Christmas? It must be a special cleaning crew, I thought. But I heard no vacuum, no sound of a trash cart being wheeled along the corridor. There were only the continuing footfalls, and then the thud of something heavy, perhaps a briefcase, landing on a surface— Dr. Schussler's desk, judging by the direction from which the sound had come.

Gott! came in a huge sigh, as the analyst (for now I knew it could only be she) threw herself into her chair much as she had thrown down her briefcase.

I dared not move. The settee upon which I lay was old, poorly built, given to creaks and moans. I was aware of the quiet in the street below, the absence of the Palace doorman's taxi whistle, which earlier had repeatedly pierced the night; of the silence in the building but for a hum I had never heard before, a strange, high whine that seemed to emanate from the building's very core.

Above all I was aware of Dr. Schussler's stillness. She had not taken off her coat, and I could clearly imagine her sitting in her chair, still bundled against the chill night, her head against the neck rest. Her weariness was palpable through the wall. I suddenly saw us as if from above, Dora and I on either side of our thin common door, neither of us here for happy reasons, the Palace sign flickering over us—Palace, P lace, Palace, P lace—our common bath of light, the unreliable hopefulness of its pink-neon glow.

I wanted the moment to stretch on and on; I thought I could remain immobile for hours, if only Dr. Schussler would do the same. But my hope was dashed when the doctor abruptly stood, removed her outer garments, and hung them on a rattling rack on the back of her door. After bustling about briefly, she sat down.

There came clicking sounds I could not identify, then a whir, then another click, after which the doctor said, Testing, one, two, one, two. There were further whirs and clicks, then the repetition of Testing, one, two, one, two—and I understood that Dr. Schussler was speaking into a tape recorder.

Friday night, she began, December 20th, one a.m. Then she laughed. Saturday morning, she began again, December 21st, one a.m. Journal of work with patients previously coded as one and two. Journal of consultations with Dr. Gurevitch concerning the patient coded as three.

She clicked off the machine.

I could barely constrain my body. Patient three! This Gurevitch was the doctor she had turned to for "consultation"! For I instantly remembered the urgent calls, always about a "patient three," always after difficult sessions with the patient—our patient, *my* patient. To whom else could Dora Schussler be referring? Patient three! I had to still myself in that creaking settee; had to calm my heart; had to ignore the electric adrenaline that shocked me as if I were a dead frog galvanized into twitching on the dissection table. I heard the scrape of Dr. Schussler's match; smelled the burnt phosphorus, then the tease of smoke from her Viceroy. She exhaled: a breath of exquisite slowness and depth. I had to, had to, had to constrain myself! She inhaled and exhaled again, then again, and yet a third time.

A clack: At last Dr. Schussler switched on the tape recorder. She cleared her throat then said into the machine:

Patient one remains cathectic upon his former wife, V.

The therapist went on speaking, but I had the sense that I had suddenly lost the ability to understand English. It seemed that V had a new husband, E, and there was a teenage son of someone called B, whose boss, W—no, that couldn't be right. W must be the boss of patient one. There were several cathexi, and characters named E, V, M, and W. If my patient's life had once seemed a story begun at random, this journal entry was nothing more than a scattering of Scrabble tiles. And its very incomprehensibleness seemed hostile to me, a narrative that refused to engage me—refused to distract me from my lone and sharp desire: Patient three; tell me about patient three!

Time wore on. I was cold. My coat, which I had thrown over myself as a blanket, was not sufficient to ward off the chill of the unheated office. The night seemed too still, as if no one existed but Dr. Schussler and I, and the doctor were speaking of the vanished. Patient two. A young man who could not separate from his mother. His "childhood fixations" and "transitional objects" and "organizations of reality"—I hated them, hated him, hated that he had been coded as "two," which ordinally stood between me and the object of my desire: "three."

Dr. Schussler had not turned on the light. She had barely moved. She was smoking constantly, one cigarette lit from another—no further scent of phosphorus had slid under our common door. And yet again I asked myself, Who was this Dora Schussler, this analyst in consultation with another analyst; this woman sitting beside me smoking in the gloom, in whose hands lay the patient's fate?

She stopped speaking of patient two. Moments passed in which nothing happened. Then:

Note to transcriber, she said at last. Close now personal journal. Please to add the following to the journal of consultations concerning the patient formerly coded as three.

Patient three!

As we discussed, Dr. Gurevitch, said the therapist with a sigh, I continue in the analysis of this uncontrolled countertransference. I am taking careful notes in an attempt to make conscious to myself the areas in which I am overidentifying with the patient, and the effects of that overidentification.

However, she continued after a coughing spell—her deep sigh had disturbed her smoker's inland sea of phlegm, which roiled while the doctor struggled to calm it. However, Dr. Gurevitch, despite our work, I am not certain if the client's analysis is proceeding toward a successful outcome. I continue to feel that the damage is grave. I cannot undo my conviction that I have done irreparable harm to patient three.

43.

Irreparable harm! I wanted to shout. What harm? What! How dare you do irreparable harm to my beloved patient! I wanted to leap up and pound on the doctor's door. Yet I was powerless. What good would it do to intervene now? The patient would not be served if I broke into Dr. Schussler's office and dragged the woman away.

So I remained still, cold on the settee, suppressing my breathing. The tape recorder ran on in a low whine. The doctor switched off the machine. She sighed as one in grief. Then:

Clack. The machine came on again.

Yes, I know, Dr. Gurevitch, the therapist continued. I know. My guilt is part of the countertransference. Yet, as we are telling our patients always, understanding a feeling is no protection against actually feeling it.

To summarize, she continued after another long sigh, I have come to concurrence with the idea that it was not inappropriate for me to encourage the patient to explore the fact of her adoption, specifically exploring her feelings of not belonging in her family. Unconfronted, this has led her into a neurotic pattern of letting herself be chosen by inappropriate partners, since the feeling of "wrongness of match" is what she associates with love, is what is "familiar" to her.

There is some disagreement as to whether or not her lesbianism is part of this neurosis, said the therapist. The DSM has not yet specifically addressed female-to-female relationships—the recent delisting of homosexuality as an illness relates most directly to male homosexual relationships. Yet you and I agree, Dr. Gurevitch, that patient three's sexual love for women is not necessarily part of her internal organization regarding inappropriate partners. The specific choice of a woman partner is what is at issue here, not the choice of a woman in principle. I will therefore continue to treat the breakup with her most recent girlfriend as an opportunity for the patient to examine her affective choices in the context of her larger psychological issues.

("Opportunity!" I thought. Her grief over this breakup is not an "opportunity," you damned therapist!)

You have helped me to understand, Dr. Gurevitch (the doctor went on as I calmed myself), that it was not necessarily an error to confront the patient with her continual evasions concerning her adopted status. Where I erred was doing so before I had prepared the psychic groundwork. I continued to believe that her resistance, her refusal to discuss the fact of her adoption—her habitual protection of her adoptive parents, another set of inappropriate partners, so to speak—was part of the neurotic pattern. My unconscious motive in doing so, as we discussed, was my wish that she would enact my deepest desire: to escape the sins of my Nazi bastard father.

This last statement was said with such venom that it seemed not to have come from the woman who had been speaking with such assurance in the cold argot of psychotherapy. Dr. Schussler slammed off the recorder, stood, then paced about her office. She continued to smoke, and again I saw her as if from above, the doctor circling, a trail of smoke glowing pink in the nervous light of the hotel sign.

Then she abruptly stopped and turned on the tape recorder.

Note to transcriber, she said. Delete the sentence containing the phrase "Nazi bastard." Then: No. Keep it. STET, I believe you say. Keep it. *Ja*. Keep.

The doctor took a long drag on her Viceroy. Then, still standing, she said:

Transcriber: Please to note my pause, my initial instruction to delete the "Nazi bastard" sentence, and my subsequent decision to retain it. Now, continuing with the journal of consultations with Dr. Gurevitch concerning the patient previously coded as three:

I have already spoken to you, Dr. Gurevitch, about my family history. But this aspect of our discussions was quite brief, as we were necessarily focused upon the patient. However, before we can understand fully all the factors at work in this countertransference, you should know that my father was not simply an officer in the German army, as I perhaps led you to believe. He was not merely a foot soldier in the Wehrmacht, not merely one of those men who fulfilled what he believed was his duty to his native land . . . *Nein* . . .

Wind gusted at our windows, which shuddered in their old frames. The doctor fell into her chair.

My father was a member of the Schutzstaffel, she said. An Obersturmbannführer. A true believer in the Führer and the Master Race. When he was at home, he wore his uniform at the dinner table, so proud of his collar insignia with its three diamonds, his hat with the twin light-ning bolts of the SS. Hitler had just come to power. *Vater* made us to stand behind our chairs and shout *"Heil Hitler!"* before we could eat, a new form of saying grace, said our mother. Even our little brother, five years old, saluted perfectly with a stiff hand and an upraised chin.

The doctor laughed.

I was fifteen, very sheltered, still a girl. My sisters were nine and seven. We could not help but find all this saluting very funny. We shouted *"Heil Hitler!"* and giggled, to *Vater's* rebukes, which made us only to giggle the more . . . *Aber* . . . But of course . . . it was not funny . . . You see: My father was instrumental in the deportation and murder of the Jews of France.

This last statement was spat out to the best of Dr. Schussler's Ger-manic abilities: the *F*-sound start of *Vater* like hot steam through her teeth.

Before the invasion of France, she went on in the same mode, *Vater's* job was to get money to amenable French candidates for office. Fascist rightists. Anti-Semites. Nationalists who wanted to purify *la belle France*. My father did his work well, evidently. By the time German tanks had poured through the Ardennes Forest, and the Wehrmacht had erased the Maginot Line, the friends of Germany were waiting for him.

But, ah! I do not suppose he had to work so very hard. The govern-ment of Léon Blum—when was that? 1935? '36? What a trauma it must have created for the French to have been led by a Jew! What nightmares it must have engendered to have had this Jew—so Jewish-looking!—at the helm of their nation while the rest of Europe could not wait to throw their own Jews into the fire. How ready they must have been to rid them-selves of this psychological stain upon *l'honneur de la France*.

Dr. Schussler stopped; stood.

I am sorry, Dr. Gurevitch, for this tone of cynicism, she said. But to know one's father was at the heart of it . . .

The therapist remained standing, mute, as the recording machine ran on, the threading tape flapping against the take-up reel. Finally Dr. Schussler slowly sank into her chair and said:

You may recall, Dr. Gurevitch, that I had to watch the war from afar. I was in this country when Hitler invaded France, beginning my studies for the doctorate at Columbia University in New York City. There I met Helmut Schuessler—still spelled with its Germanic *E* to reflect our lost umlaut—Helmut, who was already an American citizen, and who would soon become my husband. And then I, too, became an American. So it happened, Doctor Gurevitch, that all at once I became a candidate for a doctorate in psychology, a wife, an American, and a registered enemy alien.

The doctor paused.

Our neighbors would not speak to us, she went on. Only our colleagues at the Analytic Institute would befriend us.

She paused.

Mostly Jews.

And paused again.

We were imprisoned as enemy aliens. Perhaps you do not know this: Many Germans were imprisoned throughout the war, not on the scale of the Japanese concentration camps, but imprisoned nonetheless. We went to . . . Never mind. The point is that we might have remained imprisoned for the duration of the war had not our colleagues at the Analytic Institute worked so hard to see us freed. Then we did our best to stop being Germans. We dropped the *E* from our names. We became the *SHOE-slurs*. Helmut changed his name to Harold. Can one cut off one's inheritance so easily? Perhaps not. We never managed to lose our accents.

The doctor breathed haltingly, as one about to cry, then said:

I worried about the welfare of my family, *naturlich*, as would anyone whose loved ones—mother, sisters, brother, cousins, aunts—lived in a war zone. And I was anxious to hear from them. In the beginning, said the doctor, sighing and arranging herself in her chair, before the Americans entered the war, my brother and sisters sent letters in which they bragged: about Hitler, about how Germany would conquer all of Europe. And, most of all, about our father's successes. Such praise for *Vater*, his life in Paris among rich, powerful men whom he now could dominate. To this very day they believe in all that claptrap; they defend him. They say, He saved us from "those anti-German elements."

Dear *Vater*. He was the one who soothed the tiny consciences of the French. It did not take much, I should say, to convince that nation they should surrender their Jews. Father only had to assist in the maintenance of a little fiction. Send us only "foreign Jews," he said, not "French Jews." Such a small crumb to throw them: only the riffraff of Belgium or Poland, Czechoslovakia or Russia. Foreigners. Not decent French men and women such as yourselves. He helped to spread this nationalist strategy, which would come to be so useful everywhere.

And then my father asked for more Jews and more. The French resisted only briefly: They tried to shield the Jews who had lived in France for generations, the aristocrats, the "French Israelites," as they preferred to call them. And the decorated heroes who had served France during the Great War. And the war widows. But their resistance was nothing, a tissue. As *Vater* knew, it was but a balm to soothe what little was left of their better natures. Soon the French sent everyone: the veterans, the war widows, the "French" Jews of old families; the bearers of *l'Insigne des Blessés Militaires, la Médaille d'Honneur, la Croix de la Valeur, la Croix de Guerre, la Croix du Combattant*—all those Jews with all those crosses, even grandfathers clutching *les Médailles Militaires*—their service to *la France* meant nothing. Their medals went into the flames along with them.

The threaded tape flapped on as Dr. Schussler paused.

Meanwhile, the doctor continued, what elegant dinner parties *Vater* attended. Parties arranged by a fool named Louis Darquier de Pellepoix—that idiot with his monocle and the ridiculous "de Pellepoix" he insisted upon appending to his name, as if he were something more than a scheming boulevardier. There *Vater* was, drinking champagne with Pierre Taittinger, who contributed his wealth to the cause. And with Eugène Schueller, owner of L'Oréal, another grand contributor. I can never again drink champagne, Dr. Gurevitch. I will never wear products from L'Oréal or indeed—

Forgive me . . . I am ranting. All I meant to say is that the family letters came, and then they came more rarely, and then not at all. Yet I knew what was happening. And here I remained as the death machine rolled on.

I am tired now. It is—what time? One? Two in the morning? I have been Christmas shopping—the packages are all around me on the floor—and I thought, while I was downtown, I might record my thoughts. I am glad I did, despite the hour. I see I must return to my own therapy if I am to do decent work for patient three. I cannot simply turn her away—as you said, Dr. Gurevitch, such a move would be experienced by her as a casting out, yet another abandonment, inducing yet more harm. So I must make conscious my own internal crosscurrents, all that churned inside me as I read the letters from München, and when they came no more, and when the war was over and everyone knew what I had known.

The doctor switched off the machine; stood; walked about the office. Then came the sounds of paper crackling, plastic bags rattling. She must be leaving, I thought, gathering her purchases, her Christmas presents, going home to Helmut or Harold or whatever his name was now, returning to her life—absolved! cleansed!—forgiven by recounting her sins to this Gurevitch, this therapist-confessor. I would follow the doctor, I thought, accost her in some way—but how? And what good would it do? If I did . . . the therapist would know of my existence, my precious existence as the watcher over the patient . . . my dear patient . . .

The crackling stopped. Then there was only the sound of the wind, the scrape of a match. Smoke slid under the door, the snake of smoke. The doctor went to her chair, sat down, turned on the recorder.

Dr. Gurevitch, she said in a hoarse voice, you asked if I could recall a distinct moment, or a series of moments, when I believe the deviation toward extreme countertransference began. I am embarrassed to say that I knew the answer immediately, even before you had completed your question. No, I should not say "embarrassed." Of course not. The moment, as it had unfolded in time, had been just one of many vivid instances that occur during the course of a patient's therapy. It was your question that brought its significance into relief.

It took place but a few months ago—how can that be? But yes, it was only last September. We had returned from the summer hiatus, and I had led the trail of talk back to the central unexamined trope of the patient's life: I was urging her, once again, to explore the emotional effects of her adopted status. She resisted, as usual, and I pressed on. I thought I was in control of the session. I believed my motivations were clear: to help the patient see the pattern that had been imposed upon her, this endless repetition of being selected yet judged to be not exactly what was wanted, a purchase the buyer wished to return.

It was a bright day. The sun pierced the blinds, painting lines across the floor and walls. I remember this because of the way the light struck her, as you will see, because it is the light that brings the moment back to me with such clarity.

I said to the patient, Do you see? Do you see how your relationship with your girlfriend Charlotte mirrors your relationship with your mother?

She squirmed and resisted, and finally replied: Every child thinks it must have been switched at birth, these can't possibly be my real parents, it's all a big mistake.

At that moment she leaned forward into the light. She had been in shadow, only her body—did I mention, Dr. Gurevitch, what a very thin body she has, all sinew, so that one instinctively worries if she is well?—only her body had been illuminated, slashed by the beams through the venetian blinds. Now she leaned forward so that her eyes, too, entered the light, while the rest of her small, triangular face narrowed down into the shadows. In that moment, her eyes were nearly the hazel color she and her family persist in believing them to be. For they are actually brown, medium brown, with flecks of yellow, the flecks now catching the light so that her eyes blazed at me from the darkness. And her hair— also brown, not the fictional "dirty blond"—her hair suddenly haloed, a nimbus of frizzy light around her blazing eyes.

Every child thinks it must have been switched at birth, she said to me so fiercely from the shadows. Every child thinks these cannot possibly be my real parents, it's all a big mistake, I do not belong to them. Well, I just happened to have more evidence than they do. Mine really are not my parents.

What envy coursed through me! Yes, Dr. Gurevitch, I see now it was envy. She was right: She could shed her family and I could not. Her attachment to them was not "real," they were not *blut*, she had inherited nothing from them but experience, which can be discussed, analyzed, understood, changed. But I carried in me—what? What have I inherited from the Obersturmbannführer? A stain—which cannot be removed? For I belong to him, to them, my family: the defenders of the murderers of the Jews.

I believe it is from that moment that my determination grew to detach the patient from her adoptive parents, said the doctor. Yes, it was envy, certainly. She would enact for me what I could not do for myself. She could leave her family, find another, a kinder one, perhaps, one more suited to her. How could I know I was throwing her back into . . . all that.

The doctor sat quietly for a full minute, as the tape whirred and the building hummed from somewhere in its depths. Then she switched off the machine and abruptly left the room—going to the ladies' lounge, I assumed, since she had neither put on her coat nor taken her packages.

The urge to follow and accost her was overwhelming. I could station myself in the stairwell, I thought, and as she came by—what? What would I do? I had visions of strangling her—with what? My tie? Had I come to that? Could cudgel her . . . with a phone . . . ?

The phone.

I picked up the handle and dialed the number she had left in her messages for Gurevitch: five, five, two, fifteen, nineteen. At last the nine circled back to its position, at last the connection was made, finally the ringer came alive on the other side of the door. How loud it seemed, shrilling in the empty room in the dead night: five rings, six rings, seven, eight. Finally Dora Schussler's footsteps sounded in the corridor—nine rings, ten—she ran now to catch the phone, tore into her office, picked up the receiver:

Yes, I know the hour, Helmut, she said breathlessly. I am finishing and will be on my way home now.

(So she still called him Helmut!)

I told you not to worry, she went on.

She paused.

I told you I—

She said nothing for several seconds.

Helmut? she said finally. Then: Who is this?

I only breathed into the phone, loudly, to be sure she knew that someone was there, someone who was not Helmut.

She inhaled as if to speak, then let go the breath. *Attend*, she murmured in French.

She put down the handle and slowly moved toward our common door.

I put my finger on the hook. I stopped breathing. It had been too loud, my breathing—too loud!

She stood inches from me—I could almost taste the tobacco on her breath. My God, how long could I stand there without breathing?

Suddenly her phone began cawing: the quick, loud shout of a line off the hook.

Sheiss, she whispered, turning away from the door and returning to her desk. Pervert, she spat, as she dropped the phone back into its cradle.

44.

What delight it gave me to taunt her! Yet how I feared that my behavior would expose me. I had to endure Dr. Schussler, I told myself; she was my only conduit to the patient; whatever her errors, whatever her deficiencies, I needed her as badly as did the patient. For the doctor had said the patient would feel "cast out." And I . . . I could not contemplate what should happen to me should I lose my dear patient and all her sorrowing goodness.

I went to the office daily during Christmas week and did not encounter Dr. Schussler, which was fortunate, for I was not certain of my self-control, of what I might do should I encounter her alone, without her patients, without *my* patient. I might . . . no! Her absence was a relief; although it was with many bitter thoughts that I imagined Dora and Helmut holidaying in some Teutonic cottage in the Austrian Alps, reverting to their Germanic type amidst the sort of people who could very well forget the Obersturmbannführer who oversaw the murder of the Jews of France. My own family—what was left of it after the suicides— would have enjoyed Dr. Schussler's company, a cultured woman with whom they could share their greasy prejudices, their ugly words dripping from their tongues like saliva from rabid dogs.

Christmas Day itself was much like Thanksgiving: the city deserted but for the lolling alcoholics and desperate Vietnam War veterans. The sale-shopping frenzies followed; then the madness of New Year's Eve. Office workers had opened their windows to toss the pages of their desk calendars into the street, a practice I had never seen anywhere else. I walked ankle-deep through a snowfall of past appointments, random phone numbers, part numbers, names, addresses, check numbers, dollar amounts, cryptic notations. I picked one up: Give Gary the name, it said. Another: Tell Suzy no. I wondered over this Suzy—for what was she being refused? And what madness made San Franciscans dump the details of their daily lives with such abandon, such delight?

Finally came the dead day of the New Year itself, the whole world shut and sleeping—a Wednesday, but without the patient. I dared not even turn on my torn radio with its drifting tuner for fear of the dark reports that might issue therefrom; and of the static, the curtain of electronic noise that resembled too closely the whir of the hated sound machine.

I went to the office early on the following Wednesday, January 8th, hoping beyond hope that Dr. Schussler's Christmas hiatus was for but two weeks, not the three that my own nefarious practitioners had always taken, leaving me adrift at the worst time of year. (And why do they do that? What other profession absents itself exactly at the moment its services will be most needed, when patients are confronted with the absurdly neurotic idea that family holidays should make them happy? Would a medical doctor go on leave after a plane crash?) Only silence reigned in the adjoining office, and I passed the week scouring the halls, peering into offices where real people seemed to be going about the actual acts of living.

I cannot describe the feverish excitement with which I prepared to go to the office on Wednesday, January 15th. I bathed elaborately; shaved, even my chest, determined that my presence in Room 807 should be so slight as to leave not a scintilla of odor-inducing molecules upon the air. I sat still, so still as to be nearly incorporeal. I had survived her absence without deathly consequence. Any moment she would return and release me.

And finally it happened as always: elevator, ding, footfalls, slam of the door. (Oh, how I loved her slam now, the force of her very arms!)

And how was your vacation? asked Dr. Schussler.

Oh, my God, said the patient. I can barely describe it. It was . . . beyond belief. I can't thank you enough.

Ah! said the therapist. You finally swam in the sea.

That's not quite it, said the patient.

She paused. And lowered her voice. And said:

I had the best sex I've ever had in my life.

45.

The story the patient went on to tell was so direct, so . . . specific in its descriptions, that my male member grew—I should say "sprang"—at a rate unlike any other time in my experience.

She began with the word "breasts."

Breasts, she said. The whole evening started when I was at the bar on the hotel patio. Alone, except for a couple at the far end. And I thought, Breasts come out in hot weather.

Andie and Clarissa had long ago gone upstairs, she went on. They'd stayed with me as long as they could. But when they began tracing their fingertips up and down each other's arms, and a flush bloomed on Clarissa's chest, I told them: Go. I'll be fine.

Now I was alone at the bar but for the couple, the patient said. The woman was wearing a lime-green strapless, her bosoms pouring out of the top, and she was bending over in just the right way to show them off to her man—the way you'd offer a sippy cup to a baby.

I felt my own nipples tighten, I confess, the patient said. It was all I'd hoped for: breezy nights, silk dress against my almost naked body.

She giggled after she said this to her therapist.

I hope this is all right, she said.

(Of course! I thought.)

Of course, said the therapist.

Then, just as I was enjoying it, she went on, I saw the expression on the man's face—his jaw was just askew, his eyes slanting down, not listening as the woman talked—and Charlotte's ugly voice jumped into my head.

Leering jerk! Charlotte said.

I'm leering, too! I shot back at her in my mind. It was the old argument. The woman *wants* to show her breasts, I said. They're sexual organs. And men are *supposed* to want to see them.

Leering jerks!

I had to shut her out of my head, the patient told the doctor. She somehow wanted to take all the weirdness out of sex. She couldn't accept the part of it that was wild: where sex is animal.

The patient sighed.

Earlier in the evening, she continued, the bar had been filled to the edge of the pool. Men in expensive business suits, a few exquisitely dressed women. They were packed in so tightly that the circulating waiters were invisible, and the trays of champagne glasses seemed to float above the crowd on their own. Overnight markets, I heard. Inflation hedges. Interest-rate arbitrage. British accents, German, Spanish, French. Then I remembered the sign in the lobby: an international economics conference.

They were all around me, sweeping in all at once from some forum just ending. I was almost overcome by the scents of aftershave and powder in the tropical heat. Their hands were flying in the exchange of ideas. Their faces were flashing like lightning bugs. I can't tell you how jealous I was. I thought: These are the sort of people I belong with.

Then there was Charlotte's nasty voice again: *Pigs!*

And I asked myself: Were they pigs?

And then this probably ugly thought came to me: the new Jews.

I tried to stamp it out, but you can't take back a thought. And the idea finished itself in my mind despite my attempt to stop it: There was a time when only Jews did my sort of work—protected the treasures of kings and pashas and sheiks. When only Jews minded the fruits of taxes, allegiances, tributes, raids, robberies, wars, sieges, rapes, murders. And I suddenly saw myself in the long history of money: successor to the millennia of Hebrews who had handled filthy lucre to keep "clean" the consciences of pashas and popes.

The patient laughed.

So maybe it's right that I'm a Jew. Maybe I've been training to be a Jew my whole life.

It got late, she went on. The couple at the end of the bar left. The wind picked up. Dead palm fronds scraped the paving stones. I intended to drink, lose myself in a few martinis, like Mother. Why not? There is some glamour, some easing of life, that can come from sitting at a good bar with a well-made drink. The martini, for instance. The bartender made it just as I'd been trained to do: a little ice slick, clear and light, resting on the surface in a dead man's float.

But then the barman stretched and yawned. *Yawned.* And any hope of glamour vanished into the maw of that yawn. Now I could see there was only the empty patio, a man behind the bar wanting to go home, another man sweeping, a maid shining the leaves of a rubber plant. At the reception desk across the patio: a single person, a man, his head on his chin.

The patient settled her bill and walked down to the sea, first along a lighted path, then through a phony "jungle," then past a phony "lagoon," and finally came to the real sand.

The beach was empty; there was no moon. She removed her shift and stood still, wearing only her underpants. The breeze was colder than she'd expected. Goosebumps came up on her arms. Her nipples hardened. She took her breasts in her hands and softly kneaded them, for the warmth, she told herself. But then for the pleasure. Without moonlight, the sand was barely paler than the sea, which was at low tide, drained, unable to lift itself to lap at the shore. She walked out thirty paces before the water got to her knees. She wouldn't get to a good swimming depth until she'd walked a hundred yards out to sea.

Then she remembered what Dr. Schussler had told her. Be careful with yourself, the doctor had said. And she turned back.

The pool was lit with soft green underwater lights, the patient noticed as she walked back to her room. She wasn't ready to sleep, she realized as soon as she had closed the door behind her. She put on a bathing suit, then went back to the pool, where she found a low diving board. She performed a swan dive, then surfaced and tried to sprint in the too-warm water. But the pool's curving walls made any serious swimming impossible, and she was aware, anyhow, that her aggressive splashes echoed too loudly against the hotel facade in the quiet night.

She stretched out on the surface, trying to be as light and clear as the wisp of ice on her last martini, to be nothing, a slick held up by water.

When suddenly something skimmed the underside of her body, like a large fish—

She jumped upright.

Laughter came from the dark side of the pool. Then a woman's voice saying, I'm sorry. It is only that I cannot sleep.

The patient paddled toward the voice, which had spoken with a soft accent the patient couldn't identify. In the shadows was a woman holding the edge of the pool, the ends of her hair floating on the surface.

The woman turned her head. She had large eyes. Bold-stroke brows. A wide, dramatic, high-bridged nose. Full lips, like the wax lips children put on their mouths.

Then she turned her body. And there were her breasts. Bare.

Easy, the patient told herself. Europeans go nude all the time.

The woman made no effort to cover her breasts, only crossed her left arm beneath them, which had the effect of raising the nipples so that they played hide-and-seek, hide-and-seek, with the lapping surface of the pool.

My name is Dorotea, said the woman, who seemed to be in her mid-thirties. They exchanged pleasantries, how long they'd been here, how they liked it, where they were from.

Argentina, Dorotea said. Nice to meet you, she went on, laughing and extending her hand under the water.

The woman was so striking that the patient could not stop gazing at her. She seemed to have been painted by Picasso during his cubist phase, with all the planes of her face broken into sharp angles, each eye so powerful that it needed a separate space, four planes for her nose, six for each high cheekbone. But the mouth, the mouth: blooming dark red amid the hard angles. The patient finally took the offered hand. She said a bit more about herself. She tried not to look at the breasts Dorotea was cradling, not at the dark-pink aureoles as they tightened in the cool night air, not at the nipples, pebbled, erect.

Dorotea held on to her hand.

I saw you earlier, Dorotea said. I was with the group—

The economics conference?

Yes. And I saw you . . .

I was at the bar, said the patient.

Earlier, said Dorotea. With your friends. There was a long pause. She was still holding the patient's hand. Then she said: Your friends. They are . . . *together?*

Is this happening? thought the patient.

Yes, she said. Together.

Dorotea released the patient's hand, then slowly, and with some sense of demonstration, let go of her breasts. And you? she asked.

Now the patient allowed herself to look down at the full forms hiding like slick fish beneath the surface of the water, ready for the net.

I'm alone, the patient said.

Dorotea took a step closer.

They stood facing each other, saying nothing as water lapped at the rim of the pool.

Then a hand was tracing the patient's hip.

Okay? asked the woman.

The patient gasped.

Under the water, Dorotea's fingers were wandering to her waist, her belly. Slowly they circled the rim of the pelvic bone, down the thigh, across the gap between the legs, then back up again. The patient felt her clitoris grow, flourish, in the center of this circle, being the object of this circling, some kind of shrine the fingers had to walk around seven times, eight, nine, but could not enter. Finally one fingertip stopped on her pelvic bone, a spot just above the clitoris: the crown of the clitoris.

Oh! exclaimed the patient. She felt her clitoris must be inches high. If she got out of the water, everyone would see it, a finger poking out of her suit. She could barely focus on Dorotea's face, which showed something triumphant. What was the patient supposed to do? She had never done anything like this before. Something in her said, Don't do this. Be careful. Who is this woman? What are we doing here, outside, in public, in this pool? But then that fingertip slipped a little lower. And she had no more thoughts.

Meanwhile Dorotea's free hand went to the patient's breast, which was smashed under the spandex of the tank suit.

It comes off like this, the patient said to her new friend, undoing the clip at the back. When the water licked at her nipples, the patient's legs went weak, and she could do nothing for a moment. Then she roused herself and reached for the breasts that had lured her here. Her companion rewarded her touch with a long, low moan.

Dorotea's exquisite finger began massaging the skin below the crown bone, the skin that was connected to . . . everything. The patient fell against the wall of the pool.

Is this all right? she asked. I mean, what if someone sees?

What will they see? said Dorotea. As long as we don't kiss.

They let their nipples touch, part and touch under the water; nothing else, only the nipples.

I can't stand this anymore, said the patient. I'm going to faint.

Come to my room, Dorotea said.

46.

Oh, God! said the patient to her therapist. I'm sorry. Maybe this is too graphic?

(Not at all! I thought, to my disgrace.)

Of course not, dear, said the therapist. But I would only care to know—

(what happened next!)

—why you wish to tell me this. Why do you think it is important that I know you in this way?

The patient hummed; then was silent.

(In the quiet of this pause, I struggled to contain my excitement. The problem was not merely my tumescence, the possibility of a consequent need for repositioning, the sounds I might make. The problem was . . . oh, God . . . my shame. The person who had had the sexual encounter— please God, let me not demean her!—was my dear patient, whom I had come to love as a daughter.)

Said the patient at last: I think you will see what it means, if you let me go on.

Why, of course, said the doctor. It is not a question of "let." Please go on as you will.

(I prayed again to God: Help me, remember she is the patient, my beloved patient, not like the others, nothing like them at all!)

47.

Dorotea's room was enormous, said the patient. A living room. Kitchen. Dining table with four armchairs.

How did you rate this? I asked her.

She turned, put her hand on the nape of my neck. Darling, she said with a laugh. I was just promoted to managing director. It was a horrible crawl. So let us not discuss this now. Except to say I at least get a suite.

I'm also . . . I am a "quant," an econometrics analyst, I said.

So we are . . .

Together, I answered.

She laughed and touched my cheek. Instantly I knew I'd met a person of substance, said the patient. Her direct gaze. The forthrightness of her sex play in the pool—I knew it must have come from somewhere. Someone confident, substantial, accomplished.

And the obstacles you had to overcome, I said to her. As a woman.

The bedroom is here, said Dorotea.

There was an enormous bed. A patio, its door open, sheer curtains floating up like they were breathing.

Yes, said Dorotea, as she stroked my face. As a woman, she said.

We turned, gazed at each other, inches apart. I said to her: Kissing is very important to me.

Now why would I say that? the patient asked Dr. Schussler. In the middle of . . . Why would it matter to talk about kissing?

As you said, replied the doctor. She was someone of substance, you sensed. As are you. Two women of substance. About to have sex.

There was a pause. Yes, said the patient. Yes. I suppose you're right. I suppose that's why I said to her:

Kissing is very important to me.

She replied by exploring my cheeks with her her lips—God! what succulent lips!—all around my mouth.

Sshh, Dorotea whispered. No more talking.

Our kiss was soft, exploratory. We pulled back, delayed; then kissed again, this time much more . . . urgently.

I don't remember how this happened, said the patient, but at some point I tore off her robe, she tore down my bathing suit. Then we roamed our hands all over.

The patient looked again at Dorotea's breasts, then at the rise of her belly, the dark ruff that hid between the swelling bell of her thighs. Now she could feel it: the soft density of her skin, the curve of her hip, the womanly weight of her backside, a soft layer over a hard-muscled core.

Suddenly Dorotea fell to her knees. (*A posture of subservience!* yelled Charlotte in the patient's head. *Women should not do this!*) The patient's bathing suit was still around one ankle when Dorotea took her ass in both hands (*Shut up, Charlotte!*), pulled her hips toward her, then drove the patient's clitoris through those wax-red lips.

Oh, God! the patient moaned.

She had no choice but to yield to Dorotea's plans, to the hands at her ass that were driving her forward, to those lips over her inner lips, the tongue that circled and licked and flicked. Dorotea pulled the patient's hips forward, then pushed slightly back, forward and back, then around, and around again, so that the patient was performing a sort of belly dance, the performance all for the sake of Dorotea's mouth.

Then suddenly the dance stopped.

Dorotea let go of her. The patient was so aroused, confused. She looked down.

But Dorotea did nothing, only sat there, five seconds, ten. Then she reached forward and gently spread the outer lips: The clitoris was now naked, exposed. It seemed to have grown, in sensation, to enormous size. The slight breeze teasing the surface was almost more than the patient could bear. Her legs trembled. Then Dorotea slowly licked the inner lips, around and around, and finally, slowly, circled the clitoris again.

Oh, my God! said the patient. I can't stand it!

Dorotea took the clitoris back into her mouth, sucked it, flicked her tongue at it, fast, faster, a furious ululation: lo-lo-lo-lo-lo-lo-lo-lo . . .

The patient felt her insides contract. Tighter.

Tighter.

Until the muscles could hold no more.

And a wave of contractions moved through her; her entire pelvis: vibrating in time with Dorotea's tongue.

Lo-lo-lo-lo-lo . . .

Finally, she was too sensitive—on the verge of pain. The patient cried out: Stop! Oh, stop! Don't touch me anymore!

Dorotea stopped, but held on to her, both hands on her ass. And when the patient became still, Dorotea placed her tongue gently on the patient's clitoris. Oh! the patient called out, as another wave of contractions began. Then another pause, another gentle touch of the tongue—Oh, God! She was still coming—pause, touch, pause, touch, contractions slowing each time, down and down to a single last one: Dorotea licking all the orgasms out of her.

She tumbled onto the bed.

And now you, said the patient after a few moments, reaching out for Dorotea.

Are you mad? said her friend. Enjoy. Rest. Recover. There is plenty of time. All night. Why don't we shower, see what will happen then?

I nearly cried, the patient told Dr. Schussler. This was all I'd ever imagined in being with a woman. But all those years of obeying . . . what? Some proper way women were supposed to have sex. My turn, your turn. You haven't even enjoyed your orgasm for a minute when it's time to turn around and take care of her, pretend you're still hot, excited, when all you feel is a longing to . . . enjoy, rest, see what will happen later.

The patient paused. A sob escaped her.

This means so much to you, said Dr. Schussler gently.

Oh, God. Yes.

She paused.

I was beginning to think I was not really a lesbian, since I didn't really enjoy the sex. And now . . .

She sat quietly for some seconds then said:

We showered, played with the soap, emerged from the bathroom still half-wet and trembling. I made love to Dorotea as best I could, but I felt my lovemaking was crude compared to hers, inept, inexpert. The women I'd been with were like adolescents compared to her, still learning how to love. And here was this full-grown woman, free, open to receiving whatever I could give her. At that moment, I think I understood what a teenage boy must feel the first time he has sex with a real woman: a trembling, fumbling excitement.

We slept and then made love again, and again. Hands, mouths, positions, we tried all we could think of until we were exhausted. Finally we fell back on the bed, shouting: "No more! Don't touch me! I can't take any more!"

Hours later, Dorotea woke up, told me to sleep, she had to pack. She was leaving on a morning flight. She kissed me, left me her card, with a sexy note on the back.

You must have been disappointed, said the therapist.

By the note?

No, said the therapist. By her leaving.

There was a pause.

No, said the patient. I already knew she'd be leaving. Somewhere in the night we'd discussed it. We'd agreed we would see each other the next time Dorotea would be in San Francisco, which may or may not happen. I know how these things are. But the note . . . I was fine.

What was in the note? asked the therapist.

There was a pause.

Oh, said the patient. I don't think I can say.

She paused again.

(In the silence, I struggled to keep myself from imagining what else the patient and Dorotea could do with their mouths, their hands, what positions and actions could be more than the patient could say.)

All right, said the therapist. I do not want to embarrass you.

The patient laughed.

This may not make sense to you, she said, but after I read the note, I fell back and touched the sheets, with all the evidence of our lovemaking, and right then—then—I decided I had to find my birth mother. Don't you think that's strange? the patient asked Dr. Schussler.

There was a long pause.

(I wanted to shout: Yes. It is strange. Do not do it! Only grief will come of it! Dr. Schussler is not up to the job of guiding you!)

I do not think it is strange at all, the doctor finally said.

(Damn you!)

I think you had found something you always hoped would exist, said the therapist. The sort of sex you imagined, wanted, then found. And with a woman like yourself: accomplished, in business, feminine, with no boundaries to her sexuality and lovemaking. So I would think it is not strange that you would take the leap to another longed-for hope.

A real mother, said the patient.

No, said the therapist. Your adoptive mother is real enough. What I meant was, to belong somewhere, to feel you belong, to someone you want, who also wants you.

48.

She did not want you! I wanted to scream. Your birth mother did not want you! If she had wanted you, you would be with her today!

What was Dr. Schussler thinking? She was leading the patient to disaster! The doctor's family story had compromised her; she should have recused herself, no matter the temporary setback for the patient. In a few months, a new, better analyst would take the patient across this bridge; would guide her away from this dangerous search for "blood." Or, if the patient shunned therapy—a superior option!—she would find a new lover, someone like the stunning Dorotea, whose lovemaking would be so overwhelming, so physical and delightful, so "animal" (as she had put it), that the patient could not possibly see it as a metaphor for her perfect, lost mother. Given such sex, "mother" would be the last word that would come to mind!

But now . . . the die was cast, was set in stone . . . all the expressions of regretful permanence whispered themselves in my ear. In the weeks that followed, I was forced to listen as the patient imagined the path to her birth mother, wondered over its possibility, the method of finding her, who might have the records, and who, having the information, would indeed reveal it.

I trembled at her determination. But then, to my relief, I saw that the patient's research skills were undeveloped. This brilliant woman who could tease meaning from masses of financial data: utterly at sea in the face of archives. Oh, these poor latter-day graduates who have never read Greek or Latin; who look up dumbly if you mention a Latin root in English; who read the corrections in the margins of their papers but still cannot fathom the difference between transitive and intransitive verbs— never mind their total ignorance of the delicious subtleties awaiting them in the subjunctive mood! With such a poverty of language, how can they reap the riches of the library? One surely must pity these deprived Masters of Business Administration, sent out into the world without an understanding of card catalogues.

The patient's first effort was sorrowfully naïve: a call to the Catholic Archdiocese of Chicago. *Please could someone tell me who can answer*

my questions about adoptions of baptized Jewish children after the war?—
as if they would possibly reveal their nefarious plan, if indeed anyone there
even knew about the plot. Did she think someone would contact her to
say, Yes, dear, we have a list right here of the Jewish children stolen from
their parents? She called four times, on each occasion being directed
elsewhere. She wrote several letters. There were no replies but one: "I
am not certain where you heard about such events," said the letter
writer, one Father Joseph, "but they have no basis in fact."

This written denial led her to question the story her mother had told
her, which in turn led to several anguished sessions during which she
related painful phone conversations, her mother at first helpful, reiterat-
ing details she had previously relayed, adding only inconsequential elab-
orations: the color of her father's suit on the day her mother had uncovered
the file, an elaborate seal on the birth document with the letters *H.S.*
But then a cold curtain fell. "Mother" reverted to the woman who, confronted with the unpleasant topic of her daughter's homosexuality, had
slammed down her teacup to say, We will not discuss this! We will say
nothing more about the adoption. I have told you all I know. And I expect you will not put this matter before me again!

Oddly, the patient obeyed. She stopped calling her mother for information. Odder still, she complied with her mother's demand that "You
will not tell Father!" She wrote letters to every Catholic adoption agency
still extant in the Chicago area but did not call her mother and father to
learn more about her origins. It was as if she had severed her emotional
connection with her adoptive parents. My poor patient! She was cut adrift.
Her parents were no longer her parents; her girlfriend Charlotte was
gone (along with all her Holly Near posters, said the patient); she worked
ten hours a day, went home, slept a little, and repeated the schedule.
Weekends for a while were filled with compulsively scheduled dinners
and movies; then, as the patient wearied of her plan-making, she had little
but an empty apartment and lonely hours.

I maintained only one hope for the patient: that she would abandon
the idea of finding her "birth mother." How I wished she could see herself as made from whole cloth—as the self-created creature I'd hoped to
follow into my own release from ancestry. This she might have achieved
if that damned Dora Schussler were better at her job. But the therapist
did not have the skills to bring the patient across to the other shore. Her
patient was therefore caught in a downstream current, flowing relent-

lessly toward one goal—finding her "true" mother—and its corollary: the possibility of being loved by her. I believed this goal to be a disastrous one, as I have said; I thought it would merely bring the patient under the tyranny of another set of parental needs and desires—tie her through the horrible, placental prerogatives of blood.

The sessions wore themselves away. February rains battered us; March was moody, humid for San Francisco, seeping into our seams until life itself seemed bloated and gray.

Then a literal hood was drawn over us. The OPEC oil crisis had panicked the nation. Ostensibly to save fuel, President Ford had ordered that daylight savings time should begin two months early. And so we moved our clocks ahead while still in winter light. All of us on the N Judah at 7:30 in the morning found ourselves in the lingering dark, our bodies and senses telling us everything was wrong, the light was wrong, the very earth itself was out of kilter, the axis not yet tilting toward spring. We might try to convince ourselves that life was getting better—last year, under the now banished President Nixon, we were forced into daylight savings in January. But the wrongness of the sky prevailed over everyone's mood. To live under this pall of darkness made us all feel impoverished: beggars shivering in the black morning, paupers in the cold dark.

Meanwhile I listened to the patient's sessions in a growing state of terror—yes, terror overtook me. She was alone, vulnerable, unloved. She had licked clean the happiness of her one night with Dorotea (so to speak). And her path to her "birth mother" seemed hopelessly closed.

So of course they came, the crows, fluttering at our windows in the last of the rains; banging at the glass with the forces of the wind; rattling our tender doors—depression's ministers, sucking away the ancient cool core of the building. This time, however, they came not for me but for my dear patient.

She must abandon this fruitless search for her mother! I thought. There was no other way to drive out the creatures! But she did not, could not. She went on contacting this agency and that, to no avail. The pecked-out days went on, week after week. The Furies kept chattering through the voices of our trembling doors, through the rattling of our windows.

And finally I could bear no longer the patient's suffering. I could not stand this death-in-life. She was to be my icon, my champion. And the more mired she became in the muck into which Dr. Schussler had shucked her, the more determined I became to save her. She would not abandon her search; the doctor could not guide her. Now only I could help.

I could not let the monsters get her! I would not let them in! I was a professor; I had research skills. I reasoned that I could learn much more than could my dear patient, even given the sparse nature of our clues.

Therefore my project was launched. There was no choice, I thought; I could not just sit and listen. I had to abet the search for the birth mother.

My new hope was to find her dead.

TWO

49.

I began my search at the San Francisco Public Library, which was not as useful as I had hoped. Their literature of the postwar period was entirely focused upon the Marshall Plan: heroic tales of America saving Europe from chaos, financial backing, food aid, and so forth.

There was but a single volume about European displaced persons. It was not a scholarly work but a personal account by a Polish Jewish woman, one Anna Sobieskva. She had survived the Sachenhausen concentration camp, and after liberation she returned to the Polish village in which her family had lived for more than three hundred years. The town was named Kielce (pronounced *KYEL-chuh*, she helpfully advised the reader). Before the war, the town was home to a Jewish community of twenty-seven thousand people. Those who returned numbered two hundred.

They were not exactly welcomed by their former Polish neighbors, many of whom were living in the houses of dead Jews. All the same, these stragglers, whom the author called "the remnant," struggled to rebuild their community hall, in which they also lived until they could reconstruct their lives. Then, on July 4, 1946 (while we in America were preparing the rockets' red glare of our first postwar Fourth of July), thousands of the Polish villagers surrounded the Jewish community house. They were armed with knives, pitchforks, hunting rifles. Whipped up into an anti-Semitic frenzy, they invaded the hall and killed forty-two of their former neighbors. Fifty more were seriously wounded, meaning about half of the returning Jewish people were killed or maimed. Meanwhile, the police stood by and watched.

This was not the only pogrom against Jews returning to Poland, the author informed us. In the two years after the war, thousands of Jews were killed by their former neighbors.

The survivors of the Kielce pogrom—the "remnant of the remnant," the author now called them—tried to make their way to the Western democracies. But the policy agreed upon at the Yalta conference was that displaced persons should return to their countries of origin—a disaster for the Jews of Kielce, an impossibility for most Jews. Not until

1948 did the United States begin admitting refugees of any sort. The British limited emigration to Palestine to about two thousand. With nowhere to go, the former residents of Kielce fell under the protection of the Allied Forces: in displaced-persons camps, once again behind barbed wire.

What a story! Why had I never heard any such thing before? Like all Americans, I was shocked and horrified by what we learned after the concentration camps were liberated. (I myself had not served in the armed forces, having been rejected as "unfit for duty" due to my psychological history.) But once VE Day was declared, I confess I stopped noticing Europe, as if that matter were settled, especially since our country still faced the prospect of a bloody war in the Pacific.

I was now determined to learn more about the postwar experience of Jewish survivors—the patient's mother among them. Given my university credentials, I was able to obtain library privileges at San Francisco State University, the University of California at Berkeley, and Stanford University, a difficult but worthwhile commute an hour and a half south of San Francisco.

I soon learned that, by the time three years had passed after V-E day, a quarter of a million Jewish survivors found themselves in situations like that of the Kielce survivors: interned in displaced-persons camps in Germany.

I did not know how, amidst this mass of suffering humanity, I might find the patient's mother. It seemed that all of Europe was on the move, Poles returning to Poland, Sudeten Germans trying to go back to Germany, the French to France, Spaniards to Spain. Each type to his own; Slavs to Slavs, Greeks to Greeks. But the Jews: If not in Palestine, where did the Jews belong?

Now I understood that a whole new disaster had befallen them. Their former lives were gone. They were no longer Poles or Germans or Austrians; they were stateless. They were free neither to live in Europe nor to emigrate to the United States nor to join their fellow Zionists in Palestine. They were stuck in the mud of the camps.

The more I learned of this period, the more I despaired of conveying it to the patient. Even if I should find a method of getting my research to her—which seemed wholly unlikely—what effect could it have but to depress her spirits further? The information could only show the futility of finding her mother. Among the quarter million stranded in Germany: Where was Maria G?

Thus we came to April, to the end of the Easter break. The patient had not gone anywhere during the holiday, reasoning she was better off with the routine of work than some imagined (and disappointed) pleasure amongst millions of carousing college students. She had not heard from Dorotea; she was not in communication with Charlotte. Her good friends Andie and Clarissa had sustained her (to my relief, as week by week I learned of their steady support). The rains had gone on unusually late in the year; we lived under the unnatural extension of daylight savings time; the continued rains made the afternoons as dark as night. Our whole environment seemed unreal, a stage that had been set by a bored and irritable god.

It was the weekend following the spring break. The sands of Ocean Beach were suddenly littered with medical waste—used syringes, tubing, IV bags—that had washed up on shore from some mysterious source. I walked along, believing that some overwhelming disaster had befallen the Western world, that our way of life was on the verge of extinction. Oil crisis, unemployment, stagflation, a fruitless war in Vietnam slowly coming to an end. San Francisco seemed a dark and frightening place. Patty Hearst's kidnapping. White people all over the city had been murdered in the Zebra killings. The Zodiac serial killer was still at large.

When all at once, as my footfall squeezed fluid from an IV bag and I was overcome with disgust, a memory surfaced. It was the patient's adoptive mother speaking: Somewhere in the story she had told her daughter. The part about a form she had found in the locked desk. Information about the birth mother. Date of birth: May 17, 1921. Place of birth: Berlin. Last known residence: Celle.

Celle! I raced back to the cottage, to the wall where I had hung up a map of Europe, pins in every place where there had been a D.P. camp. Celle! The British called it Celle Camp or Hohne, but the internees insisted upon calling it by the name that had dishonored the place: Bergen-Belsen.

50

I had found the patient's mother! Amongst all the million refugees criss-crossing Europe, there she was: in the Bergen-Belsen displaced-persons camp. There could be no other explanation for her last known residence being Celle, for it was both a British name for the camp and the largest nearby town. I was certain: It was to Belsen she had come after surviving the war, and it was there that she had surrendered her child—my child, as I thought of her. My dear patient.

This alone should be enough to cheer her, I thought. Having an avenue of investigation would rejuvenate her spirits, reignite the intelligence that was her rope line, the faculty that always saved her from the depths. How like me she was, I thought: never properly loved, not trusting therefore, believing only in the picture of the world constructed by her analyzing mind.

My problem was how to communicate my finding. There being no mechanism immediately revealing itself to me, I decided to continue my investigations, reasoning (optimistically, against all my native impulses) that such a moment would appear. It seemed impossible to me that I might be in a position to help my dear patient yet not find a way to reach her. I believed I was her sole hope, as I have said, and, to my surprise, I found that being so needed was a tonic for the personality, drawing one away from contemplation of the abyss and into the daylight of necessity. Normal people know this, of course. They have begotten children and are, in turn, needed by them. And in like manner, I had adopted my child, my dear patient.

I therefore passed my days at the various libraries, first reviewing newspaper photographs, listening to recordings of BBC radio reports, and watching the films made by the British brigade who were first to come upon Bergen-Belsen and liberate the camp, on April 15, 1945.

All the horror I had felt when first learning of the camp came back to me. The forty thousand unburied corpses. The living scarcely more alive than the dead. The picture of a local German boy strolling pleasantly down a country road, bodies lining the margins like a hedgerow made in hell. A woman crouched among the dead, naked. The dead all around her. The dead children.

The dead, the dead, the dead. As the Nazis retreated from the Red Army, they tried to cover up their crimes. Any inmate still living was forced to move west: to walk, most dying along the way; to ride, shoved like cargo into boxcars. In the last week before Belsen was liberated, the Germans dumped thirty thousand human beings into the camp. Then, three days before the British reached Belsen, they abandoned them. The living corpses were left to their own devices: No water. Little food. The only thing available in great abundance was typhus.

The British soldiers were overwhelmed. Many to whom they gave food died of eating it, their wasted bodies unable to digest it. The typhus epidemic raged. The dying continued their short path to death. In the first week after "liberation," ten thousand more died. A BBC journalist reported what he had seen and ended his broadcast with "This is the worst day of my life."

And yet there was also the miraculous: Five days after liberation, a Friday, the Jewish Sabbath, a religious service was held in the open air, reported the BBC. For most of those attending, it was the first time in a decade that they had prayed in safety as a congregation of Jews. Knowing they were being recorded, the group of survivors, many still too weak to stand, gathered to sing the Hebrew song "Hatikvah."

I sat in a carrel; I put on headphones; I listened to the recording.

At first it seemed they would not be able to sing. There was a rumble, low voices in many keys, the words unformed, a confusion. Then one woman's strong voice emerged: *Kol od ba'le'vav*. How long had that voice waited to sing this song? How brave she was in her reach for the high notes! The others followed her, found the key, found unison, breaking now and then into aching harmonies. I found a translation of the words. *Od lo avdah tikvateinu*. Our hope is not yet lost.

I was in tears before the song ended. I sobbed in the library carrel as I had not cried since my boyhood, with a sorrow that seemed as clear and pure as the bravery in that voice. Now I looked anew at the films and photographs, for there was more to see than horror and death. There was life to come, and hope. Somewhere was the patient's mother. Some photograph might show her. Her face might appear in the British-army film, flashed by as the camera scanned the crowd. There she might be, very much alive, healthy, strong enough to bear a child. Our child. The patient.

There was one photograph I returned to again and again: a group of women in a rustic room, peeling potatoes. One woman, her hair covered by a scarf, is smiling at another. It was the sole image in which a camp inmate was smiling. In my mind, this was Maria G. This was the mother who had endured. If not she exactly, then someone like her. I decided I would send this picture to the patient, should find some way to deliver my findings, for through this woman's smile, the patient would be able to see beyond the horrors of the camp.

Two more weeks went by: two patient sessions during which her life force continued to ebb, the therapist unable to kindle in her a motive for living. Please God, let her not attempt suicide! What a torture it was for me to know that I had information that might help her—and no means to convey it. Why did Dr. Schussler not direct the patient to parse her adoptive mother's words more carefully? The answer was there, right there in front of her: Celle! But the doctor now had a more difficult task before her: keeping her patient alive. Both sessions ended with tremulous calls to Dr. Gurevitch.

Such was the situation as we came to April 16th. The session ended. Dr. Schussler left for her luncheon break, then I, too, left the office.

A piece of paper was lying on the floor in front of the elevator. It was a letter, I saw, as I drew closer. I glanced down casually, as anyone would. Then a name caught my eye: Charlotte. I knelt down. It was an envelope. Addressed to one Charlotte Cage. There was a penned slash through the address, and a hand-scrawled notice: Moved. Forward.

Charlotte.

Moved.

Forward.

This Charlotte had to be the patient's ex-girlfriend! She who had maneuvered the patient into ending their affair, this coward's mail still being delivered to the patient's house, an affront. Now goodbye, Charlotte. Slash! Moved! Forward!

I picked up the envelope, then stood staring at it. The very words on the envelope penned by my patient, her mighty slashes ripping the paper. In my hand: my dear patient's current and actual address.

51.

In my hand, I also held danger. The patient's address: a temptation beyond all others. There could I follow her; there could I wait for her; there could I watch through the windows and hunger at the doors. This had to be the perverse work of the crows. They had flown through the very air of the building; dropped at my feet this bit of paper: to tempt me, to mock at my attempts to stay away.

I let the letter fall from my hands. It fell face up, the address staring at me: 732 Alpine Terrace. I stepped over it, into the elevator that had finally arrived, hoping to leave that street and number behind. The cab lowered me down the shaft and finally disgorged me into the bright white of the lobby. The guard turned his handsome face upon me. He must have seen the turmoil in my eyes, in my body. I stumbled stupidly into the street.

732 Alpine Terrace—the address would not leave my mind. The N Judah rocked westward, the numbers and letters as if engraved on the opposite wall, as if written on every billboard and sign. I locked myself in my cottage. I ate delivered pizzas and Chinese food; I drank only water. I feared that, if I left the house, I would, against all my better wishes, find my way to 732 Alpine Terrace.

The weather was indistinct, hazy, neither warm nor cool. So fair and foul a day I have not seen, I thought, as I gazed from my window, feeling as toyed with as Macbeth had been: the Fates dropping their hints to test us, to see if we could resist the deeds that would lead us to damnation. In a kitchen drawer was a map of the city; somewhere on it was the location of Alpine Terrace. The work of the crows in my very house! I was afraid even as I reached for the folded paper. I burned it and watched, still in fear, until there was nothing left but ash.

Five days went by. I could not sleep, fearing my own dreams. Desolation came upon me as the hours ticked away. Then, on Monday, as the world was awakening around me, a plan announced itself in my mind.

How simple!

I would pretend to be one of the agencies the patient had contacted.

Any one of them would do; none had replied to her. Given all the time that had passed since her query, I reasoned that I could assume they never would reply. I merely had to choose a suitable agency name.

I hurried to the public library's reference room and took down the Chicago yellow pages. Between Adjusters and Adult Care came the heading Adoption Services. Approximately thirty agencies were listed; only four advertised themselves as Catholic. And then a name leapt out at me: Greater Chicago Catholic Adoption Services. The patient had written to them!

I knew at once the identity I was to assume: a helpful clerk at this agency on Madison Street in Chicago. It did not matter that I did not know the patient's name. I would simply address the envelope and letter using the formal and impersonal "enquiree," claiming some excuse of confidentiality.

I rushed to a stationery store to order a letterhead and envelopes large and small, using the correct address for the agency in case the patient had maintained a list of her attempted contacts. The man who took my order paid no mind to the Chicago location, indeed helped me to pick out a font and a logo from his stock set of symbols. I chose Palatino Linotype and the Virgin Mary cradling the infant Jesus.

I spent the night feverishly gathering the materials to send. I chose the image of the women peeling potatoes; another of children in the Bergen-Belsen nursery, one swaddled baby in the arms of a British nurse. Of course I would have to include a few pictures of the camp as the British found it, but I felt I could minimize the depressing effect by writing a cover letter emphasizing the hope that had grown out of such desolation. And of course I would send a cassette copy of the voices singing "Hatikvah"—this above all would comfort her.

The stationery was ready early the next morning, a Wednesday. Using a typewriter at the library (which had a room reserved for just this purpose), I composed the following:

Dear Enquiree:

I am in receipt of your query concerning the circumstances of your adoption. I hope you will excuse the impersonal address, "enquiree." It is used to ensure confidentiality among the office staff.

While we cannot at this time provide you the specific details of your own origins, from the information you provided us, we were able to discern the following:

Given your mother's last residence in Celle, Germany, and your statement that she was an inmate in a displaced-persons camp, we can state almost certainly that the camp in question was Bergen-Belsen, otherwise known as Hohne Camp, in the British Zone of Occupation. British soldiers came upon the Belsen concentration camp and liberated it, thereafter administering it as a displaced-persons camp.

I have enclosed a brief outline of the camp's history, photographs, and what I think you will find most moving: a cassette recording of inmates singing the Hebrew song "Hatikvah," which is introduced by a reporter for the British Broadcasting Corporation. While the images of the camp, as it was first found by the British soldiers, are disturbing, I would urge you to listen to the enclosed recording and to notice the hope in the voices of the survivors. One might indeed be your mother.

I will continue to research your situation and will send along any new information as I uncover it. As I shall be traveling extensively, it is best to wait for my correspondence, rather than sending mail to me, which may be lost amidst the piles of paper that will gather in my absence.

Sincerely yours,
Colin Masters
Archive Clerk,
Greater Chicago Catholic Adoption Services

I had spent a great deal of time deciding upon my name, in the end choosing one sounding formal and "English." I gave myself a lowly title; it did not seem likely that a higher-up would bother with such a matter. I placed the letter, photographs, and cassette in a large envelope (wrapping the cassette to cushion it); then I stood in a long line at the post office. How I feared I would not reach Room 807 in time for the patient's session! I worried over the postmark: Would she notice the letter had come from San Francisco? I fought to keep my worry at bay, reasoning that her excitement would overcome any impulse to scrutinize the postage.

Finally it was my turn at the counter. The postal clerk weighed the envelope; I paid; I saw the postage strip applied; I watched as Colin Masters's reply fell into a bin. And I felt I had achieved a great triumph. I had not given in to my demons. I had not followed the patient home. I was helping her to find her origins, which I hoped would soothe her.

I reached the office in time. But the patient's session was sorrowfully like the recent ones. How hard it was to hear her despair, knowing that my parcel was on its way but not yet in her hands. It would reach her next Monday or Tuesday, before her next session on April 30th. And now there was nothing for me but to wait—wait to see just what sort of deed I had done.

52.

The patient was early. The ten o'clock client still had eight minutes remaining in his session; then the therapist would take her ten-minute intersession break: eighteen minutes to wait, during which there was nowhere for the patient to be but in the hallway, marching up and down that long, dim corridor, under the watchful eyes of the marble sentries.

I thought I heard the crinkling of paper. Yes: Surely she carried the envelope I had sent her. In her very hands the paper I had held! Was hers a march of anxiety or excitement? Each time she retreated down the corridor, I feared it was the former, anxiety, and I rued sending the envelope so precipitously. But as the patient turned back toward me, I encouraged myself to believe that her early arrival, so unusual and un-characteristic, was a sign of happy anticipation.

Up and down she walked, my spirits rising and falling, when finally the door to Dr. Schussler's office opened. She bade goodbye to her ten o'clock, then, seeing the patient, said:

I will be just a few minutes. You can go in if you like.

The sound machine went silent. The doctor left. The door was open. The patient went in, took her seat. The envelope rustled in her hands.

For ten minutes we sat, the patient and I, each on our respective side of our common wall—this time with the door to the corridor open. I could hear each breath she took, each slight sniffle, each tiny crease of the parcel she held—my parcel! I had no choice but to sit absolutely still, for surely, should I even breathe deeply or shift a leg, she would hear me just as clearly as I was hearing her. It was a delicious intimacy: this side-by-side anticipation.

At last I heard the doctor's limping footfalls on the carpet. At last she crossed the threshold of her door, closed it shut behind her. And in that instant the patient said:

I got something!

Yes?

I got something back from one of the agencies, about my adoption! (It was a cry of happiness!)

Let me read this to you, she said to the therapist.

Then she read aloud the letter from "Colin Masters."

(My words in her mouth!)

The therapist gasped upon hearing the name "Bergen-Belsen." Then she sat immobile until the letter's end.

Isn't that wonderful? said the patient. I know where my mother was. I know where I came from. The Bergen-Belsen displaced-persons camp, in Celle, Germany. And maybe he'll send me more information. Here. Look at the pictures he sent.

I could hear the rest of the papers being withdrawn from the envelope, the sound of the doctor shuffling through them.

Finally Dr. Schussler said: Some of these pictures are quite shocking. Are you sure you are not dispirited by them?

No, said the patient. Not at all. I looked at the women preparing food, at the babies. One of them might be me! I can't explain my excitement. Here. I existed here. I don't come from some vague unknown gray space in the universe, but from this particular place, a place on a map. I can't explain it. I felt a kind of realness that I had never experienced before. *Physical* realness.

She paused.

And I wish I could play for you the cassette I received, she went on. It's a recording of the just-liberated inmates singing a Hebrew song. I have never heard anything so . . . heartbreaking in my life. If one of the voices was my mother's, I couldn't be prouder of her than if she'd been—I don't know who, the Queen of Sheba. Do you understand? I come from these extraordinary people, I realized I am . . . overwhelmed with . . . Oh, God. I can't express it.

The patient stuttered softly, as if she was considering, then discarding, words that might describe her state. Joy! I wanted to supply. Joy is what you are feeling!

The therapist said nothing for a full minute, which allowed her patient to experience the moment silently, a change of technique for the doctor, for in the past she would have pressed in by now with "Any words?" or "Do you feel this is related to . . . ?"

Then, being the horrid woman she was, she said:

Have you told your parents?

Huh? said the patient, awakening from her joyous dream.

Your mother and father, your adoptive parents. Have you told them about your news?

The patient bolted upright in her chair.

No! she said in a dark, ugly voice, one that seemed to come from a creature other than the young woman just finding her happiness. Why should I tell them? she went on, speaking as a dybbuk. Mother forbade me to discuss this matter further. "Forbade": her word.

Well, said the doctor, because they are the ones who raised you and think of you as their daughter. And I do not believe it is in your interest to keep shutting them out of your thoughts.

How dare the doctor do this! The patient immediately reverted to the depressed creature she had been. Her joy was banished; her newly found life was roped to the old one; her sense of being real suddenly made false again. It had to be the work of Dr. Schussler's guilt, I decided. All that angst over her Nazi father's misdeeds—the moment Dr. Schussler saw the pictures of Bergen-Belsen—up it rose.

It was more than I could bear. I shut my ears to the rest of the session!

53.

I was more determined than ever to get information about her mother to the patient. I could not leave her alone in the clutches of that Nazi daughter. The therapist's professionalism had crumbled at the very idea of Bergen-Belsen. I thanked God that the patient had not been adopted out of Drancy, the transit camp into which the doctor's Obersturmbannführer father had dumped the Jews of France. Who knows what ugly motives hide in the shade of guilt?

I continued my research and soon found information I believed would hearten the patient.

After liberation, the camp disappeared from the news. Then it reappeared in dramatic fashion: with coverage of the "Lüneburg trials," British military tribunals at which the guards and commandants of Bergen-Belsen faced justice. It was not the content of the trials I wished to communicate—the transcripts made for grim reading—but an event that happened concurrently: a meeting in Belsen of hundreds of Jews from the British zone.

The organizers did not ask for permission from the British; it would have been refused in any case. But a Jewish leadership had arisen spontaneously, in the earliest days after liberation. Taking advantage of the Lüneburg trials and the arrival of many foreigners, they organized the "First Congress," as they called it. By the time the meeting was over several days later, the Jewish internees had elected their own leadership, their own governing councils, their own committee members. At the head of this "government" was one Yossele Rosensaft.

I thought it remarkable that the survivors should outwit their British overseers and establish, so quickly, a self-governing community. It was this dynamism I hoped to convey to the patient. Perhaps she could see that this Bergen-Belsen, the D.P. camp, was no longer Bergen-Belsen, the concentration camp.

There was a newspaper photograph of Rosensaft. It shows a compact man in a dark suit whose body, in another life, might have been that of a gymnast. His hairline is receding; his brow wide and noble; his head and face distinctly triangular in shape; his eyes intense. The reports describe him as a charismatic, a "man of the people." I thought the patient would be proud to know the stock from which she came—rebels, organizers, fighters.

I quickly assembled this information, including copies of news reports and photographs, and mailed it to the patient the day after her session. But the postal clerk could not promise delivery by the following Wednesday morning. It might not arrive before her next session!

I therefore passed a fitful week. Temptation lured me into thinking that it might be best, in the future, to deliver the parcels directly to her door, even to risk her noticing the complete lack of a postal cancellation. There would be no time lag, whispered my demons. You could reach her before she gets back to that Nazi-daughter doctor. You will arm her with hope! they declaimed in my mind.

But I was stronger than they were; the patient was my shield; the demons did not ensorcell me. I put my energies to better use, continuing to assemble information about Belsen, also contacting the agencies that had provided aid to the camp. I wrote to them as a professor doing research for a biography. Did they have any records pertaining to a Belsen internee whose name was given only as Maria G.? I told them all I knew of her—her birth date, the birth date of a child born to her in the camp, the date she surrendered the child for adoption, anything I could recall from the adoptive mother's story—and begged them to provide any further details their files might reveal.

Still, as busy as I was, the demons kept up their whispering. What will you do, they chided, if Wednesday comes and the patient still has not received your envelope? Will you finally heed us and go to her?

54.

I got another parcel! the patient said gleefully.

(Thank God! I thought.)

She had barely sat down when out came the envelope.

It's fascinating, she said. What happened there. Amazing!

(I nearly cried aloud with relief.)

The patient withdrew the photographs and passed them to the therapist, all the while relaying (quite accurately) the information I had sent her, going on to extol the achievements of the Belsen internees, their endurance, their determination, their bravery.

The therapist—for once—kept her own counsel. Aside from a few polite invitations for her client to continue—Yes? Really! How interesting!—she said nothing, allowing the patient to talk without interruption for nearly the entire session. The result fulfilled all my hopes: the patient now heartened, able to see beyond the darkness of the Holocaust into the time that followed, the time and place from which she came, about which she could feel pride. And since the information was new to the doctor as well (I presumed), there was nothing she could say to mediate the patient's newfound happiness. Perhaps it even lightened her own sense of guilt: to know that the remnants of Europe's Jews were not an entirely defeated people, that her father's work had not achieved its exterminating goal.

Finally the patient ended her soliloquy, sitting quietly for several minutes, breathing deeply. Until she said:

I had no idea they—we—had such heroism. It's not something you normally associate with Jews, is it?

The therapist started in her chair, shaken from what seemed her imposed detachment.

Are you referring to me, personally? she asked. Something *I* do not associate with Jews?

No, said the patient, with a laugh. You. One. It's not something one associates with Jews, is it?

The therapist paused before answering.

There is the stereotype, she said. Such as those we have talked about. The stereotype of the weak Jew, yes.

Lambs to the slaughter, said the patient. Isn't that what everyone believes, that the Jews went to the Holocaust like lambs to the slaughter?

The therapist gasped. Then coughed.

Excuse me, she said. No, they did not go to the slaughter, she said in a hard voice. They were taken by force.

Of course, the patient said. What was I thinking?

Patient and doctor sat without speaking for a full minute, the tension between them palpable through the door. This therapist has to reveal her bias! I thought. She must not leave the patient with this sense of being unfeeling and uninformed. Just when the patient was making progress in her self-identification as a Jew—how dare Dr. Schussler presume to lecture the patient about the sufferings of the Jewish people!

But the damage was not complete, thank God. The material I had sent the patient prevailed. I heard the rustling of paper, then the patient saying:

Don't you think I look like him?

The therapist hummed. Let me see again, she said.

Look at the shape of his head, said the patient. Triangular. Like mine. The same narrow chin. Also the brow: very broad, like mine. And the eyes: deep set.

(Yossele Rosensaft!)

Of course he's darker than I am, the patient went on. But I keep coming back to that distinctive head. It's rare. So much like mine. It's what always made me feel like an alien in my family—nobody but me has this weird triangular head. You can't imagine how hard it is not to look like anyone. And then I saw this picture and . . . don't laugh.

She paused.

It came to me that he could be my father.

When the therapist said nothing immediately, the patient jumped in to say:

Or some relative of his. I mean he may not exactly be my father, but . . . It seemed to me I was part of this family.

(I was filled with joy. How much better that the session was over and the therapist could do nothing to ruin the moment.)

Ah, but look at the hour, said the doctor. We will have to discuss this next time.

55.

All of this was happening too quickly, I thought when I returned home. I was delighted at the patient's reaction to Rosensaft. Yet her sudden identification with him—the need to see him as her father, instantly, with the evidence of just one photograph—communicated to me the urgency with which I had to find Maria G. The patient had to know her relatives, have hard information about them, what had happened to them, and soon, or else begin to drift into fantasy; thence, I feared, back into depression.

She had said to Dr. Schussler: You can't imagine how hard it is not to look like anyone.

And I thought of my dear boyhood friend Paul, whose singularity had been a release from oppressive parents—or so I had always supposed. Now, in light of the patient's words, I relived that distant summer afternoon with Paul's clippings from his boot boxes. I now considered what anguished energy had driven him to create that collection of aging family faces, in secret, over the course of years: what hard work had gone into convincing himself that looking like one's kind was not a comfort but a nightmare.

My motives fell into confusion. I had posited Paul as an icon for the patient, and for myself, an image of the self-created individual, freed from the ownership implied in the inheritance of one's parents' genes: You are not of them; they do not own you; you owe them only the normal gratitude for having been raised up and fed by them; you may become what you need to be.

Yet now I wondered: Was I doing the right thing in aiding the patient's search for her mother? I thought of her twenty-ninth birthday. Celebrated in Puerta Vallarta. Quietly? Privately? Not telling the sexy Dorotea? The patient did not say. On the day of her birthday, December 26th, I had sat alone in my office, pondering her experience of that singular day: the first in which the "birth" portion had acquired flesh.

Now she knew she had come out of the body of a particular woman, a Maria G., in a physical act, at a specific time, in a specific place. Did this fact overwhelm all the prior birthdays? Did the old birthdays

182

suddenly seem to be vaguely superfluous affairs, parties with cakes yielding over the years to dinners with wine, all the while detached from their origins, the physical facts, from the blood and guts of *birth*?

At none of her prior birthday parties could her mother—the woman she called Mother—at no time could this woman embarrass the patient with tales of her hard labor, the hours of pushing and breathing, the pain of the child actually coming out of her loins, the months following wherein she knew she would never again have that taut belly, those pert breasts. Therefore she had no guilt to lay upon her adopted child, who did not owe anything to this woman for a body robbed of youth.

But now there was a body, a mother to whom a physical debt was due. And not just any mother, but a Jewish one. The patient was thereby lashed not only to Maria G. but, through her, to an entire tribe, thousands of years of history, familial relationships going back in time—if one believes it—all the way to Avram, who took the name Abraham as he accepted the One God.

Was it wrong of me to abet the patient's search, to "flesh out"— literally—the reality of Maria G.? It had all happened stepwise, I told myself. The adoptive mother was cold and rejecting. The patient was alone. The therapist could not divert her client from a quest for origins. The patient had fallen victim to the dark, circling birds of depression. And I had to help her; I was the only one who could help her. And now that I had stepped upon the path of information-giver, whetting her appetite, it was more urgent than ever that she receive an answer to the question she had posed above all others: Where did I come from?

I spent the night feverishly assembling another packet. I had to send something—anything, to extemporize until I had the hard information I needed. Fortunately I had already gathered information related to the orphaned children at Belsen. The patient herself was not an orphan. As far as we knew, her mother was very much alive when she had been surrendered. Yet I thought the patient would feel closer to her origins if she saw the photographs of the children at Belsen, and their caregiver, the camp doctor, Hadassah Bimko.

In the summer of 1945, Jewish institutions in Britain tried to move some of Belsen's children to England, in a humane gesture. Yet Bimko and the rest of the camp leadership ferociously fought this plan. They wanted their children to go to Eretz Yisrael or else stay with their own people in the camp. And they achieved their goal of emigration. In April

1946, about a year after the camp's liberation, the British issued special certificates for children, and Hadassah Bimko led a hundred of Belsen's orphans to Palestine.

I thought the patient would be cheered by this story and moved by the example of Hadassah Bimko (the only woman in the camp's leadership, as far as I could tell). The next morning, Thursday, as soon as the stores opened, I rushed to make xeroxes of the photographs at a copy shop, and then was first in line at the post office with my envelope. I had enclosed a note saying, "From the information you have given us, we do not believe you were orphaned in the Bergen-Belsen displaced-persons camp. However, we thought you might wish to see what happened to other youngsters who, like yourself, had spent their early days in the camp."

That would hold the patient for a week, I hoped. Then what relief I felt when she did not begin the next session with questions about her mother. Instead there came a panicked cry about her work.

It's pandemonium! she said. You'd think the world had come to an end. May Day, May Day! everyone keeps shouting, because the change took place on May 1st, and we feel like we're going down.

Evidently there had been some change in rules surrounding brokerage trades. If I understood the patient correctly (something that required great concentration on my part, as I had never traded stocks and bonds in all of my life, an inexperience shared with most of the United States population), commissions on securities sales had been a fixed percentage, no matter how large or small the trade. Now, however, the percentages could vary and could be negotiated. I did not see how this mattered so very much, but to the patient and her colleagues the change was "momentous" and "deal-changing" and "a jolt to the industry."

We will need to recalculate everything, she exclaimed.

But the therapist—damn her!—did not allow the patient to continue talking about this "momentous" change in her client's working life. All too soon, Dr. Schussler posed the how-are-you-really question. And the patient replied: I got another packet in the mail. About a woman in the camp. Bimko, Hadassah Bimko, a doctor. Of course I wondered, despite myself, if she knew my mother. And if I should try to find this Bimko.

How would you go about it? asked Dr. Schussler.

I'll write to that nice Colin Masters, she said, to see if he knows anything about where Bimko is.

No! I thought. She could not write to the agency—of course there was no Colin Masters there.

I could no longer wait for replies from the agencies I had contacted; I had to make progress, and quickly. I began making phone calls: to each agency, to different departments in each agency, to different people in the different departments—I would make a pest of myself, I decided, until I found someone with information about the mysterious Maria G.

The days went by. I did not go to the office; I stayed home in my bare, mean cottage with my telephone. My calls became more urgent. Another week passed. I put together some random information for the patient— pictures of the camp schools, youngsters doing calisthenics—any photograph showing a child in Belsen, buying myself further time. My efforts were successful; the patient spoke favorably of the parcels. Yet concurrently with her growing knowledge of the camp there grew in her a surging desire to know the true facts of her origins. She became impatient with the therapist; she was annoyed by her work; she was restless and anxious. She began to question the motives of "that Colin Masters." Why was he being so helpful? she wondered. What role had he played in my abduction? I was afraid for her, for myself; I kept up my calls.

Then, after two weeks of telephoning and being transferred from extension to extension, I reached a Mr. Linder in the New York offices of the Jewish Agency. It was nine in the morning New York time, and I found him at his desk. I told him I was working on a biography of a woman who had lived for a time in the Bergen-Belsen displaced-persons camp. I knew but a fragment of her name: Maria G. I explained I wished to chronicle her experiences after her release.

Great! he said. Terrific. You professors haven't done much about what happened to Jews after the war. So what you need to do is send a request letter on university stationery. I think to a Mrs. Knobloch in Tel Aviv. Wait. It's just about four p.m. in Israel, and she might still be in. It's no problem to call her—we make calls to Israel at the drop of a hat; we have everyone's number. If she's there—or an assistant or a secretary—I'll found out if she's the right contact. And I'll get her address.

A request on university stationery.

I panicked while I waited three long minutes until Mr. Linder came back on the line. Did I have any university stationery with me? Yes, I told myself, yes, I would find it, somewhere in my dreadful cottage, I would find it. But if the stationery is not there! Make a fake letterhead, I told

myself. Like the one for the Chicago agency. A print shop: a fake. Better
yet, I would say that I had already delivered my formal letter of request—to whom? Whom else had I called? The Immigrant Hebrew Aid
Society. Why not? Yes, I'll say that.

Thus somewhat becalmed by the last resort of deception, I did not
fear Mr. Linder's return to my call.

I talked to Mrs. Knobloch, he said. A meeting ran overtime, so
she was there. She's the right one. I told her what you wanted. And she
laughed. Said we should go ahead right away. Said someone must've
made sure of you, or no one would've transferred you all around to get
me. I mean me, who you're talking to.

Of course her surmise was wrong. But there was no need to say that.

Mr. Linder said, Hold on. I'll transfer you.

In no time at all, a woman's cheerful voice with a Hebrew accent
came on the line. Hello, Professor! she sang out. Please to wait a little.
Some papers I must sign now. Please to hold.

56.

The line was strangely quiet—no music, no static—so that I feared the connection had been broken, and I would have to call again and again and never find my way back to her extension. I was alone on the line for perhaps a half minute, but a half minute during which my heart pulsed fifty times—more, for I started counting to distract myself.

Are you there? she asked, finally coming back on the line.

I had not yet composed myself. But I managed to say, Yes, yes. I am here.

What good fortune to find me today, Professor. The Belsen roll of internees. I was looking at it two hours ago. The file is on my desk still. So. Mr. Linder told me you were looking for a Maria G.

She turned pages. She hummed; said something in Hebrew; hummed some more.

I waited. The pages turned.

I have to say I am sorry, Professor, she said finally. Your good fortune was for the timing only. Not good for the result. In the list, I see no one named Maria G.

She smacked her lips. Was she eating? Eating while she destroyed me!

You see, said Mrs. Knobloch, to the sound of paper crinkling—wiping her sloppy lips? Belsen was not completely Jewish until some months after the British soldiers came upon it by chance. Notice, I do not say "liberated" because . . . I shall stop. Another story for another time, Professor.

You should know, she went on, that many Polish people were in Belsen at the beginning. Mainly Catholics. They were German political prisoners, suspect collaborators, women kept for pleasure—who knows why? So your Maria G.—Maria, a Catholic name—she must be one of them. Polish Catholics, I mean. And you may assume that she went back to Poland. Why not? That was not the graveyard of her people.

She said nothing for several seconds. And I thought: Do not stop there, you heartless woman! Then I was ashamed of the thought. *The graveyard of her people.*

Is there nothing more? I asked.

Ach! Such impatience! The search through records by now thirty years old, and the tumult of that time—this is not so simple. Maybe British records can help you. They were in charge of the camp. Maybe they cared enough to keep such records. Our concern, you must understand, was taking care of the Jewish people imprisoned there and seeing them safely to Eretz Yisrael.

Hold on, please, she said, then clicked me off into another ether of silence. I am not sure how I endured that moment—and it was but a moment—during which I felt despair enwrap me.

Then she returned, apologizing, going on to say:

Do not believe I am lazy, Professor. We are alike, yes? People who search to find truth. Is not that who you are?

Yes! I answered. How good of you to say so. Yes. We are kin.

She laughed. Are you Jewish? she said.

Ah. No.

Then I am afraid we are not kin. We are people with abilities and values we hold in common. That is not a little thing, ah?

Certainly. Thank you. An important thing.

Now, she said, sighing, I went down the list through all the Ms, with last names starting with G. I found two more women with the initials M.G. This is not much, I think you would agree as a researcher. But we must wait until Sunday to continue.

I do not understand, I said. Why must we wait?

She laughed. Professor, you have reached the Jewish State. It is Friday. *Shabbat.* I am not very practicing, but I should have left hours ago—we are officially closed since two.

My mind screamed: Sunday! Two unendurable days until I find M.G.

Yet I steadied myself to say: Is it possible for you to call me in the morning? As early as is possible?

It will have to be a collect call, she said.

Of course, I said (however alarmed I was at my growing debt to the Bell System).

So do not fear, Professor. I will call you. But please to remember, our Sunday morning will be your middle of Saturday night.

This is perfectly all right, I said. At my age, it is difficult to find sleep in any case.

Ach! she said. This I understand!

57.

How the Fates were making sport of me!

I do not know what transpired in what remained of Friday's daylight. I have no memory of it. Perhaps I lapsed into a sealed darkness, as I had but five times before, and many years ago.

I emerged into memory as dusk fell from the sky. Thick flocks of gulls circled the shore and set upon the seawall. Their black outlines filled me with dread; such that I began to wonder if I should avoid Mrs. Knobloch's call altogether, for she might reveal yet another damning episode in the patient's early life. In which case I will have failed the patient, and the crows will have had their victory over me.

I slept fitfully, and come Saturday morning I knew that my only hope was the office. I found the elevators under repair, compelling me to climb sixteen flights of stairs, two flights per floor. By the time I reached eight, I was fighting for breath. I stared, dizzy, down the long, empty hallways. I touched the cold marble walls to steady myself. I walked up and down, saw no one, heard no one, and could not face the confinement of my office. As I went by the mail chute, a letter came fluttering down. There was no story above eight! Where had the letter come from! I raced down the corridor and locked myself in Room 807.

Saturday evening came. I went home, where I was surrounded by whisperings. The radio's static-dashed reports of war in Cambodia. Far-away calls of gulls, now conflated with my crows. Hisses and cries; and, outside, the crash of the surf.

I must have dozed off, for I was awakened by the jangle of the telephone.

58

This is the Bell System long-distance operator, said a nasal voice. Will you accept a collect call from Israel from Mrs. Orna Knobloch?

Orna, I thought.

Yes, yes, I hurried to say.

After several seconds of static, the connection cleared, and I heard the bright voice of Mrs. Knobloch. Orna.

You did wish me to call first thing in the morning, yes? she said, no doubt hearing the sleep in my voice.

Yes, yes. Just a short nap.

Ah, a little sleep is better than none, yes?

She drew in a breath and quickly said: We will begin where we left off for the *Shabbat*. The other women with initials M.G.

The first is Miriam Gerstner. As you are not Jewish, Professor, you may not realize that Miriam is a very common name for a Jewish woman. Very common, like Ruth and Sarah and Naomi. And the last name. Gerstner: a name that may come from anywhere in the Western European Diaspora.

Nevertheless, you may believe—

I believe there is not much for you here. All I can learn of this Miriam Gerstner is that she was in Belsen. And the date she left. After that, there is nothing more of her. It is, how do you say in American? A dead end.

I can add only one thing, she went on. Since Miriam Gerstner left Belsen before the founding of the Jewish State, she could have gone only on an Aliyah Bet ship.

Aliyah Bet? I asked.

Vessels making illegal runs to Israel.

Pardon, Mrs. Knobloch. Perhaps you mean Palestine. At the time, it was Palestine.

Excuse me, Professor. I do not intend rudeness. Always for us it was Eretz Yisrael. Which soon came true in 1948.

Of course. My apologies. Eretz Yisrael.

A *humph* came from Mrs. Knobloch's end of the line. Then she quickly said, Apology accepted.

And the conversation moved on.

All right, so let us say that Miriam Gerstner is on an Aliyah ship. But all the ships were intercepted by the British, and everyone on them was sent to transit camps. However, there is no record of our Gerstner being in any transit camp.

Oh, she said with a laugh. One ship was sent back to Germany. The famous movie ship *Exodus*. But that happened later, '47, after Gerstner left Belsen.

The date she left.

You said you know the date of her departure.

Let me see. Yes. She left on 18 May, 1946.

One day after she surrendered the patient. Yes. This must be the mother. I have found her, I have found her!

Wonderful! Mrs. Knobloch. Wonderful! Exactly the woman I am seeking. After so much research, yours and mine, Mrs. Knobloch, together we have found her.

As you wish, Professor. But what you have here is the date Gerstner leaves Belsen. Then she vanishes. Is enough for you?

Yes, I believe—

Before you believe anything, let me tell you of another M.G.

Excuse me, she said after a pause. Please do not mind. My travel today was delayed and I must be taking the breakfast at my desk.

Not again! I thought. Chomping and chewing and rustling paper as she tortures me!

Now . . . Here is the next M.G. She is a woman with the Israeli name Michal Gershon.

She pronounced it *mee-CHAL ger-SHUN*, with a gutteral *CH*.

She swallowed.

As with Gerstner, she left Belsen on 18 May, 1946.

Again. The day after the surrender!

But I am sorry, Professor. She also disappears from our files. No records from transit camps, no arrival information, no housing assignments, no work assignments, nothing. She has an Israeli name, I am thinking, but I cannot find her anywhere in Israel. So, I think, another dead end.

But Professor! she went on. You will see I did not give up your cause. I am as determined as you seem to be. I am bloodhound. I am Sherlock Knobloch of Tel Aviv!

Oh, please tell me you found her, Mrs. Sherlock Knobloch.

I am next thinking, Many were injured in the War of Independence. Maybe that is why we do not have all the usual information. So I am going next to health and hospital records. And there she is! Our Michal Gershon.

Oh, Mrs. Knobloch. You are my savior!

Of course, Professor, I cannot tell you what is in those records. Even I cannot see them. But what we have is her name on a file, also a date of admission and release. I cannot give you the actual dates, but I will say they are both in 1948. So maybe she was injured in the war. Or simply suffering from some other newcomer ailment—who knows?

Is there nothing more? I asked, almost begging. No continuing contact? Perhaps a follow-up with a doctor? Where she went after she left the hospital?

Professor, please to be happy to know she left the hospital and so in 1948 is not dead!

Dead. I had never considered it. Thirty years from the patient's birth date: her mother might be dead.

Where shall we go from here, Mrs. Knobloch?

She sighed. From here I do not know. Let me think a moment.

Another bite. The rustle of a napkin to wipe her mouth. Get to it, woman!

All right. Sherlock Knobloch will not give up. Perhaps the next step is the Jewish Agency. Let us say our Michal Gershon received absorption assistance from the Agency—absorption, to help new immigrants get settled. If so, the Agency should know where she was at that time. But, Professor, as a researcher, you know that "let us say" indicates we are starting with a supposition. Finding her address in this manner is— how do you put it—something long . . .

A long shot.

That is it, a long shot. In any case, I am now thinking you should contact the Agency. Or we will do it for you. Yes, better we do it. To us they will answer much sooner.

I told myself: I will succeed! Despite the supposition, despite the long shot, I would find the mother of my dear patient. There had to be a clue somewhere in all that I had learned.

Thank you so very much, Mrs. Knobloch. You have given me a wealth of information with which to continue my research. I believe that one of these women—Miriam or Michal—is the she whom I have been seeking.

Are you sure, Professor, because—

Yes, I interrupted her. I believe I have found her. With your help, I hurried to add.

So, said Mrs. Knobloch. Let me with you review. You came to me looking for a Maria G. As we discussed, Maria is a Catholic name. Then: no later record of her. Probably back in Poland.

Then you think maybe it is Miriam Gerstner. Common name, as common as the name Maria for a gentile. Her last name from Europe anywhere. Gerstner leaves Belsen on 18 May, 1946. Then disappears.

Then we come to Michal Gershon. All we know is the date she left Belsen. And some hospital records.

Finally, what do we have? The initials of the three women are the same. Two dates are the same, the Belsen departures. Then nothing at all for one woman. And for the other only a hospital file. Excuse me, for a researcher that is not very much certainty for you.

No! I thought. How can she sit there—drinking something again!— and deny all the work I have done. No. I refuse to be disrespected. Somewhere in there is my elusive Maria G.

Nonetheless, I said, I think there is enough for me to continue my search.

Mrs. Knobloch sighed heavily.

All right. I will send you copies of the files in question. You maybe can see details I cannot. Do not worry if a few weeks pass—all the papers to be put together and copied. Meanwhile, we will try for Gershon's last known address. It will be in the packet, if we find it.

Mrs. Knobloch, I said to her, I very much appreciate the scrupulousness of your reply. But I do believe—

You want to believe?

Yes. I do believe I am very close to finding the woman I am seeking.

She laughed. Who am I to tell you what to believe?

59

Stung by Mrs. Knobloch's sarcasm, I returned to the libraries, as I am always pleased to do, there to find several authoritative histories of German Jews during the Holocaust. I learned there was an order (if one may use the word "order" in this context), a sequence the Nazis followed in their attempt to eradicate European Jewry.

Jews outside of Germany were taken as those nations were conquered. But the murder of the German Jews was done in stages, a "slowly closing noose," as one source said. There were some suggestions that Hitler delayed taking German Jews en masse to avoid horrifying his own citizens—who preferred order and rules: *Ordnung*. Therefore he took his own Jews step by step, to spare the "sensibilities" of "good Germans."

Within Germany, the Nazis established a perverse hierarchy of Jewish "privilege." The least privileged, those taken first, were Jews who had come into Germany fleeing pogroms in Eastern Europe—*Ostjuden*, as they were called. The sensitive German citizens saw them as a sort of insect invasion; therefore any horrors visited upon them were not disorder, in their eyes, but a pest extermination.

Taken later, over a year or more, were German Jews who were "useful" to the Nazis: those working in defense industries, in labor camps.

Going up the line of privilege were Jews who were married to so-called Aryans.

Rounded up last were those German Jews, primarily women, who were married to good Germans, had converted to Christianity, and assumed their husbands' Christian names. But in the end, marriage or conversion or name-change meant nothing. They, too, were taken.

I was about to shelve the last volume I had consulted—its proper place right before me—when a series of thoughts rushed into my mind, thoughts as orderly as a logic proof.

First, Maria G. surrendered her child in Belsen, in Germany.

Let us therefore assume she was a German Jew.

Then, I asked myself, which of the German Jewish women were most likely to have survived the Holocaust and found their way to D.P. camps?

Those taken last.

German Jewish women Christian converts married to "Aryans."

And a calm certainty washed over me. I had found her.

Maria G.

She was no Polish Catholic going home to Poland. She was Jewish, she had married a German, converted, and changed her name.

The name: The name was the clue! I read further and learned that many survivors in the camps took back their Jewish names. And it was just as Mrs. Knobloch had said. Miriam: a common name for Jewish women. Gerstner: a good last name for a German Jew.

The clues fell into alignment. My deductions had brought me to a firm conclusion:

A converted Jew named Maria G. comes into the camp then takes back her Jewish name—which is exactly why Maria G. disappears.

She reappears as Miriam Gerstner.

Next clue: Miriam Gerstner left Belsen the day after the surrender of my dear patient. This could not be a mere coincidence.

And I was sure: *Miriam Gerstner and Maria G. were one and the same.*

She was the mother. I had found her.

Then, in just a tiny slice of time, my hopes evaporated. I thought: Wait. Wait. There is no record of Miriam Gerstner ever having been in Palestine, later Israel, or anywhere else, for that matter. The evidence trail goes cold. Mrs. Knobloch's words returned: *dead end.*

Defeated—I felt the past had defeated me. History refused to yield its secrets. Oh, I cannot help her, I thought, I cannot help my dear patient find her mother. "Colin Masters" must give off writing to her; Dr. Schussler would have to manage the wreckage.

But then, against my lifelong habit of racing to the bottom reaches of pessimism (my love for the patient propelling me up and forward), I forced mysef to persevere. Go on, I thought. There is one last M.G.

Gershon, like Gerstner, left Belsen the day after the patient's surrender, making her a candidate. And this M.G. does not disappear. We know she is in Israel in 1948. But where to go from there? Was there truly a chance the Jewish Agency would find her?

I knew my only hope was the library, to read on. The librarian of Berkeley's reserve section was my genius, my guiding star. Half an hour after I had queried her, she handed me a monograph: an anthropologist discussing the cultural environment among Jews in Palestine and Israel from 1945 through 1959.

Many Jews shed their European names during this period, said the author. The purpose was to break free of their long stay in Europe, which had ended in disaster. They took names that were more "Middle Eastern," also names of places in Israel, to establish themselves, once and for all, in Eretz Yisrael.

Michal Gershon.

Which Mrs. Knobloch had described as an "Israeli name."

And there it was: the only logical conclusion.

Maria G. became Miriam Gerstner who became Michal Gershon.

One woman, three names, moving through the twisted path of history.

60.

I was startled awake by the phone, then the voice on the other end. The Bell System operator. Would I receive a collect call from Israel from Mrs. Truva Golan?

I do not know this person, I replied.

Softly in the background, I could hear the operator conferring with the caller, soon coming back on the line to say: The other party says she is the assistant of Mrs. Orna Knobloch.

Yes, yes, I said in anticipation of some further developments in the story of my patient's mysterious origins.

Good morning, Professor. We are about to send out the material Mrs. Knobloch promised for you. I would like to make sure we have the right address for you at the university, the exact building and room number where mail is received.

I am on leave, I told Mrs. Golan. Please take down my temporary address.

I am not calling the university now?

No, madam.

There was silence on the line.

I am afraid I have broken protocol, she said. We have a duty of confidentiality, which I'm sure you understand. We have vetted your university affiliation—

(they contacted the university!)

—and the department secretary verified your position on the faculty. But we cannot speak so freely without proper identification, without a formal letter of request, which I cannot seem to find. Forgive me. But I must send all the information to your verified university address, since . . .

I understand completely. There is no problem. I will simply have a colleague forward it to me.

61.

I was doomed. What colleague would sort through my mail and forward it to me? Who there still trusted me? Particularly as I was tracing information about a woman, a young woman . . . If the parcel was to be opened by the secretary, the department head would question the contents, and then . . . Oh, God, I would be banished from the university forever.

Thus did I work myself into a panicked state, as was my wont. It was three o'clock in the morning. I could not go back to sleep. Nor could I sleep the entire day, one that seemed inordinately long, as the sun of springtime lingered, slanting into evening.

Five days of isolation followed.

At the end of which, I knew: I had to find Michal Gershon. To stop here, and deliver nothing more, was to add another abandonment to the patient's life. I would find a way to receive the files. I had to believe they contained Michal Gershon's address. This I would send to the patient. She would find her mother.

My new hope, though dim, was to find the patient's mother alive and well and open to loving the daughter she had surrendered.

62.

I emerged from my isolation. I walked along the margin of the dusking ocean, wondering how I might retrieve Mrs. Knobloch's files. An hour went by. Full dark fell upon us. Bonfires bloomed along the sands. I let the problem recede from my direct consciousness and listened to the surf, the rhythm of the sea. And by the mysterious process through which these thoughts arise, a plan came to me.

There was a postdoctorate student, a young woman who had remained friendly with me throughout—or at least civil and polite. I would call her, I decided, and tell her a near truth: I would say I was searching for the birth mother of a cousin who was adopted, a story that closely followed the path of my heart.

I was surprised when her telephone answered with a recorded message: Please let us know the date and time of your call, and leave a message at the beep. The beep came. I babbled. Another beep sounded, and the line hung up. I called again. At the beep, I tried to make my message more coherent, and was again cut off by the second beep. Answering machines were illegal, and rare; the Bell System owned all the equipment and had forbidden the use of the devices on their lines. Under normal circumstances, if no one was home, the phone simply rang and rang until the caller gave up. I therefore did not know how to behave in the face of that machine. I froze at the thought of being recorded; my words sounded stilted to me; I was aware that I was leaving a record of a lie.

She returned my call nonetheless, sounding quite at ease. She thought it "touching" that I was helping my cousin and asked no questions about the matter. Yes, she would stop by the secretary's office often and "keep an eye out" for the envelope; yes, she would forward it; no problem, she said. I gave her my address in San Francisco. Then, at the end of the call, her voice grew tentative, and she asked:

But how *are* you, Professor?

I am . . . doing all right, I said.

She said nothing for several seconds, then:

I hope everything works out, she said. I would enjoy working with you again.

I nearly broke into tears. This was said so freely, so openly—the first hint that my life at the university was not a complete ruin.

Thank you, was all I could choke out in reply. And she rang off with another promise to forward my mail.

63.

The patient's next session proved to be inconsequential. She spoke of
the major event that had just happened in the world, the fall of Saigon, the
dramatic and humiliating exit of the helicopters from the embassy roof.
She discussed a matter at work, however desultorily. She spent a little
time puzzling over the relationship between Clarissa and Andie—they
never fought, it seemed. It appeared the hour would end with little accomplished, I thought with relief.

Then, as the session neared its close—as always, we analysands
dangle ourselves before the fire only when we know it is about to go
out—the patient suddenly sighed, sat quietly for a time, then said:

You know, Dr. Schussler. I can't help thinking about my adoption.
And it's come to me that, not only have I been abandoned, but that I've
been abandoned twice. First by whatever mother gave birth to me. Some
Jewish woman named Maria—how odd, a Jew named Maria—a widow
too desperate to raise me, or not ever married—or a prostitute, even.
Why stop with nice mothers? Mothers come in all varieties, don't they?
Witness Mother, Mother with a capital M.

And then I was abandoned—junked!—by my grandfather. Whoever
he was. Mad Catholic patriarch. Funny to think of how I could have
bumped around in the world during those first months of my life. Why
stop at two abandonments? Maybe others took me up and left me—nuns,
priests, village ladies—why not? A whole Europe full of people ready to
abandon little Jewish babies.

As I listened to the patient, I understood that all the pretty parcels
I had sent, showing a decent life in the camp, could not wash away
the stain. Only her birth mother could remove it. Perhaps by giving a
mother's love? Or, at the very least, a decent explanation of why she had
never come for her.

Eight days later, Mrs. Knobloch's parcel arrived, courtesy of my graduate student.

It contained a thick pile of papers. On the last sheet: Michal Gershon's
last known address.

64.

I have it all, said the patient. Everything I need to find her.

It was not the joyous voice that had greeted the first parcels about her mother.

Name, address, everything. It would be so simple. Just write a letter to this address and see what happens. I mean, maybe . . . maybe it'll just come back saying, Moved, no forwarding address. Or, No such person. Or a letter saying, You've made a mistake. I'm not your mother. Or the worst: Nothing. The worst thing is that nothing at all comes back.

She laughed.

Watch out what you wish for, she said. I wanted to know about my mother, and now I do. But now what? Is this a ticket to a new understanding of my life, or a bomb that's going to blow up everything?

Consider one more possibility, said Dr. Schussler. That you remain essentially the same person you were, neither new nor destroyed.

The patient laughed again. You mean it's all a lot of trouble for nothing?

Not at all, said the doctor. It is a challenge.

The patient sat silently for several seconds, then said:

But what happens if I find her and she rejects me all over again? She could just say, I didn't want you back then, and I don't want you now.

Do you really think anyone would say that to you?

Yes, said the patient. I do think someone will say that to me. *Has* said that to me. I mean Mother.

Your adoptive mother.

Yes. Capital-M mother. She didn't want me then, and she doesn't want me now.

That is not true. Why are you punishing yourself again? Your mother was conflicted, put in a situation not of her own choosing. And now she is afraid of your father and unable to handle her own feelings.

I've spent my whole life looking out for Mother's feelings! It all amounts to rejection for me.

This last was said in her cold, angry voice. After which she sat back, mute. One could imagine her arms crossed over her chest, the glum expression on her face. The seconds ticked away as traffic noise filled the space in the therapeutic conversation.

Finally the therapist said: And so you believe your Michal Gershon must do the same.

Of course.

But why? Why would she?

She gave me away. Isn't that enough evidence?

Perhaps she wonders what became of her child.

She could have looked for me, if that's what she wanted. Like I said a couple of weeks ago, mothers come in all varieties. Maybe she's a shit.

So then, said the therapist, it will be she who is lacking. Not you.

Ah, said the patient. Yes. I suppose so.

Her voice drifted off, so that the "I suppose so" was a near whisper.

I sat pained as I listened to her indecision and fear, the awful sense she carried inside her, ontologically, of being unwanted. I saw how adoption, far from liberating a person, could inscribe a sense of defect inside one's heart, as deep and indelible as any work of the genes. She had "inherited" her feeling of being unworthy; she had come to consciousness with the knowledge of having been given away. I could not imagine any path for her but toward the truth. Nothing could possibly cure such feelings of unworthiness except understanding why: Why had her mother given her away?

What should I do? she asked her therapist.

Do you really want me to give you the answer? replied the doctor.

The patient sighed. Of course not. No one can do that for me. But . . . I've barely digested the bad meal fed me by one set of parents. Why subject myself to another mother? Maybe I can just put all this information aside. And wait.

You are not required to do anything at all, said Dr. Schussler.

Yes, said the patient. I'm just going to put all this on the shelf. And see how I feel after a while.

A perfectly realistic decision, the doctor said.

65.

How could she! The therapist had pulled her client relentlessly toward the birth mother, and now—after all the hard work I had done to find her, laying my overcoat across the therapist's mud swamp, so to speak—now the doctor thought to say: Well, never mind.

It was the therapist's guilt and fear. What relief Dr. Schussler must feel to put it all aside, go back to "Mother" and "Father," the two parental figures who predate the whole dark, messy, terrifying connection to the exterminated Jews of Europe.

The month of June ended; July went by; the August hiatus loomed. Throughout, the patient never again mentioned her birth mother.

As the sessions wore on, my feelings about her denial began to evolve. Initially I was merely angry at Dr. Schussler and felt somewhat forgiving toward the patient; such reticence seemed natural, protective, given the scar upon her soul. Soon, however, by the time we had come to the fourth session, and the patient still had not said a word about her mother, my emotions began to take on a more sinister cast, which, given my history, should have been a warning to me.

The patient began to bore me. What dullness she revealed as, week by week, she ventured nothing more daring than a discussion of work issues (things far too technical for the therapist to remark upon), thoughts about finding a new apartment (without taking any action whatsoever thereupon), rants about lesbian-feminist politics (she was against separatism, a position unchanged since the second session I had overheard), current events about which she could do nothing but moan (the FBI shootout at the Pine Ridge Indian Reservation, the congressional report on CIA abuses in spying upon Americans).

Such timidity! Such a lack of curiosity! With all the new avenues opened up to her by the knowledge of her origins, she had withdrawn into the safety of the quotidian. It was one thing for her never to have set off on this road. But now that she had begun—was indeed close to her goal—her repression and denial was outright . . . cowardly!

She had toyed with my emotions, I felt. She had presented herself as a complex person of merit, someone who might understand me. I had been fooled. Betrayed! Could this dull person possibly be the young woman I thought I loved as a daughter? My god. She had revealed herself as spineless, shallow, listless—*common.*

There remained but one more session before the August hiatus. I did not care to attend. Why waste an hour listening to the patient's vacant chattering? I decided instead that I wanted to see what she looked like, in the flesh, for real. My goal: to erase the ideal image of her I had been carrying within me all this long year.

I wanted to see with my own eyes that she was an ordinary girl. Perhaps she really was the common-looking woman I'd seen in the elevator, she of the matted brown hair, flushed cheek, and sweaty brow. Unlovely. I would be released from caring if she did not conform to the lovely vision I had constructed in my mind: if her movements were not graceful and delicate; if her eyes were not intelligent; if the swell of her lips was not the perfect portal for the creamed-coffee flow of her voice. I thought of the patient's flaws as I had learned of them through the eyes of her mother and the therapist: the frizzy hair, "dirty" blond; the eyes that go "dark"; the low, "disgusting" gums; thinness to the point of seeming ill. The "weird" triangular head she had ascribed to herself, Yossele Rosensaft's head: ugly on a woman. I would station myself before the elevators at the end of the patient's hour and wait to lay eyes upon this flawed, disgusting, unlovely creature.

I stood before the three elevators at the appointed time. The eyes of the cherubs rolled left then right, following the path of the cabs as they rode up and down the shafts. The center car made a slow descent: stops on seven, four, two; on the mezzanine—could they not walk down!—finally at the lobby. At last the doors rolled back: to reveal the plain woman with matted hair! Her hair, still matted and unruly. The flushed face now red with a pimply rash. She duck-walked forward with rounded shoulders.

Immediately the car to the right opened and disgorged its passengers. And a young woman emerged: another woman who might be the patient! Brown hair, skinny, curly hair—who could tell under such a mop of hair if a head is "triangular"? Perhaps she was indeed the patient, fluffing up her hair to hide the shape of her skull. She, too, walked toward me, her step martial, strident, ungainly.

I turned and followed them out of the lobby. Which one was my patient? Oh, God, why did I not think to say good morning, so that each might reply and reveal herself through the sound of her voice? I trailed behind them as they walked toward Market Street, at which point each turned and went a separate way. I stood there dancing from foot to foot, unable to decide in which direction I should go, feeling such disdain for them that it came into my mind to think, Unworthy bitches! When suddenly I realized the elevators were not done for the day; car upon car would yet discharge its passengers.

I raced back to the lobby. I was sweating, still shifting from foot to foot. The guard fixed his gaze upon me.

He came at me in two long strides.

What is the trouble here? he demanded, his powerful body towering over me.

He knows what I am about! I thought desperately. He knows I am a threat! Yet I managed to reply:

I am late. Meeting someone. And I am agitated at my tardiness.

I heard a deep chord of skepticism rumbling in his chest, saw his eyes running over me like those of the cherubs, his beautiful, frightful countenance as unmoving as their bronze faces.

Then, behind him, the left elevator opened its doors.

Over the guard's shoulder I saw her: the young woman who had lived in my mind all these months. Slim as an iris stem. A nimbus of brown hair suddenly ignited by a band of sunlight. Delicate cheekbones. Chin pointed like the fulcrum of a heart. Movement as elegant as a willow. *Shall I compare thee to a summer's day?*

Is there a problem? said the guard.

He must have seen it: the sudden lightning of desire on my face.

I found myself in front of the building, next to the patient, about to move toward that lovely form. All the disdain had been drained from me; my plan to hate her had utterly failed. She was all my imagination had created, and more. And I would have followed her anywhere, if she would have me.

A hand gripped my elbow.

Get along your way, sir, said the guard, his eyes fierce with threat, his arm turning me away from Market Street.

But I am a tenant here, I said weakly.

I said, Get along your way!

The patient was leaving me! I watched her shape recede as she crossed Market Street, where she would disappear into the crowd. I tried to tug my elbow away from the grip of the guard. I looked down at the hand restraining me. And I was about to protest again—when suddenly it came to me that I was being held in the hand of Providence.

Truly, I was not a believer. Before that moment I had no faith in divine intervention into the world of men. Yet right then I knew some force had been sent to save me from my fearful desires. There was no reason this guard should have left the building to accost me. I had never seen him challenge anyone as he had challenged me. Now I knew why he was placed in our building; why his beauty so unnerved me. *Each angel is terrible.*

Thank you, sir, I said to my angelic guard.

He screwed up his eyes. He had not expected this gratitude. He hung over me, still holding my elbow.

I suppose I missed my niece, I said to him. I should go in and phone her.

He said nothing, only continued to hold me by the elbow to escort me inside, then see me into an elevator car. I rose up the shaft knowing I was being watched over: the guard watching the eyes of the cherubim, as they watched me ascend to eight.

66.

The August hiatus was an orgy of self-recrimination.

I had thought I would be safe as long as I could hear the patient's voice. Her story, my desire to know it, was all that was decent in me; all that kept me from the trail inscribed in my blood. Yet I had succumbed to the crows—or nearly. I had been on the brink of following her! Who knows what I would have done if not for the intervention of my frightening angel?

Dr. Schussler was gone. The patient was where? At home? On vacation? Traveling for work? How tempted I was to find 732 Alpine Terrace and watch for her. I locked myself in my cottage and forbade myself to go.

It was a time of the truest of lonelinesses (since loneliness is plural, various in its aspects and effects); and by this I mean not simply the absence of companionship but a complete estrangement from all feelings except self-loathing. The world tolerated me, I believed, only because of my subterfuge: the fraud I perpetrated which fooled them into thinking I was human.

67.

Labor Day came, and ten days lay between me and the patient's return. Was I worthy of her? Could I return to her? Each night my imagination was invaded by hideous images. In my dreams I opened my eyes yet remained blind.

Finally came Wednesday morning, the tenth of September. I awoke in a sweated puddle of fear. Yet, as if enchanted, I found myself dressing, leaving the cottage that had been my prison all the month long, climbing onto the N Judah for the long ride downtown. It was a blisteringly hot day. The wind came from inland, from the dry hot valley, and standing in the sun merely to cross Market Street was nearly intolerable. My gargoyles labored under the eaves. I came to the door; I entered the blind white of the lobby.

The guard was not there! The podium and desk: bare! The sign-in book: gone! Had the guard been let go? Fired? Had the building management decided it did not need a guard or could not afford one? Or had the guard never existed at all, his presence and intervention in my life having no more reality that the unnatural images of my nightmares? I knew I should have feared the disappearance of my observing angel. I knew I should have worried for my sanity. But a calm washed over me. For no reason at all, I was certain the good Eumenides had spared me. The guard's absence, I felt sure, was proof of his Providential purpose: He had been sent precisely for the one duty he had performed.

In my pocket was the notice requiring me to renew my lease else vacate the office. I should have returned it weeks ago. Up until the moment I stood staring at the empty podium, I had not been certain if I would sign the form or tear it up, leave the building, leave the patient and all that tempted me. Now I climbed to the mezzanine up the narrow stair I had not traveled for more than a year—the marble steps worn yet more concave—hastily signed the form, and dropped it into the manager's box. Then I rode up to my dear office.

The cool interior of the building's breath enveloped me; the cold marble reassured me once again: *Everything will be all right.*

I took my chair as always. First came the bongs of the church bell, then the patient's footsteps. At last: The extinguishing of the sound machine. The breathtaking silence that followed.

Into which the patient said: I found her. Michal Gershon. I found her.

The therapist started in her chair.

And immediately a chasm opened between the patient's last words and those still to come.

Was the woman named Michal Gershon truly her mother? What was my evidence? Initials. A date. Historical patterns. Almost nothing.

The laughing voice of Mrs. Knobloch mocked me: Who am I to tell you what to believe?

THREE

68.

Your mother, said the therapist. You found your mother.

No, said the patient. I can't call her that. Mrs. Gershon. I found Michal Gershon.

(Please tell me she is your mother!)

Ah? How? What? piped the therapist.

Completely on impulse, said the patient. I bought a ticket from a travel agent, flew standby to Tel Aviv the next day.

And?

A mistake. A disaster. The worst experience of my life.

(No! This cannot be the whole of the story!)

The patient was silent for several seconds. Dr. Schussler's venetian blinds banged against the sills in the faint hot breeze. The street was strangely quiet, deserted because of the heat.

There's only one good thing about it, the patient went on. I don't have to worry about mothers anymore. I'm free of all mothers. Adoptive, birth, natural, first, second, blood, not. She laughed. I'm *Mutterfrei*. You've heard of *Judenfrei*, free of Jews? Of course you have, being German. Europe cleared of all the Jews. Well, I did better than Hitler. I'm *Mutterfrei*.

(What a horrid way to express it. And a nice barb at the therapist, too. But yes, I thought from behind the protection of my wall. This is where you want to be, my dear patient: rid of them all.)

Suppose you tell me what happened, said Dr. Schussler.

What's there to say? When someone says to you "Get out of here! Never try to contact me again!" what else is there to say? Want to hear it in her own voice? Here. I brought a cassette recorder. It's all cued up.

There was a click, then a voice in a scratchy recording shouting:

Do not look for me again! I beg you: Never again try to contact me!

The patient immediately clicked off the recorder.

Okay, so I got it a little wrong. She didn't exactly say, Never try to contact me again! She said: Never again try to contact me!

The patient said nothing more for several seconds. The venetian blinds rattled and bumped. All the while one could hear the slish of

Dr. Schussler's stockings as she crossed and recrossed her legs—one could almost feel the stickiness of her thighs as they suffered in their nylon casings. She was extemporizing: What should she possibly say in reply to that shouting voice?

Let us put aside the recording for the moment, the therapist said finally. First let us talk about your decision to go to Tel Aviv. Tell me how the trip came about, how you made your decision.

It was an impulse, said the patient. As I said. The city was fogged in. Andie and Clarissa went to Las Vegas, a place I hate. It would cost a fortune to fly to Tel Aviv at the last minute. But I'd just received a bonus. Why not go? I walked into a travel agency. Plane, hotel, done.

I had to change planes in New York, and all the while there was a little whisper in the back of my head saying, You can turn around; you don't have to do this. Just the same, I kept going, in an out-of-body state.

The patient stopped, coughed, adjusted her position in her chair.

And so you went on, said the doctor.

Yes, I went on.

Then what happened?

Tel Aviv was not what I expected. I don't know what I thought it would be like. But I wasn't prepared for everything being new, white, concrete, a city built all at once, it seemed. And then there were the soldiers, young men and women everywhere in uniform, carrying Uzis. People my age and younger, walking around with machine guns slung over their shoulders the way kids here carry a book bag. There was a beachfront, also unexpected. Hotels lining a crowded shore on the Mediterranean. Sparkling sun.

The receptionist at the hotel told me how to get to Michal Gershon's address. She didn't live in Tel Aviv proper, but in a suburb. I had to take a long ride in a stifling, crowded bus. My stop was on a dusty road. There were no shops, only a drive-in restaurant advertising "shashleek." The counterman spoke some English, and he directed me to a narrow street of three-story apartments. They seemed shabbily built, not old but already showing cracks. It was midday, the sun directly overhead. Cool breeze. Hot sun. I was the only one out on the streets. I found the house number, walked in, went up two flights, and was facing the apartment door: Mrs. Gershon's last known address.

Again it was an out-of-body experience. I felt nothing at all, no fear, no anticipation, nothing, as if the concrete that built Tel Aviv was in my veins. I was just this body performing an action. Knock, knock, knock.

There was no reply. I knocked again and waited. Still no one.

Then a voice called out something in Hebrew, then in English, Who's there? And the head of an old woman—about seventy, seventy-five—poked out of a neighboring door.

I'm looking for Michal Gershon, I said.

Who's asking? she said.

I'm a friend from America, I told her.

She eyed me a moment, then said that Michal Gershon had moved to what she called "a nicer place in Jaffa." I had no idea what she meant, where or what "Jaffa" was, and simply asked her if she would write down the new address for me. Which she did, finally saying, Tell Michal she could remember once in a while where she came from.

I thought it was a strange thing for her to say. I left with a non-committal nod.

I went back to the hotel to rest, and fell asleep. When I woke up, it was dark outside; the clock said eight. With my jet lag, it took me a few seconds to remember that I was in Tel Aviv, and on the dresser was the real address of my birth mother.

Then the words of the woman at the door of the old apartment came back to me. Tell Michal she could remember once in a while where she came from.

It seemed to be a warning.

The patient paused.

A warning not to go. It told me Michal Gershon is a person who likes to leave her past behind.

Then the patient said nothing for several seconds. She sighed and shuffled about in her chair, scraped her feet on the carpet, withdrew a tissue from the nearby box, coughed, sighed, and coughed again. Moments floated by on the heat.

But you did go to Jaffa the next day, said Dr. Schussler.

Yes.

And there you found her.

Yes.

69.

I took a bus to Jaffa, the patient continued. There were little cobbled alleys going off in all directions. I got turned around, lost. I sat down at an outdoor cafe, ordered iced tea, and handed the waiter the scrap of paper with Michal's address. Did he know the way? He was a tall man of about fifty, an Arab, clean-shaven, wearing jeans and a shirt open at the collar. He laughed and pointed across the narrow street.

There is a courtyard, he said, just to the right. Michal's little house is at the far end. Under the curving stone wall. And tell her Schmuel says hello.

You're Schmuel? I asked him.

He laughed again.

No. But that is what she calls me.

He waved away my attempts to pay for the tea. I thanked him with the little bit of Arabic I knew.

Shokran, I said.

Afwan, he said, with a small bow.

This Schmuel suddenly seemed . . . well, propitious. I had no plan. I didn't know what I'd say when Michal Gershon opened her door. I couldn't say, I'm your daughter. Or Hi, Mom. Now I felt he'd given me a sort of passport. I could say, Schmuel says hello.

I followed Schmuel's directions. I crossed the road. Went into the courtyard, turned right. And it was just as he said. A curving stone wall. Under it a house. Made of the same stone, so it seemed part of the wall. But with a door. And windows. A fairy-tale house.

The door was a hard, solid piece of wood. With an iron latch, an iron handle.

There was no choice now: Knock, knock, knock.

I don't know how long I stood there until I heard steps, a voice, a young voice, with a thick accent saying something, maybe in German.

I said: Do you speak English? I'm here to see Michal Gershon.

The door opened a crack. A young woman looked at me. She had blond-gold hair, green eyes, white skin, cheeks like apples.

Schmuel sends his greetings, I said.

Ah, Schmuel, she said, laughing, opening the door and waving me in. Schmuel: my magic word, my open-sesame.

Then I saw things in flashes. A dark room. Heavy wood furniture. Embroidered tablecloths. Doilies on chair arms. Bare walls. No pictures, not even family photos. I followed the young woman who'd let me in. A big strong girl. She called out in German to "Frau Gershon," maybe saying someone is here, I don't know, I'm guessing.

She led me around a corner, then into a small, dim room. The window shades were drawn, but there was a gap. A slice of light broke through it—brilliant, dusty, opaque—like a scrim. Behind it was a figure. All I could see was a shape, bent over, but otherwise only a shadow. For some seconds, nothing happened. The figure did not move.

Behind me, the girl sang out something in German.

Then suddenly a face burst through the light. Her mouth was frozen open. Her eyes were startled wide. They rolled back and forth over me.

Otherwise her face was still, a rictus. Then tiny muscle movements began rippling over her features—the muscles twitching but paralyzed, the way a dreaming dog trembles in its sleep—as if waves of emotions were running through her, but in fast-forward, so it was bizarre, almost comical.

What? I wanted to shout. What! What are you seeing! Because I knew whatever was going on was set off by the sight of me. I was a part of those racing expressions, a player, but with what role? The ripples of memory kept running across her face. Meanwhile, her body was fixed, hidden behind the beam of light, so that the whole drama was being played out with this head suspended in a cloud.

Gerda! she abruptly screamed, going on to yell curses in German at the girl who had led me in—even I understood they were curses.

Then she stepped forward through the light.

Now I could see her, head to toe, in the low, even shade of the room. She was sturdily built, broad-shouldered, of medium height. She had blond hair, high cheekbones, a broad, clear brow. She looked young except for her bent posture—I noticed now she held a cane. She would be beautiful, I thought, weirdly, if her face were not tied into a knot of rage. Suddenly a kind of fist grabbed my insides: disappointment. Dreadful disappointment. Until that moment, I hadn't realized how much I'd hoped to look like her.

All the while, she kept screaming in German, walking toward me, waving her cane, until I understood she was trying to force me out, the way you'd use a broom to shoo a dog. I was instantly angry, thinking, How dare you treat me like this!

But you know me! I screamed at her, walking toward her, putting up my arm to ward off the cane. I saw it on your face. You recognized me immediately. You know who I am!

No! No! she answered me. Go away! How did you get in here?

You know me! I kept shouting. You know me!

The girl Gerda came up beside me.

Please to leave, she said, taking my arm.

I jerked it away and said, No! You know who I am!

Michal raised her cane as if to wave me away again. And then, all at once, she deflated. That's the only way I can describe it. A long breath came out of her; her head and shoulders shrank down; her back slumped. She said, "Ay! What is the use?" then stumbled toward an upholstered chair and sank into it, head down, eyes focused between her knees, her left arm hanging limp over the cane, like a rope.

Gerda, bring me something to drink, she said in a mixture of German and English, still looking at the floor. Tea, she said. And whiskey. Then she looked up at me and said, And something for . . . something for this girl.

I don't have a recording of this—I didn't buy the cassette recorder until the next day. So what I'm telling you is from memory. What happened next was that I sat down—there was another upholstered chair, catty-corner to hers. She looked straight ahead, not at me, and we said nothing. This gave me time to look at her more closely, and I saw that her eyes were very brilliant, maybe blue or green—I couldn't tell exactly in that light—and that her skin was exquisite, pale, translucent, without lines except for a few delicate sketches at the sides of her eyes. At first, because of the cane, she seemed older than Mother, big-M Mother. Then I realized that without it, without the cane and bent posture, Michal would look younger, probably five years younger.

Suddenly it came to me: Big-M Mother wanted me to be pale like Michal, pale and blond and light-eyed.

I don't know how long I sat in that chair wishing I were dead. Two blond mothers and there I was: an alien, not appearing to be the spawn of anyone.

The tea appeared on a tray. The whiskey. Teacups and saucers and little pitchers of cream. Gerda served me a cup, put in sugar and cream without asking. She did the same for Michal, but with a shot.

Michal took her first sip. Then she said, very slowly, each word like a stone hitting concrete:

I hoped you would never know about me.

She had a beautiful voice: low, resonant, accented with a smooth blend of several languages I couldn't identify—a voice so beautiful that the meaning of her words did not penetrate for several seconds.

So you just wanted to be rid of me, I said.

She winced. That is not it at all, she said.

She sat back and sighed. How did you find me?

A librarian at a Catholic adoption agency in Chicago.

You are an *American*?

Yes. I live in San Francisco.

Too bad, she said. Americans. Ignoramuses all. Ill-educated, over-confident people. I had planned for you to be a European. How did you get to America?

All I know, from my mother—my adoptive mother—is that the Church was looking for Catholic homes for babies, some of them Jewish, who had been sheltered with the Church during the war. Europe was in tatters, and there were more takers in the U.S. than in Europe.

I see, she said, staring away from me.

Well, she went on, at least you are a Catholic.

No, I said. I was brought up Presbyterian.

Ah! Even better!

What do you mean? I asked.

Now she turned to look at me, calmly, surveying me for the first time. Emotions played across her face again, but slowly now. Tiny frowns, surprised eyebrows, fleeting smiles—they might have meant anything. Then she simply gazed at me. She looked at my hair, my mouth, my chin. And then into my eyes. On her face was an expression of love so powerful, so open, that I realized I had never been loved in the whole of my life. Then the emotion moved on.

I wanted to make sure you would not be a Jew, she said.

70.

I was shocked, the patient told Dr. Schussler.

(I, too, was shocked, and nearly gave myself away by starting in my chair.)

I mean, there she was in Israel, the Jewish State, the patient went on. Why wouldn't she want me to be Jewish? But when I asked, she only laughed and said, That would take more than a teatime to explain, my dear!

Then Michal turned to me with that tender look again and said, So tell me. What is your name?

And I told her. After which she sat thoughtfully for a moment, then said, Very nice. Very good. I am very happy for you—she gave a nod with each "very."

(Why did you not say your name aloud to the therapist! I wanted to cry out from behind my wall.)

I realized right at that moment that I might have had another name, said the patient. So I asked her.

Her face went through those changes again, memories running over her features—more like lightning strikes this time. Finally her eyes went cold, and she said, No. Never. After which she sat back in her chair, stone-faced, and looked away from me.

Somewhere in the house a clock was ticking. Children were playing in the courtyard; I could hear their squeals of delight. I knew she was lying, that I did have another name, one she gave me, or intended to, a name she carried around in her mind all these years—or one she wanted to forget. In any case, I was angry. I felt my names belonged to me, and that I should have them, know them. I couldn't stand being a person dealt out in little pieces, different people owning parts of me, different ideas of me. Michal's abandoned infant. My grandfather's rejected Jew-baby. My parents' unsuitable daughter. I wanted to gather up all the pieces and own myself. Does that make sense to you? That I wanted to own myself?

Yes, of course, said the therapist. That is why you were doing all that. Why you went there in the first place.

(Yes! I thought with joy as I listened in my room. Own yourself!)

So I confronted her, said the patient.

I am sure it was difficult, said Dr. Schussler.

Oh, God, yes, said the patient.

But I am sorry, said the therapist, I am afraid you will have to tell me about it next time.

Oh, God, said the patient. We're done, aren't we? I wasted time. All that crap about the city and the beach. I wasted the hour.

You did what you needed to, said the doctor gently. But let me propose something. I have an opening on Monday nights. Nine o'clock. It will be temporary, a few months. But I would like to offer it to you, so for a while you may come twice a week.

The patient hummed. I don't know, she said. Monday night. Let me think about it.

Yes. Think about it. Call me, and let me know. I will keep the hour open for you.

71.

Monday night could not come quickly enough. How I hoped the patient had indeed accepted the hour. Joy: I would be with her twice a week.

I sat in the office on Monday listening to the hiss of the sound machine and the screech of brakes in the street, and I thought the earth had somehow stopped revolving. Would the sun never set! Would dark never come!

At last Dr. Schussler's eight o'clock patient left. The doctor moved about her office, then turned off the sound machine, as she normally did when her workday was at an end—and as she did before the patient's arrival. The silence, therefore, could indicate either condition. Yet I had to calm myself, remain exquisitely still, for at that late hour the building was quiet, the only sound being the low hum that seemed to emanate from the core of the place, from the basement, or the elevators, or the roof, or perhaps was the life-thrum of the building itself.

When suddenly something shrilled through the silence.

The doctor's phone.

She jumped up before it could ring again.

Yes, she said into the phone. Good evening, Dr. Gurevitch. Thank you so much for returning my call.

(So she was still in "consultation" with this Gurevitch.)

Dr. Schussler occasionally murmured "yes" and "I see" as she listened, finally saying: I am relieved that you agree with my assessment. It does seem the most efficacious method of proceeding.

(What were they talking about! What method? By the glow of my watch, I could see that we were fast approaching the top of the hour. Was the patient coming or not?)

I concur, she said at last. Yes. Her cynicism is key. Cynicism and self-punishment.

(This had to be about the patient.)

And I must, if possible, guide her toward reconciliation with her adoptive family.

(No! Help her leave them!)

Otherwise she will have no base, no home. However, it may be that such reconciliation impossible, given the mother's schizoid personality and the father's emotional distance.

(Footsteps were coming down the hall.)

And therefore—

(There were knocks on the door. Yes! She was here!)

Ah, but there she is now. I must ring off.

(The knocking continued.)

Just a minute! the doctor called out. Then said softly into the phone, Thank you, Dr. Gurevitch.

She hung up the phone and walked to the door.

Come in, she said to the patient.

72.

This building is really strange at night, the patient said. The hallways are so long and dark.

The therapist laughed. Yes, it sometimes does feel that way.

Twenty seconds of silence followed, after which Dr. Schussler said:

Let us return to where we broke off last session. You were about to confront your birth mother.

No. Not my mother. Michal.

Let us please agree to call her your birth mother.

The patient exhaled her annoyance.

Since it is a fact, the therapist continued. If only to facilitate your ability to discuss the issue.

The patient stalled. One could hear her defiance through the wall: her body shifting in her chair, her feet dragging over the carpet.

No, she said at last. I'm not ready to. I'll call her my birth mother when I'm good and ready to.

Do you really want to keep going back and forth to clarify which mother you are talking about?

The patient replied with no small amount of sarcasm: So. You mean something like big-M Mother versus birth mother.

Yes, said Dr. Schussler. I mean something like that.

But I need to call her Michal when I'm talking about her. I can't keep saying *birth mother.* Takes too long.

Agreed, said the doctor. So you felt Michal was lying to you and would not reveal your name.

Right.

You felt divided, that your identity was divided among your birth mother, your grandfather, your parents. By the way, have you told your adoptive parents about finding Michal?

No.

No?

No. You know we're hardly in contact. A call on Christmas. When someone's died. So I don't feel any need to go through all this with them.

But you will tell them eventually.

Yes. Eventually. Once I know how *I* feel about it.

Of course, said the therapist. This must go first. So let us return. You were angry at your birth mother. You confronted her. And then?

And then she was just like . . . big-M Mother, trying to warn me away.

73.

We were still in the living room, said the patient, sitting in the catty-corner armchairs. Michal had just told me she didn't want me to be a Jew. And I replied something like, I don't get it, which made Michal laugh. It was my "I don't get it," which she repeated with an exaggerated American accent, making me feel stupid. Stupidly American.

Then she just sipped her tea and her whiskey, and didn't say anything. A long time went by like that: Michal blowing across her tea, that clock ticking from somewhere, the children shouting and playing outside. Finally Michal stirred in her chair, put down her teacup, and suddenly cried out:

Oh! Why do you want to go into all this! Why must you? There was so much . . . *unhappiness* in that time.

When she said "unhappiness," her face fell. Every feature was drawn down as if weights were hooked onto her eyelids, cheeks, mouth. And I immediately returned to the habits I'd developed with Mother, big-M Mother. That is, I didn't want to inflict unhappiness on her, I wanted to protect her from all those sad feelings I aroused simply by existing.

And when I realized *that*—that I was doing it all over again, sacrificing myself for my mothers—something broke in me. I actually shook. I found myself jumping out of the chair, almost yelling: I don't care if it makes you unhappy to remember! I don't care! You have to tell me!

I kept yelling it over and over. You have to tell me! I have to know where I came from! It's horrible to live without knowing. Like starting from a blank. You have to tell me!

I found myself crying—shaking, out of the blue—and I fell into the chair.

Michal stood slowly, with difficulty—I saw her in my peripheral vision. She came over to me, took my chin in her hand. And she lifted my face to her. And again I felt that I'd never seen such a look of warmth and caring in my life, such sympathy. And she said,

Oh, my poor dear. Is it so horrible not to know?

I told her yes. That there was this space that had . . . nothing in it. Like my whole being floated on . . . nothing.

Oh, my God, she said. I never meant to hurt you. I only meant for you to have a better life.

She sighed and turned to sit down. I stood and helped her. Then she said, Oh, all right. If you feel you need to know this, I will tell you the whole story.

She stopped and looked at me.

But you may not like what you learn. Do you understand that? Life was hard, almost inhuman, and people did what they had to do to survive. When you are humiliated until your humanness leaves you . . .

Oh! she sighed. All right. I will tell you the whole thing, the whole . . . ugliness of it. But not today. No. I am in shock. Let me recover. Come tomorrow, and we will begin.

74.

My poor patient spent the night reviewing the waves of memories that had seemed to wash across Michal's face. She could not sleep, only drifted off in tiny sips of the night, meanwhile wondering: Who was it that Michal recognized right away? Who is it that I look like? *Who?*

The next day, as she was about to leave the hotel, it occurred to her that she was unlikely ever to visit her birth mother again, that she should record whatever it was that Michal was going to tell her. The hotel deskman told her there were many places selling inexpensive cassette recorders and directed her to the nearest one. There she bought a nine-by-six-inch portable with a leather shoulder strap.

Then I went back to Michal's house, the patient told Dr. Schussler. Once again, Gerda led me into the dark room with that slash of light. To the two upholstered chairs set at right angles, Michal in the same seat as yesterday. Everything the same as if nothing had happened between this time and the last.

But before I could ask—demand!—all I wanted to know, Michal turned to me with that open, sympathetic face. Her skin glowed. Her eyes were kind and soft, full of light. And she said: I spent all night wondering over you. Wondering who you have become. You are a grown-up woman with a life. Almost thirty, yes? So tell me, for instance, what do you do? I mean as your profession.

Suddenly, again, I wanted to please her, the patient told the therapist. How damnedly deep is this desire to make your mother love you! Love me, love me, love me. Tell me what I must do to win your love. So I succumbed. I told her I was an economics analyst, to make it simple, since who knows what a "quant" is?

And she immediately replied:

You are not an artist?

Hardly, I said. Was I supposed to be?

On my side, she said, we were all artists and writers and art dealers. But, oh! There was my uncle on my mother's side, the architect, and his son, the engineer. Is economic analysis anything like architecture or engineering?

I felt I was auditioning for the role of daughter, the patient said to her doctor. For the role of the daughter she had imagined. Even though— through no fault of my own—I'd become an American. Even though—through no fault of my own—I'd failed to become an artist, still: I would have her see me as creative, interesting, worthy.

I told her that what I did was a lot like architecture. Architects imagine and analyze space, engineers turn that into numbers. I told her that I envision and analyze money, which is a completely imaginary space.

The patient went on to give a witty, detailed description of her work (which I found utterly fascinating, as it clarified many points that had confused me as I had sat listening to her sessions).

I'm not sure how much of it Michal understood, the patient said to Dr. Schussler. I tried my best to make it all clear to her, a "civilian," as we call them. I wanted her to see my work as stimulating, inventive. I didn't want to find another Charlotte, who would wave me away as being on the wrong side of life. I didn't want to be rejected because I wasn't an "artist."

I played the role of "creative quant," if there can be such a thing.

It's all an elaborate belief structure, I told her, a structure based on reputation, in which the players must trust one another. In other words, a house of cards. My job is to try to understand the stresses—yes, like architectural engineering—to try to prevent the house from falling down.

And I got my "bravo!"

How marvelous! Michal cried out. How intelligent you must be to do such work! I am utterly delighted!

I looked hard at Michal. She was beaming. Pleased. Admiring. My God! I thought. Finally a mother who approves of me.

But then came the next question, the inevitable question, the one that always sends me into hiding.

She asked: And are you married? Or perhaps "with" someone?

I answered: I just broke up with someone.

Normally I would have gone on in the usual gender-indistinct way. You know, saying "this person" and "someone." Or always sticking with the plural. But here I was with my birth mother. And I couldn't stand it anymore. So I came out and said:

The person I broke up with was a woman. A beautiful woman. But she was a Marxist-Leninist-Maoist-Lesbian-Separatist bicycle messenger, and I am an economic analyst with a Wall Street brokerage.

Michal burst out laughing. So you're a lesbian! she said. Isn't that just wonderful! My sister, my older sister Gisella, was a lesbian. She brought home the most marvelous, strange girls. We lived in Berlin—in a big, beautiful house. My mother was the most gracious and interesting hostess, and everyone wanted to visit us. And there was Gisella with her exotic creatures, one after another, each more beautiful than the last. I think half of our visitors came just to look at her conquests. I was so jealous that I did not have an attraction to women. It seemed by far the more interesting way to be.

She laughed again, then I laughed, both of us giddy to find we were really *related* to each other. And I . . . My God, it was the first time in my life I felt I had come from somewhere, where I was normal, not an alien. Then it came to me . . . Then I realized . . . That world didn't exist anymore. The world of artists and writers, architects and lesbians and marvelous strange girls—my ideal life—gone.

I think the feeling of a lost life came to Michal at the same moment. We sat and didn't say anything for a long while. Again I was aware of the clock ticking, the children playing in the courtyard. Reality seemed to press on us. We were undeniably in Israel, a long way from her house in Berlin.

Finally she said: You cannot understand what happened to me, to you, unless you understand my life in Berlin. Oh! she said with a gasp. It pains me even to remember it, the wonder of it. Could such a life disappear from the face of the earth?

75.

Here's where my recording starts, the patient said to Dr. Schussler.

There came clicks and whirring sounds, then a voice that penetrated the scratch and hiss of the tape.

And what a voice it was! Just as the patient had described it: low, resonant, a choir of sound. Now came a creamed-coffee alto, now a bourbon baritone, here and there a sprinkle of soprano laughter. The accent was too complex and blended for me to place. German, British English, Hebrew—but others seemed to play below the surface. Which? I did not know. Yet the accent was all the more alluring for the hidden identities of its components: a caravan of languages reflecting Michal Gershon's sojourns through the world.

On the tape the patient and her mother are drinking tea—one could hear the occasional clicks of cups and spoons and saucers, the pauses as one or the other stops to drink. I imagined them in their armchairs, the tea set between them on a low table, the dim room surrounding them, the scrim of light that curtained the space.

Slowly I was able to strip Michal's voice of its accent, of the age that had roughened the tone. And I was overcome by the recognition: It was the patient's voice!

The patient was not an alien on this earth. She did indeed "look" like someone. Except it was not on the mere surface. She had inherited the more profound interior configuration of the body, the subtle crenellations of lung and diaphragm and sinuses, the delicate architecture of the airways; all of which combine to produce that aspect which is last noted but finally most determinant of one's overall feelings about a person: that which produces a sense of pleasure or displeasure in her presence, an awareness of her graciousness or lack of it, a tug of intrigue or a drone of boredom; that which makes the plainest woman magnetic, the one most visually lovely an irritant: the voice.

Did the patient know this? Was she aware—when she described her mother's voice as beautiful, low and resonant—that it was so similar to her own? Fixed as she was—as fixed as her adoptive mother had made her be—upon the surface features, the colors of eyes and hair, it was unlikely that the patient understood the quality of her own voice: its divinity. Had no one told her?

Our house had twelve bedrooms, her mother began, in the warm sound that was the ancestor to the patient's voice. Eighteen fireplaces, a ballroom, Michal went on. Can you imagine this today? A very large room reserved for the rare social occasion called "a ball"? Four servants lived on the attic floor. Oh God! What a vanished world! Sometimes I wake in the middle of the night and still hear the Berlin of my childhood.

She spoke of horses neighing, the ring of bicycle bells, the drone of organ-grinders. Trams rumbling down the boulevards. Cars racing in the streets, jamming the roads, backfiring and stinking.

My father was an art dealer, she said. Not that he made any money at it. He collected art out of a passion for it. Grandfather was very rich. And he did not mind funding my father's artistic pursuits. My grandfather's idea was: What is the use of having all this money if we cannot subsidize the artists and dreamers in this damned family?

She took several sips of tea.

We were the Rothmans, you see. Of the "Joseph A. Rothman and Company" Rothmans. The maker of the finest textiles. Established in 1809 by my great-great-great-grandfather. But you don't even know my original name.

She laughed.

I was Margarette, Margarette Rothman. Oh, there was another whole life in that name. For seventeen years, I had that esteemed name and that wonderful life, from the "before time." I saw my last ball in our ballroom when I was fourteen, the last swirl of dresses, the last incense of perfumes, the last salons.

The Rothmans, Michal continued. My father's side of the family. They had lived in and around Berlin for three hundred years. My mother's family was a more recent arrival.

She laughed.

Only a hundred years.

You see, she said after a pause, we were later called anti-German elements. I ask you, how many hundred years does it take to become a German?

We did not think of ourselves as Jews, you must understand. We considered ourselves to be . . . in English you would say, "Germans of

Hebrew Heritage." What we inherited: so many silver wine cups and little spice boxes. Otherwise no different from the Germans who were Protestant or Catholic.

The German Jewish community was very, very rich, very established. You must understand this, what the world was like for us then. Imagine it: the synagogue on Fasanenstrasse. A magnificent structure. Crowned by three domes. My parents told me that the emperor himself attended the opening in 1912. Seats for seventeen hundred people. It was our cathedral. Seventeen hundred well-dressed German Jews gathered for the Jewish New Year.

Her voice became bitter.

Our cathedral did not stand for long. I last saw it just before my parents left. It was destroyed by the Nazis on Kristallnacht.

You see how they came to hate us.

Why would they come to hate you? the patient on the tape asked her mother.

Because we were doing too well. Ah. Here is the new pot of tea at last.

See the pattern on this set? said Michal after she had served the tea to the sounds of clicking cups and clanging silver. Look at the roses, the tiny roses. Each painted by hand. This is Rosenthal porcelain. From before the war, I mean before the first war. I searched and searched in the Sunday markets until I found it: the pattern my mother had for her dinner service. I have just these two cups and saucers and the creamer.

All gone. My mother's beautiful things. Service for twenty-four, all the pieces you can imagine on a table.

She said nothing for several seconds; there came the sound of her settling back in her chair.

All gone, she said again. Looted by my husband's family with the help of the Nazis. All the china and silver and crystal and linen. The feather beds and sofas. The mahogany furniture and the paintings—let's not forget the fortune in fine art carried away by the Nazis—all the things they were jealous of and hated us for. Looted by that band of thieves.

I don't understand, the patient said. Your husband's family?

Michal sighed, almost a sob.

I'm getting ahead of myself, she said. Let me go back. Let me stay awhile longer in that . . . in that "before time."

She stopped to drink her tea, then said:

Oh! We knew everyone. All the famous artists of Weimar, and the ones who would become famous, some of them because of Father. There was Max Liebermann, of course. Max Beckmann, Otto Dix, George Grosz, Christian Schad, Hannah Hoch, Oskar Kokoschka, Ludwig Meidner. But do you know even one of these painters?

The patient must have shaken her head no.

Ach! Of course not, she said. American cultural limitations. I am sure you know no one but Monet and Picasso.

Renoir? said the patient weakly. Degas?

Her mother laughed.

I am sorry, dear. Most everyone loves the Impressionists. But hatred of them was one of the liveliest parts of our evenings. Our drawing room was crowded every night my mother was receiving—Tuesdays, Thursdays, Fridays. The artists and their girlfriends—or boyfriends, in some cases. Musicians and poets. My sister's beauties. Hangers-on and would-bes. Desperate former members of Russian nobility and society. Intellectuals. Professors. Not once did the question of our being Jews have any part of these evenings—oh, yes, there was one time.

Ludwig Meidner was drunk, said Michal. Meidner, the painter. He held forth one night, excoriating Max Liebermann for having altered his scandalous portrait of Jesus in the temple. It was an old painting, from 1879 or 1880, but it remained controversial among the artists in the drawing room. In it, Max originally showed a twelve-year-old Jesus talking to the elders. One elder wore a Jewish prayer shawl. But the real problem—for the crown prince of Bavaria, among others—was that Jesus was portrayed as Semitic, swarthy. How brave! How new! It was maybe Max's best painting, because so much of his work was derivative of Corot and Manet. Too many *Münchner Biergärten* and *Bäuerinnen*. And in the middle of all that work was this daring painting: Jesus as a Jew. Of course, what else could Jesus have been—a Hindu?

Max wasn't there that night. This took place in about . . . Let's see. I was twelve. Max was an old man by then, and he had retreated to his country house on the Wannsee. Huh! The house on the Wannsee. Expropriated later, of course. Only to become the site of the Wannsee Conference. You know the Wannsee Conference?

Where the final solution was planned, said the patient.

Ah! said her mother. This you know.

There came the sound of clicking silverware, someone shifting in her chair, sighs.

But I am getting ahead of myself again, said the patient's mother. Let me go back . . .

A long pause followed, the tape hissing.

So everyone was there that night, in the drawing room, Michal went on, her voice striving but just failing to reach its former energy. And drunken Meidner was shouting and swinging his glass about, she said. He was in his late thirties, a madman; his paintings were challenging, dark, angry. He began railing about how Liebermann had repainted the picture. The coward! No painter with respect for himself and the craft would do such a thing! Repainting the finished canvas—what kind of coward does such a thing? Repainted Jesus, turned him into a little blond darling. A blond boy! To satisfy the fine German sensibilities—Jesus had to be a *Münchner*, German, Aryan. Why not just put a Bier stein in his hand?

Everyone was yelling. Why go into this now? Aren't things bad enough for Jews? Meidner was a Jew. Max Liebermann was a Jew, but only as the Rothmans were: just barely.

Every good memory leads to the bad, Michal went on, her voice almost a whisper. It is impossible to keep "before" and "after" separate in one's mind. Weren't things bad enough for the Jews? Ah! If only that had been the worst. One looks back and sees that there were fissures through which we might have seen the future, but of course one lives drenched in the past, that wet cloak that weighs around one's shoulders.

The patient stopped the tape.

Michal shuddered, she told Dr. Schussler. Just as if a cold wet cloak had actually dropped on her. Then she called for Gerda to come and take away the tray and told me, You have to leave now. I'll tell you the whole story, but it must come slowly. Come tomorrow at the same time and we'll resume.

I rose without question and walked toward the far end of the room. Obeying, allowing myself to be sent away. Then—maybe because I had put some distance between us—before I left the room, it came to me that I still did not have an answer to the one question I'd been determined to ask. So I walked back and stood over her.

But I have to ask you, I said. You must tell me . . . When I walked in here, you knew me right away. I know you're tired. But you can't understand what it's like to live not looking like anyone. Not related to anyone. Please: You knew me immediately. So who is it? Who do I look like?

Her face went blank for a moment, and I was afraid she would shout and wave me away again. But then she smiled, very slowly, very sadly. My sister, she said finally. You have her face exactly. Her figure. Her grace. Your pointed chin, the haze of hair around your face. It was as if my sister had come back from the grave and stood before me.

Nothing of my father?

Her face hardened. She snorted. Ha! Whoever that might be.

76.

I looked down at my watch and was shocked to see that the session had gone well overtime. I had been so engrossed in the story that I had lost track of the hour; perhaps this had happened to Dr. Schussler as well, I thought. But then in a soft voice she said:

We have gone overtime tonight because I thought it best not to interrupt you. Sometimes a session is that critical, and I wanted to let you continue as long as possible. But I am afraid we must stop now.

I understand, said the patient. And thank you.

But before you go, let me ask: Did you believe what your mother told you?

About?

About your looking like her sister.

Well . . . Yes . . . I did. And I have since. But now I suppose . . .

She stopped speaking, and there was hardly a sigh or a crinkle of leather issuing from the neighboring office. This went on for a good half minute, an eternity in a conversation, until the patient said at last:

I guess it all fit so well with my fantasy. When big-M Mother first told me the whole story, she kept asking me if I really wanted to know the truth. Remember? And I had a moment where I wanted to cling on to one last fantasy. The rich woman in her house in Berlin who held salons. A grand house full of the intelligentsia of prewar Europe. And here was my actual birth mother fitting right into that dream. But something in me knew it was all too good to be true. A mother so beautiful, still young-looking but for that problem with her back or her hip—oh, that just makes the story better: a war wound of some kind, from a bombing, maybe. Then add artists of Weimar. And *then* the beautiful lesbian sister. And I look like her!

She paused. I really did want to believe her. But now that you ask . . .

She was quiet for perhaps twenty seconds, then said:

Why are you asking?

It only seems odd, said Dr. Schussler, that she would not have told you right from the beginning. Why not, when you walked in, say, My

God! The image of my beloved sister! Or when she told you Gisella was
a lesbian—why not then?

The patient hummed. Maybe I sensed that. Maybe I did. So you
think . . . You think she's not saying . . .

She could be telling you some things she believes you would like to
hear, said Dr. Schussler. Also perhaps what she would prefer to remember.

I don't understand. Is there something else you think was, well, a lie?

Weimar was not . . . Germany was . . . It was a very difficult time.

77.

And that is how the therapist left her patient! On that note of doubt! The one solace the patient had gained during the visit—the knowledge that she looked like a daring lesbian with her gorgeous girls—obliterated by Dr. Schussler. What kind of doctor sends one out the door saying, Perhaps you have cancer. Perhaps not. Come back in a few days. Yet this is exactly the condition in which my poor patient was turned out into the street past ten o'clock on a Monday night, when Market Street was returning to its seedy core.

Dr. Schussler finally gathered her things and left about fifteen minutes later, after which I found myself curiously agitated. I waited for the N Judah. The air was cool, the wind down, the fog having completed its invasion and now blanketing the night. The city lights played against the thick, low clouds—here blue, there reddish, there the dun color of hopelessness—so that I seemed to stand not under a natural sky but encased in a metallic dome. The streetcar rumbled toward me out of the fog; it screeched to a stop; the doors yawned open. Yet I remained rooted to the platform, unable to induce myself to climb aboard. After some interval, during which time the car gently rocked on its tracks, the driver did not look at me, and the three people in the car did not speak, the tram shut its doors and rattled off into the night.

Without intention, I found myself wandering "outbound" on Market Street (or such is the direction as calibrated by the good San Franciscans, who seem not to travel east or west, north or south, but into the city center and out of it). Beyond the wide boulevard of Van Ness came the no-man's-land of vacant lots and abandoned buildings. And an unbidden thought came to me: The city through which I walked was a sister to Weimar Berlin. Two wild, depressed cities in a nation stupefied by inflation and unemployment, two countries humiliated by lost wars—World War I, Vietnam—chafing under the decline from greatness into shabbiness.

And all at once a gimlet eye opened in my mind as I reviewed Michal's story. Something was amiss, as Dr. Schussler had sensed. Margarette Rothman may have been youthful during the time of Weimar, but not so young that she would not have been aware of the larger world. There was something of the fairy tale about her story—yes, the patient had hit upon it exactly. All that was needed was a viscount or two to turn the whole thing into a bad Victorian novel. The three-hundred-year presence in Berlin. Ballrooms, the art gallery, the famous painters, the salons. What about the hyperinflation, the poverty—all the misery shown in the work of the Weimar painters—the desperate whores and ugly fat cats of Otto Dix's paintings, Grosz's amputees and maimed war veterans—where was all that in her story? How many lies had she told the patient? Or to herself?

Suddenly my chest began to reverberate. *Doom-bah, doom-bah, doom-bah, doom-bah.*

Someone shouted at me, Come on up, Pops! Come on up!

What was happening? Where was I? I had been lost in my own thoughts, and now I looked up to see an open balcony, the source of the *doom-bah* rhythm pouring down upon the street. The sign on the balcony said "The Metro," and it was from its second-story patio that the shout had come. A dense crowd of men filled the patio, all of them naked above the waist but for something crisscrossing their chests—leather straps studded with metal, I saw.

Come on up, Pops! yelled the voice again amidst hoots and whistles and proffered beer bottles, and men bumping hips and groins.

Where was I? I asked myself again, wheeling around and back until I found the street signs above the three-cornered intersection: Market, Noe, Sixteenth Street.

You're in the Castro, old man! came the voice, as if understanding my confusion.

The Castro. Yes. I had walked out far enough to have entered "the Castro," the "gay Mecca," as it was called, a district I had not visited before nor had intended to visit now. I looked down at my watch. Eleven-ten. At midnight, the "owl service" would begin on the N Judah line, at which time a bus would be substituted for the streetcar, using a route I did not know. I should ask someone for the nearest tram stop, I told myself, and ask soon. I continued walking outbound on Market toward Castro Street itself, where there was a great crush of people, among whom, surely, would be someone who could direct me to the N Judah.

But when I turned the corner onto Castro, I was so amazed by the scene before me that I forgot my intention to ask after the streetcar. It was as if I had entered yet another city, this one inhabited by lumberjacks, cowboys, leathernecks, roughriders, policemen, firemen, musclemen, bikers—such was the demeanor of the hundreds of men (thousands?) who thronged the street. As I tried to negotiate the sidewalk, I was thrown from store window to gutter, into groups of lean, bare-chested men, then into ones covered in leather; next set amidst youths in tight T-shirts and jeans; then put shoulder-to-shoulder with stout, half-naked, extremely hairy men; and so on through the many types, each expressing such a stark and heavy masculinity that my senses were assailed with odors of maleness—now sweaty, now cologned, now something I could not identify but which seemed concocted of leather and tobacco and the chlorine of ejaculate. I thought, I must get off this sidewalk!

At that moment, a bar door opened and I was swept inside by the crowd.

Deafening music assaulted my ears. It was dark but for strobing blue lights, which revealed the bar's inhabitants in epileptic flashes. So displayed, each face suggested menace—a false impression, I struggled to see, as it was soon clear that this bar catered to the milder tight-jeans-and-T-shirt types—but a suggestion clearly intended by the establishment, which had painted the walls black, and the floor black, and had illuminated the back bar with the sort of red one imagines as the color of Hades. Many eyes turned toward me. I did not belong there, they seemed to say. And I very much wished to leave—desperately wished to leave!—but again a scrum of bodies swept me along, and I soon found myself pressed against a stool at the far end of the bar.

I turned a shoulder in an attempt to slide through the crowd. And before me was a face that stopped me as if I had been turned into a pillar of salt. My dear student! I thought.

I looked into the face. I could see it only in blue flashes. Was it he? As the lights blinked over him, I looked at the eyes: childish rounds. At the body outline: slim, still adolescent. No! It could not be he! See! This youth sitting here does not know me, and besides, my dear student could not possibly be here, now, in San Francisco. He had returned. He had completed his "pilgrimage," he said. He was back at the university. No! It was not he!

I pushed my way through what seemed a wall of flesh; was cursed at and elbowed and scoured by nasty glances; and finally reached the street.

I fought my way back toward Market Street. But as I approached the corner, I remembered that I did not know where I was going. It was nearly midnight. Where was the stop for the N Judah?

Before me, as if magically, was the most improbable of stores: a bead shop. I all but shook my head in disbelief at seeing this slip of a shop on such a street. Supplies for stringing necklaces and bracelets and earrings. Was this truly here?

The shop was empty but for an elderly woman, who sat upon a stool behind a vitrine filled with beads of various descriptions.

Can you please direct me to the nearest stop of the N Judah? I asked her.

Oh, yes, she replied in a sweet voice, going on to say that I should cross Market Street and go uphill until I passed a hospital on my right. Then, turning right, I would find the stop on Duboce, just below the crest of the hill.

It is the last stop before the tunnel, she said with a smile. But you had better hurry, dear. You'll want to get there before the owl.

Her way of putting this—that I must get there before the owl—seemed to say that a dark, winged creature would descend upon the tunnel at midnight. And in that mood of dark enchantment, I hurried across Market Street as directed, then marched up the steep hill leading out of the intersection.

The night overtook me: the dunnish sky, its metallic dome, the cold of the fog. The higher I climbed, the more empty became the streets, until I seemed to be the sole creature about. Even the hospital, as I passed by it, appeared stilled and shut. Then, just as my good witch had predicted, I came to Duboce. I turned right, and glanced down the hill: She had not deceived me.

The platform was deserted, its lights enswirled in fog. My watch said 12:05, but I put aside my panic by reminding myself that midnight referred to the time when the last car left downtown, and surely it would need more than five minutes to travel this far outbound. I stared into the maw of the tunnel, at the dark outline of the hill rising above it, then back at the street, my eyes following the line of the tracks until they, too, were surrounded by fog.

When suddenly out of the mist swam a police cruiser. It slowed as it neared me, stopped. The officer riding shotgun gave me a once-over, and I felt guilt drip from me like the condensing fog. I am the one who did it, I thought, whomever you are seeking, whatever the crime. Then I saw him mouth "Zodiac."

I began to shake; I thought I would fall down. A rumble rose from the tracks. Something creatural wobbled toward me: the one-eyed light of the streetcar. It screeched to a stop; I climbed aboard the too-bright car; the doors shut behind me. I saw the police cruiser drive off.

The streetcar entered the mouth of the unlit tunnel, its stone walls painted black. At moments, the tram lost its electrical connection, and we rode in utter blackness under the hill.

Finally we emerged at Cole and Carl, the first stop at the other end of the tunnel, on the west side of the hill. We had left the world of the Castro. From here, we would ride farther and farther away from the gay bars, into more respectable neighborhoods, where families huddled in their apartments and houses, worried over jobs and budgets, struggled against the stagnation and dereliction that had been visited upon our country, carefully locking their doors against the serial killer who was still at large.

At that moment, I thought of the patient and my dear student, and I ached with envy. They belonged to the wild world of San Francisco: to their very own Weimar of danger and carousing men and marvelous strange girls. Whereas I did not belong in the Castro, nor was I welcome at A Little More; and neither was I respectable, proper, productive. I have no family, I thought, no firm connections. I am dross, a castoff. Only the crows know what I am.

78.

Two days slouched along at a dilatory pace. My mood was not improved by the fine fall weather that descended upon San Francisco, the very air betraying me with its fresh feel of a new semester. I could not help but remember my feelings at that time of year, the hopefulness of beginnings, the happy sight of students holding books they had not yet read but soon would. And I felt how far away I was, banished, haunted by the eyes of the boy in the bar, the round childish eyes in the strobe of blue light.

Then my loneliness grew teeth. My only defenses were thoughts of the patient. I told and retold myself Michal Gershon's portrayal of her early life in Berlin, like a bedtime story one reads to a frightened child, a story that must be repeated exactly with each retelling. In this way, I suppressed my suspicions about Michal's version of events—closed my gimlet eye upon them, as it were. Otherwise, if I persisted in my skepticism, I would find no comfort in the tale.

At last came Wednesday. Finally the session began. And a great tranquillity settled over me, for the story resumed: The patient was back in Tel Aviv. There she was to see her mother again, the mother I had helped her find. The scene was Michal's little house, the patient told us, a room we had not previously visited: a small dining area that adjoined the kitchen.

79.

The table was too big for the space, said the patient to Dr. Schussler. It was a big, heavy mahogany table with ornate legs. It had to be shoved into a corner to fit into the room, and the chairs on two sides were pinned between the table and the wall. Michal sat at the foot, where she could look out the window, and I sat catty-corner to her again, my chair nearly under an arch that separated the dining room from a small kitchen.

It was an odd arrangement because Gerda, that young girl, was sitting in the kitchen—right next to me but not "in" the room, if you know what I mean. She sat on a high step-stool with her hands on her knees, just sitting, staring forward. That loud clock I'd been hearing hung above her head. I was uncomfortable because I still didn't know what the relationship was between Michal and Gerda, who seemed to be a sort of servant or maid.

(Ah! I thought, one of those German youths doing penance in Israel.)

Michal began by saying: I suppose we now must leave the "before time."

She looked at me steadily, so unblinkingly that I could barely meet her eyes. There was something accusatory in that gaze, an accusation that *I* was the one making her leave the "before time." *I* was the reason she had to remember all this. It was all *my* fault. And it was clear why she never wanted me to find her. She wanted to leave behind everything that happened to her, and I was part of that "after" life. And again I went through my whole inner drama: wanting to protect her from bad memories, hating myself for wanting to protect her, and so on. But before I could get to the anger—the rage, it was almost there, that impatience that explodes into fury—you know what I mean, Dr. Schussler?

I do, said the therapist.

Before it came flying out, Michal suddenly softened. She gave me the sweetest smile. That loving look came onto her face. So, my little American, she said. Do you know any history? Do you know when Hitler came to power? When the Nürnberg Laws were passed?

I was confused by this sudden shift in feelings. Again. Just like the day before: hate, then love, any moment hate could come back. I mumbled something like, Early thirties.

And she said to me, good enough. Hitler came to power in 1933. The Nürnberg Laws were passed in 1935. There wasn't a Jew in Europe who didn't know that something terrible was coming.

Then Michal reached into her pocket and took out a coin. She held it by the rim, between the thumb and forefinger of her right hand—squeezed it hard, moving it back and forth, pressing grooves into her fingertips. It was a funny gesture, administering a little pain to herself, it seemed, like the pinch you give yourself when you're getting a shot. All during this time—you'll hear it on the tape—she picks up that coin, cuts grooves in her finger, then slaps it down on the table. Picks it up, slaps it down. Let me start the tape.

There was a long hiss, and finally, above the annoying drone of the poor-quality machine, came Michal Gershon's beautiful voice.

Let us be clear, Michal was saying. I am only going to talk about what came just before the war, and what came after, where you are born and enter the story. Understand that. The middle, the Holocaust—too long, too dark, too many endless things to say. I would like to start just as you enter the story, but you cannot understand the "after" unless you know something of the time just . . . before all that. Do you agree?

What choice do I have? asked the patient.

Michal laughed.

None.

My parents left in 1938, she continued on an intake of breath. The whole family left. Only I remained.

Where did they go? asked the patient on the tape.

To the Netherlands, Michal replied. Then she stopped speaking.

The tape whined and hissed for fifteen long seconds. One could hear the ticking of the clock that hung in the kitchen. It seemed that all Michal Gershon's resistance to remembering her "after" life had been distilled into those sounds: the clock tick, the machine drone, the sinister whisper of the tape.

Then came a loud clack—the coin slapped down on the table? Yes, that must have been it, the slap signaling Michal's determination to continue. For now her words tumbled out in a monologue:

They went to the Netherlands, she said. They were sure they would be safe in Amsterdam. Such a mistake. The Dutch are still seen as such nice people. They get a "good rap," as the Americans say. And all because of Anne Frank. The world thinks the good Dutch people hid her. Ah! But they also betrayed her. Consider that the Germans needed only two thousand soldiers to keep the entire country subdued. The Dutch police did all the work. Eichmann himself was dumbfounded at how easy it was: at the willingness of the good Dutch people to turn over their Jews.

She laughed.

My parents rented a house on the Prinsengracht, she went on. On the canal. They settled in. They received funds from—I'll get back to that. I'll just say that all seemed well for while. Then . . . the roundups began. Roundups of the Jews, done with the quiet but thorough compliance of the Dutch police and bureaucracy. What else could they do? the good Dutch people told themselves. Poor us! We are conquered! Well . . . My parents were rounded up early. They were too prominent, too visible.

For a while, I still received letters from them. They tried to be reassuring. They said at first they were only going to be resettled. Then that they were "only" going to a work camp. Finally I received a strange, cheery postcard that said, We are resettled in a lovely valley.

She paused.

Then nothing, she said. I never found my family again.

I turned off the tape at that point, the patient told Dr. Schussler. Michal stopped speaking for a long time, and in that silence, with the clock ticking away madly over my head, it seemed somehow wrong to keep the recorder going. I didn't dare say a word or ask a question, because Michal's face had fallen in on itself again. She picked up that coin and pressed it hard, then harder; I could see the tendons flexing. Finally she cleared her throat and said:

Anne Frank was sent to Bergen-Belsen.

This startled me and I said:

Did you see her there?

She gave me this terrible look.

How naïve you are! How stupid! By the time I got to Belsen, Anne Frank and her sister were stinking corpses in tattered clothes, half returned to the earth.

I just sat stunned, the patient told Dr. Schussler. What could I say to that? The clock ticked, Michal said nothing, and Gerda shifted around on her clanking stool.

Finally I thought to ask Michal:

But how is it you stayed in Germany when your whole family left?

Ah! she said, with a long breath. Then she gazed out the window for some seconds. Finally she turned her cool light eyes on me and said:

Start up again your little machine.

Now comes the first part of the story.

80.

My grandfather was a smart businessman, said Michal on the tape. He understood the firm was about to be "Aryanized"—stolen from us. So he and Dieter Gerstner, one of his plant managers, came up with a plan: I would marry Dieter's son, Albrecht. I would convert. And the firm would be assigned to the Gerstner family, good Catholic Germans since the dawn of time.

I should say that I once loved Albrecht, in the romantic way, when we were in *Gymnasium* together. He was fair-haired, tall, athletic: a quite beautiful man in the Germanic sense, which was also my ideal. I truly believed that such a blond god of a man was superior to the dark Jews who lived in the Scheunenviertel district, who had been filtering in from the east, from Poland and Russia. They were uneducated, poverty-stricken. I was embarrassed by their horrid black hats, their ugly clothes, their poverty—yes, I was embarrassed to see the naked face of Judaism in those people.

Don't be shocked. We all felt that way. We were, after all, the Rothmans, rich and cultured and fair-skinned. Look at my hair, my eyes. Many of us were like this. You could not tell us from the most Aryan of Germans. Even Hitler said so. Ha! So perhaps that is why I did not protest my grandfather's plan too very strongly. Maybe that embarrassed part of myself, stupid girl that I was, welcomed it: my chance to *be* German, not German of Hebrew heritage, but simply a German German.

She laughed, sighed, called out for more tea and whiskey.

Then there came the sound of the coin slapped on the table.

The patient stopped the tape.

Gerda rattled dishes behind me, said the patient to Dr. Schussler. And I sat there, again seeing myself through the eyes of my birth mother— through the eyes of the woman who bore me. I was too Jewish! No wonder she gave me away. I nearly laughed out loud. I thought it was only my WASP mother who could feel this way.

If not for Gerda standing over me with a sweet smile, I think I would have run from the house and never returned. But events have a way of keeping you in rooms you wish to leave, don't they? Just when you think

you've had enough and are going to run away, right then normal life—
teacups and creamers, two sugars or one—cement you in place. And you
have no choice but to say please and thank you and just go on with what
you hate, the life you'd like to abandon, the people who don't love you
and you'd like to leave.

I went ahead and took my tea. Michal took hers with a shot of whiskey, and then I turned on the recorder.

So I converted to Catholicism and married Albrecht, said Michal.
The conversion was not at all taxing. By then the priests had had a great
deal of practice converting Jews, and were all too happy to capture another soul about to marry into a Catholic family. I agreed to read three
books. I learned four prayers in Latin. I was tested in a recitation of the
Credo, which of course I already knew from all the great choral music of
Mozart and Beethoven and so on. The priest prayed over me. I accepted
the trinity of God, Jesus as God's incarnation on earth, the holiness of
the Virgin Mother. The sign of the cross was sketched above my head. A
little sprinkle of holy water, and it was done. I was now Maria. And then
I married and became Maria Gerstner, wife of Albrecht Gerstner.

(Ah! I thought. There you are, my little German Jewish convert. My
elusive Maria G.)

Well, said Michal, sighing. Grandfather executed all the paperwork
to assign the business to me and Albrecht and Albrecht's father. Then
my family packed up and left. My mother, father, sister, uncles, aunts,
grandfathers, cousins—everyone went to Amsterdam.

There came the sound of tea being sipped, once, twice.

Weren't you sad when they were all gone? the patient asked her
mother. Terrified? Desperate?

There was a long pause, then:

Yes.

Michal clacked down her teacup.

Albrecht's father, Dieter, had worked for my grandfather as a plant
manager. He was not an educated man but a shrewd and ambitious one.
At first he acted as if he were honored by my grandfather's trust in him.
Because, after all, it was all based on trust. Dieter, Albrecht, and I may
have been the legal owners, but the understanding was that three-
quarters of the profits were to go to Grandfather in the Netherlands, for
further distribution to our exiled family. Look at it: The Gerstners received our magnificent house and one-quarter of our esteemed and very

profitable firm, and for nothing, making them richer than they ever could have imagined in their dreams.

But Grandfather did not realize the hatred the Gerstners had nurtured over the years. And most of all, he underestimated the effects the Nazis were having on even the most moderate of anti-Semites. Dieter Gerstner, under all his pretenses of faithful service, was a nascent Jew hater who came to full bloom, shall we say, under National Socialism. He resented our family's wealth. The wealth had been honorably earned. *Mein Gott*, Rothman Textiles made fabric for the Kaiser during the war of fourteen-eighteen! Nonetheless, as soon as my family was gone, that rat Gerstner began making comments about "Jewish theft" of Germany's resources, about "Jewish cunning" and "Jewish pollution of the race." Each time he would look at me accusingly, as if I had polluted *him*, despite the fact that *he* was the thief.

There came a long pause.

But I did not see all this from the outset. A strange kind of normalcy reigned in the household. Each Sunday, I covered my head with lace and knelt down before the great crucifix. I listened to the prayers intoned in Latin and the sermons thundered in German. I endured the incense. I took communion. I went to confession and lied.

After six months had gone by, Herr Gerstner proudly bought tickets for a performance at the Deutsches Opernhaus Berlin—the opera house.

By then all the Jewish players had been banished. And Goebbels, that puny propaganda minister, had forbidden the staging of any works by Jews. Most of the talented conductors refused to participate and left the country. But that traitor von Karajan stayed—he later went on to world renown, as if he had never collaborated, the hands that held the baton now cleansed. He was conducting that night, Mozart, *Die Zauberflöte*. Officials of the Reich marched in and filled the first row. As one, the audience stood, thrust out their arms, and roared: *Sieg heil! Sieg heil! Sieg heil!*

It was at that moment that I understood the life that lay ahead of me. There I was, standing in the balcony, my arm out, feebly, covertly resisting, I thought. My dear father-in-law watched me closely from the corner of his shrewd little eye, and I had to mouth the words and hum softly to add some sound: *Sieg heil!* Then I sat through the performance. In the end, I stood and applauded with everyone else.

So began my double life.

Then she called out: Gerda! *Mehr Tee!*

Und whiskey? asked Gerda.

Ja, mit whiskey.

Again Gerda stood above us, said the patient after stopping the tape, that apple-cheeked young woman cheerfully bringing the teapot, the cups, the sugar, the creamer. Michal didn't say anything, prolonging the rituals of sugar and cream and stirring, it seemed. Once she had a teacup cradled in her hands, she looked at me and went on:

I should tell you that Albrecht truly loved me. He was a kind and good man, and I could be myself only with him. He was very brave; he withstood the great danger that he would be declared a *Rassenschande*, a race defiler. He defended me against the barely disguised slurs from the extended Gerstner family. We both agreed we would just let them talk, not answer back. We decided I would behave like a good Catholic: go to church with a headscarf, kneel and cross myself. And like a good German, heartily shouting *Sieg heil!* when the occasion called for it.

She was silent for several seconds, drinking her tea, then said:

All right. Time goes by. I pretend to be Maria Gerstner, and my family is still thriving in Amsterdam. I don't know if Dieter sent all the funds he was supposed to send, but whatever it was, it was evidently enough.

Then . . . then. May 10, 1940, Germany invades the Netherlands. Hitler bombs the hell out of Rotterdam and threatens to do the same to Amsterdam. The Dutch surrender in five days.

Now come the roundups, the letters from my parents, finally that strange, cheery postcard. We are settled in a lovely valley. Dieter stops sending funds to Amsterdam. I saw that he was happy about it. Now he owned it all, except for me. If only I did not exist. It was the thought I saw in his mind every time he looked at me: How can I get rid of this one last Jew?

Now comes another terrible year, 1941. The Nazis slowly begin "cleansing" Germany of its Jews. But the full force of Hitler's death machine does not take aim at us immediately. Regulations strangle us. We cannot use public transportation. We cannot have certain professions, then we cannot work at all. Jews are wearing yellow stars. Not I—I was a convert, protected by my marriage to an Aryan. I walked the streets of

Berlin and saw my former schoolmates, my old friends, their families, wearing the yellow star. And they looked at me.

The patient stopped the tape.

Michal said nothing more for a long while, the patient told Dr. Schussler. By the changes in her breathing, and the twitches of her eyes and mouth, I could tell she was remembering the scene. I could not imagine what she felt at that moment when she stood there, protected, and everyone she knew from her life as Margarette Rothman walked by wearing the yellow star. I hoped she would go on and characterize her feelings, but she was shut up tight.

The patient sat quietly for some seconds.

The hour is almost up, isn't it? she said.

Almost. A few minutes more, said Dr. Schussler.

You're a German, said the patient. How do you sit and listen to all this? What do you feel when you hear it?

Ah, that is not the point, said the doctor. The question is how you feel.

Right, said the patient. You'll never tell me. But I'm not alone in the room, and knowing who I'm talking to is pertinent in this situation. I'm not asking, Did your mother love you? I'm asking how you, as a German, think about the events of the Holocaust.

(Yes! I thought. Demand to know!)

Dr. Schussler sat back and sighed before answering.

I am a human being, she said, and of course there will always be things in my patients' lives that will evoke personal reactions. However, whatever my thoughts and feelings, my every concern is for your well-being.

(Liar!)

Can you see that? asked the therapist.

I suppose.

And whatever personal reactions I may have, the doctor continued, if they interfere with our work together—if—it is then my task to manage such issues. My task, not yours.

I see, said the patient flatly.

(She suspects, I thought. Good!)

All right, said the doctor. Let us resume on Monday night.

81.

For five days, I looked forward to the confrontation between the patient and Dr. Schussler: She must learn her therapist's bias! But then again I wondered: Could it be that the patient did not really wish to know the details of her therapist's life? I thought back to my own therapies and remembered how, in many ways, I wanted the analyst or counselor or doctor to be little more than a blank wall. The therapist who insisted that we had a personal "relationship" was the one I detested most. So perhaps the patient, too, would be content to remain ignorant of the doctor's private life.

These ruminations were interrupted by a letter.

It came through the mail slot in an odd fashion: alone, many seconds before the other mail, as if it had frightened away the advertising circulars. I saw the Gothic typeface in the return address. The silver seal above it. The motto: *Per Aspera Ad Astra*. I knew it at a glance: the university's stationery.

It was a thin envelope. Only one sheet inside, it seemed. Therefore it could not contain a firing, because surely any such action would be accompanied by documents requiring signatures, including my own. (I laughed to myself as I considered how this reasoning was the opposite of that used by university applicants, who knew to be happy at the sight of a thick envelope, the sign of acceptance, and to feel dread at a thin one, the one-page letter of rejection.)

I put the unopened letter on the kitchen counter and could not bring myself to so much as touch it. The sight of the boy in the bar, now this letter: I felt that the university had begun to stalk me, had followed me to San Francisco, where I was a different person, I longed to think, a loving friend to the patient, a good man. As the days went by, I convinced myself that a thin envelope could indeed signal disaster, was perhaps a note saying, "You are fired. Paperwork to follow." So I left it lying there amidst the embedded greasy remains of food whose preparation had preceded my tenancy in the cottage.

By Sunday night, I felt my resistance falling. The patient's session was but one day away. I convinced myself that whatever the effect of the letter, I would be returned to health by the sound of my dear patient's voice. I could pull her life over my head like a blanket covering (smothering, superceding, replacing) my own. Therefore I might open the letter and subject myself to whatever fate was contained therein.

It was late, nearing one in the morning. The traffic on the Great Highway was sparse; the ocean seemed tame, perhaps at ebb tide. My own breathing was the predominant sound in the house.

I went to the kitchen and opened the letter.

This is to inform you that the Professional Ethics Committee has taken up your case. Investigations will proceed through the fall semester. The Committee hopes to complete its work before the start of the spring semester; in any case not later than the beginning of the 1976–77 academic year.

As you have been interviewed previously, your participation is not needed at this time, and you should not expect further communications from the Office of the Provost until the matter is resolved. However, the Professional Ethics Committee may, or may not, keep you apprised of their progress, as they deem appropriate.

Sincerely yours,
Bill Selyems, for the Office of the Provost

What kind of special torture was this? A committee that may—or may not—see fit to keep me informed. An investigation that may be completed within a semester—or an entire calendar year! What was the point of this letter except to remind me that I had been hung by the neck. And yet provided with a tiny footstool that might hold my weight for a time—then any moment be kicked away.

I paced throughout the night, realizing I had underestimated the potency of the letter, underestimated how much hope—in the very back of my being, before the patient, before anything that had happened in San Francisco—how much of my future depended upon the university. Oh, God! I called aloud. Oh, someone! Oh, something! Show me there is a reason for my life! I should have opened the letter late on Monday, I told myself, not on Sunday night; for now I had to endure an entire day before I might receive the medicine of the patient's voice.

I closed the curtains. It was a gray day, and I managed to sleep. I awoke at five in the evening; ate a sandwich; went to the office and waited. She was all that could save me, I thought. She must distract me from whatever was (or was not) happening at the university.

And thanks to God (or to whomever, to whatever Providence might or might not exist in the universe), here she was finally, not confronting Dr. Schussler, not demanding to know the details of her doctor's life, abandoning that battle as I had thought she might. Instead she resumed her story right where she had left off: in Michal's little house, where she sat with her mother in the dining area that adjoined the kitchen, at the table that was too large for the space.

It seemed as though we had been sitting there for hours, said the patient to Dr. Schussler, although less than an hour had passed.

82.

Michal was telling me about her friends who now wore the yellow star, the patient went on. About having to walk right by them. She was afraid to associate with them. Her father-in-law watched her constantly, she said. He never said it exactly, but the implied threat was that if she did not behave herself, if she brought even a whiff of Jewishness into the family, he would somehow force Albrecht to divorce her, and then she would be on the next train to Auschwitz.

Some of her old friends and acquaintances tried to go underground. U-boats, they were called, after the submarines. They tried to disappear, blend into the woodwork, pass as regular Germans, helped out by sympathetic non-Jews. She was terrified when she ran into one of her friends who was not wearing a star—terrified that her recognizing them would give them away. Because everyone knew she was an ex-Jew, and her knowing them would be suspicious.

The patient clicked the recorder on and off, on and off, cueing the tape. When it played again, we heard Michal saying:

Slowly they all disappeared. All the old friends and acquaintances, with and without the yellow stars.

Then came a long pause.

And as all this was happening, Michal continued, I just went about my life as Frau Gerstner. Frau Maria Gerstner.

Dieter Gerstner barely let me leave the house, she continued. I should describe him. A very undistinguished-looking man. Short and stocky, with a pockmarked face under a brush of thick, light-brown hair. He was not an Aryan god of a man. Albrecht got his good looks from his mother, Swanhilde, who was beautiful but a meek, weak person who ceded to her husband in all things. Dieter was a brute. One day he walked into my private dressing room unannounced, without knocking, stood looking me up and down, and said: Beware, my son's fake little wife. The race laws are changing, and you are not as well off as you think you are.

What relish he took in reporting this.

Until then, being married to an Aryan was enough to make me *privilegiert*, to give me privileged status. But now the most privileged

Jewish women were those who had children with their Aryan husbands. It was not enough just to be married; you had to have a child.

That night, Albrecht and I decided I would become "pregnant." We didn't want a child. We agreed we didn't want to bring children into the world as it was, and we were very careful in our sexual activities. But we had to pretend I was pregnant. And then I would have a "miscarriage." If necessary, I would get "pregnant" again.

So began our subterfuge.

My father-in-law had filled the house with spies. He wanted to be sure I was not secretly being a Jew—as I explained, for fear of losing the company. So the servants watched me constantly. I had to hide all evidence of menstruation from the maids. I had to be careful not to stain the sheets. Albrecht carried out my bloody cottons hidden in his briefcase. After three "dry" months, we announced I was having a child. One of my old school friends was a doctor. I told the family he was my physician, and luckily for us, he did not live close by and was not part of the Gerstners' circle.

The Gerstner family threw a big party for us, which was exactly what Albrecht and I had hoped for. All Dieter's friends in the Party now believed I carried the child of an Aryan. So I was golden! Nothing could touch me now.

I had to begin "showing," so I bought a girdle that was too large for me and filled it with stuffing. I was terrified that Marta, the housemaid, would find it. She afforded me no privacy. She went through my closet, my drawers. I still believe she stole my mother's cameo. She wanted to come and help me dress, help me in the bath, and it took all my conniving to keep her from seeing my naked body.

Albrecht and I then determined it was time I had a miscarriage. We waited for my next menstrual period, and I purposely stained the sheets. It was quite a scene as I held the bloody sheets up to Marta and cried over the lost child. I really did manage to cry. It was not hard to find in myself great sadness and desolation.

This meant, of course, that I was now childless, and vulnerable, so Albrecht and I made quite a deal of the fact that we would try for another child immediately, as soon as it was medically safe for me. I had to present myself as an Aryan vessel-in-waiting, a walking womb about to be filled any day with a good German child. My father-in-law's dear friends in the Party began making jokes about when I would become pregnant again—didn't I know it was my responsibility to the race?

So I soon became "pregnant" again. My whole life was subsumed by this subterfuge. And poor Albrecht, there he was carrying off my bloody cottons, my stained underwear, in his briefcase, finding ever more clever excuses to take a ride in the country, where he could bury the evidence.

There was a pause, then a command in a cold voice:

Turn off that machine.

She called for Gerda to come help her, the patient told Dr. Schussler. She wanted to stand, move around, take a walk, she said. Gerda came and, with Michal leaning on the girl's arm, they walked toward the front door, then out into the courtyard.

83.

The sound quality was poor on the next part of the tape. One could hear the cries of children, a faint rumble that might have been passing trucks, but mostly one heard the wind rushing across the microphone.

Albrecht had been my hero, Michal began. My rock, my only true companion. The only person on earth with whom I could express my feelings and my fears. And of course we were bonded by the drama of my "pregnancies," my supposed desperation to be what a good German woman should be: a mother.

The wind lashed at the microphone. What she said was not clear, until she said the word "sick." Then:

Pneumonia. In those days it was not like now, where you take some pills, go to bed for a few days, recover. Albrecht's lungs had never been strong to begin with; he had suffered from asthma as a child, and was always a little wheezy.

Again the wind overcame her words. What one heard next was:

. . . to the car. Fainted in the street. It was the fever, you see. He was running a high fever, although he told no one. I heard Marta cry out, and I looked out the window to see Albrecht sprawled out on the pavement. Next to him was his briefcase. And I remembered: He was carrying away my bloody underwear and rags! Marta ran out the door, and I had to race behind her, not only because I was afraid for Albrecht, but also to get that briefcase before Marta could put her hands on it.

She paused. The shouts of children rose in the background, the *boink* of a ball bouncing.

Finally she said, I had to go to the briefcase before I could go to my husband.

Another pause.

Which I did. And then I nursed him, as best I could. He was all to me; I was in terror of losing him. Gerda, *bitte* . . .

And the wind took away the rest of the sentence.

The patient stopped the tape.

Gerda helped Michal take a turn around the courtyard, said the patient. When Michal sat down again, I asked her what happened next.

He died, she said. Just like that she said it, very flat: He died.

Then she said nothing for a long while, just sat there, vaguely looking at the children, as if her thoughts were far away.

I asked her to go on.

And she said, On? What else is there to do but to go on?

She laughed.

Here is the part where I am caught.

84.

It was Albrecht's funeral, said Michal as the tape resumed. There were very few of us at the graveside, just the immediate family, a few cousins, a friend or two of the Gerstners.

I felt lost, desperate, was sobbing, having only Albrecht's mother, Swanhilde, for support, otherwise I really would have fallen into the grave with him.

Suddenly Swanhilde tightened her arms around me. I followed her gaze to the edge of the graveside circle. Two men—Gestapo. With them was a woman, her arm linked with one of the men, hanging on him like a gang moll. She wore a wide-brimmed hat, but you could see a swirl of gold hair peeking out. And her eyes: just visible below the brim of her hat. The eyes.

I knew at once who she was; we all knew who she was: Stella Gold-schlag, "the blond poison," notorious traitor. A Jew. She was a "catcher": she hunted down other Jews for the Gestapo. They promised, if she co-operated, that her parents wouldn't go to Auschwitz. Ha! Later her parents were taken anyway.

And staring at me: those terrible hunter's eyes.

I nearly fell. I grabbed on more tightly to Albrecht's startled mother. I watched as Stella pointed me out to one of the men. And he came toward me. Marching. I couldn't believe it: Were they going to take me away directly from a burial? Were they that callous? Of course they were, I answered myself.

The Gestapo officer grabbed my arm and said, Come with me.

Then Frau Gerstner said, What are you doing?

It was not like her; she was usually so meek; but even she could not believe what was happening. And she said again, What are you doing?

The officer said that I was no longer *privilegiert*. With Albrecht dead, I was now just a Jew like any other. A Jew by blood. And Swanhilde, sud-denly brave, answered him back by saying: But she is carrying my son's child! She is pregnant with a good German child!

I nearly fainted. Oh, God. A child.

Michal stopped speaking; the wind rushed into the pause; there came the sound of something tapping, perhaps Michal's cane against stone. After some seconds, she resumed, her voice lowered, flat, drained.

I got away that day, she said. But now I had to keep the subterfuge going. But how long could I do it? I was already supposed to be four months pregnant. I would have to begin to "show" again. I had managed to keep my girdle, but the stuffing had been thrown away, and now I had to smuggle in some stuff, bit by bit, in a handbag. Without Albrecht, I had to find a way to dispose of my menstrual pads, again in my handbag, which became stained one day, a stain I had to explain to Marta as a cut on my hand. But there was no cut.

It was inevitable. My spirit had already surrendered. One day, while I was in the bath, Marta broke in—broke the flimsy lock on the door. She saw the girdle, the stuffing. She reported me to the Gerstners.

I must tell you this scene, she went on. We are in the great drawing room in which my mother once held her salons. Dieter calls me in. Frau Gerstner is there, Marta is there, and her husband, Hans. Dieter says, You cur! You liar! There never were any pregnancies, were there?

It must have been all arranged, because right then the officers were ushered in, and I was taken away.

There was a long pause. On the tape, the patient then asked, Where did you go?

I was taken to Theresienstadt, then to a labor camp in Poland.

There was another long pause.

And what happened to you there? the patient asked.

I told you, said Michal. We would not discuss this part. Nothing happened to *me*. It was nothing about me, personally, as a human being. The point was to humiliate us and take away our personhood. What happened to me is what happened to everyone.

But you survived, said the patient. I think it's . . . heroic.

Michal laughed.

Heroic! That is ridiculous. All I had to do was convert and have my husband protect me for years, while the Jews of Berlin slowly disappeared. If he had died a year earlier, I would be another rotting piece of flesh in some mound in Poland. Heroism! Living through that time had nothing to do with my heroism. The heroism was all my dear Albrecht's. He endured the taunts of his family. He defied the race laws. He kept me alive.

The tape whined on, as if empty. The patient clicked off the machine.

She made me stop taping, she said to Dr. Schussler. Gerda helped her up, and they started back to the house. At the doorway, Michal turned and said to me, Come back tomorrow, and I will get to the part where you come in. After the war. To Belsen.

85.

To Belsen, to Belsen. The words rattled in my thoughts in the rhythm of a rushing train. I was the one who had gotten us here, on that train hurrying to the site of the patient's birth. And what awaited us?

I did not fall asleep until the sky was brightening; I awoke past three o'clock in the afternoon. I am not certain why, but I switched on the battered radio my landlord had left me, something I rarely did, since, as I have said, its defective tuner drifted along the dial. I must have wanted to hear a sound, any sound, to vanquish the words that had installed themselves in my mind. *To Belsen, to Belsen.* Through the static came bits of traffic reports, sports scores, commercial advertisements, weather forecasts; when suddenly there came the jangle of a fake teletype, then a man's excited voice shouting:

Bulletin! Bulletin! Patty Hearst captured!

After which the voice, the fake teletype, the news reports, the ads, all drifted off into the static storm.

I tried to retune the station but succeeded well enough only to hear "fugitive heiress," "FBI," and "house in the Outer Mission." I rushed out to a nearby electronics store, where televisions normally were tuned to each of the five stations received in the area. All the channels had interrupted their normal programming, their announcers excitedly reporting the story.

The newspaper heiress Patty Hearst, who had been dragged screaming from her Berkeley apartment some seventeen months ago by a group calling itself the Symbionese Liberation Army—its motto "Death to the Fascist Insect That Preys on the Life of the People"—who apparently had joined forces with her captors, taking for herself the nom de guerre Tania, banding with them in a bank robbery and murder (appearing on security cameras sporting an assault rifle and looking rather jaunty in a beret)—the fugitive Patty Hearst had been captured by the FBI.

A month earlier, there had been a shootout in Los Angeles between the police and six members of the SLA, and all six group members had been killed, either by bullets or as a result of a fire that had been started by police tear-gas canisters. Patty Hearst's reaction at the time was to send a tape saying that the "fascist pig media" had painted a distorted picture of her "beautiful brothers and sisters." Now, however, when the FBI came for her, she walked out quietly, saying, "Don't shoot. I'll go with you."

The late edition of the *San Francisco Examiner* (her father's newspaper) reported that Patty, upon leaving her arraignment, raised her handcuffed hands in the black-power salute. Her hair was died a brassy red. In an AP photograph taken through a car window, the top half of her face is obscured behind large, tinted aviator glasses. But her mouth dares you. The lips are drawn back to form a perfect triangle; the lines of her even white teeth exposed, upper and lower—a shark's smile, a mouth you would not want to see swimming toward you out of the depths.

The story of Patty Hearst had fascinated me—it was one of the few news events I had followed while in San Francisco. How could I not? How did this heiress to the Hearst fortune, granddaughter of the legendary scoundrel William Randolph Hearst, she who was set up for a life in high society—how did she go from kidnap victim to the rifle-wielding "Tania"?

And how had the transformation been achieved within fifty-nine days? For that was the mere slip of time between her capture and her first communiqué saying she had joined forces with her captors. Was a person so malleable? Could sweet Patty, engaged to a wispy man with the unfortunate name of Steven Weed, be swept away so easily, so quickly?

Or was Patty Hearst one of us, her fate already inscribed within her, an inheritance from her notorious grandfather. Perhaps that shark's smile was always there, merely waiting for a salty sea.

86.

The patient returned to Michal's house as directed.

So now we come to the time after the war, said Michal's voice on the tape. As we agreed. Just before the very end. Where it was supposedly all over.

Mother and daughter sat in the same upholstered chairs they had occupied the day before. It was early morning, the patient told Dr. Schussler. The room was in shadow. Without light, it was cold, smelling of ancient damp from the stone walls.

There were rumors that the German army was in retreat, Michal continued. The skies were filled daily with bombers, and from the look on the faces of our torturers there was suddenly—how shall I put it? Suddenly they looked like men and women in whose dark minds something had lit up. I don't mean their consciences. I mean they knew they were going to be punished. The effect was for them to hate us all the more. Because one day we were useful to them, doing things they wanted done. Then—I cannot give you the exact moment—then suddenly we were . . . evidence.

But where were you? the patient interrupted her mother. In what camp was this?

I told you it does not matter! Every one of us went through the same thing, internally, the ripping-out of every shred of self-respect. What is this constant need to retell the stories in horrific detail? That child frozen. That woman experimented upon. That man electrocuted. All the many ways humans can be humiliated. Why tell everyone how to do this! It is practically pornographic. Yes! It's pornography to keep disclosing exactly what was done.

She had been ranting; now she was breathless; she said nothing more for several seconds.

All I know is this: One day I was called to an assembly and immediately pushed onto a train. It was a regular passenger train, but we were packed in, so that no one could move. People were sick, emaciated, exhausted, many half-naked—all jammed in together.

I cannot tell you how long that trip lasted, she continued. When you have to remain on alert at every moment, time stands still, is a constant present, and duration has no meaning.

Eventually the train stopped, and we were ordered to march down a road. Ahead I saw barbed wire. I thought: another imprisonment, yet another. The guards pushed us through the gate and left. No one led us to a barracks. No one said when food would be given. No one ordered us to do anything. We were just left there.

Nothing, not even the labor camp or the transport, could prepare me for what lay before my eyes. At least the camp had had rules. There were boundaries, duties, orders, lists. People were used up systematically. The evil was deliberate, conscious, human.

But here . . .

Before me there seemed to be a field of corpses. Arms, legs, feet, heads protruding from the mud. Wisps of cloth, the remainders of clothing, shivering in the breeze.

Then I saw the blink of eyelids, the tremor of a hand. And I realized there were still living people among them—no, not living exactly. Here a man, there a woman, sitting, staring, vacantly, not turning a head, not a shred of attention for us, the new arrivals, we who had been tossed in among them. They simply fell, as if their joining the dead were inevitable. A process that began with being dropped into the camp, sitting down in exhaustion, falling to one side, dead.

I do not know how long I stood there. But suddenly there was a commotion at the gate. Shouting, screaming, then gunshots—shots fired into the air. Burly guards, not in German uniforms, came rushing toward us. They spoke Hungarian, a language I understood. And after the scene had quieted down, one of the guards came over to me. He stared at me, looked me up and down. His eyes slithered over me like an anxious Midas counting his possessions. *Neck, breasts, belly: all mine.* And then he circled me, once, twice: a snake sliming around me. And then he said—slowly, I will never forget it—he said:

You are as fat and rich and yellow as a big stick of butter. And I want to lick you.

Michal paused. The tape wound on. There was a cough, a sniffle—was she crying? Suppressing tears?

Then she laughed.

Do you know how hard it is to learn Hungarian? It has no relationship to Romance languages, none to Slavic languages. I stood there with the stupidest thought. I thought: I wish I did not understand what that man had just said.

He took me to his barracks, where he raped me for the full day. No sense describing it. It was like all the other rapes, all the other times I had to give up my body to survive. Yes, I slept with them all: guards, inmates, kapos, jailors, kitchen help, it didn't matter. You see, because I was taken later in the war, and had done what I could to keep eating, I still had breasts. Real, full, suckable breasts. Among all the skeletal women, there I was with two round, soft breasts. What gold I had in them! What I could not exchange for sucks at those nipples!

Finally he brought me food. Then he kept me for two more days, raping me and, in between, feeding me. It was only because of him—and my breasts, and I had those only because Albrecht had kept me safe—for those reasons I am still alive. Outside there was no food, not even any water, as my tormentor kept telling me, saying how lucky I was he had taken me. A typhus epidemic was raging. Hundreds were dying by the hour. See? he said. Compared with death, what is being here with me?

On the third day after my arrival, I was alone in the barracks— locked in—and I heard the rumblings of heavy trucks, maybe tanks. I was afraid it was the German army, and they would come into the camp and just shoot us all. These rumblings went on for some time—hours— then a loudspeaker came on with a screech of, what do you call it, feedback. A howling screech of feedback. And then a big booming voice said:

Ihr seid frei!

You are free, said the patient.

Ah, said her mother, at least you understand a little German. Yes, the voice said we were free.

So it was April 15th, said the patient. The day the British liberated Bergen-Belsen. The day of your liberation.

Liberation! said her mother. You Americans, with your idea of *liberation*. Sailors kissing nurses in Times Square. Ticker-tape parades down Fifth Avenue. Happy families moving to Levittown. How glorious for you to be the victor with not a speck of damage to your homeland. Oh! Has there been a war victor since Rome in which the winning armies went home to such a pristine land?

She paused.

Liberation, she muttered, then fell silent.

87.

At that, the therapeutic session ended, early, for reasons I did not know. The church carillon was not yet done sounding the three-quarter hour when doctor and patient went their separate ways.

The next days proved difficult. Thoughts of the university, of my banishment, swept through my consciousness at what seemed to be regular, four-hour intervals. There was nothing to do but endure it, since, as I have said, such internal processes had a way of suffusing themselves throughout my body, leaving me with as little control over them as one has over glucose absorption, for example. My sole relief was the anticipation of Monday night's session, the continuation of Michal's story, its effect upon my dear patient.

I therefore arrived on Monday during Dr. Schussler's evening break, which she normally observed between 5:00 and 6:30. Her custom was to return no later than 6:45 to receive her three late-night clients, the patient being the last of these.

I sat reading a professional journal for perhaps an hour (by flashlight, of course, for fear of revealing my presence to Dr. Schussler), when I was startled by a sharp rap on my door.

I had no idea who it might be. It surely was not Dr. Schussler, whose walk I would have recognized in an instant.

The rapping came again.

Be calm, I told myself. Whoever it is will go away.

Yet again a fist rapped at the door.

Quiet, I told myself.

Now came a pounding upon the thin center panel of the door—so forceful that I feared for its tender fruitwood.

I saw you come in, said a man's voice between two bangs on the door.

Who saw me? *Who was watching me?*

I know you're there, said the voice.

Who is it? I felt compelled to answer.

The manager, he said. I must speak to you.

I opened the door a crack to see a very short man with bulging eyes—but he was not the manager as I had known him!

270

Are you new? I asked him.

What do you mean? he replied.

I do not know you.

Of course you know me, he insisted. You negotiated your lease with me.

Now I believed I must have lost my mind, because I was certain that I had never before seen this odd-looking man, who, as I examined him further, became stranger yet, with his wild eyebrows and mouth twisted down on the left side. Surely I would have remembered such a creature. In his right hand he held a lit cigar. He took a long draft, then blew foul-smelling smoke into my face.

Let's go inside, he said.

I felt there was nothing to do but comply.

Hey! he said upon taking a step into the office. Why are you sitting in the dark?

My eyes, I said, extemporizing. A medical problem. I must use low-level lighting else harm my eyes.

He hummed. I feared he would flash on the lights. But happily he remained standing in the opened doorway.

This won't take long, he said.

Yes? I asked.

I need to inform you that we're moving your office, he said.

What? I all but shouted.

Move you. Downstairs. Same footage, same orientation, just down a floor.

I thought my heart would stop. Move me? I thought. Away from my dear patient!

How is this possible? I argued. My lease term runs through August.

The man who may or may not have been the manager said, Look at your lease.

What should I see there? I asked him.

He reached into his back pocket, from which he retrieved a sheaf of folded paper. He opened it, held it toward the hall light, and pointed at a paragraph.

See here? he said. It says we have leased you Room 807 *or compara-ble space.*

I leaned over. I tilted the sheaf of paper to catch the light. My God! The words were actually there!

But are you sure this is the same as my lease? I asked him.

Look, fella, he said. This is the deal. The guys next door want to expand into your space, and I can do it by moving you downstairs. They've been here for ten years, you only since last summer, and I'm obligated to accommodate my long-term tenant if I can. And I can. Anyway, they've already got your room number.

What was he talking about? Who had what number?

See, your room here used to be 805, he said, stabbing his lit cigar at me as he spoke. Those guys originally occupied it, and when they took the larger office next door, they took the number with them. And then this room didn't have a number. So we gave it 807.

He laughed.

So you see, you are not even in your own room's number! Which was supposed to be 805. Look, you move down to 705, since, as I said, 05 was the original number of this line. And the guys expand to fill their original 805, which is now your 807. Then goodbye to 807, since it will be part of 805, its original number. Done. Everyone has a space, everyone has a number. End of story.

I stood swaying; I reached out a hand to my desk to steady myself. Yes, all this taking of room numbers had been explained to me when I first engaged the space, but I never believed it could be forced upon one. Forcefully taken from one space and moved to another! Numbers marching behind like a retinue!

Then I should be in 707, I said, reaching for an argument—any argument—in my favor. At least I should be able to retain the 07!

Sure, said the man with a laugh. Why not? If you like playing James Bond, keep your 07. There's no 707 at the moment. Sure. If that's what it takes, we're done.

No! I thought. *We could not be done. This cannot happen.* But what could I do? Argue with him further? I had to get him gone before Dr. Schussler's return.

May we discuss this tomorrow? I asked him.

I don't know why, replied the man.

You see, I cannot move, I said. I absolutely cannot change offices!

But you said. That 707—

I am in the midst of a project. And any interruption of the sort you suggest will ruin my work and cause me to miss a deadline. Material harm! I lied. You will cause me material harm!

I paused, and thought it would be best to add:

I am begging you, sir. Surely we may find another solution.

He hummed again, puffed on his horrid cigar, and finally said:

There is some possibility—possibility—that the architects on the other side of the engineers are moving. In which case, the engineers might . . . Well, we'll see. In any case, even if we take your room, I can give you ninety days, at least.

Ninety days from—?

From the first of next month. See? That gives you nearly three months and a half.

I thought of all that must happen in the patient's life, and how I might have to leave her in three and a half months. I nearly wept as I stood there.

In any case, the man went on, I'll let you know . . . lemme see. The architects have to give notice by . . . lemme see . . . end of October. Yeah. October 31st.

At that he turned and left.

Not thirty seconds later, Dr. Schussler's footsteps sounded in the hall.

88

The patient settled into her chair, and we soon heard Michal's voice saying: I was locked in. That Hungarian beast—he left me locked in.

I could hear people shouting in every language. The roar of heavy trucks, or tanks. I kept pounding at the door, Let me out, let me out, in every language I spoke: German, English, Polish, Hungarian, Czech, Slovak, Russian. But people kept running past me; there was too much noise for anyone to hear. This went on for hours—I don't know how long. Hours. The announcement *"Ihr seid frei"* had come in the afternoon. And from the cracks of light around my door, I thought it had come at three o'clock, maybe four. All the while, the shouting kept on, the heavy treads—boots, I thought. Eventually the light faded: twilight came, then dark.

Something momentous was going on—what?—and there was nothing for me to do but shout "Let me out!" until I was hoarse, until I had no more energy, until I sank down exhausted by the door. Then, sometime after nightfall, I heard shots—pistols? rifles? machine guns? This terrified me because I could not know who was shooting, who was being shot, what new terrors lay outside my locked room, and now I wanted to stay where I was, thinking myself safer inside than out. No sooner did I have that thought than I heard pounding at the far end of the row of barracks, then scuffles, a man's voice shouting in Hungarian "I had to! I had no choice, they made me, I had to!" Then a shot and a thud, and the voice was stilled, and I knew what was happening: the now-free prisoners were looking for their former guards, and executing them.

I kept hearing doors being kicked in, one after another, each time coming closer. A second guard was found in his quarters, and shot; then another door was splintered, and another. I took off my kerchief, opened my coat, unbuttoned the top of my shift, stood with a hip out—anything to make it clear at a glance that I was female. Because most men, not all—most men, no matter how evil, will hesitate before killing a woman. Something in the bones and blood says no, speaks more quickly than even the desire for revenge. So there is sometimes a moment, the merest slip of a second, during which one might turn or lunge or shout and somehow fool death one more time.

They destroyed the door of the room next to mine. Then they came to me.

I shouted, in the highest voice I could manage, a wail, a puppy-dog cry. Either they did not hear or their thirst for killing had closed their ears. They heaved themselves against my door, once, twice. With a crack, the frame gave way. And they tumbled into the room.

Three men, one rifle, pointed at me.

Hungarian whore! shouted the man with the rifle, in Polish.

Kill her! shouted the second man, in Yiddish.

I had my hands up. No, no, I am a Jew, I said in Polish, then in Yiddish. No, I am a Jew!

Liar!

Shoot her!

We were all shouting at once, and I thought I would be killed in all the confusion. I could smell their bloodlust—they had just come from killing, and they smelled of it. Any moment the trigger would be pulled, inevitably—I nearly laughed that I had come this far, survived this far, only to be killed by fellow prisoners—really, such a thought went through my head. They kept shouting "Hungarian whore!" and "Kill her!" They were shaking. Possessed. Hungry for revenge. I kept repeating, I was raped! He took me and kept raping me! Finally I yelled out, Do you want me to show you the damage, the bruising, the blood?

They fell silent. In that terrible moment I realized I had put the wrong thought in their heads. I could see in their eyes that they did want to see the damage, wanted to undress me, that they were imagining . . . And I thought, Oh, God! I am going to be raped again, but this time gang-raped, a fate I had managed so far to escape.

Then a voice outside the room shouted in Yiddish, What's going on in there? And someone pushed his way into the room.

He wasn't a big man, but there was something powerful about him, his solidity, his bearing. He stood with his back very straight, holding a rifle. His eyes were dark, and as he turned intently to each of the men, he seemed to draw all the light out of the room and into his eyes—what little light there was, so that it seemed to grow even darker around us— which put a sort of spell over the other men. Their emotions were suddenly rearranged, calmed, flattened. The rifle pointed at me fell. All three men turned to this new man. And in measured voices—thank God! I thought; they sounded sane—in measured voices, in Yiddish, they discussed me. Was I a collaborator, a kapo, a whore?

The man who had just walked in—he was clearly a leader; the others were deferring to him—turned to me and asked me what I was doing there.

I told him my story, in broken Yiddish—the one language I understood but did not speak well. I told him my story, that I had come on a transport, had been taken immediately by the guard and raped for three days, that I had heard the announcement *"Ihr seid frei!"* in the afternoon, but had been locked in, wondering—afraid of—what was happening. Then these men . . .

He said nothing for a long time, seconds, which seemed to me a pause in time itself, a cavernous room in which my fate was being decided. No one moved. I could hear the men breathing, their breath almost echoing, so vast seemed this hole in time.

Then he suddenly shouted, Let her go! Then: Let's go!

The three men left. I pulled my coat around me and was about to go out the door when the leader said to me, Stay close. Things are very . . . the word he used meant something like "fluid" or "boiling."

I followed him down the row of barracks. I heard gunfire, shouting, screams. We turned this way and that, and I could see there were crowds ahead. I had no idea where all those people had come from, they looked like prisoners but healthier, not the living corpses I had seen. I didn't know then that there was another part of the camp where conditions were better. I only knew that there was a great surge of bodies pushing in all directions, and I struggled to stay close to this leader, this haunting man with his rifle and his penetrating eyes.

We turned a corner at the end of the barracks. The back of the structures had these sorts of eaves, and the barracks were arranged in a line, maybe fifteen, maybe twenty. From each eave hung a body.

Kapos, said the leader in my ear.

We continued on, the leader forcing his way through the crowd, but in a way I found almost magical, because in all that bedlam, he did not push or shout, only touched people and spoke into their ears—or maybe this is merely the way I am remembering it. Because the entire crowd was in a mood as murderous as the men who had forced down the door of my barracks-prison, shouting, Get the kapos! And, To the kitchens! And, Feed us, you bastards! Everyone was shouting. People all but trampling one another in the crush forward, which I soon understood was the way to the kitchen and pantries that had fed the soldiers and guards.

All at once, we were being raked by machine-gun fire. Everyone was screaming. I saw people start to fall—a machine gun was raking the crowd, starting on the far side of the space in which we were caught, a kind of plaza in front of a large building. There was something horribly synchronized about the way people fell, one section after another, dominoes falling, one area and then the next around the plaza: people shrieking, bloodied, downed. I looked up to see where the fire was coming from—it is a stupid reaction but irrepressible; something deep in your nerves wants to know, *Who is killing me?* I looked up, and I saw, standing on the roof of the building, a guard.

My guard. And at that moment, he saw me. And, for a shaved speck of a second, he hesitated—took his finger off the trigger. Because once they rape you more than twice, something in them adopts you, as a sort of pet, or at least a belonging, a possession. They make some animal connection, even if it is only disgust, or dominance, or a desire to prolong the time of possession. He saw me, my face, my body, the body he had owned, dominated, violated—and, for a mere skip in the progression of time, he backed off on the trigger.

I ducked. Beside me, the leader ducked. And everyone in our quadrant—no, not a quadrant; what do you call the smallest slice of an area? Everyone in our tiny angle also ducked. And was saved.

That shaved second now over, the machine gun resumed its raking to the right of us: the screaming and the falling and the dead.

The leader, next to me, stood and aimed his rifle. A miraculous shot! My guard fell dead.

Was that the one who took you? the leader said into my ear.

How did you know? I said in my broken Yiddish.

He only smiled and said, You saved my life.

89.

How did he know that? said Michal. Among all the things one could say after such a narrow miss with death: Why that? Why the belief that I had saved him?

I never knew. I only knew there was some . . . potency about the man, some aura that made him seem more than real, charmed. You will see this in all the stories of us survivors: improbable moments like the one I just described, events that turn on luck, on nonsensical holes in the fabric of logic, tears in reality itself. Otherwise, if we had followed the inevitability of normal events, one thing expected to follow another, the way the world works most of the time, we would be dead. There would not be that moment when the guard hesitates. The disgusting tenderness the tormentor feels for the object of his evil deeds—it could not exist. A small, compact man should not be able to take aim with a standard-issue rifle, and, with one clean shot, kill the man determined to kill us.

But so it happened, and we lived.

She paused.

The rioting went on for three days, she continued, her voice now striding on in a faster cadence. Hundreds died by gunfire. Meanwhile thousands died from typhus, from starvation. The kitchen was raided, and people could not be stopped from stuffing down everything they could get their hands on. But their bodies could not digest it all. Many choked. They died. Death by eating—who could imagine such a thing?

The British gave us aid, yes. But they also betrayed us. They had made a deal with the Nazi officers. The Germans did not surrender outright. Instead, the camp had been declared a "neutral zone," and inside it, the Germans and their Hungarian guards were allowed to remain armed. Armed! The British army's excuse was typhus, confining the epidemic to the camp. But typhus isn't spread person to person. Lice spread it; to people confined to lice-infested buildings, like ours. The purpose of the guns was to keep us locked up, to shoot us if we did not behave.

And we did not behave. I should say it was the leader, and those he led, who formed the disciplined core of our misbehavers. I cannot un-

278

derstand how they did it, but within hours of the British soldiers' arrival, they had captured weapons, taken up positions, gained control over parts of the camp. Who were these men? I asked myself, because I had never before seen such Jews: warlike, organized, tough. They were Polish Zionists, I learned, with lifelong commitments to creating a Jewish state in Palestine, and they had spent all their days training to take it by force, if necessary. These were the men who went on to organize the camp, who eventually joined the Irgun and Hagganah—the Jewish militias that fought the British and the Arabs in Palestine—and who now run Israel: these same warlike, organized, tough men. Whatever Israel is or will become, we have inherited their warrior nature.

She laughed. And look at the trouble it has gotten us into, she said.

There was a long pause.

All during the rioting, she continued, I tried to stay close to the leader. He kept stopping to take aim at the rooftops, where the Hungarians still patrolled, meanwhile trying to calm the half-mad prisoners who were starved and parched and desperate for help, telling them where to assemble, where to find food and water, whom to ask for when they got there. Somehow everyone believed him and trusted in him, and he knew how to express himself with his eyes, his hands, his body, and people did what he told them to do. And I, too, did what he had told me to do: I stayed close. I stuck myself at his side.

So we came to the evening of the third day, Michal went on. At twilight the camp seemed to be stilled: no more gunshots, no more mobs. I had stayed with the leader all this time, and on that third evening we found ourselves in an empty barracks. There was no forethought: Suddenly we grabbed each other. Desire simply exploded from somewhere deep within us. One moment I was overcome with the realization that I was free—my God, free! Alive!—and the next my body demanded its pleasures. Sex! As battered as my body was, I wanted it, wholly, completely. I ached for it: sex, life, which at that moment seemed the exact same thing. The act was quick, hurried, fumbling, greedy. But it was sex. With desire, the first sex I'd had with desire since . . . everything.

She laughed.

And then he simply buttoned up, walked out, and told some passing men where the food-distribution point could be found.

She paused at length; the tape machine droned on.

Weren't you upset that he just left you? the patient asked her mother finally.

Oh, no, said Michal with a laugh. Not at all. I admired it, admired him. His charisma, his sangfroid—you do know what that means, my little American ignoramus, *sang-froid?*

I'm not an idiot, the patient replied to her mother.

Of course, said Michal.

And I don't appreciate your calling me an ignoramus. Yes, you went through a great deal, but still: That doesn't give you the right to treat me as if I'd spent my life on a marshmallow.

A long hiss of empty tape followed. There was not a rustle, not a cough. How surprising was the patient's sudden expression of resentment! How long had she been sitting there chafing at Michal's mild derision, which I had thought almost affectionate?

The patient on the tape broke the silence and said: The leader you're talking about is Yossele Rosensaft, isn't it?

A sudden rustle and thud: Her mother jumping up in her chair?

What do you mean? said Michal. How do you know about Yossele Rosensaft?

I told you, I'm not an idiot. I told you I did research, that I read about Bergen-Belsen. And so of course I'd find out about Yossele Rosensaft. And your description fits him: compact, charismatic, steely.

No! said her mother. It wasn't Rosensaft. Not him! There were other leaders. He wasn't the only one.

So which one was my father? the patient asked her mother. Rosensaft? Another "leader"? The Hungarian guard? Some kapo right before you were put on the transport? Maybe even someone on the train? Don't you think I can do the math? Math, the one thing you know I'm good at. I can count the months from April 18th, 1945, the third day after liberation, and get close to December 26th, 1945.

She paused.

My birthday.

90.

Another long silence ensued. The recorder whined; the tape hissed. In the therapist's office, neither patient nor doctor moved.

Then a faint sound emanated from the tape, which might have been a whimper—whose?

Finally there was a cry, and Michal's voice saying:

Oh, my dear! Can you forgive me? I am describing events I have not even allowed myself to think of for many years. Of course you would want to know who your father was. It is natural, yes. Natural that you would want to know.

The tape stopped with a click.

And did she finally tell you? asked Dr. Schussler.

Tell me—?

Who your father was.

No, said the patient. She wept. She said she was sorry she didn't know, couldn't know. That I had it right. There were four men she had to have sex with right around the time of my conception—and the one man she did want, the "leader"—and she could not be sure which was my father. She kept weeping. But I did not apologize for making her cry: one victory at least. I didn't "take care of her feelings." I let her cry. And after a while she looked up, her eyes puffy, her cheeks wet, her beautiful skin slicked with tears, and she asked again if I would forgive her. And if I could leave and come back the next day.

She paused.

I did, and I left.

We only have a minute, said the therapist, but did you believe her? That she really doesn't know?

I did then. But now . . .

Now?

I still think that when she saw me for the first time, she was stricken with a bad memory. She saw in me someone she didn't ever want to see again, or someone who hurt her deeply. It couldn't have been her sister that she saw in me—you're right. She would have cried with delight if I looked like her sister.

She paused.

So I'm probably the child of some rapist. Or else of a hero, maybe Rosensaft. Or maybe not.

Does it matter?

Of course it does.

What difference does it make? It does not change you.

Dr. Schussler's voice had slipped into the tone that invariably tells the patient, The hour is over.

91.

Does it matter? Does it matter who your father is? Your mother? Who are the exact people who dropped their blood into the container that is you?

The patient and therapist had come to the dreadful nub of the matter, the awful question that had haunted my soul since I had become a conscious being at twelve years of age; the question that had hovered over the patient since the moment she had tried, and failed, to defend her declaration *I am not adopted! I have mysterious origins!* For if it mattered who had spawned us, and mattered too much, I was doomed; and if the patient's unknown and unknowable ancestor possessed the sort of genes that predominated, resonated, indeed conquered all opposing chromosomal challengers—everyone knows of such individuals, whose unlikely red hair, for example, reappears generation after generation—if her father were of that variety, she was consigned to a lifetime of fearing what resided within her: the heart of a rapist? A hero? A brute?

Tuesday morning I awoke with the feeling that something was wrong. I had a sudden, strange headache. And when it passed, I noticed that the edges of things were more rounded than they ought to have been. The window frames were bowed, the doors had gone concave. The light was dusty, chalky. The base of my skull went numb, as did the bridge of my nose: such odd places for numbness (my nose!) that I feared my brain sensors had become hopelessly scrambled, and it was really my leg that had fallen asleep and not the bridge of my nose.

I reacted as I have in the past to these sorts of events: with an attempt to resume normal activities. I went to get myself a glass of water. (I do not know why a glass of water is always offered as a cure for strong sensations, but so it is.) However, on the way to the kitchen, I noticed a rug out of alignment. Tugging it straight required moving the chair that stood upon it. As I did so, I noticed a tear in the cushion fabric that had been mended with strong tape, and I left the cushion upended while I searched for the special tape the landlord had provided. I went opening drawers to find the tape and came upon a file for which I had been searching over days and weeks. I opened the file and tried to read a paragraph but noticed that the paper, too, had become bowed in shape, which caused me to remember the water. But on the way to the kitchen once more, I felt the need to straighten a window shade. But what about the crooked calendar that hung on the wall?

I stopped. I looked about. The rug, the chair, the drawers, the calendar, the window shade—the litter of my obsessions.

I sat down and held my head in my hands, hating the very fact of my existence. For I was caught, once again, in the spider's web of compulsion. And I did not know if, on this occasion, she would eat me (so to speak); that is, did not know when this particular episode would end, if the night in its entirety would be spent picking lint from a suit jacket, or perhaps I would be doing so into the morning light, perhaps into the days ahead. And even as I pondered these questions, I felt my eyes wander to the trash that had to be put out that night, a task interrupted by the thought that the landlord had not paid the scavenger bill as he had promised, a thought that in turn was interrupted by the idea, once again, that I ought to have a glass of water. It was as if I were trying to write a sentence and had become distracted by the thought of the em dash, and why not an en dash; and why must the question mark contain a period, implying finality, when all one wishes is a momentary pause for doubt or wonderment (the question mark should be placed here, but I do not want it!); that is, if one tried to write and became seized by what creates, shapes, and ends sentences—thereby making it impossible to write; or, applying the metaphor, to live.

In this state did I pass the night—all the long hours until the patient's next session.

Wednesday morning dawned. The attack was yet in full form. My arrival at the N Judah stop was something of a victory in itself, the entire house ransacked in search of a missing quarter for the fare.

As I rode downtown, a terrible question came to me: What was about to transpire in the room toward which the streetcar was ineluctably carrying me? What would happen in the therapeutic hour that was rapidly approaching? *Does it matter?* Patient and therapist would inevitably return to the question. And everything hinged upon the skill of the therapist. If she did not guide the patient well! If she could not help her cross the river of blood ties! If she could not lead her to a self-created existence! Oh, God, if I should lose my icon, my champion, what would I do? Shout? Tear open the door? Threaten the therapist? Harm her?—

A screech. The streetcar stopped at Market and New Montgomery. The doors opened; I stepped down. I approached the building, and the gargoyles seemed to mock me: You wish to avoid something? they seemed to say. Why, then, come up here and hold the roof! Similarly did the cherubs roll their eyes in hilarity at the sight of me: What a loser! they chuckled. You'll never make it!

Not even the white purity of the marble could wash away the dark influence of my affliction. It seemed the crows had gained entry, had gotten past the podium without its guard. I had become one of them, I thought; I carried darkness everywhere; no one could escape me (so melodramatically had my nervous condition taken hold of me). Elevator cars came and went. If I did not step into one soon, I would miss the patient's session.

The cab seemed to float upward to the eighth floor. All the while my anxiety rose with it: What if I should lose my last protections? The protection of the patient, all that stood between me and the spider who even now legged her way toward me? What if, upon hearing the patient's voice, I remained unchanged, unbecalmed, still the dark creature who might descend upon her? *Her! Her! Her!*

92

Convince me, said the patient to open the session. Convince me it makes
no difference if my father was a monster.

(Yes! I thought as I heard her statement. This is exactly what you
must demand from the therapist: exoneration from the very nature of
your ancestors. Fight for yourself! Fight for us both! Make Dr. Schussler
do for you what she cannot do for herself: escape the evil of a father.)

Said the therapist:

Let us put the tape aside for the moment. Do you agree?

Yes, said the patient. Funny. I didn't even bring the recorder today.

Good, said the doctor. So we both know what is the work for today:
the question of your father. So let us return to the thought with which
we ended last time. I asked, What does it matter if your father is a hero
or a brute?

Right. That's where we ended. And I said it matters.

And I was about to say that it matters very little, except as one thinks
about it.

What do you mean, thinks about it?

What I mean is this: Your father, since you cannot know him, is
therefore a thought, an idea, a feeling. And the thought, the idea, the
feeling, is something we can talk about, a subject about which your
opinion may change over time.

(Yes! I thought. Excellent work, Dr. Schussler!)

Humph! came from the patient. If Michal is my mother and I don't
look like her, then I must look like my father. I have *inherited* my body
from him. It is not an idea. It's in my *body*.

But what is in your body that predicts your behavior? You have been
alive all these years, become the person you are. If you were to find out
your father's identity tomorrow, what possible difference could it make?

(Oh, no! The doctor had made a terrible mistake with that "possible.")

Possible difference! the patient cried out.

(As I feared.)

Possible! That's exactly the point. The probabilities and possibilities
I have inherited from my father. Inclinations to respond one way or

another. Temperament. My physical reactions. How do I know what's hiding inside me, genetically? Given some jolt to my system, some extraordinary pressures, how can I know what might explode out of me? Bravery? Selflessness? *Brutality?*

But why on earth would you become brutal? asked the therapist.

Look at what happened to Patty Hearst.

(Ah! I thought as I listened. She believes as I do about Patty Hearst.)

But that was purely a product of confinement, replied the therapist, a set of severe social pressures which produce temporary—I repeat, temporary—psychological changes.

Oh, that's just some drivel from Hearst's defense team, said the patient.

(For that was indeed the line of defense her father and lawyer had begun to promote.)

But it is a real effect! said the therapist, nearly shouting.

(Most unusual behavior from the therapist.)

Two years ago, there was a bank robbery in Sweden, Dr. Schussler went on in a more subdued tone. Employees were held hostage for six days, during which time they became sympathetic to their captors, even rising to their defense after the robbers were captured and the employees were released unharmed. Since then, psychologists have studied this very closely.

Maybe they were accomplices, said the patient.

Not at all, said her doctor. Captivity, complete and enforced separation from regular society, fear of harm and death, a perverted social norm: These combine to coerce almost any sort of behavior in a human being. We are social creatures, born helpless. Our survival depends upon our living within a group. And our entire psychology is based upon that need: to be accepted within a society. So this has a very powerful influence upon behavior.

But some people resist.

Rarely. Given enough separation from other influences, almost no one resists. You know the Milgram experiment.

The one where they gave shocks.

Yes. Perfectly decent people, kept isolated, willingly administered to an unseen person what they believed were deadly shocks.

So what you're saying is, I shouldn't worry about my father because we are all brutes.

Potentially. Temporarily.

A long pause followed. The therapist shifted in her chair, again and again, as if uncomfortable in any position.

All right, Dr. Schussler, the patient said. You've proven to me that any decent person can become a brute. But are there any studies that show brutes becoming decent? Becoming heroes?

The doctor sighed and softly laughed.

Is there any evidence so far in your life that you are a brute?

Silence.

No, the patient answered finally. Of course I've been rude at times, insensitive, but no, there's nothing particularly brutish about me. On the contrary, I think I'm too meek. That I don't go up against things. That I haven't seized life and turned it to my will. That I don't even have a strong will.

Nonsense, said the doctor. You defied your parents when you went to Wharton. You defied convention by being a woman in the financial world. You have truly defied convention by being a lesbian. *Gott,* you have even resisted the norms of that demimonde! Do I have to recite any further risks you have taken? How much you have not conformed? How much internal bravery this implies?

(Bravo, Dr. Schussler!)

So if you are descended from a hero, the doctor went on, you have his bravery. Well and good. If from a rapist, you have certainly found a different way. As I said, What does it matter which one was your father?

The patient inhaled time and again, as if stopping herself from saying one thing or another. Then she said at last:

Yes. But you can't help but thinking. Can't help but wonder who he was.

Of course, said the therapist. You will always think about it and wonder over it. It is part of your history, and quite an unusual history at that. I imagine you will tell many stories about it as you meet people over the course of your life. But I don't think you necessarily have to *feel* too much about it, if you understand my distinction.

I think I do.

It is an interesting and distinctive fact about you, but says nothing—

About who I am now.

Then good. We have done our hard work for the day. Of course I suppose we will have to go over this—

Over and over, said the patient with a laugh. Back and forth. Many times. Retreat and forward again. Yes, I think I'm now getting how all this works.

There was a long silence, then again came the patient's laugh.

Ah! See? she said. I still have something left of my mysterious origins.

93.

Miraculous! The therapist had done her job! Dr. Schussler had separated the patient from her father—returned her to the mystery of her origins and the mysterious creation of herself! I nearly cried. I did not think
Dr. Schussler had it in her, indeed that any therapist could be effective
in this manner, and I instantly regretted that I had quit all those analysts, doctors, counselors, social workers—perhaps too soon?

The therapeutic discussion continued until the completion of the
hour, but, with the climax of the session behind them, patient and doctor were languorous, like lovers after sex.

Yet I grew increasingly uneasy. I kept hearing her mother's denial of
Rosensaft's paternity, a denial that seemed ever more absurd as I replayed
the scene in my mind. Why had her mother dismissed it so very ada-
mantly, so oddly (come to think of it)? Perhaps Michal did indeed believe
that Rosensaft was the father, and she did not want the patient to seek
him out—wanted to keep Rosensaft out of the patient's life and her own.

But was any of this true?

If Rosensaft is her father, I thought, then the patient was right: She
would have to look like him. But did the patient (as I thought I knew
her) look like Yossele Rosensaft (as I had seen him in news photos)?

No, I answered myself. They looked nothing alike.

Then came another invasive thought: Had I ever seen the "real" patient? That lovely woman who emerged from the elevator the day my
angelic guard detained me: Was that glowing vision truly she?

Which reopened the question of Rosensaft's paternity: Perhaps the
actual patient—whom I had never seen—had indeed inherited Yossele
Rosensaft's inner and outer substance.

All of which led back to the original question: Does it matter? Does
anyone's father, especially an absent father, make any difference at all in
one's life?

Then I knew I had not escaped my spider. For I found myself spin-
ning like a wrapped fly, stuck in fruitless, circular, obsessive ruminations: I must know who the patient's father is! I thought. To which I
replied (to myself), No! It doesn't matter who the father is. Yes, it does

matter (I contradicted myself). Maybe Rosensaft truly is the father. And the patient should seek him out, learn more about her origins. No! She should retain her sense of mystery! Of self-creation! It doesn't matter if he is the father! Then again, perhaps it does matter?

Suddenly the therapist's voice broke through my chain of thoughts.

Remember that you will always wonder over your father, she said to the patient.

(As if she could hear my obsessions!)

This is normal and inevitable, the doctor went on. The best approach is for you to allow the thoughts to arise yet not become *attached* to them. Do you understand?

(Help me understand!)

Yes, I think so, said the patient.

Have the thoughts, and let them go, said the therapist.

(Let them go. Let them go.)

If you try to suppress the questioning, you will only strengthen your attachment to fragments of "evidence," and you will come to "certainties" which most likely will be false. So, neither suppress the questions nor—

Become too attached to them, said the patient.

Yes, said the doctor.

(Just let the thoughts circle. Just let them be.)

We must end here, said Dr. Schussler.

I know, said the patient, rising from her seat.

As she did so, the night seemed to rise up with her: the doorman's taxi whistle with its yearning cry, a truck thundering by, a man happily shouting, See you soon! It was as if we were suddenly lifted up from a deep cave, from its permanent crepuscularity and gloom, and returned to an ordinary, normal night.

The patient left; the sound machine resumed its play. As the elevator doors closed in the vestibule—with their *shuss*, like a mother's calming sound—I felt that I had indeed been released, that the doctor had freed me from the spin of my own mind; may God bless her!

And so my thoughts were free to turn to the next session, to Wednesday, to actual happenings: to Maria Gerstner's story. Which had been suspended at the point at which "the leader" had buttoned up his fly and left her, and she had admired him nonetheless; at the moment when Maria was about to begin her life in a liberated Bergen-Belsen—the patient already growing in her womb.

94.

There had been no Monday-night session. Dr. Schussler had communicated this change of schedule during the langorous part of their last meeting. A seven-day separation might have panicked me. But not now. I was stronger—the doctor had becalmed my mind.

The patient did not set the scene on the tape. After some brief chatting at the opening of the Wednesday session, she simply clicked on the machine and said: Here is what happened next.

I am not sure how I survived the next few days, said Michal's voice on the recording. I was on my own from the moment . . . after the encounter I described to you.

By the fifth day, she went on, the British had imposed some order on the camp. The dead were buried in mass graves—tossed in with bulldozers—just as everyone has seen in the magazine pictures. But if you have never seen anything like it before, you can search the depth and breadth of all you have ever learned about language, and you will not find a word or a figure of speech, or a form of rhetoric, to help you pronounce in your own mind what you are seeing.

Said the patient: The BBC radio reporter called it "the worst day of my life."

Did he? asked her mother.

Yes.

Well, her mother replied as if tossing the word over her shoulder. Maybe for him.

The tape went silent, as if empty, unrecorded. The machine whirred on, for five seconds, ten. There was a cough, probably Michal's. After which Michal said:

Then there was a miracle.

95.

I sat on the ground in a quiet corner of the camp, Michal continued. This is still the fifth day, I'm talking about. Twilight approaching. But overhead and to the east, the sky was still a clear blue. I could not remember the last time I had simply sat and contemplated the arc of the day.

Then I heard murmuring. At first I thought it was an hallucination, a product of my senses suddenly awakened to the possibility of the loveliness. A murmuring and whispering like the stir of dry grass. But there was no grass anywhere. And then I really did believe the sound arose from my imagination, which frightened me. Maybe this was an early symptom of typhus. Or of starvation, since I had eaten so little, like everyone else.

The sound became a sort of chanting interrupted by shouts, and I was not sure if I should run away or find its source. My desire to know overcame my fear. I walked toward the center of the camp, the direction from which the murmuring or chanting or shouting seemed to be coming. Finally I went around the side of a building, to a large open space, and it took me a long minute to understand what I was seeing.

A group of men, maybe forty of them, stood tightly together, with shirts or rags or coats covering their heads, rocking on their feet, sometimes bowing slightly and abruptly coming upright. To their left stood a group of women, of about the same number, also packed tightly together, also with their heads covered, not rocking like the men but looking down into their hands. I had not been to a synagogue in decades, and even in the days when I was still a Jew, the practices were foreign to me. So not even the sight of a man with a blue prayer shawl could explain what was happening before me. I understood only when the entire group's voices rose up in unison to chant:

Shema, Yisrael!
Adonai Eloheinu
Adonai Echod

The single Hebrew prayer I knew. The Shema, the proclamation of the One God. Even I, a "German of Hebrew heritage" and a convert to Catholicism, knew this prayer.

Hear O Israel!
The Lord thy God
The Lord is One.

And it came to me that it was Friday. And this was a Sabbath service. Tears streamed down every congregant's face. Women sobbed; men sobbed, some so uncontrollably that they could barely intone the second "verse" of the prayer, which I never knew well and have mostly forgotten, only that it begins with something like *Baruch shem c'vod—* something like that, I could be wrong.

I stood in astonishment as I watched the rest of the service. Gradually I took in the presence of some British soldiers, standing by, watching, maybe protecting the congregants; the rabbi in a British uniform leading the service, probably a chaplain, a Jewish chaplain; and others on the edge, watching as I was, some moving their lips along with the prayers, their eyes also wide in astonishment, because many congregants were so weak, so thin, some thin as rails, barely able to stand, and others clearly ill, so everyone seemed to be holding up everyone else, there was no other way this service could be happening. And last came the realization of where we were, Bergen-Belsen, Germany. And the question, How long had it been since a *Shabbat* service had been celebrated in Germany?

Michal paused for several seconds.

That's amazing, said her daughter. Are you crying?

No, said Michal, but with a sniffle and a catch in her throat, perhaps truly crying. Then she said: But I have not even come to the miracle yet.

The service went on toward its conclusion, said Michal, and it ended with the singing of a Hebrew song. It had a pretty, uncomplicated melody, it seemed cheerful. Many alongside me clearly knew it well, because they slowly moved in closer and joined in the song.

And soon everyone was crying. I, too. Although I could not have told you why. There was nothing in me, up until that moment, that would have made a *Shabbat* service moving to me, nothing that I had ever cared about in the rituals and prayers: the men rocking on their feet—*davening*, it's called—which I always thought was funny and stupid; and the separation of men and women, because supposedly men talked to God and the very sight of a woman would arouse them, take them away from God—what a stupid idea. You see, I had always scoffed at the rituals, thought them backward, embarrassing. But there I was, suddenly overcome with a sense of belonging to these people, to everyone who knew even the slightest bit of the Shema. And I cried—sobbed—for the first time since . . . everything.

Then a larger group joined us, very hale and hearty people by comparison. By now we were perhaps a hundred, and everyone was crying and laughing and crying—we did not know which to do first. And the ones who joined us started up another song, called "Hatikvah"—

I heard that sung at Belsen! said the patient to her mother.

You what?

I have a recording of it. Of the Belsen survivors singing "Hatikvah." Made by a BBC reporter.

You *heard* it? The actual singing?

Yes, yes. A recording of the actual singing. It broke my heart, really. And I wondered if my—if you were part of it, if what I was hearing contained your voice.

Oh! said Michal with a great sigh. How strange is the world. But no, my dear, no. You did not hear my voice. You see, "Hatikvah" is now the Israeli national anthem, but at the time I did not know a word of it.

A quick intake of breath: a sob from Michal?

I was surrounded by the rising chorus of this song, this beautiful song, said Michal, the first time I had ever heard it, or the first time I was aware of hearing it. One woman in particular leading, a very strong voice, a steady alto, and everyone followed. All around me such singing, so much energy coming from those who were so physically weak, and I could not join in, could not sing with them. I thought: Who *are* these people? What sort of people have such determination and courage, even before all the dead have found their graves? What was giving them such strength, such hope? And the tears ran down my face, this time not with joy but with regret, and heartbreak, and longing.

Why? What happened? asked her daughter.

Well, her mother replied with a catch in her voice. This was the miracle.

The patient's silence held the question, What was the miracle?

You see, said Michal: At that moment, and for the first time in my life, I wanted to be a Jew.

96.

Neither mother nor daughter spoke for several seconds. The tape whined and hissed. Finally the patient said:

But now I am really confused.

Yes? replied Michal.

Confused by what you just told me. You suddenly found—*joy*, I suppose is the right word. Joy in being part of the group. In being one of them. A Jew. So why wouldn't you want that for me?

Michal laughed softly but said nothing.

The singing of "Hatikvah," said the patient, it happened right after Liberation, in April. And I was born in late December. By then, you didn't want me to be a Jew. That's why you gave me away, you said, so I would not be a Jew. So how did this change, then change back, so quickly? All within eight months, eight and a half months.

The situation changed, said Michal. Everything changes.

But so quickly.

Yes. Quickly. It was a time of extremes. Anything could change into anything in a moment.

At that, the session came to an end.

97

Monday night found me sitting restlessly in the dark, reading by flash-light. The sessions were ticking away. The possible loss of my office loomed over me like the blinking pink neon sign of the Hotel Palace.

I had arrived at the office early, at six in the evening. Dr. Schussler had left for her dinner break. When suddenly there came a sharp rap on the door.

Saw you come in! yelled out the voice I had hoped never to hear again.

Let us in! went on the man who had represented himself to me as the manager.

Us? I wondered. *Who else was with him?*

The sharp rapping came again.

Hey, fella! Let us in.

I thought, What chance did I have? I opened the door.

Reading in the dark again? said the little man with the bulging eyes and wild eyebrows and twisted-down mouth.

Behind him were two men in overalls.

They need to measure the space, said the manager person. *And*, he said with emphasis, they will need to turn on the lights.

At that, his hand flew to the wall plate.

The overhead fluorescent bulbs winked to life—let Dr. Schussler not be in the street now! I prayed; let her not look up!—and the two work-men shunted me to one side of the room then another as they stretched out their metal tapes and called out the numbers to the manager, who recorded them in a spiral-bound notebook no larger than his hammy palm.

Now move over there, said one workman as he pushed me to the wall behind the door, which was fortunate—provident! I might say—for not two seconds later came the limping tread of Dr. Schussler.

She stopped at the opened door.

Is that office to be leased? she asked, looking into the room.

I pressed myself against the wall. Could I hide in this narrow V be-hind the door? *Please do not see me!* I cried out in my mind.

Then a second fear rose up behind the first: *Mr. Manager! Please do not say that the room is already leased!*

It seemed he said nothing for minutes—hours! Had he not heard her?

I hung in time, a dead man.

Then the manager's brusque voice said: Huh? What's that?

And Dr. Schussler replied: I said, is the room to be leased?

He coughed—another delay!—and finally said, The engineers in 805 are thinking of expanding into here. I think they're going to use it for their copy equipment.

(*Thinking of it!* Then it is not settled, I dared to hope.)

Said Dr. Schussler: You mean I will have to hear the thump and clack of Xerox machines all day? Not to mention the smell.

Well, if it becomes a problem, said the manager, we can always move you, find you a more accommodating space. Nothing available right now. I'll let you know if something suitable opens.

(*Even Dr. Schussler might move!* I thought. Everyone moving. Everything fluid. What kind of place is this?)

Well, replied the doctor, I certainly hope not to move. It disorients the patients. And then there is the problem of one's preprinted stationery and all.

Oh, there might be a room on this floor, said the manager. You never know. And if there is, you can take your number 804 with you.

The doctor said nothing, only gave a sort of *humph*, and took the two steps to her own door.

The workmen lashed in their measuring tapes and left. Then the manager said to me, I'll let you know, fella.

My legs were trembling. My mind, however, kept clear its workings. If I said nothing in reply, I thought, only nodded, Dr. Schussler could believe one of the workmen was still in the room, might believe the manager was talking to one of his men. So I therefore stepped out from my little enclosure behind the door, raised my chin to acknowledge him, and turned out the lights as he left the room.

I was still safe, I told myself. For now. She still did not know I was there.

But a sword hung over us, I knew.

98

The patient remained skeptical about her mother's sudden embrace of Judaism, and the rejection that had followed just as suddenly. Yet Michal persuaded her daughter to suspend disbelief, as it were, until she could continue her story. And the patient complied.

Michal then moved quickly through the early days of Belsen's establishment as a D.P. camp (which speed gave me some hope that I might yet hear the end before losing my beloved Room 807). Within several weeks of Michal's arrival in Belsen, British soldiers marched the survivors up the road to what had been a Panzer training school. Clean and deloused, she emphasized. Then the army burned down the original camp.

The British goal was to "get out of the D.P. business," as Michal described it in American slang. They wanted everyone to be repatriated as quickly as possible.

But as for me, said Michal to her daughter, where was "home"? Germany? Was I going to knock on the door of my former father-in-law? The door of Albrecht's cousins who had hated me? They would throw me into the street.

The life I had led in Berlin had been demolished. So what was I? A person without an identity, someone with a made-up name. Stateless. I was exactly where I was supposed to be: in a displaced-persons camp. I had no choice but to accept the fact that the next turn of my life would take place in Bergen-Belsen.

The tape rolled on through a period of silence before Michal finally said:

One day shortly after I was settled in the new camp, I was summoned by a British soldier. Two soldiers, she corrected herself. They walked me to a building they called the Round House. It was in a wooded area, on a rise by a small lake, lovely, mid-morning of an exquisite spring day, of the sort you never forget: the aroma of the greening earth, the scent of blooming hyacinths like a drug.

The building rose before me like a vision from a former time—my life in Berlin—an imposing structure with rounded wings at each end.

We walked up a porticoed entryway, across a wide foyer, the wood floor creaking and echoing, finally to a room of palatial proportions. And for a moment my knees went weak. One young soldier accompanying me—he had a pencil mustache and deep-set eyes, very sympathetic—had to hold me up, because a sudden hallucination had come over me: I believed I was walking into the ballroom of our grand house in Berlin.

Then I saw a desk and three side tables. Four seated officers. Three or four more junior soldiers. A ledger, papers, pens. Light dancing in the shine of the wooden floor. Dancing exactly as dancers do, swaying, and swirling, so that for a moment the hallucination of the house and the ballroom returned. I think it must have been the effect of near starvation—thin soup, a little bread, was all we had to eat—inducing moments like this one, when I did not know who I was, where I was, what I was doing there.

Someone spoke. The question to be addressed, he said, is your status: Are you an enemy collaborator or a victim of the Nazis?

This question gathered up my senses, focused my attention, dissolved the vision of the dancers. And immediately I answered, Victim! I was in a labor camp, arrived on one of the last transports, was dumped into Belsen three days before liberation, taken by a Hungarian guard, raped.

Raped: Once more I should not have said the word. Again a man circled me. Once more a man eyed me, evaluated me, looked me over from my head all the way down—no, this man stopped at my ass, much diminished in appeal by that time. I was skinny, wan, my hair like dead grass. Huh.

She paused.

It occurs to me just now—now as you sit before me—that I was already carrying you—

Me.

—was pregnant by then. Not yet started on special rations, so—

Me, repeated the patient.

Yes. You. A tiny ball of starving cells inside me as I stood there, thin and tired and frightened, barely able to nourish myself, let alone you, as this British officer circled me and circled me. And discussed me, and questioned me. And eventually decided: Victim. I must have been a victim.

99

The patient, having heard the first mention of her earthly existence, seemed to grow more relaxed. During long stretches in the narrative, she allowed Michal to go on without interruption. In fact, we barely heard the patient's voice on the tapes during the next two sessions.

And Michal seemed to be more relaxed as well.

Now, she said, we come to the almost happy time of my internment in Belsen.

I was young, she said, dazzled by the camp leaders, fascinated by their audacity, their ferocious determination to take control of their own lives. The best, the strongest among them, was Yossele Rosensaft—see, my dear? Now he truly enters the story. And not far behind Rosensaft in resolution was his second-in-command, Norbert Wollheim—a cultured Berliner like myself. They and their followers opened schools and kindergartens; organized the hospital; set up a commissary; formed a theater company, writing and acting in their own plays, giving performances of cabaret—cabaret in that place!

Above all, the camp leaders demanded that Jews be recognized as a group, which the British had refused to do.

Internees had been housed by nationality, said Michal, meaning Polish Jews were locked up with Poles, who were more Jew-hating than even the Germans. Or maybe they just lacked "German discipline," unable to control what came out of their mouths.

The good Brits had thrown me into a barracks with German women, said Michal, half of them non-Jews. These women had been sent to Belsen by the Nazis because of "suspicious political activities." But somehow they still believed they were part of the master race. One night I woke up and walked around the barracks, not able to get back to sleep. And this—all right, you know the word—this bitch starts muttering under her breath, I thought Hitler got rid of all of you.

The leaders organized, marched, made demands, and soon released us from this humiliation. Jews came to live with Jews. And the leadership fought and won the battle to get aid from Jewish agencies into the camp.

We were no longer beggars at the feet of the British; we took care of one another.

Again Michal thought, who *are* these people? What sustains them?

Most of them were Polish Zionists, she learned, young people who, before Hitler, had spent their summer-camp days learning Hebrew, marching in the forests with wooden rifles, training to be soldiers who would fight for a Jewish state.

Maria (as she was still named) moved into a barracks with ten other Jewish women of various ages. They cleaned and scrubbed; found bits of cloth, made curtains; picked wildflowers that grew at the foot of the fence that imprisoned them and brought them indoors to cheer them-selves. Maria was popular. Because of her language skills, and relative health and energy, she was elected to be assistant block captain, which meant she went about the camp wearing a little blue-and-white armlet with the Yiddish words *Segan Hablock*. She attended committee meet-ings; helped distribute clothing and shoes; painted scenery for the Yid-dish theater.

Gradually, she became integrated into the life of the camp, while the camp itself began to take on the characteristics of a town. There was a main plaza, called Liberty Square, with a loudspeaker giving news and information in Yiddish. The Jews formed their own police force, to counteract the bullying of the Polish police that had ruled the camp. Couples married; groups formed themselves into *kibbutzim* and gave parties. Along the streets, small stores, called "canteens," were set up in an ad hoc fashion, offering shoe repairs, haircuts, cleaning, tailoring. Business was done on the barter system: Individuals traded the rations they received from aid agencies for goods and services. The gold coins of the realm were coffee and cigarettes.

This will sound very strange to you, Michal said to her daughter. There I was an internee. But somewhere around the fourth or fifth month in the camp, it came to me that I had somehow healed a bit, healed from . . . all that.

You felt better because . . .

Because for the first time in my memory, even going back to when I was fifteen—for the first time, my life was under my own volition, my own direction. I wanted to join in these activities. I wanted to contrib-ute. I wanted to be one of those brave, strong people who had snatched life from the Nazi hell.

There was a Yiddish newspaper, said Michal. I do not know how they did it. Found paper. Mimeographed the pages. People rushed up to grab a copy, overcome at the sight of this newspaper that seemed to have materialized out of nothing.

One day I found myself standing before Rafael Olevsky, said Michal, one of the founders of the newspaper, saying to him, Please. Teach me Yiddish. Teach me to read and write Yiddish.

What is your name? Olevsky asked me.

And I was embarrassed to answer. What was a Maria doing there in the camp? He would never teach such a Maria.

Miriam, I answered him. Miriam Gerstner.

(Joy! My trail of names had come true. Maria to Miriam, as told by Michal.)

And that was it? asked the patient. Nothing more formal? No papers? No ceremony?

Michal laughed. Do you think I should have applied to the magistrate in Celle? Asked the Germans to allow me to be a Jew?

100.

Let me show you how far we came in a short time, Michal continued. How quickly we took control of our lives.

Just six months after the British had come upon the thousands of living corpses abandoned in Belsen, the bastards who ran the camp were put on trial in a nearby town called Lüneburg.

The camp's doctor, Hadassah Bimko, testified before the tribunal, Michal told the patient. Before Belsen, she had been at Auschwitz, and she identified commandants and guards from both camps.

And then Bimko exposed a truth that shocked the world: the existence of the gas chambers in Auschwitz.

This revelation made her famous, said Michal.

Then she laughed.

Also infamous in the dens of the Holocaust deniers. I think one of them called her "The Heroine of the Holocaust."

Then, six days later, Michal went on, just six days after the commandants and guards had faced their fate, the First Congress of the She'erit Hapletah took place in Belsen, the First Congress of the surviving remnant. Remnant. You must think what this means to a people. Torn. All that is left.

At this congress, we elected a government—our own government—to lead the camp.

I remember the closing day exactly. I was sitting in the last row. Just as the meeting was getting started, Bimko came in late, shaking hands while she made her slow progress to the auditorium stage.

Let me describe her, said Michal. She was "stout" and "plump," as the newspapers described her, which was true; she was a stub of a woman. Which did her no good when she was cross-examined by the attorney for the defense at the Lüneburg trials, whom the British had appointed.

Michal laughed.

The story of what happened at the trial went around the camp. In her testimony, Bimko described the deprivations of the prisoners in Auschwitz and Belsen. Then the defense lawyer asked: And were you subject to these deprivations, Dr. Bimko? Were you emaciated at the time of liberation?

Since it was impossible not to notice that Bimko was not at all thin, not at all recovering from emaciation, the underlying point was to question whether she was a victim or a member of the camp staff. She had worked under the evil Josef Mengele. She was well fed and healthy. What was she, victim or perpetrator?

I always knew I was a prisoner, Dr. Bimko replied.

We came to the end of the congress, said Michal. We held elections for the heads of the various committees. Hadassah Bimko became the official head of the Health Committee. Of course Rosensaft was chosen to be the leader of the Central Committee, Wollheim to be his second.

Rosensaft gave the closing speech: We are now entering an era when we must fight for our rights, he said. We have been slaves, but now we are free. May we be blessed to convene our next congress in Eretz Yisrael.

The newly elected leaders shook hands with one another. Rosensaft embraced Bimko. Everyone rose for the singing of "Hatikvah."

Michal was silent for some seconds—moved by the memory of the moment?

Then she said:

I stood up. Dizzy, sweaty. I was six months pregnant. My belly getting big. I nearly tumbled over.

Because of me inside you, said the patient, neither asking nor asserting.

Michal said nothing for two or three seconds, then answered in a bright voice, Yes, my dear daughter. You were there! You were at the very first Congress of the She'erit Hapletah!

101.

Michal's voice was too bright. And the patient knew it.

I'm what changed things for you, aren't I? Your being pregnant with me.

No! How can you say that?

You were dizzy and sweaty and about to faint—

I did not say faint.

All right. Fall over.

No, no, no.

Now you have to tell me so I believe you. How did you go from your "almost happy time" in the camp—that great Zionist creation—to giving me away so I wouldn't be a Jew? How?

As I told you, it was a time of extremes. Changes. Quick turns. Reverses.

That's not an answer.

Michal hummed through a pause, took a breath.

Yes. Not an answer. Yes, I suppose I must go on and tell you, all of it. This will be difficult, for you as well as for me. But yes, having begun, I must go on to the end.

Get to the part where you give me away, said the patient. Don't click your tongue at me, Michal. That's what you did: You gave me away.

Listen, my dear. If you remain so angry, you will stand in the way of the story. I will run through quickly, and you will never understand what happened.

All right.

You must reserve judgment.

All right.

All right, said Michal. Now . . .

I can only say that the change came slowly. Over months. Creeping up until I looked around one day and said to myself: I must leave this place.

There must have been arguments from the beginning, differences over the sort of aid we needed. Of course there were differences. These went on quietly. The general mood was one of cooperation.

But—sometime soon after Rosensaft was elected to lead the Central Committee—sometime around then, the arguments broke out into the open. Battles between ideologies: Should we go back and rebuild our communities? Refuse to have our European home taken away from us? To which the Zionists replied: Home! There is no home for us in Europe. Europe is a grave. Our only home is in Eretz Yisrael!

And then came the fiercest of battles: for control over the aid flowing into the camp. Which was growing daily into a great pile of money and goods.

She laughed. Greed. Greed on all sides. Like everyone and everywhere. Greed for money and greed for power.

The rabbis wanted funds dedicated to religious purposes, she went on. Improving the rooms and buildings used as *Schulen*—synagogues. Also more money for religious instruction, Torah studies, not just the teaching of Hebrew as an everyday language, but the ancient Hebrew of the Torah. They wanted scholars to be paid for their studies, as other leaders received subsistence living allowances. Newer Torahs in better condition, which, it turns out, are very expensive. And then there were the ritual baths for women.

Ritual baths? asked the patient.

Yes. You see, we bleed with our periods, and religious Jews consider us to be dirty—all that blood—which has to be "cleansed" afterward, to make us "pure" again.

Do not laugh, Michal said to the patient. This is true.

And the faction against the rabbis? asked the patient.

Rosensaft, Wollheim, the Central Committee. They did not care to spend funds on religious objects, beyond what was necessary for services. The idea of paying men to pray and study, while we were freezing and hungry, seemed ridiculous. They wanted shoes, clothes, food, fuel.

She laughed.

It was good they won. I was pregnant and undernourished. It was a cold, cold winter. You were born in the middle of it. Without the fuel and the warm clothes and the food, it is not certain you could have survived.

The patient breathed in and out, but said nothing.

But over time . . .

Over time?

Michal sucked in a breath.

I think it was the coffee and cigarettes that made everything fall apart.

Rosensaft pressed for larger and larger donations of cigarettes and coffee. Again, it was good in the beginning. They were used for barter in the canteens and everywhere else, between the people inside. Coins of the realm, as I told you. Trade.

But then the amounts coming in doubled, tripled. A black market sprang up. Of course, what could anyone expect? You lock up a bunch of people, give them no means of earning a real livelihood, pour into the camp the sorts of things the good Germans around it haven't seen in years—coffee, a Nazi-loving farmer would swear undying love for any Jew who could get him real coffee—and what do you think will happen?

There were police raids, to stop the black marketeering. In no time, the trade would come back, as if nothing had happened to stop it.

Rosensaft was the driving force behind this. I cannot prove it. But I believe he was. I also believed—still believe—that the underlying push came from Bimko. Hadassah and Yossele took up together. They got married eventually. And I think she poisoned Rosensaft. He was—had been—truly a man of the people. He came from a poor family. Survived on his wits and force of character.

But she, on the other hand, came from a rich family, something to do with gold, gold dealers, I think. And when Rosensaft took up with her, he was somehow corrupted. They got rich in the coffee and cigarette trade—that was generally believed. So where did she get all those cigarettes? She was lighting one cigarette from the tip of another while other people had to save up six packs for a pair of five-time recobbled shoes. Bimko. That stinking, chain-smoking little troll.

I do not have the facts, said Michal. I cannot tell you for a fact that Rosensaft and Bimko got rich off purloined coffee rations. All I know is the result. They eventually moved out of the camp into an apartment. And when the camp was closed, did they go to Eretz Yisrael? Did they join all the orphans Hadassah led into Palestine like some Moses? Did they go to the place to which we all had been urged to go, as our duty, our only hope, our God-given destiny? The place they had battled the world to create? Oh, no, no, no. The big Zionists moved to Switzerland. *Schweiz!* That pretty, *neutral* country with placid lakes and snowy mountains. They lived in Montreaux, on Lake Geneva. What a nice life! They also had a house in San Remo, on the Italian Riviera, the *Riviera dei Fiori*. And for a while in New York, an apartment on Fifth Avenue, where your precious Renoirs and Gauguins hung on the walls.

All this I learned later from a Bergen-Belsen survivors' group. The members remained in communication and knew where many of the internees had gone, particularly the leadership.

Even then, while still in Belsen, I did not see a future in the camp. Belsen was quickly becoming a place of rich and poor, the well-connected and everyone else.

In the end, it was a scandal. Of all the camp leaders, only one, Rafael Olevsky, the cofounder of the newspaper, settled in Israel. All the others made easier lives for themselves. Wollheim went to America and became an accountant—an accountant! Trepman went to Canada. Laufer went to Canada. Rosenthal to Philadelphia. Oh, they all sent money to Israel. They all felt "deeply connected" to Israel. Ha! One of the Orthodox rabbis even had his dead body shipped here from Europe, so he would have his final rest in Israel. But did they live in the place they were demanding for all the rest of us? Did they settle here? Take up the hard life of building Israel? What brave pioneers!

She spat.

It was becoming clear that the leadership was doing far better than everyone else, she said. There were grumblings. About Rosensaft. Accusations that Rosensaft and his cronies controlled the coffee market. I cannot say if it was true one way or another, but where did he get the money to rent an apartment in Celle while we were all behind barbed wire?

And there were complaints about Rosensaft's near-dictatorial powers. No one questioned his motives. It was the concentration of his authority that was at issue. His insistence that all aid be funneled through the Central Committee, which he ruled. That all major political decisions be approved by the Central Committee, which he commanded. That the organization of the camp itself be under the control of the Central Committee, of which he was the undisputed king.

Her voice was suddenly bitter.

Behind his back, she said, people called him Little Stalin.

102.

Stalin! I thought as the session came to an end. How quickly did Rosen-saft, who had dazzled and fascinated the young Miriam, become Stalin!

Something was wrong. Michal's bitterness, her cold cynicism, was too strong to be caused by mere politics. But what lay behind it? The patient did not press her mother. And, in the next series of sessions, Dr. Schussler did not intervene to discuss the question.

To make matters worse, Michal's narrative at this point became oddly disjointed, proceeding by theme, not by chronology. It would have been no matter if she were relaying only a brief portion of the story. But she was portraying eight months of her internment in Belsen: three months from the First Congress in late September 1945 (the establish-ment of Rosensaft's power, Michal had said), to the patient's birth in December. And then another five months until Michal left Belsen in May 1946.

Michal told and retold the events of this period, going over and over the time that followed "the almost happy days." But the story came in lightning strikes, a phrase here, a paragraph here, wild spikes in random order. Rabbis were "fat, bearded, crabby old men." Wollheim, whom she had described as aristocratic and learned, became "Rosensaft's poodle." The joint leadership of Rosensaft and Wollheim was "autocratic," "un-scrupulous," "tyrannical," "self-serving." She laughed and jeered, spat and snorted and clicked her tongue. Something more than camp politics had to be behind this bitter, bitter mood.

And what emotional swordplay was responsible for the most drastic change in Michal's characterizations: the transformation reserved for the doctor? Hadassah Bimko, who began as the ministering angel saving the camp from typhus, became the heartless rich girl, Rosensaft's cor-ruptor. Finally to become "that stinking, chain-smoking little troll."

Why did Dr. Schussler not probe her client? How could she not no-tice the fundamental change in Michal Gershon's narrative? Two weeks went by, and I awaited her entry into the therapeutic conversation, to no avail. And it came to me that she had not said anything of consequence for some time. Had the doctor fallen victim to the sweep of Michal's narrative? Was her guilt preventing her from intervening? There was no telling, as I heard none of the usual indications of boredom, no creaking leather as Dr. Schussler shifted about her seat, no slishing stockings as she crossed and recrossed her legs. She simply maintained her silence for reasons I could not divine.

As a consequence, a powerful need developed within me: I had to hear her voice once again. The shushing Ss and spat-out Ts that had first intruded upon my consciousness; that had first informed me of the doctor's existence—that had lured me into my relationship with the patient!— I must hear them again. Yet the therapist persisted in her all-too-brief ritual phrases, good morning, good afternoon, as-we-were-saying-last-week, our time is up.

Come back to me, Dora Schussler, I thought. But the silence wore on; and the longer the doctor remained mute, the more her passivity seemed hostile, a willful withdrawing from me. For she had turned me into her creature, a sort of patient. Not one of my many therapeutic practitioners had ever cured me of a bout of obsession, yet Dr. Schussler had accomplished just that. I had come to trust her, need her—she had engendered in me this trust, this need—and now where was she?

103.

The last of these sessions drew to a close. Given my agitated state, I dared not move until Dr. Schussler was safely out of the office. Then I quickly gathered my things and left.

Despite our having arrived at autumn, it was a blistering hot day. (I had utterly given up all attempts to understand San Francisco's climate; aside from summer fog, the good people of the city inevitably described whatever weather was present as "very unusual for this time of year.") The days were shortening, however, and I soon found myself strolling toward Union Square in the cooling air of approaching sundown.

I came to a bench (perhaps the very one from which I had followed the Indonesian girl and boy, all those many months ago). And suddenly it was as if a veil had fallen from my eyes; or, more accurately, a muffler from my ears.

For no sooner did I feel the cool of the stone beneath me than Michal Gershon's story leapt into clarity. It was exactly as if the recording of her voice had been cut into a hundred pieces and then reassembled as a coherent, linear narrative. And I knew the precise instant when Michal's feelings toward Belsen had changed, the fulcrum moment that had bred Miriam Gerstner's hatred toward Rosensaft, Wollheim, and Bimko. And I understood Dr. Schussler's silence, how blessed it was; why she had not pressed this understanding upon her patient.

104

The fulcrum moment came, I was certain, on the closing day of the First Congress of the She'erit Hapletah.

I could all but see Michal, then Miriam, sitting in the last row, watching Hadassah Bimko shaking hands, nodding hellos, being adored, as she made her way to the stage.

As Michal described Bimko's entrance, why did she feel obliged to mention the doctor's testimony at the Lüneburg trial? Bimko's being stout and plump? Her near-humiliation by the defense counsel? The implication that Bimko might have been not a victim but a collaborator with the infamous Josef Mengele; her collaboration accounting for her survival and good health? Why use the lawyer to defame her?

And then the story of the congress's final minutes. All the newly elected leaders shaking hands. *Rosensaft and Bimko embracing on the stage.*

Miriam rises to sing "Hatikvah." She is pregnant and dizzy and sweating—and watching the embrace. She nearly tumbles. And then I understood: It was not merely her physical balance that was lost. It was the moment when her life in Belsen—the first time she had ever wanted to be a Jew—turned back upon itself.

From the moment I had first heard the story, I knew that something was wrong, off. But I could not bring it to consciousness, could not understand exactly why I was so discomfited. And immediately thereafter, Michal had begun to relate her story in fractured pieces, as I have said. Straining to understand her, I did not have time for reflection, review. And I was preoccupied with Dr. Schussler's absence from the conversation.

But now, as I sat upon the bench in Union Square, it was as if each fragment of Michal's story glared at me nakedly from within the circle of its own spotlight:

A mention of a "difficult pregnancy." Something about "spotting," premature contractions, fluctuations in blood pressure. Waiting in endless lines for extra rations. Resentful stares, jealousy, as she received additional food. These details had been dropped like salt grains into other stories, and thereby quickly dissolved in the overall wash of events. And, as if she had not already obscured the story sufficiently, into this mix she stirred suggestive mentions of Rosensaft and Wollheim and Bimko. The presence of Dr. Bimko in a tale of a difficult pregnancy was to be expected. But what did those men, Yossele Rosensaft and Norbert Wollheim, have to do with the gestation of my dear patient?

I sat in the square and reviewed the other clues Michal had left behind, over the course of many weeks, traces that had resided in parenthetical remarks, asides, snickers, bits of dialog, flashes of anger. The mufflers having fallen from my ears (so to speak), my review required but fifty or sixty seconds; after which the real thread of the story revealed itself to me. The secret lay in five separate scenes, previously mentioned by Michal weeks apart, cut away from the broken time line and aligned in narrative order.

First was a brief interaction between Miriam Gerstner and Yossele Rosensaft. It came following some committee meeting. She said something personal to him. Personal how? She did not say. And she felt quite hurt when he was dismissive, or else he had dismissed her; in any case, she felt dismissed, dispensed with, discarded.

The next scene is more elaborate, again played by Miriam and Rosensaft. The place: a camp building, a hall, after a wedding. Miriam danced with Rosensaft. Afterward she took his arm, wanting to walk out for a breath of air. He dropped the triangle that had supported her arm, turned to her, looked into her eyes, then—as she returned his gaze—he gave her "a little chuck under the chin." After which he "walked away laughing." If this was not bad enough, he returned to the floor, danced with another woman, to whom he also gave "a little chuck under the chin."

Lothario, Michal had whispered on the tape.

Had Miriam been romantically interested in Rosensaft? The third and fourth and fifth scenes, all involving Norbert Wollheim, brought the question into relief. It was not clear where those interactions took place—Michal reported only shards of these conversations with him. In one, Wollheim is saying that she can have "no claims" upon Rosensaft's time (or else he said she had "no claims" upon Rosensaft himself; Michal spoke too quickly for me to hear it clearly). In the next scene (also played upon a blank stage) Wollheim says something on the order of: You and I have more in common than you have with Yossele. And finally, on another bare stage, he tells her: "Rosensaft is with Bimko. They are going to be married."

Suddenly it was all so clear. How could I not have seen it? Hidden beneath the dry brush of political meetings and committees, underneath the passions of Zionism and the debates about the future of the Jews, another story smoldered: Wollheim wanted Miriam; Miriam wanted Rosensaft; Rosensaft wanted Hadassah Bimko. The eternal tale that could play itself out anywhere: a prosperous city, a country estate, a displaced-persons camp.

What a sad story it was, I thought, as evening came on and Union Square began to bustle with office workers hurrying home. For the longer I contemplated my scenario, the more convinced I was of its veracity:

A woman survives what seems a lifetime of horrors and is surprised—stunned—to find herself still healthy, young. She begins to discover a new identity, a new life, one in which she is popular, active, involved; in which she learns new languages; where she is valued for skills she never imagined she possessed. She falls in love, reaches out for a husband when she discovers she is carrying a child, most likely his child. Then her new identity as Miriam is slowly forced to shrink, as if her range of motion must contract in proportion to the expansion of her belly. She is envied for her special foods and rations, and her popularity fades. The man rejects her. Her difficult pregnancy keeps her from the activities in which she was engaged. She has to give up her places in groups and committees. Slowly, what overtakes her is a sort of nineteenth-century confinement, literally a confinement in the hospital, wherein she falls under the care of Dr. Hadassah Bimko, the lover of the man she desires. And it is precisely at this point—when she is forced to remain bedridden, overseen by her rival—that the good doctor, that angel, becomes "that stinking, chain-smoking little troll."

I whispered a passionate "thank you" to Dr. Schussler. And this gratitude was for her gracious silence; for relinquishing her therapist's imperative to probe, and probe ever deeper; and, most of all, for allowing the patient some degree of ignorance about the story of her inception. The patient certainly had intuited the starkness of her origins. But it would have been cruel to inflict upon her the knowledge that her very existence had snuffed out a nascent life. For Maria-become-Miriam was barely born when her newfound joy was drained from her. Her moment of belonging, of wanting to be a Jew for the first time in her life, was taken from her by the being she called "a tiny ball of starving cells."

It was not the patient's fault, of course. But she had come along when she had come along. Her mother was about to be judged: Was she truly a victim? She was hallucinating from hunger; barely able to stand. And inside her was the tiny patient, her starving cells awash in her mother's fear.

The patient grows toward birth, submerged in the noxious brew of the dying Miriam's emotions: a flood of vengefulness, bitterness, hatred, cynicism, sorrow, and despair. O my dear patient! Even in your pre-life: consigned to the tribe of the inherently unhappy.

I put my head in my hands and cried. People walking by me in Union Square gave me a wide berth, as I sobbed uncontrollably, how long I do not know, only that night came on, and the square filled with frightening characters, and yet I wept. I was overwhelmed with the depth, breadth, urgency, and sheer inescapability of my kinship with the patient. We were born to darkness. It was our task—our imperative!—to think, plan, use our minds (the only strength that remained to us) to fight for the life of our flesh. And—to hell with our ancestors; we will show them; they do not rule us—to thrive! Or, at the very least, remain alive.

105

The next session confirmed—indeed made me certain—that I had arrived at the truth about the patient's birth.

The patient had barely settled in when she said to Dr. Schussler: Michal told me I almost didn't make it.

Make it? asked the therapist.

Almost didn't get to live.

(Not one of us moved, none drew breath; as if we, too, if not careful, might fail to achieve life.)

I was thin, Michal told me. Lethargic. Cranky. Irritable. In her exact words: I was "delicately devoted to being alive."

There the patient stopped; and the doctor asked:

And how did you feel when your mother said this?

The patient laughed. That all my emotions now made sense, she said. It's just as I am now. I'll never change. I'll always be stuck in this irritable self, unsoothable and uncomfortable in my skin. I'll always have a delicate devotion to being alive.

(No! I thought. You must resist this thought. We can, must, overcome the life of the womb.)

The therapist hummed, as if deferring a response.

Michal said I was born in a freezing *Kinderbaracke*.

Children's barracks, said the doctor.

Well, of course you'd know the word, said the patient.

Dr. Schussler sighed. She was not about to be drawn into another discussion of her German heritage.

It was the dead of winter, of course, the patient continued. Born in December: a very bad idea if you're in a displaced-persons camp, in a freezing children's barracks. With a mother who was glad to be rid of you.

What makes you say that? asked Dr. Schussler.

She told me she had no milk. She had to beg one woman, then another, to nurse me. Beg. Because those other women also had children at risk, if not as delicately devoted to being alive as I was. Wet

nurses! Was this some nineteenth-century novel? But Michal claimed—
she swore!—my fragile state had nothing to do with why she gave me
away.

Again the doctor deferred a response.

She claimed it had to do with that Hadassah Bimko, the camp doctor, the only woman in the Central Committee.

(Now here is indeed the nub of it, I thought.)

According to Michal, it all started with something I'd read about in
one of the packets from the Chicago agency. Some British Jewish organization wanted to take Belsen's orphans to England, where they'd find
homes for them with Jewish families. But the camp leadership protested,
saying the children would either stay with them or else go to Palestine.
As I said, I'd read about it—which surprised Michal. Anyhow, it was
considered a big victory when the British caved in and granted emigration
visas for the children.

Here. I've cued the tape. Where Michal's reaction startles me.

Shameful! said Michal as the recording began to play. Using those
poor children as pawns in their Zionist games! The children would have
been much better off in Britain. England was not in great condition after
the war, but at least the war was *over* there, finished. Imagine those children toddling in peaceful English gardens, she said, on the stoops of
friendly streets. Now picture them in Palestine, where the Irgun is blowing up British installations, where there is a nasty little war brewing between Jews and Arabs. Why would they take those poor orphans there if
not to make a political point? It had nothing to do with the welfare of
the children!

So, Michal continued, Bimko travels with a hundred orphans from
Belsen, and then she's given another *thousand* children who came from
God-knows-where in the British zone. And when she gets to Palestine,
she is suddenly enraged to find various Zionist organizations interview-
ing the children, trying to send them to appropriate homes. Bimko
wanted them to stay together. But she'd arrived without a plan, and what
did she think was going to happen? That the children would be placed
in an instant kibbutz?

And there she is, said Michal, that savior, that great leader, taking
eleven hundred children into a war zone for the glory of Zionism—or for
her personal glory?

Michal paused, then said: It was Bimko's trip to Palestine that made me decide.

Decide what? asked the patient.

To give you up for adoption.

I don't understand.

I refused to let you be a pawn in the Zionist cause.

106.

I saw no future for anyone, Michal went on. I had lost my illusions about the Zionists. Power was concentrated in a very few hands, as I have told you. Also about Bimko poisoning Rosensaft.

(Said the woman who had lost her lover to her rival.)

The only course was to leave Belsen. And the only possible place I could go was Palestine. And I did not want that life for you. Every time I thought of taking you there, the image of Hadassah Bimko and her orphans rose before my eyes, and I decided, each time, that I would find a better future for you.

(Bimko again, I thought sadly. If only I could find a way to tell the patient how this Bimko had changed her mother's life.)

There was a Polish woman I had befriended in the camp, said Michal. A Catholic, therefore free to roam about and find her postwar fortune. She had found employment of a sort at a nearby . . . monastery, convent, I cannot remember which. They donated food to Belsen, and because I volunteered in the kitchen, I spent time with her. Her name was Bibianna Lobzjeska. One day we were working side by side in the pantry, and she began talking about some group that was gathering up Jewish children who had been left with monasteries and convents before the war.

I know about this group, the patient on the tape interrupted her mother.

You *know* this group?

Yes, the patient replied. My mother—my adoptive mother—told me about it. That they essentially stole the children. Before any Jewish people could come for them, they farmed them out, clandestinely.

I did not know that! Are you sure? I thought the children were truly orphans, that no one had come for them, and—since the children had been baptized and had spent the better part of their lives as Catholics—it seemed logical and generous to find them Catholic homes.

No, said the patient. Not all of them. Some had people looking for them, maybe aunts or cousins, not parents but relatives. But unless it was the actual parent, they refused to give up the child. Sometimes not even then.

My God! But you see there were hundreds, said Michal. Hundreds of children given over by parents who were being rounded up by the Germans, parents who hoped their children would survive even if they did not. Well. I have to say, if the choice was between a good Catholic home and some distant cousins in a displaced-persons camp or a dusty farm kibbutz in Palestine where the children would have to learn to shoot rifles, I would choose the Catholic home. Otherwise, it is no better than what Bimko did: put children in harm's way for the sake of a principle.

For the sake of a religion, said the patient quietly.

There was silence on the tape.

Pooh! said Michal finally. *Pooh* on religion.

You mean the Jewish religion.

Her mother said nothing for several seconds.

Knowing only what I knew, knowing only what I *could* know, said Michal finally, I asked Bibianna to put me in communication with the group.

And they came and got me.

Yes.

And how long until they came?

One month.

So quickly?

I was glad. I was relieved. I put you into the hands of a priest and told him I had been baptized as a Catholic, that your father was a German Catholic, and that I wanted you to be baptized and raised within the Catholic faith.

Wait! said the patient. You said you didn't know who my father was.

That is only what I told him. I wanted to be sure they would give you to a good family. I wanted to be sure they did not see you as just another spawn of a converted Jew. It was not as if anti-Semitism had disappeared with the death of Hitler, you know.

Oh, I know, said the patient to her mother. I know. Anti-Semitism is why I am with my parents, my adoptive parents, and not with some insane, Jew-hating, fundamentalist Catholic sect.

What are you talking about?

Oh, yes. I didn't tell you, did I? That nice Catholic life you put me into? I was first adopted by the man who is the father of my adoptive father. He was the chief nutcase in a fundamentalist Catholic cult that was about to remove itself from the sin of the cities to some compound in rural Illinois. And when he found out I was Jewish, that I had a Jewish mother, he wanted to dispose of me.

My God! whispered Michal.

Yes. God. It was all about his "God." My father and grandfather were completely estranged, and somehow my father took me because of some bizarre struggle between them. I don't know any more than that. Mother—my adoptive mother—was not exactly forthcoming.

The tape whirred; neither woman spoke.

I . . . said Michal. How . . . How could I know?

Of course you couldn't know. You just dropped me into this priest's hands and sailed away.

More whirring; more silence.

Okay, said the patient to her mother with a breath, that's over and done with. I didn't come here to berate you.

Really, replied Michal flatly.

There was a pause before the patient replied: Really.

Then what did you come for?

Another pause ensued.

Just to know, the patient said. To know where I came from.

The tape rolled on for several seconds.

Oh, I am so . . . completely sorry, said Michal at last. I only wanted what was best for you, what I thought was best for you. But I can only tell you the story as I know it, as it happened to me, and as I understood it. That is what you wanted, yes?

Yes, said the patient. That's what I wanted. That's what I came for. So, she said after a pause. You just picked me up out of a crib and handed me to a priest you'd never met. And he simply walked out of the camp—no questions asked? When this baby just disappeared from the *Kinderbaracke*—this little baby only how many months old?

Five months.

When this infant—me—when I disappeared, what did you tell them?

I told them I had sent you on to Palestine with a Catholic group, and that I was joining you there.

And off you went.

Yes. I was a convert. To him, I was a Catholic. He helped me get an emigration visa. And I went.

So you traded me for a visa! Everyone else in Belsen is stuck there, but you make a deal with Mr. Priest: I give you this baby, now get me out of here. God! Everyone traded me for something!

Oh, no, no. You must not think like that. The way I saw it, you were off to a good life and I was going to hell, at least to a different hell, one not surrounded by barbed wire.

107.

The tape wound on, neither the patient nor Michal speaking. Five seconds, ten. Dr. Schussler had drawn a breath as if to initiate a discussion when the patient's voice on the tape returned.

I may—may—understand why you gave me up when you did, she was saying to her mother. Why you *surrendered* me, is the proper term I think. But why didn't you ever look for me? Why didn't you ever contact me? Try to reunite with me. After all, you now have a good life in Israel.

You think so? replied Michal.

Well, it seems so, said the patient.

Seems. *Seems!* Michal exclaimed. We *seem* to be fine. What you *see* is a lovely, prosperous city, gleaming buildings, white-sand beaches, young people lounging in cafes. And do not forget the luxurious villas our politicians built for themselves. Seems. This is what you see when you look at us with your naïve eyes. You have a nice hotel?

What?

Your hotel. Which is it? Never mind. It is not the shabby little seafront place where just a few months ago Fatah murderers came ashore in a dinghy, took eight hostages, then killed them. Did you even read about this?

I . . . no. I don't remember.

You don't remember, don't remember. Do you remember reading about the guerrillas who broke into a school and took hostage a hundred and twenty children. *Children*. This was a first for us. Did you read about it?

I . . . No.

I am sure you were never even aware of it. And how about . . . Never mind. The incidents are too many to tell you about. One thing: Do you at least remember reading about the Yom Kippur War?

Yes, replied the patient. Of course.

Ah, well, at last! Of course. Because we were surprised, nearly overrun. If not for a handful of berserker tank fighters in the Golan, who held off the entire Syrian army, there would be no Israel now. Do you know what it is to live with this? With the knowledge of such a fragile life, such a fragile existence as a country?

She paused.

It is good you do not even try to answer because you cannot. No person living in the United States can feel this. You do not live moment to moment thinking your country might disappear, your life will be over, everyone will be dead.

The bomb, said the patient. I grew up thinking any minute we'd all be dead from nuclear war.

But that would happen to everyone! said Michal with a laugh. It is a madness that would take down the whole world. But here . . . it would just be us, the little state that is the Jewish remnant: obliterated while the rest of the world goes on about its business.

You cannot imagine what happened to us, Michal went on after a long pause, the trauma when we nearly lost the Yom Kippur War. We are a country that lives by the sword. A desert warrior nation. Remember I told you: The people who founded this country were like the mad, unyielding men of Belsen. We believed in our army, the invincible Israeli Defense Forces. Then, for the first time, we understood that the IDF was not magic, was only an army. We understood that we could be beaten. Now we all sit and shudder and think, When will the time come? When will we not prevail? Someday our enemies will no longer be the pitiful armies of feuding sheiks. Someday they will come at us from all sides with modern armies and real arms and unified purpose. Then who will help us? Who will save us?

America? posited the patient.

Michal laughed until she coughed.

Do you not see what is happening? she asked. Young people all around the world have replaced the Vietcong with the Palestinians as the current cause célèbre of anti-imperialism. I see the young Americans come here. The nice, liberal American Jews who walk through the King David Hotel wearing Arafat's *keffiyeh* as a scarf. And I think: Here come our American saviors!

And all this because we will not go back to the pre-'67 borders, she continued. But what were those precious pre-'67 borders? Some grand internationally negotiated settlement? Some U.N. resolution? Some solid black lines on ancient maps? No, simply where we stopped in 1949. At the end of the War of Independence. Then another war. And another. War after war after war.

She grew quiet. The clock-tick filled the silence, seeming to grow louder as the seconds passed.

And not a pretty war, that first one, Michal finally said. There were horrors on both sides, I will admit. There is cause for the Arabs' bitterness. Many were driven from their homes.

Well, she said with a sigh. I cannot ask you if you remember that, because the story has not been written down yet. We are still living in the fantasy that we were all heroes. Someday—should we survive—we will be allowed to be a normal country, with good and bad, with skeletons in our closets, like everyone else.

This city, she went on after a pause. Jaffa. Two hundred thousand Arabs lived here before the War of Independence. Now they live in some wretched refugee camp in Gaza. We are ringed with their encampments, refugees sitting in their warrens, seething with hatred for us. Do you think we can hold them off forever?

Ah! she said with a sound that might have been her hand slapping the table. Somewhere down a maze of hovels in Gaza is a woman, a woman sitting there brimming with fury, holding the key to this house. My house.

I often think, Michal continued after a long pause, What am I doing living in this rough country, speaking a language that feels flat in my mouth? And with yet another name: Michal Gershon.

Again she seemed to slap the table.

Sometimes I detest it here, she said, her *T*s like little knife stabs. Truly. Detest it. Which you may have supposed by now. So why would I want to bring any child here? Where we are ringed by enemies. Tell me, skinny girl who has come all the way from America to find me. Where exactly are we wanted?

108.

For many seconds, the patient said nothing in response to her mother. The sound of the ticking clock in Michal's kitchen somehow managed to interweave itself with the clicks of the cassette, so that, for a moment, the time then—the patient with her mother, and Michal's first arrival in Palestine—seemed to merge with the time now—the patient with her therapist (and with me). It was as if we all sat in some room together outside of normal duration, where we could not stop asking ourselves: Where exactly are Jews wanted?

So you are telling me, the patient said to her mother (time returning to its proper depth), that you didn't come for me because your life was so dismal here?

Well. No. Not exactly dismal, said Michal. But. Yes. But more. As I—

As you what? *What?*

As I have said, over and over. I did not want you to be a Jew.

But why? Why should I not be a Jew?

Michal did not immediately reply. The tape continued with its rhythmic thumping, as if the end of the tape, and their conversation, were bearing down upon them.

I wanted you to enjoy the world, Michal said at last, wearily. And by the world, I mean . . . God . . . Europe . . . my long-lost, beloved, still dreamed-of Europe.

If you are not a Jew, she went on after an enormous sigh, you can sit in a bistro in Paris, drink a Kir, smoke a stinking cigarette, and never have to look around and wonder, Are these the people who turned us over for deportation? Climb the Tour Eiffel, walk the Champs-Elysées. And never think: How quickly they all succumbed to save their precious Paris. Even Hitler loved Paris so much he was relieved not to have to destroy it. Ah! Go to the spa at Evian. Enjoy the waters. Eat supper in the elegant dining rooms. Drink the cool, clear, miraculous water and never associate the place with the conference at which the Western powers learned of the fate of the Jews and decided to ignore it. Be massaged by sturdy women, and never once stop to think: These are our murderers.

Travel south to Provence. Walk the foothills of the Pyrenees, and never think of the Jews who walked there to escape France only to arrive in Franco's Spain. Go! Go in the early summer! Eat mussels by the seashore, watch the local military academies march to honor the local war veterans. See the good *burghers* expand their breasts laden with medals. All this, and you never have to think: Vichy. This was Vichy. All around me are the people who were only too happy to rid France of Jews.

And . . . the Netherlands. Lovely Netherlands. See the charming houses of Amsterdam. The canals filled with boats. The sturdy women pedaling bicycles. The placid lives they lead. The happy children playing in the street: Imagine that someday those will be your children, tossing balls in security, skipping rope, if someday you will care to have children. You may dream so! And no need to defend the Dutch for their weakness, for their fears, lacks, collaborations, for being accessories, trembling accessories, to the murder of your people. You can see them as normal people who behaved less than honorably under the pressure of intimidation, flattery, fear of their own deaths.

Now . . . I cannot even think of it . . . but Germany. Germany so beautiful I cry when I think of the life I lost. The forests, the *bier* halls, the new summer wines served at tables set under the trees—terrible, tart, sour wine but everyone happy, drinking, singing. Oh! The hills covered with vines. The tidy, *heimlich* towns, all tucked in, hiding their garbage where no one can see it. You can gaze upon the Rhine and Danube, upon the breathtaking confluence of the Rhine and Mosel. And think only of the beautiful music they inspired, the waltzes, the ladies swept around the floor by dashing men. And Bavaria at Christmastime: Go to a *Christkindlmarkt*, the little shacks that appear in every church square selling tree ornaments, *Glühwein*, *Lebkuchen*, lights shining in the dark of a winter night. By God! You can enjoy the whole canon: Goethe, Schiller, read all the masterworks without once wondering: How did such a culture, in which we were so intricately woven, how did it cast us out? What am I saying—cast us out? Murdered us! If you are not a Jew, my darling, you are free from all this. You can look at the peasants bringing in the crops and never think, Were they devoted Nazi Party members? Are they living in grandmother's summer house? Did they take all the old silver?

Europe! It can be yours to love. The cathedrals, the ancient city centers, the twisting streets, so picturesque. Eat a Sacher torte for me when you are in Vienna while you gaze at the great St. Stephen's. And never imagine Hitler's exuberant welcome into Austria. Listen to the lovely voices of the Boys' Choir, high and clear like angels, and never have to think: What joy the Führer took from hearing those tender boys!

And the Italian Riviera. Where Rosensaft and Bimko went to forget their Jewishness. Rent a villa! Swim in the Mediterranean! Rent a car and drive the Amalfi Coast. Go there and never have to think of compromise, defeat, embarrassment. Go there and simply enjoy it without a moment's thought that you are betraying your people. How can you not understand? I wanted to give you merely what Rosensaft and Bimko stole for themselves: Forgetfulness. Obliviousness. The ability to live, without guilt or sense of obligation, among those who murdered your family. Whereas . . . if you were my daughter . . . if you were a Jew . . .

If? intruded the patient. What is this "if I were"? I am your daughter, and you do admit that, don't you?

The clock slashed away at the seconds.

There is nothing to admit, said Michal at last. Admit—as if it were a crime. Yes. You are my daughter.

So I am your daughter. Born in Bergen-Belsen. Given away to a priest. But you at least agree: I am—

My daughter. Do you need me to say it again?

I do. I need you to say it!

Yes. I cannot say it more directly than this: You. Are. The. Daughter. I. Gave. Away. In. Belsen.

Therefore, said the patient, I am the daughter of a Jewish woman. So then: How can I not be a Jew?

You are not a Jew just because I bore you.

A Jew is something I *am*!

No. It is not inherited—

—everyone believes it is.

So to hell with them. That is some nonsense made up by racists and old rabbis. In any case, why does anyone have to know anything about it? It is no one's business. You just decide! Decide right now. You simply do it. From then on, you are what you always thought you were: Protestant. *Protestant!*

Michal slapped the table.

Make up your mind to it, she said. Now. Then it's done, finished, over: You are not a Jew!

109.

And what followed, in Michal's next breath, were the shouted sentences with which this encounter was fated to end:

Do not look for me again! she cried out. I beg you: Never again try to contact me!

Yet now we heard those words in a different light.

The patient clicked off the tape recorder, then said nothing for ten or fifteen seconds. The sounds of the night rose from the street: the complaint of the hotel doorman's taxi whistle, the church carillon playing the three-quarter hour, cars idling on New Montgomery Street. From deep inside our building came its systemic hum.

You know, the patient said finally. I really can't think of her as my mother. She threw me out of her life—twice—and what sort of mother does that? No. She is not a mother. Not really my mother.

Said Dr. Schussler: Yes. That is right. She is not a mother to you.

But I can't hate her, the patient said. Because she hates her own life more than I could ever hate her. I think she really believed she was saving me from it, from her, from everything that had happened to her.

Dr. Schussler hummed in agreement.

It's sad, said the patient.

Sad how? asked Dr. Schussler.

The patient hesitated. Then she said:

The whole story is more about her than about anything else. It's the good and the bad news: Her shoving me out was not about me; it was about her.

I see the good news, replied the therapist. But how is it bad?

Oh! sighed the patient. All that angst about should I find her or not. Then, if I wanted to find her, how could I possibly do it. Then, having found her, should I go see her. All that: years of suppression, then examination, then suspense, then action. Funny. And after all that, finding my birth mother turns out to be all but irrelevant.

Whatever I was or wasn't didn't matter to her, she went on. Her story and mine do not intersect.

Then both sat silently as the truth of the patient's statement permeated the night.

We will meet again on Wednesday, said the doctor.

Yes, Wednesday, said the patient.

A long pause followed. The night sounds—the horns, the taxi whistle, the tires whispering by—reinhabited the room as the human voices retreated.

Her story and mine do not intersect.

The patient's words lingered behind her, rustling in the air like felicitous banners.

And I thought: If only the world could be stopped, right here, in this calm harbor of time, as the patient sails on without her mother. For what a perfect ending we had come to for this chapter of the patient's life.

FOUR

110.

So did we come to the patient's final session before the Thanksgiving hiatus. She would break no new ground, I thought, as was normal for analysands on the verge of being deserted by their analysts. I expected the hour to dispose of itself lightly: fifty minutes of chitchat amounting to a delicate farewell.

Right on schedule, the loudspeakers reappeared in the lobby (one week before Thanksgiving somehow signaling to unknown authorities the official start of the Christmas season). Lights twinkled along the high moldings; poinsettias bloomed unnaturally in green plastic pots planted upon the podium; "Jingle Bells" played to distraction. As I approached the elevator—the music treacling a quarter tone out of tune, the speakers buzzing, as they had a year ago—I realized this was a time when I should be succumbing to my familiar despair. The crows should be taunting me: *laughing all the way.*

Yet where were they? Perhaps they were hiding, as they often did, the wily ones, the cowards; hovering just below the sensory limit, or so they thought. They did not know that if I stilled myself I could hear them, sense them, taste their bitterness.

I ascended in the crowded cab. It was damp from wet coats; eyeglasses fogged in the sudden heat. All felt normal: people going to work, pleasant people who made way for one another as they reached their intended floors, some even wishing the departing passenger a good day. Perhaps all this civility was a clue, a phony niceness, a prisoner's village designed to make one relax vigilance.

But something seemed changed in the very atmosphere. For the first time in many years—how many I did not wish to name, for the days wound back to my boyhood and the onset of my condition—I felt no sense of menace. Things seemed, oddly for me, just as they were. The fogged eyeglasses were just that. The damp coats were only wool and polyester and dye. They signified nothing. Nothing hid in the fog; lurked in the folds.

I dared to think: Perhaps I had indeed undergone a miraculous cure. Perhaps the therapist's teachings about my circling thoughts (*Let them go! Let them go!*) had robbed the demons of their power. Perhaps the patient's presence in my life, and mine in hers, had transformed me.

I thought back to the prior session, to what the patient had said about her mother's life: *Her story and mine do not intersect.*

As the cab rose floor by floor, the fear that I had done her harm began to evaporate. By the time I stepped out on eight, I was convinced that my intervention had been salutary; that I had given her the gift she had come to want above all else: knowledge of her mother, and—much more—freedom from her.

I sat in my office. The hours floated away, and at last my dear patient arrived. She sat down. But where was the opening chat? There came only silence, then the patient's words:

There has been a complication.

Oh? replied the therapist.

One could hear the patient take a breath, then stop to retrieve whatever further words she was about to speak.

And? the doctor prompted.

Then finally the patient said:

I saw Mother.

(Oh, no! I thought.)

Big-M Mother? asked Dr. Schussler.

Mother. Big M.

(Mother! I wanted to shout. Just when we were about to dispense with mothers for good, why did this other mother have to return to our narrative?)

But of course this was precisely what Dr. Schussler had been waiting for! I thought with some disgust. This return, this hope of rapprochement with the stiff couple the patient called Father and Mother. Hadn't the therapist said as much to Dr. Gurevitch? One could hear the doctor's happy expectation in the quick creak of her leather seat, in her sudden, small intake of air, as if she had taken a sip of a drink about to give her pleasure.

And? she asked.

The patient said nothing.

I think I've only come back to where I started, the patient finally said.

111.

Immediately following last Wednesday's session, my dear patient had received a phone call.

Did someone die, Mother? she asked upon hearing the familiar smoke-huskied voice.

Why would someone have died?

You never call me unless someone has died or is sick enough to be on the verge of it, said the patient.

Nonsense, dear.

The mother went on to say that she and the patient's father would be in Pebble Beach over the weekend.

That is near you, dear, isn't it? her mother said.

Yes, Mother. A two-hour drive at most.

We're going to be there this weekend. All expenses paid!

A large building-supply corporation was rewarding architects who specified their products, said her mother. Friday seminars for the men. Coffee circles for the ladies. On Saturday the men would play a round of golf at what the patient's mother called "that fabulous, famous course," while the wives attended "golfing clinics." "Clinics," thought the patient, as if the women were ill and in need of rehabilitation while their husbands braved the brisk air of the Monterey Peninsula.

They promised us a suite with a fireplace, her mother rattled on. A view of the ocean. On Saturday night, a formal gala. I shall finally get to wear that midnight-blue gown that has been hanging in my closet all this time, waiting for my life to catch up to its glamour, she said, laughing at her own little quip.

The patient's heart began to thump irregularly. It was the pressure of all that she could not say, she told her therapist, the avoidance, the pretense.

Surely you didn't call to invite me to a gala, the patient said to her mother.

Of course not, dear! What would you do at a gala? In any case, we don't have an invitation for you. But I was thinking: You'll come down here for lunch. It will be lovely. You will enjoy it.

The patient laughed to herself. You will enjoy it!

Then she thought: I probably should lie about prior plans. Or say I have to work.

I knew that if I went, she said to Dr. Schussler, I would have to tell her about finding Michal. And suddenly I wanted to tell her—bash her with it.

Bash her? asked the doctor.

Yes. Fling it in her face.

The drive down to the Peninsula took just a little over an hour and a half. By eleven a.m. Saturday, the patient was taking the turnoff from Route 101 for Pacific Grove.

But here things went awry. The low-hanging marine layer obscured the narrow, curving roads. The wind-stricken cypress trees, black in the fog, seemed coiled up, ready to spring upon any car whose driver was not paying exquisite attention. And the signs were demonic; they seemed designed to keep her circling forever in the shrouded lanes. She followed the turns for the Lodge at Pebble Beach, where her parents were staying, but somehow always found herself at the Inn at Spanish Bay. Three times she made the circuit, and three times the sign for "Spanish Bay" came looming out of the mist like some inescapable fate. She retraced her turns, and decided to go left at what had been a right, where the signs pointed to the "Scenic 17 Mile Drive." The direction seemed wrong, vectoring away from the Lodge. And yet, inexplicably, not five minutes later, there was the correct driveway and the valets taking keys from the arriving guests.

She pulled into the long driveway in her 1966, much-dented Volvo, her squashed bug of a car lining up behind Cadillacs and Lincoln Continentals, bargelike Buicks and Pontiacs, a few BMWs and Mercedes-Benzes, and some modest rented Fords and Chevrolets. Finally she reached the entrance. The valet tried to put her car into reverse, and failed.

You have to double-clutch it for reverse, she told him.

His face was blank. She took the keys and parked it herself.

A concierge in the lobby directed her to the area reserved for the ladies' golfing clinics, and she followed his directions to a foggy hillside where fifteen ladies were, variously, practicing chip shots, putting, and driving. At the far end, whacking a ball off a tee, was her mother.

She seemed to glow out of the fog. She was wearing beige slacks with a slightly golden hue and a cashmere sweater in a soft salmon color. She was only a little less bejeweled than she would be for a gala: two rings, a heavy gold necklace, teardrop-shaped pearls dancing on diamond-encrusted wires—earrings so familiar that the patient could recognize them at a distance. The only concessions her mother seemed to have made to the sporting nature of the occasion were the shoes, spiked golf shoes, and an old madras-print bandana around her head, to prevent her teased and sprayed hair from blowing about in the wind.

The patient tried to keep herself standing there, watching her mother, hoping to see that woman there in the salmon sweater as a separate person, someone she could examine and evaluate as if she were a stranger. Her mother was not a bad golfer, she saw. Her stance was good; she kept her head down and addressed the ball; her swing was balanced. Her drives sailed high into the fog then arched down far across the narrow little valley below; and the patient could see the pleasure that the woman—there, the person she was seeing for the first time—was taking in her expertise.

But immediately, her mother—her internalized big-M Mother—took hold, and the patient saw herself through the surveying eyes about to slide over her. She saw the inadequacy of her own outfit; of the gray shirt that had been chosen under fluorescent light which now, in daylight, was revealed to clash with the gray of her pants. Most of all, there was the disaster of her hair, which, with the wind and humidity, had become a mass of frizz.

(Run for your life! I wanted to shout to my dear patient, as if the story had not already happened; as if disaster could still be averted.)

Mother! she called out.

Her mother, who was addressing the ball as the shout came, looked up for a moment. Then she returned to the tee and took her hit.

A massive drive! her mother whooped. Darling! Did you see that?

Terrific, Mother, the patient said.

She walked up to the tee. Her mother stood and watched her come closer. And already the once-over was beginning: the scrutiny, the tightened eyes searching as if down a bombsight, enjoying the hunt for the exact spot to destroy.

Are you sure that top goes with those pants, dear?

You should mention my hair right now, replied the patient.

All right. Can't you comb it or something?

Hello, Mother, the patient said, going up to her for the obligatory kiss on the cheek.

How nice of you to drive down, her mother said.

Her mother bent down and put another ball on her tee. As she arranged her stance, she said, I hope you don't mind. I've invited one of the other ladies here to join us for lunch. Quite a lovely lady. You'll like her.

Whack! went the drive, and her mother watched it sail over the hill and into the little valley.

I'd rather it was just the two of us, said the patient.

Her mother placed a new ball on the tee. Oh, why is that, dear? I hope you're not going to bring up . . . Well.

She looked up into the haze, briefly distracted from her golfing. Then she returned to her tee.

The patient's focus was so acute that her mother's movements seemed to unfold in slow motion. The little wiggles of her mother's behind as she adjusted her stance. The club head easing toward the ball for the near-kiss of the address. The arc of the club, gently, gently rising toward its apogee. And just at that point—just as her mother was about to uncoil her body and unleash the forces of physics, the patient said:

I found Maria G.

The club head wobbled at the top of the arc. The stroke was enervated. The club barely hit the ball, which wobbled off the tee.

Her mother looked around as if to see whether anyone had seen her bad shot; if anyone were listening; if anyone could possibly wonder over the cryptic "I found Maria G."

Her mother threw down her club. It's the hotel's equipment, she said. Then she strode off, her back to the patient as she called out, Let's go to the room.

112.

The patient chased her mother up and down corridors that seemed to her all alike but that signified something to her mother, she supposed. They spoke not a word, as if any conversation would poison the air of the hallways, seep under the doorways, into the suites where rewarded clients stared into their fireplaces or gazed upon the restless Pacific.

Her mother's room was luxurious, the patient saw, as her mother gave her a perfunctory tour: a small kitchen, a central area where three small couches surrounded a fireplace, a sliding door onto a patio that overlooked the ocean, a vast bedroom, a marble bathroom as large as a normal person's dining room. Laid out upon the bed was her mother's gown, the midnight-blue one she had waited so long to wear, its sheer organdy sleeves flung upward, like a woman waiting to be ravished.

So, her mother said, sitting on the bed to change the golf shoes for her blue satin, wedge-heeled bedroom slippers. So . . . You have found her. Your—what did we agree to call her?—your *birth* mother.

Yes, said the patient. Birth mother.

Her mother rubbed her ankle. Then she untied the bandana.

How's my hair? she asked, patting it all around. Not too blown out?

It's fine, Mother.

With a sigh, her mother stood, checked her face in the mirror over the dresser, then left the bedroom for the area by the fireplace, where she opened the sliding door an inch or two. Immediately the crash of the Pacific filled the room, along with cold, damp air. Fog obscured the view.

Her mother dropped her weight onto the sofa that faced the sliding door. Her back was to the patient as she said:

Was it difficult? I mean finding her?

Not really.

And you saw her.

I did.

Her mother took a cigarette from a pack on the coffee table and lit it. Then she patted the sofa cushion next to her.

Come sit down, she said.

They sat side by side, saying nothing for several seconds, her mother

341

dragging on her cigarette and blowing out smoke, and the ocean below thrashing beneath its clouds. Looking back at mother and daughter were their pale reflections in the door glass: two outlines against white-out, and the dancing red spot of her mother's cigarette.

Finally the patient said: I found her through the Catholic agency Father used—well, it was his father, I suppose—the one he used to adopt me.

Her mother turned, shocked.

What?

Through the agency that arranged my adoption.

But—she took a drag on her cigarette—but I don't think there ever was an actual agency. I mean, not a real one, not in the sense of social workers and so forth.

But didn't you tell me that? That I got adopted through a Catholic agency?

Her mother smoked. Well, maybe I did. I don't remember that time too clearly. As I told you, I never wanted to remember it at all, until you—

The patient all but saw her mother's censor leap onto the stage: a fig-ure in a black robe, priestly, rushing in to clip out any deep, hard emotion that might have the audacity to express itself.

They have a bar here in the room, her mother said. Completely stocked. We could have martinis.

No martinis for me, Mother. I'm not drinking. But you go ahead.

Not at all?

No. Not at all these days.

It was a rebuff. Her mother stubbed out her cigarette, stood, took the four steps into the kitchenette, where she opened the freezer and re-trieved a small bottle of vodka. She simply poured the liquor over ice, as if too annoyed to go through the cocktail ritual herself.

She remained standing, leaning on a counter, sipping her drink.

So, she said after several seconds, I suppose she is living in some hor-rid circumstances.

You mean my birth mother? Not at all, said the patient. She has a charming stone house in Israel. South of Tel Aviv. Her name is now Michal, by the way, not Maria. And the G stood for Gerstner when she was in Germany. But now her last name is Gershon. She changed it to make it more Israeli.

Of course, said her mother. Now it sounds even more . . . *Jewish.*

She had flung out the word, and left it hanging there. Then she returned to her drink and asked:

And is she pretty?

The patient laughed. Yes, she said.

Prettier than I am?

The patient sighed.

Mother. Please.

Well. Naturally, I'm curious about her looks. Last I knew of her, from the records, she was slim and blond with "Aryan" features. Is she still?

Yes.

Still slim and fit?

Still slim. But not as fit as you are. She walks with a limp, using a cane.

Poor woman.

She drank. Then she went to sit on the sofa next to the patient, her focus on the invisible ocean.

How was it? she asked. Did she . . . receive you well?

Not at first, said the patient. She laughed. At first she tried to throw me out—

Throw you out?

Yes. Look. I just walked into her life and scared her to death.

Well, said her mother. That I can understand. The sudden upset—

Before her mother could condemn her for creating "upset," a terrible breach of Mother's extensive social code, the patient rushed in to say:

But Michal eventually told me her whole story.

Her mother listened with a noncommittal face, smoking one cigarette after another, as the patient relayed Michal's history in some detail, from her early days in Germany to her landing, finally, in Israel. The patient did not leave out the circumstances under which she was conceived, under which she was born and given away.

What a dreadful story!

Hard at times, yes, the patient said. But Michal's experience wasn't all dreadful. The camp organized itself into a sort of village. She made it to Israel. All those horrors she was able to survive and overcome.

For all of her . . . surrendering you, said her mother, it seems you still think her noble.

Yes, replied the patient. Now that you bring up that word, yes. I might say her surviving was noble.

The patient's mother hummed and stirred her glass, setting the ice to clinking.

Well, then. You got what you wanted from the experience, I'm assuming.

Maybe, said the patient. I don't know yet.

In any case, you've gone and done it. You found the mythical birth mother. Maria G., who is now—what is it?—Michal Gersh-something.

Gershon.

And you know all about her and where she lives.

She paused.

And what comes next? asked her mother.

She took a short sip of her drink.

Can we expect that we'll be losing you? asked her mother with a toss of her head. Are we to think that you'll be—ha! ha!—"running off" to her?

What was this? thought the patient. Could it be that her mother feared losing her? Had she really spent all those years afraid that some-one would appear, some family person from the darkness of Europe, and snatch her away?

Right then, the patient told Dr. Schussler, I thought it might even be true that this mother loved me. In her way.

No, Mother, the patient said. I'm staying here. I'm not going off to live with her.

Ah, said her mother.

Meaning what? the patient thought.

But, darling, her mother continued, doesn't it bother you that you come from . . . all that?

All that.

No, it wasn't love, the patient decided. That "ah" was relief that she retained, for herself alone, the prerogatives of "mother."

You're the one who's bothered by it, dearest Mother.

Don't say that, darling.

You're the one who doesn't want anyone to know that your adopted daughter is really a lesbian daughter of a Jew.

Her mother clacked down her glass. Why must you always throw this in my face! Can't you understand how much it upsets me? That you're not going to have a husband, that—

That I'm not going to produce grandchildren for you. But in any case, Mother, they would be Jews too. All of them. Jewishness goes from mother to child. The father doesn't matter. I could marry stuffy Prince Charles, and your little grandchildren would still be Jews. Jew after Jew after Jew.

Her mother bolted from the sofa, opened the sliding door so forcefully that it shook. She took one step onto the patio. But when she saw her drink was nearly gone, she raced back in to "refresh" it. Then she strode back outside.

The wind invaded the room. The long curtains bordering the door were flung to and fro. Something in the kitchen blew off a shelf; it was a plastic napkin holder, the patient saw, and white cocktail napkins were swirling up and around before settling to the floor.

The patient went out to the patio and stood next to her mother, who was leaning on a railing, drink in hand. They said nothing for a long while. The crash and hiss of the dangerous North Pacific rose up to fill the silence between adoptive mother and daughter. Occasionally, the mother sipped her drink, the tinkling of the ice adding a high, clear ring to the air. Alcoholic wind chime, thought the patient.

Maybe you should go live with her, said her mother finally.

What?

Maybe you should go live there. Maybe there you'll be better . . . placed.

You mean it would be easier for you.

No. I'm thinking of you. It's so obvious you're not happy with me.

The patient grabbed the railing. It seemed cruel to come right out and say, It's true. I was never happy with you.

But it doesn't matter what you think, she finally said. Or what I think. Michal doesn't want me.

She doesn't want you there? asked her mother, her head whipping around. Doesn't want you . . .

Either. That's what you're going to say, right? She doesn't want me either.

Don't say that! How can you say that!

The patient laughed. I know you, Mother. Don't think I don't know you. But it makes no difference anyway. Either, neither, both. Doesn't matter. Michal thinks I'm better off here. You think I'm better off there. Well, at least my two dear mothers agree on something.

Oh! said her mother. Why do you keep talking about all this? Why do you want to go and upset everyone? Because that's what you've done. That's exactly what you've done.

She whirled her whole body around to face the patient, then stood tipping sideways when she came to the end of the turn, the vodka having gotten to her.

That poor woman in Israel, she went on with a hint of boozy anger. You went barging into her life. No warning. Here I am, here I am, your long-lost daughter. And you've upset yourself with all this questioning. And most of all, you've upset me—brought this all up out of the past, made me go back into all that . . . muck, that nasty business, when it all could have been packed away in a clean little box and put away for good.

She wheeled around to face the ocean, then the door again. You were always like this, she said. Can't you ever leave well enough alone?

Then she wobbled off the patio in her blue satin slippers.

After several seconds, during which the patient swore to her therapist she felt nothing, she, too, left the patio. She found her mother in the bedroom.

So it's all my fault, the patient said, walking into the room.

Her mother ignored her. She was arranging and rearranging the skirt of the midnight-blue, silk-and-organdy dress.

Now what in the world will I tell Father when he sees I'm so upset? What will I tell him? He'll take one look at me and see I'm all upset. Oh! she sighed, stroking the sleeve of the gown. How can I possibly enjoy myself tonight?

113.

My dear patient drove home through the foggy lanes, again going around and around her lost circuit, this time returning perpetually to the Lodge at Pebble Beach rather than the Inn at Spanish Bay. The repeating sight of the stone driveway, valets leaping at the head of it, made her neck sweat. For each circuit gave her another opportunity to decide whether or not to see her father; and each time she had to remind herself that he would be in the bar by the last hole, whatever they called it here, the Nineteenth Hole or the Hole in One or the Caddy Shack or the Driver or the Mulligan or the Cheap Shot Inn—she had visited him in all of them. Her father's hale-thee-well greeting. The back-slapping men. The introductions to Jims and Joes she would never see again. Once more she would tell herself, Why bother? And then she would try to leave the place, only to keep finding it again and again.

Dr. Schussler tried to soften the effect of the visit. She told the patient that she was right to wonder if her mother did indeed love her. Because her mother did love her, as best she could; which was to say not very deeply or very well.

Do you think your sister basks in the glow of adoring love? she asked the patient. Could your mother truly see a daughter, any daughter, without also seeing someone to serve her, adorn her life, reassure her that she was beautiful and lovely and loved?

You're right, replied the patient. But it makes me feel monstrous.

Monstrous? But how?

Not being able to feel love. What sort of monster doesn't love her mother?

You could never, ever fulfill her, replied the therapist. You know that.

There was a long pause.

You know that, repeated the doctor.

Yes, the patient said in a whisper. Yes. I do.

And at that the session closed.

114.

The therapist was taking an extended holiday. And so fourteen days of the Thanksgiving break stood before me, each a stake in a high fence (for so I envisioned it) over which I had to leap if I were to survive without my dear patient. Despite believing myself bettered by my association with her, I knew I could not rest. Long experience had taught me the wiliness of my demons, the strength of my crepuscular self, and how swiftly it might return to claim me.

For the holidays fell upon me as they had a long year ago: the smiling cardboard Indians and Pilgrims taped to store windows everywhere; the disgustingly cheerful music; the twinkling lights on streetlamps; the empty lobby wherein vacant elevators continued to ride up and down, up and down, ogled by the cherubs; the building's long, silent corridors where dusk gathered at the far ends. And Thanksgiving Day itself dawned as unpleasantly as it had the year before: cold with intermittent rain. Once more the streets were filled with haunted men who smelled of terrible things.

I feared I might not sustain myself through the day. Yet I did not fall. I was not fine, but I did not fall. And during the immediately following days—the panic of post-Thanksgiving shopping, the frothed atmosphere as Christmas approached—I seemed to hover just at the margin. Some current, some sort of magnetic field, hummed below me, like a net stretched above the dark zones, into which I did not tumble.

Yet, come the Friday before the patient's Wednesday return, my supports threatened to desert me. It might have been the rain, which fell with deluvian determination; or the ceaseless wind; or the ocean's roar outside my cottage, which kept grating upon my ears like an amputating saw cutting through bone. Adding to it all, a report that braved the static of my radio: an atomic submarine that had released radioactive waste onto the beaches of Guam, fifty times the supposedly safe dosage, which spoke to me of a despaired world where we human beings were doomed to destroy ourselves, and everything else along with us.

Whatever the cause, single or joint, I suddenly looked around my cottage and was startled by the condition in which I found it. All about:

the litter of tasks started and abandoned. Ironing board open, iron radiating heat, forgotten. Water boiled away on the stove for tea that had not gotten made. Hangers and shirts, obviously waiting to be joined and hung, lay strewn across the bed. A sandwich prepared—how long ago?—tomato leaking through the bread, its red stain spreading outward from the center. A scissors lying on the kitchen table, legs open, blades ashine: to cut what? And a slow fear grew in me. Was I regressing? If so, how far would I fall? For I had not engaged in such behavior since Dr. Schussler's "lesson" on how to release obsessive thoughts.

In this state, I heard the mail fall through the door slot. The usual junk lay scattered upon the floor. Then came an odd sound—a scrape, another scrape, then another—and I saw, coming through the slot, section by section, a thick manila envelope. The postman continued to stuff it through, a few inches at a time, until the whole legal-sized mass of it fell to the floor with a thud.

I walked over to it; did not touch it; only looked down. And once more I was forced to consider the existence of Providence, some unknown intervening force come to distract me from one trail of obsession and set me upon another. For I saw the return address: the university's Office of the Provost.

I had been expecting something, some action, some decision, since receiving the letter telling me that my "case," as it had been put, was to come up before the committee in October. And it was only because of the patient, and my engagement in her mother's story—how much I owed them!—that I had not spent the time worrying over the proceedings; had not perseverated (as I was so wont to do), playing scenes over and over in my mind, refining the torture, each scenario darker and more damning than the last, until I imposed upon myself a judgment impossibly more harsh than any verdict to come. Death. I should die.

So this, finally, was the end, I thought, taking the heavy envelope into my hands. Surely it was filled with legal papers I had to sign, where, in dense language, I offered up my resignation; wherein I attested to the fact that I was voluntarily unbinding the university from the contract of my tenure. They would crush me otherwise. My quiet going-away might at least secure for me the possibility of teaching somewhere, at a junior college, some night courses; might at least save me from destitution (or worse, I tried not to think: from jail).

I spent several minutes simply holding the envelope, as if procrastination could fool fate.

The very weight of it seemed damning.

Over my shoulder waited the abandoned tasks.

There was no recourse, nowhere else to go.

On the kitchen table: the ready, spread-legged scissors.

115.

Atop a deep stack of paper was a cover letter typed on university stationery. It contained a single paragraph:

> Enclosed please find copies of transcripts of conversations conducted with the complainants and others who voluntarily provided information pertinent to the matter.

I noticed that the typewriter's letter *P* was missing its descender. Otherwise there was nothing else to see on the page but the stamped signature of the university provost.

The heft of the transcripts loomed behind it, a stack thick enough to strain my hands, which began to shake. So much? I thought. Had they done all this because of me?

I flipped through and saw that within the stack were groups of pages stapled together, each stapled group comprising one transcript. In the top left-hand corner, in bold, handwritten letters, was the name of the "conversant." So it was that I could flip through the stack and, like one of those children's cartoon books that create a little movie if one flips through quickly, I could see a sort of documentary of my life. Everyone I had known, everyone with whom I had come in contact, student, faculty, and staff, popped up in alphabetical order as if standing before me: to remind me of who I might be to them, how they might have seen me, what I did or did not do; what I said or left unsaid; to him, to her, to him, to him, to him, to her, to her, to her.

Her! Her! Her!

Out flew the crows, as I feared they might. For in those pages was my darker self, laid bare to some, still invisible to others; and did I want to know which I was, and to whom?

I put the whole mass of pages in the dirty, unused oven, and shut the door, thinking that I would wait, wait and see until the patient's return, when I might be stronger. Yet as the hours advanced, it was as if something were banging against the grime-smeared glass of the oven door, and I knew I could not hide from those hundreds of pages, from those thousands of words.

I read through the night, forcing myself to go on and on, no matter what, not allowing myself to mark any pages or scream back with any defenses; only reading, transcript after transcript, until light glowed at the corners of the window shades and the last page was turned. And yet I still could not decipher who I was, what I was. Some saw me as a decent man; a few as an ogre. Who was right? The committee would have to decide.

116.

The next day, for sustenance, I went to the office. I asked the help of the friends who had taken me thus far: the hardworking gargoyles, the lobby in its purity, the empty reception podium, where my providential protector once had stood guard over me, the cherubs floating above the elevators, the steadfast marble sentries who lined the hall.

I came to our dear eighth floor. I touched the golden letters that spelled out Dr. Schussler's name on her door. I rubbed my hands over the doorposts of my own. For I felt—as I once had, a long year and three months ago—that it had not been guilt and despair that had sent me here. I had not fled the university pursued by the ever-vengeful Furies. I had been led here by Athena's Eumenides—the kindly ones, the gracious ones—who had brought me to this building, this office with its lucky number 807; to the thin door that adjoined my room to the one next door, through which I had become adjoined to my dear patient.

Then the days advanced toward the patient's return.

Yet the weight of the transcripts hung upon me. And I had to ask myself: Was I altogether innocent? Could I say with utter certainty there had been nothing of love in my feelings for the boy? Was it only a metaphysical love; only the charged feelings between mentor and apprentice? Was I not always on the brink of transgression, taunted by my foes, my darker nature, just as I had been with the patient?

If not for the boy's running off . . . If not for his disappearance . . . If I had come to San Francisco earlier . . . Let us say I had found him that night in the Castro . . . If it had been his eyes that looked back at me in the bar's flashing blue light . . . If we had encountered each other there and then . . . what?

117.

Such was my unmoored state as the long Thanksgiving hiatus came to an end. Perhaps it was asking too much to hope that the patient's return, of itself, would restore me to equanimity. Yet in no way could I have anticipated the next turn of events.

For no sooner did the patient take her seat in Dr. Schussler's office than she said:

I went back to Tel Aviv.

(God, no! I wanted to cry out. We have already dispensed with this mother!)

I'm surprised, said Dr. Schussler (repressing her own shock, as one could tell from the creaks of her leather chair).

I believe, the doctor went on, that you had come to the conclusion that your life and Michal's did not intersect.

(Exactly! Good work, Dr. Schussler. Remind her of her freedom!)

A silence of several seconds spread itself out between client and doctor into which car horns blared and radiators spat their steam.

Finally Dr. Schussler said:

It is because of what happened in Pebble Beach, yes?

Further silence from the patient.

Is that what propelled you to return?

Yeah. Sure. At Pebble Beach, it was clearer than ever that big-M Mother is no mother. And Michal, what kind of mother is she? What kind of mother throws out her own flesh and blood? Yeah. Going back. My last try. Last try to get myself a mother.

And did you? asked the doctor.

No.

No?

But I found someone else. Someone else I'm related to.

Oh! said Dr. Schussler. Wonderful!

The patient did not immediately reply.

Wonderful, repeated the doctor. Yes?

Maybe. Maybe not.

118.

I took a last-minute flight, said the patient, standby. I let the taxi driver suggest some hotel—it was fine. I dropped off my bag, and went directly to Michal's house.

I found the door open. A crack. I gave it a little push. It fell open all the way.

I yelled out, Hello? Anyone there? I waited. No one answered.

I walked halfway down the hall and yelled again, Hello, hello.

Finally someone in the kitchen—from the direction of the kitchen—called back: Here. I am in here.

The kitchen. I stopped at the threshold. There was a woman in an army uniform standing with her back to me. There was a rifle slung over her shoulder. I saw groceries on the table—milk, bread, apples. She took off the gun. Put it in the corner.

Hello, I said again.

And the woman turned around.

She looked like me.

Exactly like me.

I was on instant recognition. But I should check, came to me. To be sure. Each feature. Eyes, mouth, chin, cheekbones, shape of the head—the same, the same, the same, the same. Hair dark brown, little halo of frizz—the same.

Gott! whispered Dr. Schussler.

(A sister! How did I not know there was a sister?)

Then I felt tricked. My eyes playing tricks on me. Seeing what I wanted to see. Another look. Army uniform, rifle over the shoulder, strange expression on her face: Suspicion? Disdain? Not me, not me, not me.

All this is happening in—what? A second? Two? And I'm thinking, How do I know what I really look like? In the mirror. A pose. Preferred angle. Flattering expression. Maybe someone would say we don't look alike at all.

We were just standing there. Not moving. Then in some heavy accent the woman said, Who are you.

It wasn't a question. Her tone was flat, dead flat.

I'm Michal's daughter, I said. From America.

My sister—she had to be my sister—tipped back her head and squinted at me. Then she said in that same dead flat voice:

I am also Michal's daughter.

We kept standing there, just looking at each other. She scanned my face, features, body. Like I did with her. She inventoried me—that's what it felt like, being inventoried. Probably that's what she saw in me. When I was checking. To be sure.

We are similar in appearance, she said.

I think more than similar.

Yes, more than similar.

I look like someone.

My head went light. Balloon light. I don't know what expression Leni saw on my face. Leni—she told me later her name was Leni—I don't know what she saw. My face felt inert. Like my whole body. Inert. My breathing, gasps for air—maybe she understood from my breathing.

But I saw something in her. Her expression was the same as when she first saw me. Head back. Squinting. Then her mouth slowly turned down.

She said: How did you come to be here?

I came to find my birth mother. Last summer. I'm adopted. Michal— she is my birth mother.

I knew it, said Leni. I knew something must have happened. Last summer. Something changed. So it was—

Me.

We didn't know what to say after that. The clock ticked. I heard a car go by. Leni stopped scrutinizing me. Finally she said,

And how did you find her to be? I mean, what sort of reception did she give you?

Why do you ask?

She tipped her head to one side and laughed.

I am imagining she was not happy to see you.

Yes. Right. She sent me away.

So why did you come back?

I don't know.

You should not have come back. You should leave.

I was startled, a little afraid. I didn't know what to do. But just finding her—a sister, almost a twin—it never occurred to me to turn around and leave. I kept staring at her. And she stared back: Standing taller. Shoulders back. Chest high. A soldier. A soldier's stance.

Leave? Do you really think I could leave now? I said. Just when I find a sister—we have to be sisters.

Yes. Sisters. What else could we be?

It was strange. We didn't say more about how alike we were. As if it was too weird. Or something we couldn't cope with right then, or wouldn't, not knowing each other. Almost doubles—what it meant. In Leni: no sign of joy, tentative joy, or happiness, or relief. Something else.

We exchanged names. She told me then: Leni Gershon. We said what we did for a living—she's an engineer, a civil engineer. We compared birth dates—she's just a year and a half older than I am. We both said we didn't know about the other's existence.

So why do you think I shouldn't have come back? I said finally.

You may not like what you find out. About Michal. About where you came from.

My body bent over into a sort of crouch. Being tired. Maybe to defend myself. I don't know from what—yes, I knew, from her, something steely in her. How she towered over me.

And what did Michal tell you?

Everything.

Leni laughed. Well, not everything. You did not know about me. So you could not have come here looking for me. Then why are you here? What is it you hoped to gain by returning?

One thing, I said. The truth about why she gave me away. Why she never looked for me.

Heh. That is two questions.

I said nothing.

Are you sure you want to know? she asked.

Everyone has warned me off, I said to her, finding some bravery in myself. Mother—my adoptive mother. And a . . . a doctor that I see. And Michal. Everyone warning me. Thinking they'll spare me something. But I've already heard some awful things—and I survived. See? I'm back. And if there's more that's bad, I can take it.

Then I suddenly lost my little surge of courage. I couldn't go on. If I said, I don't have a mother, I need a mother, I came back to find a real mother, I'd break down in front of her. I could tell she wasn't a person who wanted to deal with sobs and tears. And I didn't want to look weak in front of her.

But she must have seen it in my face. She let go of her stance. She went "at ease," I suppose. Then she sighed and said:

Sit down. I will put the groceries away. Then we can talk.

She scraped back a chair for me, and I sat as the apples and milk went into the refrigerator. Bread, other things still in the bag, into cabinets and pantries. She picked up the rifle and put it in some other room. Then she came back, sat down in what had been Michal's chair last time I'd come.

She put her arms out on the table, leaning on her elbows, hands together, a triangle.

First, she said, before I tell you anything, you need to know a little about who I am, who I am in relation to Michal.

Her daughter.

Wait, please. "Daughter" tells you nothing. When Michal brought me here, it was very bad for me. Very bad. I was angry, furious. I hated her. Nine years old and hating everyone and everything around me to my bones.

Brought you here? From where?

Later. I will get to that later.

But why—

Later.

From her tone, I knew better than to keep asking questions. So I only said,

But you're still here.

Heh. Where else? Look. I had to come to terms with it. I am here, she is here. After all, she is my mother.

Mother, I said. Your mother. Maybe in time you forgave her for whatever happened. Maybe in time . . . you came to love her?

Leni laughed at me.

Are you still so sentimental about "mother"? Even after Michal sent you away? Between me and Michal, it is more like an armistice. We stopped fighting. We came to accept each other. Rely on each other. For day-to-day things. But love . . . Do you know what love is?

I was going to jump in and say of course. Then I thought of big-M Mother, drinking and disapproving. And about Michal, her face full of love—vanished in a moment. A few girlfriends, maybe, when it seemed like love in the beginning, the sex time. But . . . love?

I looked at Leni's face. Almost a duplicate of mine. And so hard, defended. And I saw myself in that, too.

Not really, I said.

119.

The patient seemed on the verge of tears. Yet several minutes had passed since the carillon had chimed the three-quarter hour. Dr. Schussler took in the breath that tells a patient—somehow, subliminally—We must stop now.

The days went by. The next session began. As if no time at all had passed, the patient resumed her story precisely where she had left off: after telling Leni she had no experience of love.

It's funny, she said. Leni seemed to relax just then. No, did not relax. Was maybe a little . . . friendlier. We made chitchat. About what kind of place I have in San Francisco. About where she lives, nearby, alone, "for the moment," as she put it. Then she asked about my life, my life before I found Michal, and after.

I gave her as quick a summary as I could. Born in Belsen. Michal's excuse for giving me away, so I wouldn't be a Jew. A quick trip through my nutso grandfather, the hand-off to big-M Mother and Father, all the way up to Michal, her story, her shooing me away. I tried to be a little glib about it. It didn't matter that Leni's mood had changed. She still wouldn't want me breaking down right in front of her.

But she surprised me. When I finished, she looked at me with a kind, almost mournful, face.

I am sorry all that happened to you, she said.

We said nothing for a while. I stared at the chair jammed against the wall, she out the window.

Then she said, Something to drink? Orange juice? Coffee? Tea?

Coffee, thanks.

She made instant coffee. Nescafé. I'd noticed that a lot of Israelis don't fuss over things like coffee. Seems they like things plain, quick, practical.

Now you, I said when she put the cups on the table. Your story.

My story, she said, shrugging. This will take some time.

I'm not in a rush.

She laughed. All right. But to get to me, we have to start with Michal. Did she tell you about what happened before the Nazis took her? About

360

her marriage to Albrecht Gerstner, about the false pregnancies and such?

Yes, said the patient. The whole story, starting with her family going to Amsterdam.

And did she tell you about how her father-in-law betrayed her?

Yes, that they nearly took her from her husband's graveside, then later came for her in the house.

And where did she say she went from there?

She refused to say anything about that time. Only that she was sent to a labor camp.

Leni broke into barking laughter, which utterly baffled me.

Well, Leni said, trying to stifle her laughs, labor did have something to do with it.

120.

It is an implausible story, Leni began. But survivor stories are all like that. Most of them. If not for something impossible or ridiculous or shameful—stealing bread, sleeping with guards—or pitiful—hiding in dirt basements, living off grass and weeds in the woods—or lucky—being young, healthy, with a strong constitution—or astoundingly brave—stealing guns from guards, jumping from trains—they would not have survived. So see Michal's story in that light. Is all of it true? Maybe yes, maybe no. Many survivors do not want to describe in detail what happened to them. The *Shoah* is a national bond here. But it ended only thirty years ago. Many of the survivors are just into their fifties. They were a generation that did not go in for therapy and talking cures.

So . . .

I think you already know that Michal was taken from the Gerstners' house directly to the train station. Her name was Maria then, but that is too strange, so I will call her Michal. She was about to be shoved into a packed car on its way to Theresienstadt, when an old friend came by. A former beau from her years in *Gymnasium*.

Leni laughed. I should say "another" beau from her *Gymnasium* days. There were more than a few, as she tells it.

All right. Now. This former beau was by then a Nazi officer, and he was shocked to see her being rough-handled by a low-ranking brute of a soldier. He grabbed her away, saying that he knew Michal, he could swear she was not a Jew, that she was a good Catholic who had lost her papers in a bombing raid. The duty officer did not look convinced—papers lost in bombing raids was a common ruse used by Jews in hiding. So the former beau quickly made up a story that she was pregnant with a child fathered by a senior SS officer—who would take some heads if he discovered his fiancée in Theresienstadt!

The duty officer had enough fear of the senior officer's rank that he went along, saying, if she was really pregnant with a good Aryan child, then he knew exactly where she should be. There were general orders, he said. Pregnant Aryan women who were not living with husbands or family were to be taken to a special maternity hospital.

Which, in many respects, said Leni, it was.

After spending two nights in a dormitory, Michal was transported to a small village in the vicinity of Poznán, Poland. She was very frightened. She had already been caught in one false-pregnancy scheme, and now she was on her way to a maternity hospital, where they would certainly know she was not pregnant. It was the winter of '44. The transport was a small, freezing bus. It took her east, where she could see what the war had done. Ruins, cold, somewhere in Poland—she was sure she was going to her death.

When she got to the hospital, of course the doctors knew immediately she was not pregnant. But instead of the transport to Auschwitz she expected, the doctors were surprisingly casual about the whole thing, saying something like, Oh, well. Such a pity you lost that pregnancy. It is too common these days. No fruits and vegetables. The stress of the war. Here you can rest and get a proper diet.

Just what sort of "hospital" was this? Michal wondered. It was a large stone structure, columns at the entry. There were extensive grounds around it, now covered with snow. Tall trees. Linen-wrapped hedges to protect them from the cold. When she had first arrived, she followed a nurse across the sprawling main floor, to a registration room, where they took down her particulars. She gave her name as Maria Gerstner, of course. Then the nurse walked her through a library, a drawing room, a solarium. They took an ornate ironwork lift to the third floor—Michal took particular care in describing it; something from the "before time." Then the nurse brought her to what she said was Michal's bedroom. A private room with two floor-to-ceiling windows draped with silk brocade, warm brown, tied back with gold tassels. Michal also described this in detail, again saying it reminded her of the "before time." The bed was wider than any she had ever seen before. There were many pillows, and a bedspread made of the same brown silk.

She went to dinner in a dining hall with white-tile walls. Hard walls that echoed the voices of the women. She thought there were thirty, maybe thirty-five women. They were called "patients." Michal noticed that the other "patients" were all blond, blue-eyed women like herself. Everyone spoke at least a little German. But many were comfortable only in Polish, or Czech—they were called Sudeten Germans by the staff. The women at the table did not speak among themselves except for the most commonplace things—How did you enjoy breakfast? Is your room warm enough? Do you need salt? A rule, evidently, because Michal noticed certain glances in the direction of the thin-faced matron who sat at the head.

Doctors examined her daily and found her to be in "excellent Aryan health." Despite the rules, the women found ways to tell her just what sort of hospital she was in.

It was a tranquil place. The women had soft beds, well-heated rooms, trees near the windows that would give shade come spring. They ate the finest foods. Entrecôte, veal, capon, trout. Buttered potatoes, spinach, kale, carrots, peaches, oranges—Michal described these foods in detail— fresh fruits and vegetables in the midst of war, rationing, hunger. The miracle was the fresh oranges, the mysterious golden oranges.

And then, to repay the good offices of the Reich for its munificence, if they were not currently pregnant, it was generally known that these pampered women should not be averse to enjoying the company of visiting Nazi officers. It was something called Lebensborn, meaning "life spring," a nasty little Nazi eugenics program to ensure the future of the master race.

The therapist gasped.

This is . . . unexpected, Dr. Schussler said.

Yes, said the patient. A shock.

121.

(Please God, no, I thought, as I sat listening. Lebensborn! How could I have known?)

Lebensborn, said the patient. I had no idea beyond what Leni told me later. But even then, she was sketchy, talking only about how it affected her life and Michal's. No background, nothing about why no one seems to know anything about it. When I got back home, before this session, I went to the library. Nothing, just a newspaper article from a small town in Kentucky that called it all bunk. It said Lebensborn centers were maternity hospitals. The story that they were brothels: bunk.

She paused, then said:

Do *you* know anything about it, Dr. Schussler?

The doctor said nothing, then:

I know it is . . . controversial.

You mean the argument over maternity hospital versus whorehouse.

No, said the doctor. Whether Lebensborn existed at all.

She inhaled deeply, as if needing a drag of a Viceroy.

But why would Leni talk about it? Say it's something that happened to Michal?

Well, there is some testimony from women who say they were kept there.

Say?

Most are not believed.

Rain sketched the windows, a soft rush against the panes.

The doctor took another drag on her invisible Viceroy.

The truth is not yet known, she said.

(You must tell her, Dr. Schussler. Tell her, once and for all, about your guilt at being German.)

So you say Michal is lying, said the patient.

As we have discussed, said Dr. Shussler. Michal has . . . embellished her experiences before.

And Leni? She's lying too?

She may simply be repeating what Michal told her.

You're saying everyone is lying! I can't believe it.

The doctor shifted about in her chair.

There is some hard evidence of Lebensborn, she said. I have heard about an old business registration. With Lebensborn in the name.

From that time? During the war?

Yes.

So something was there, said the patient.

One tattered record, I believe.

Doesn't that mean it existed but was kept secret?

Well, said the doctor with a laugh. You may say Lebensborn was not there. Or you may say it *was* there but kept a secret. One cannot prove something with a negative—prove that something existed because we have almost nothing about it.

(Sophistry!)

Why are you doing this? asked the patient. Why are you questioning everything?

The doctor took a deep breath. Please believe this, she said. It is my hope that you will think deeply about what you have learned. And come to know, within yourself, what is true in what your mother and sister have told you. And what may be a kind of truth they have told themselves.

(Was this some kind of excuse? Her German denial? Or had she been doing this from the beginning, asking the patient to question what she had been told?)

I'm completely confused, said the patient. Yes. No. False. True. My truth. Theirs.

I will leave you with this, said Dr. Schussler. The problem with Lebensborn is that there are too many versions. Fair-haired children kidnapped from Poland close to the German border. Orphaned Germans raised to see themselves as specimens of a master race. A maternity hospital that pampered German women, also to preserve the future of the master race. Or maybe just a normal maternity hospital. Or, yes, perhaps a place where women entertained good Aryan men to produce healthy Aryan babies. I am not sure we will ever know.

The patient inhaled deeply.

Why can't this all be true, she said. Who says Lebensborn has to be only one thing? And about Michal. Maybe she embellished things.

Maybe she said a few things she wanted me to hear, or not hear. But it was to protect me, in her mind, from things that were true. But what I don't understand is why would she talk about Lebensborn if she risked the whole world branding her a liar?

Yes, said the therapist. These are good questions.

122

I'd like to go on, said the patient. Go on with what Leni told me.

Of course, said the doctor. Please do.

The patient settled into her chair.

So, she said, after the shock about Lebensborn, I got my wits about me. And I asked Leni: Was it some sort of whorehouse?

I was relieved for a minute, when she answered, No, not exactly. The women were "free" to refuse the attentions of this man or that.

Then she went on to say:

But if they did not accept someone eventually, they were sent away, away from the warm beds and good food, so the inducement was there.

And in Michal's case, the alternative was—

There was no alternative, said Leni. It was Lebensborn or roam around Poland without papers. Or worse. Be sent to a real labor camp. Yes, the women could refuse a man who disgusted them. Not for the woman's sake. But because the doctors believed the environment of the womb would be disturbed by the mother's unhappiness. The idea was to create a beautiful environment for the gestation of perfect Aryan children.

But if Michal was safe and warm in this Lebensborn place, what happened that she was sent to Bergen-Belsen?

Ah! said Leni. It happened very abruptly. One of the "visitors" was a relative of her dear father-in-law, Dieter Gerstner. He exposed her, and that very day she was put on a train for Belsen.

Belsen. We sat there thinking of Belsen.

And the rest of the story you know, said her sister.

But let me ask you. Her being discovered, was it right near the end of the war?

Yes. Maybe so. Is that important?

Well, yes. I'm counting months. I was born in Belsen. Born a little prematurely, eight-plus months. But that seemed okay given the situation. I thought my father was someone in the camp, one of the Zionist leaders, at least I hoped so. But . . . if Michal left the Lebensborn hospital, say, somewhere near the end of March '45. If I count from there to my birthday on December 26th: nine months exactly.

Ah, I see, she replied. More coffee?

No, thanks.

Leni didn't make some for herself, the patient told Dr. Schussler, just sat there holding her cup, saying nothing more about my calculations.

So I turned to her and asked, Where do you come in? Where did baby Leni get started?

She kept staring down into the empty cup.

Oh, yes, she said, looking up at me. We now come back to where I was before Michal brought me here.

I waited for her to go on. She said nothing for what seemed a long time. Then finally:

Now let us do my calculations. Michal was taken to the Lebensborn facility in the winter of '44, in early February, she told me. Then I am born on 15 November of the same year. So now I, too, will count back nine months. Which puts my conception in February.

So you were born—

I was Lebensborn.

We said nothing. I suddenly felt ashamed. For both of us. The shame of where we came from.

Leni took a deep breath.

Michal told me she got pregnant almost immediately. I was born, full-term and fat, as chubby as a cherub, according to Michal. That is all she remembers of me as an infant. They did not even let her nurse me. She gave birth, and I was taken away. Then she did not know what happened to me. None of the women knew what happened to their babies. It was rumored that, after the babies were weaned, they were raised in some special kindergarten facilities, or else were given to the wives of high-up married officers to be raised as their own children.

Leni paused.

Well, she said. That is what happened to me.

What happened to you?

Leni abruptly stood with a screech of her chair. She began pacing: two steps, turn; two steps, turn.

I was given to a Nazi family to be raised, she said.

My God!

Leni stopped pacing.

Yes, to good, devoted members of the National Socialist Party. Not the worst of ogres, mind you. My father was not a guard at a concentration camp. He did not pack Jews into trains. During the war, he was a soldier, an officer. He led a division on the Eastern Front. Which fought bravely, evidently. Hence the reward of me, what they believed was a perfect Aryan child.

My mother was a good *Hausfrau*, Leni said, pacing again. My German parents—which is how I still think of them, although I haven't seen them in over twenty years—my German parents were decent-enough people, but very stiff and formal. And of course prejudiced. Your ordinary, everyday anti-Semites, saying the things everyone said: Complaints about being "Jewed," or "dirty Yids," and so on. We were rich. There were maids, nannies, tutors. The war itself was never discussed. *Vater*—my German father—refused to talk about it.

But you said he wasn't—

No. Not that sort of guilty past. The memory of the horrors of the Eastern Front. Death and gore. And all for nothing, he believed.

So they, your parents, your German parents, knew all about it. About—all that?

They never spoke of my origins. I thought they were my "real" parents, that I was their "real" child. All they told me was that we had an obligation to the lost Reich, to the future of the race. It was a big secret. I was never to tell anyone, now that the "American Jews" were running Germany, they said. I came to awareness with the idea already in my mind, so they must have told me when I was very young, and must have kept telling me. I was conceived as a higher being, and a higher being is what I was supposed to remain. Great achievements were expected of me, superiority in all things.

She looked out the window, at nothing it seemed.

Are you all right? I asked her.

She took a big breath and said: Yes. All right.

I saw her compose herself. Back erect. Shoulders back. But she couldn't clear her eyes of that vacant stare.

So, Leni continued, half turning to me. I had no idea that my parents—my German parents—were not my real parents. Not until Michal appeared one day and said she was my mother.

And about my father . . . Michal would never say. Only that he was decent in his lovemaking—some women were used brutally. He wanted his bedmate to have pleasure—he made sure she had it. She absolutely had to enjoy herself, another sort of tyranny, I always thought, if you do not care for a man and he refuses to stop until you climax. They spent two weeks together, then he returned whenever he was on leave.

Michal knows his name, she said hurriedly, but she will not tell me. She says she "forgot" it. Nonsense. She does not want me to find him. He was just "a depositor of Nazi sperm" is all Michal will say about it.

We sat quietly. I think we were both trying to imagine this depositor of Nazi sperm. Then I broke in to say:

He kept coming back, you said. Maybe up until the end, right before Michal was exposed?

Yes. No. I have no idea.

But about my counting months. If he was there near the end . . . it's possible . . . he might also be *my* father.

We surveyed each other's face once again, looking for evidence: Did we have the same father?

I cannot say, Leni replied finally. We look alike, and neither of us looks like Michal, which would seem to indicate yes, we look like our father. That we both came from the same depositor of Nazi sperm. But then again, I cannot comment about any of Michal's relatives, because she has nothing of them, no pictures, nothing. But of course there was once a whole family of Rothmans, hundreds of them if one counts all the generations and all the aunts, uncles, and cousins who were still living before the war. And we might look like any one of them.

We were quiet. The time "before the war": completely lost.

Finally I said to her: So am I also . . . Lebensborn?

Many seconds went by before Leni said: Maybe.

123.

I couldn't say another word, the patient told Dr. Schussler. It was more than I could deal with right then. I just sat there staring at the wall. But then something awful occurred to me.

Michal went looking for you, I said to Leni. She looked for you and found you.

Leni's response was to drum her fingers on the table, look out the window, finally turn to me. She looked so hard into my eyes that I could hardly stand it.

Yes, she said. Michal looked for me. I am sorry for you to learn this now because—

Michal never looked for me.

Leni's fingers kept drumming.

Why didn't she ever look for me?

Leni leaned forward, gripped the edge of the table.

Look. Do not compare our situations. They are not at all the same. You see, once Michal had been exposed as a Jew, she was afraid that the child she had given birth to—me—she was afraid I would become an *Ausschusskind*. Do you know what that is? What they called a garbage child. She was afraid that whoever or whatever was raising me would find out that the mother was Jewish. And they would toss me out, send me to some unspeakable orphanage, where I would become one of the castoffs upon whom the Nazis performed terrible experiments. She could not rest until she knew what had happened to me.

Leni gave a bitter laugh.

Of course I did not become a garbage child or a Nazi experiment. I was being raised in a rich, proper Nazi family who were secretly guarding the future of the race. The first that anyone in Germany knew I was Jewish was when Michal found me.

And how did they know she was Jewish? Leni went on with a laugh. She is so fair and blond. She could have passed for "Aryan." But she had to say she was Jewish or my German parents never would have let me go—guarding the future of the race, and all that.

I was nine years old. My parents could never again feel the same way toward me. They had never been exactly warm parents, were mainly dutiful. Then . . . Then Michal appears. She appears and my whole world goes to hell.

Now I did indeed become a sort of garbage child. Because my German parents were too shocked even to look at me. Their obligation was over. Worse, they barely knew what to do with me. I wandered around their house—it was their house now; not mine. I was afraid they would send me—where? Drop me on the doorstep of a synagogue? Leave me in the woods to die? I was actually relieved when Michal came back to get me six months later. She had made the arrangements, and I was off to Israel, the place my German parents had taught me should be wiped off the face of the earth, every Jew within it killed.

She laughed again. The same bitter laugh.

It was terrible, Leni continued. As I told you, I was furious. Hateful. There I was, a product of the Reich, a superior Aryan being, suddenly living in *the Jewish State.*

Oh, she said, sighing. There is no sense reliving it for you. I am sure you can imagine the rest, what awful years I had, what rebellions and scenes. Then somehow it all stopped. Maybe I just matured. Or I resigned myself to the situation. But now—now that I come to think of it—the big change might have been when I began my compulsory service. Michal had a low opinion of the IDF leadership. But when she saw me in uniform—who knows? I looked at her and saw maybe she had some pride in me. In any case . . . eventually . . . I made peace with Michal.

Peace? Or what you said before—armistice?

All right. Something in between. But to this day, I will not talk with Michal about what happened after she came for me—I did not want to talk about it with you. I still cannot forgive Michal for destroying my childhood.

We were silent for a time. Leni turned her empty coffee cup around and around.

Then she looked at me, her eyes slowly running over my face.

So now you know, she said.

I looked back at her. She was crumpled into her chair. Her eyes were vague, unfocused. And I saw what telling this story had cost her.

Thank you, I said to her as gently as I could.

Yes, said Leni, low and soft. Look what Michal had done to me. She expected to save me, not plunge me into years of self-hatred.

And when she saw me standing there . . .

It was nothing about you.

What I thought were bad memories—

Nothing about you.

What she saw was . . .

The wreck of my life, said my sister.

Immediately she stood up and began bustling around, opening and closing cabinets, drawers, closets.

With her back to me, she said: Michal will be home soon. I think you should leave before she gets here.

Yes, I said. I think I should go.

Abruptly she spun around.

Yes. Go. Leave. Forget all this. Go back to America. Hold on to the life you have there. This is no place to be looking for love. Michal gave all she had left of love when she sent you away, kept you away. Do not expect anything more.

She will be here any minute, Leni said.

She walked me down the hall. She opened the door. And I turned to her.

Should we stay in touch? I asked.

Leni put her hand on my shoulder. It was electric. Her face like mine, her touch.

I will leave the decision to you, she said.

124.

Doctor and patient sat quietly, the end of the session closing in upon them. Dr. Schussler crossed her legs. When her client said nothing, she crossed them again.

Until the patient finally said:

I don't know what to think about any of it. It's all so—

A door slammed somewhere down the corridor. Footsteps raced by.

Our time is up, isn't it?

Yes, said Dr. Schussler. I am afraid so.

The patient stood but did not open the door.

The doctor rose from her chair; walked toward the patient.

Please do not worry, said Dr. Schussler. There is no need for you to decide anything now. You will need a good deal of time to . . . integrate Leni into your life, if at all.

They stood quietly for a moment, then the patient said:

Thank you, Dr. Schussler. I mean it. I could not have gone through any of this without you.

And then she went out the door, leaving behind that present for her therapist.

125.

So did we come to the tenth of December, on the cusp of the Christmas therapeutic hiatus.

Suddenly we were deep into the rainy season. Trees writhed and shook, tormented by wind. Umbrellas flipped inside out, shoes were ruined, hats bounced down the street and lay sodden in gutters. Inside the office, the windows rattled in their sashes, the glass fogged, and the radiators spat and hissed and clanged in valiant effort against the cold. Across the way, the windows of the Hotel Palace glowed golden against the soaked gray stone of the facade. A bellman hefted up a suitcase in one room; two young girls jumped on the bed in another. One felt content to be indoors on such a day, as indeed I did, curled up like a restless child awaiting a rainy-day tale.

The patient arrived as usual. Without delay, she took her seat. And then, in an odd, tense voice, she said:

Something very strange has happened.

Oh? replied the doctor.

Here, said the patient. Read this.

There came the sound of crinkling paper, the doctor humming as she read.

God! the doctor whispered under her breath.

They say they're very sorry for the long delay. I got it yesterday. This morning I called them.

And?

They don't keep any kind of archive. There's no such person as Colin Masters.

(Oh, God, no!)

A gasp escaped from the doctor.

So who the hell has been writing to me? shouted the patient. How the hell did anyone know about any of this? Did you—?

No! said the doctor. How can you think that?

Right, said the patient. So who? I went back and looked at all the envelopes I'd gotten, and not one came from Chicago. It had a letterhead saying Greater Chicago Catholic Adoption Services, but every single envelope was postmarked San Francisco. How could I have been so stupid to not see it?

You were excited, said Dr. Schussler. Why would you look for that?

But who's been writing to me? Who? Someone arranged for me to find my mother. Someone's screwing around with my life. Who's doing this? *Who!*

A long break in the conversation followed. The radiators clanged. Car horns played. The doorman's taxi whistle wailed again and again, as if in vain.

I knew it, the doctor said just above a whisper. I knew it.

What? asked the patient.

Shhh came from the doctor.

Why?

Please keep your voice down. Be still. Do not move. I just cannot— I am sorry. Stay here.

She marched toward our common door. Where she stopped, standing so close that her angry breaths seemed to fall directly upon me.

I know you are there, she said in a venomous voice. I know what you have been doing.

Then she raced from her office and positioned herself before my outer door. Where she began pounding. Open up! she shouted. Open up! The door shook in its hinges. The doorknob rattled. Open up! she shouted again.

Help me! I screamed in my mind to my marble sentries. Send her away, my hard-stone guardians!

Yet she pounded on.

Open up! Open up this minute! I know you are in there.

I know you are in there.

I looked at the transom: shut. At the deadbolt: secured.

Open up! she kept shouting.

At last Dr. Schussler gave up her pounding, then stood still on the other side of the door. Her breath came between clenched teeth. The position of her mouth, her foot, the place where her fist had met the door— from these points, I could see the outline of her body. Feel the strength that had rattled the doorknob. She was tall—and so strong! She was not the tiny woman of a certain age I had imagined. Now only the thin square of fruitwood, so tenderly varnished, hid me from her. The brass fittings—hinges, lock, handle, worn by time—they were all that stood between me and the sudden appearance of Dr. Schussler in the living flesh.

For a slim second, I think of revealing myself, doing as she commands. Open the door, confess my existence, the role I had played. I almost welcomed it: discovery.

When abruptly Dr. Schussler stepped back, returned to her office, slammed the door.

I always knew there was something strange about that room, she said to the patient.

You mean someone was in there listening? *Is* listening now?

I should not have told you. But there were calls, breathing, I feared . . . Forgive me. This outburst. It should not have happened. But now. Now we have no choice.

Yes, said the patient. No choice.

We were all together for one long moment more.

Then came a click. And the breath of the sound machine rose like a foul mist on the air, thick as a closing curtain, designed to hide the patient from me forever, before we had come to the end.

You can hear the BBC recording of "Hatikvah" as sung by the Bergen-Belsen internees at www.fsgbooks.com/byblood#audio.